The UNBOUND EMPIRE

I'd known this was coming. It was inevitable, now that I was taking my place on the stage of Raverran politics. My friends would be in danger so long as my enemies saw them as weaknesses.

"Vulnerable?" The voice that came out of me was cold and hard. "Oh, I think not."

"Is that so?" Caulin asked, all innocent curiosity.

Once, he might have successfully intimidated me. But I had made the choice to kill my own cousin to save others, when I held the terrible destructive power of Mount Whitecrown beneath my hand; whatever soft spots remained in me had been blasted away in the volcano's fire.

"You are a fool if you think them unprotected," I said. "It's not my mother's retribution you should worry about. It's mine."

He lifted his eyebrows, affecting an expression of mild concern, and said nothing. But those black eyes analyzed me.

I stepped closer to him. "Let me be absolutely clear, Lord Caulin. I will not bury my mean_____ _____ touch my friends, I will destroy y____

D1426832

C016733583

Praise for the
Swords and Fire Trilogy

The Tethered Mage

"*The Tethered Mage* is a riveting read, with delicious intrigue, captivating characters, and a brilliant magic system. I loved it from start to finish!"
Sarah Beth Durst

"Charming, intelligent, fast-moving, beautifully atmospheric, with a heroine and other characters whom I really liked as people. (I overstayed my lunch break in order to finish it.) I would love to read more set in this world"
Genevieve Cogman

"Intricate and enticing as silk brocade. Caruso's heroine is a strong, intelligent young woman in a beguiling, beautifully evoked Renaissance world of high politics, courtly intrigue, love and loyalty—and fire warlocks"
Anna Smith Spark

"One of the best first novels in a brand new high fantasy series that I've read in ages…If you're hungry for a new fantasy series with awesome, nuanced characters, powerful worldbuilding, and solid writing—look no further. *The Tethered Mage* is the book you need right now. Absolutely recommended"
The Book Smugglers

"Engaging and entertaining with intrigue, a good pace, and strong characters. Zaira and Amalia are bright, bold heroes in a smartly constructed world"
James Islington

"Breathtaking…Worth every moment and every page, and should make anyone paying attention excited about what Caruso will write next"
BookPage

"An enchanting voice and an original world you won't want to leave"   RJ Barker

"A rich world, political intrigue, and action that keeps you turning pages—*The Tethered Mage* is classic fantasy with a fresh voice"
                                                                 Jeff Wheeler

"*The Tethered Mage* is the best kind of fantasy: intricate world-building, the most intriguing of court intrigues, and a twisty plot. But while readers might pick it up for those elements, they'll stay for the engaging characters and the unlikely friendships at the story's heart"   Rosalyn Eves

"A gorgeous, fresh fantasy debut filled with political intrigue and ethical quandary...Highly recommend"   *Girls in Capes*

The Defiant Heir

"Takes the series to the next level in every way...I absolutely loved *The Defiant Heir*"   *Fantasy Book Cafe*

"An entirely new level of awesome...Absolutely addictive"
                                                                Powder & Page

"An inspiration for geeks everywhere...Action-packed and bittersweet"   *Kirkus*

"A refreshing and lively fantasy that has characters that I just can't get enough of...Highly recommend!"
                                                            Speculative Herald

"A joy to read...Melissa Caruso is well on her way to making a very big splash in the fantasy genre."   *BiblioSanctum*

By Melissa Caruso

The Swords and Fire trilogy

The Tethered Mage
The Defiant Heir
The Unbound Empire

The UNBOUND EMPIRE

Book 3 of the
Swords and Fire Trilogy

MELISSA CARUSO

www.orbitbooks.net

ORBIT

First published in Great Britain in 2019 by Orbit

1 3 5 7 9 10 8 6 4 2

Printed and bound in Great Britain by Clays Ltd, Elcograf S.p.A.

Papers used by Orbit are from well-managed forests
and other responsible sources.

Orbit
An imprint of
Little, Brown Book Group
Carmelite House
50 Victoria Embankment
London EC4Y 0DZ

An Hachette UK Company
www.hachette.co.uk

www.orbitbooks.net

To Maya and Kyra,
my moon and sun.
Yours is a powerful magic.

A Current and Accurate Map of ERUVIA

The Winter Ocean

The Sunset Ocean

VASKANDAR

Markova

Vilskafar

Allevar

Morgaine

Kosenia

Kar

Gened

Roskoth

Eynie Lake

Atruin

Orium

The Whitecrown

The Endless

Asral

Kazerath

Urshul

Sevarch

Highpass

Durantain

Tira

Elowan

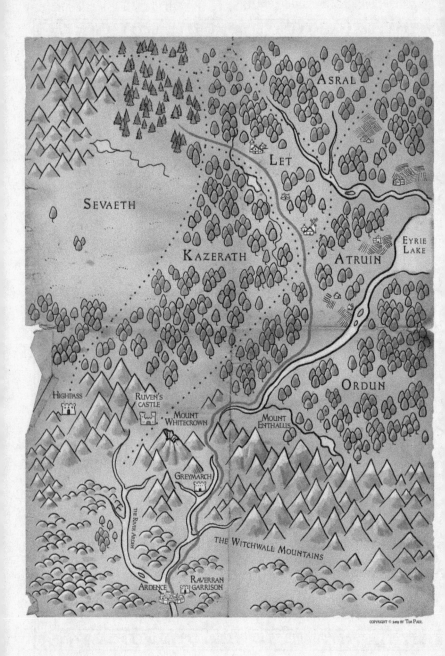

ASRAL

LET

SEVAETH

KAZERATH

ATRUIN

EYRIE
LAKE

ORDUN

HIGHPASS

RUVEN'S
CASTLE

MOUNT
WHITECROWN

MOUNT
ENTHALLIS

GREYMARCH

THE RIVER ARDEN

THE WITCHWALL MOUNTAINS

ARDENCE

RAVERRAN
GARRISON

COPYRIGHT © 2019 BY TIM PAUL

Chapter One

I had expected the prison to be darker. But the corridor down which the guard led me was awash with brilliant light.

Luminaries blazed in unadorned brackets all down the white stone hallway, which someone had swept and scrubbed spotlessly clean. A line of stout doors bore intricate artifice wards graven in broad scarlet circles above iron bars and locks. Each one represented a life sealed neatly away, bound in metal and magic.

Horrified pity stirred in my chest as I thought of the people behind those doors, locked away from fresh air and human company. I reminded myself that these cells held only Raverra's most dangerous and irredeemable criminals: traitors, murderers, and renegade mages who turned their powers deliberately against the innocent.

Or, in some cases, all three. Like the man I'd come to visit.

Still, my stomach lurched as the guard stopped before a door two-thirds of the way down the corridor. She gave me a wide-eyed backward glance that told me she knew full well who my mother was, and what would happen to her if this visit went wrong.

"This one," she said, and swallowed. "You're sure, my lady?"

I nodded, curling my hands closed to hide the sweat on my palms. He had no power to harm me, now. If this was a trap, it was a desperate and foolish one. And if it wasn't, I wanted to hear what he had to say.

"I'm sure," I lied.

The guard placed her palm on the seal, which flared with vivid red light. She turned a key, lifted a bar, and, with her hand near her pistol, opened the door.

It revealed a dim box of layered darkness, disconcerting after the brightness of the corridor. I clutched the lace of my cuffs and tried to piece out shapes from the shadows.

"Don't they give you any light?" The words burst out before I could stop them.

"I prefer it this way," came a too-familiar voice, rough with disuse or emotion.

Details emerged as my eyes adjusted: the blocky shapes of a writing desk, a chest of drawers, a bed. A slit window, thin as my arm, showed a narrow slice of night sky and a meager handful of stars. And there, in the farthest corner on the edge of the bed, slouched the lean shadow of a man.

Ignazio. My mother's cousin. Once powerful and respected, the former Serene Envoy to Ardence. My family, my mentor— and the man who had, on various occasions, poisoned, kidnapped, and attempted to murder me.

The cramped room smelled faintly of sweat and wine. I couldn't bring myself to step inside, even with the guard hovering protectively beside me. Ignazio had always been so neat and meticulous, with his sober dark velvet coats and spotless lace collars. His voice had been smooth and controlled, sometimes lightly mocking. Four months in prison had changed him—or perhaps it had all happened in that one moment when his careful schemes collapsed, bringing his life down in ruins around him.

Memories of him warred with this sour collection of shadows: Ignazio, presenting me with my first magical theory text, his eyes sparkling benignly. Ignazio, watching me with aloof regret as I lay dying of the poison he'd given me ten years before. I failed to suppress a shudder.

"Why do you prefer the darkness?" I asked.

"Perhaps I want to be remembered as I was, not as I've become." He shifted, and enough light fell on his face to pick out dark stubble on his cheeks. "You got my message, I take it."

"Yes. You said you had information." I tried to make my voice a crisp blank page, untouched by the history of pain between us, but it crumbled at the edges like an old letter.

"Of course." A bitter gleam of starlight caught the corners of his eyes. "Four months in prison, and neither you nor your mother sees fit to pay a family visit. But I say I have information, and you're here the next day, sure as the moon rises."

The guilt that stabbed me was the sort of cut only family could inflict, no less deep for its lack of justice.

"You tried to kill me," I reminded us both.

"If I'd tried harder, I wouldn't be here. But now I have something you need. Oh, you don't even know how much you need this." He rose, slowly unfolding the thin length of him. The guard shifted behind me, but Ignazio came no closer. "And you can get me out of this place, Amalia."

"If you want to negotiate your release, why are you talking to me, and not my mother?" I asked sharply.

He went still. For a moment, his breath rustled the darkness around him.

"I don't want this to become another of her victories," he said at last. "She would take what she wanted and cast me aside like a soiled napkin. But you, you'll keep your word." Ignazio turned toward the window. The feeble light cast stark hollows beneath his eyes and in his cheeks. "And I owe you this. I won't deny I've done you wrong."

"Then tell me what this great important mystery is, that you've somehow learned while locked in prison." I folded my arms, which not so coincidentally brought my hand closer to my flare locket, ready to unleash its blinding flash if he made any sudden moves. He was stalling. He had nothing, and this was a trap after all.

He turned toward me, his face falling into shadow. "I've been talking to Lord Ruven."

The name dropped into my mind like a black stone down a dark well.

"That's not possible," I protested. But the slit of a window drew my gaze, and I knew it was. Ruven had passed messages with seagulls before, to Istrella in her tower when she'd fallen under the control of his poison. The smallest opening would suffice when birds and rats and insects could all be Ruven's agents.

"You are too apt a student of magical science to believe in the impossible," Ignazio said.

"Perhaps." I stopped myself before letting the promise of secrets draw me a step forward. "Are you so close to him, then?"

Ignazio grunted. "That viper is no friend of mine. We stirred the same pot in Ardence, but I refused to ally with him then. He seems to harbor hopes that prison has changed my perspective, and he's been trying to recruit me."

"Why does he want you?" Ignazio didn't answer immediately, and I turned the question over in my mind. "Alchemy. This has to do with his command potion, doesn't it?"

"You still have a sharp mind, I see." Ignazio bowed mockingly, starlight sliding over his back. "It has come to his attention that I have some knowledge of Demon's Tears, which happens to be one of the very few alchemical poisons known to remain in the system for longer than a week. He wishes to enlist my expertise in designing a way to make his potion's effects permanent."

Hells. That potion was dangerous enough when it wore off in a few days. "You didn't tell him anything, did you?"

"I'm not a fool." The calm control I remembered had returned to his voice. He held power again at last, and he knew it. "But although you and your mother seem to wish to forget it, I am a Cornaro. I know how to manipulate an enemy. I let Ruven think I'd help him in return for my freedom, to coax his plans out of him."

I was glad the light behind me cast my face in shadow, so he couldn't see my eagerness. Ruven had been ominously silent these past two months, and the doge was certain he could make no moves with winter snows choking the passes through the Witchwall Mountains; but I rather doubted he was meekly waiting for spring. "And did you learn anything?"

"Oh, yes." Ignazio laughed, a grim, humorless rattle. "It's a good plan. If you don't stop him, he could threaten the Serene City itself."

"Then tell us how to stop him."

"Of course. The irony is too sweet, that I will become Raverra's savior." He paused. "There is, naturally, a price."

"Your freedom," I guessed. "I don't have the power to grant it to you."

"Your mother does. Tell Lissandra." He drew back into the shadowy corner in which I'd found him, his outline blurring into the general darkness. "Tell her and the rest of the Council that if they want to still have an empire to rule when the snow melts, they must let me go. I'll retire quietly to a country estate like a good boy, if they wish. I'll even let them come by to thank me if they bring along a good bottle of wine."

"I'll pass along your offer. You'd best actually have something good, though," I warned him.

"I am well aware how much my cousin despises those who waste her time. I would never presume to do so." He folded himself back up on the edge of his bed. "I want their promise, in writing, with the imperial seal. Once I'm free, I'll tell them everything I know about Ruven's plans."

"Isn't there anything you can tell me now, if it's so urgent?"

A moment's silence. Then, "For you. Not for your mother, or the Council." His voice dropped almost to a whisper. I leaned toward him, despite myself, holding a lungful of the sour air to catch his next words. "He's planning to turn our own against us. Don't trust familiar faces."

"I could already have guessed he'd try to use his potion to infiltrate the Serene Empire." I tried to sound unimpressed by this piece of information to coax out more. "Is that all you have?"

"Don't dismiss this so lightly." Ignazio's voice roughened, trembling. "I have every right to hate you, for landing me here. And I'm forced to admit you have even more right to despise me. Believe it or not, however, I'm trying protect you. So *listen* to me. This isn't some mere plot to seize a remote outpost; the Serene City is in danger. *You* are in danger." He drew a deep breath; when he released it, his usual controlled irony returned. "If I give you any more, your mother will figure out Ruven's plans on her own, and I'll lose my bargaining chip."

"Very well." Foreboding clung to me like cobwebs. I had to restrain the urge to brush myself off. "I'll attempt to impress the urgency of the matter upon the Council, and hope they respond to you quickly."

"If they don't, it'll be their fault when Ruven flings open the gates of the Nine Hells. And if he does, I doubt even Lissandra Cornaro can get them shut again." Ignazio sounded tired now, as if our encounter had exhausted him. "Good night, then, Amalia."

I couldn't quite bring myself to wish him the same, even for politeness's sake. I gave a curt nod and turned to go. The guard, avoiding my gaze, caught the door to close it.

"Amalia." Ignazio's voice floated out after me, from his darkened room. "You know Ruven better than anyone in Raverra. You know what he can do. We can't let him succeed."

"He won't," I promised.

The heavy door closed between us. The guard slid bolts and bars into place, and the seal carved into the door flared briefly with reddish light.

The guard escorted me through narrow corridors, past more locked doors. It was unsettling to think a human being lived behind each graven seal, a life full of thoughts and dreams that the Empire had deemed too dangerous to allow the simple grace of freedom. It was easy to think Ignazio deserved it; setting aside what he'd done to me, he'd also kept kidnapped children in a lightless drain and threatened a city with destruction to advance his own political fortunes. In theory, only such terrible crimes were supposed to earn imprisonment in a sealed cell. But I knew too much about the workings of power to presume that not one silenced voice behind those sturdy doors was innocent.

We passed through double sets of guarded, artifice-sealed doors and reemerged into the administrative wing. As I crossed the grand entry hall on my way out—a stern, soaring space of unadorned white marble, dominated by a single statue of the Grace of Majesty with a set of scales and a forbidding expression—Ignazio's warning gnawed at me.

Ruven was dangerous enough when we knew exactly what he was planning. If we couldn't discern his move before he made it, we might fail to block a crippling stroke.

"Lady Amalia," said a smooth, diffident voice. "I'm surprised to see you here."

I glanced up and found myself face-to-face with Lord Caulin, the doge's secret liaison with the imperial assassins and the criminal underworld, and the newest member of the Council of Nine. His slight build, mild expression, and unassuming posture made him easy to overlook, but it was perilous to underestimate him.

I forced a smile across my clenched teeth. Lord Caulin had tried to trap me into a choice between murder and treason a couple of months ago, and he was no ally of mine. But he had power, and it accomplished nothing to antagonize him. "Lord Caulin. I could say the same to you."

He modestly smoothed the simple silk cravat that adorned his chest in place of the more showy lace most Raverran nobility sported. "My business takes me to the prison on a regular basis, my lady. There is much to be learned from its inmates. As perhaps you are well aware?"

The tilt of his head invited more information. I hesitated. I needed to bring Ignazio's offer before the Council, and I could think of no reason to hide it from Caulin, but I didn't trust him.

"Come now, my lady," Caulin coaxed. "We may sometimes be political adversaries, but we are not enemies. Not when it comes to the safety and security of the Serene Empire. We're all on Raverra's side, are we not?"

"I am always on the side of the people of the Serene Empire," I said.

"Then we cannot possibly be opposed." His mouth moved in a perfunctory smile, but his eyes flicked across my face, assessing. "Did your mother send you here?"

"I was visiting Ignazio," I said reluctantly. "He has information on a plan of Ruven's. This is only a guess, but given that he spoke of turning our own people against us, I suspect it's a scheme to use his command potion to sabotage the Empire."

"Ah." Caulin nodded. "That fascinating potion. I'm not surprised. It doesn't take much imagination to think of a hundred ways he could use it, and he'd be a fool not to try."

I didn't doubt Caulin had thought of a hundred ways *he* would use it, if he could. "Ruven is no fool. Have your own connections learned anything relevant? If he's attempting to place someone in a key position in the Empire under his control, he might well hire a Raverran poisoner."

"Investigating that angle is precisely why I'm here." Caulin's lips thinned in a smile. "You think like a true daughter of the Serene City, Lady Amalia."

I shifted uncomfortably. Somehow that didn't feel like a compliment, coming from a man whose methods I despised. "Thank you."

His eyes took on a gleam I didn't like. "You should use that mind to the Empire's benefit."

"I like to think I do, Lord Caulin."

"Do you?" He raised his brows. "One might argue that your current attempts at lawmaking serve no one but our enemies."

He meant my proposed act to end the forced conscription of mages, into which I'd been pouring countless hours and every crumb of political influence I had. *Attempts at lawmaking* shouldn't have stung, coming from a man who'd never tried to pen a law in his life, but it set my teeth on edge.

"One might argue that," I agreed stiffly, "if one lacked both the wisdom to recall that the mage-marked are imperial citizens and the foresight to realize that it only strengthens the Empire to free them."

Caulin's tone shifted, becoming softer, more dangerous. "It's a waste to bend your efforts toward foolish gestures that could deprive Raverra of its most formidable weapons just when we have greatest need of them."

"The mage-marked aren't weapons. They're people," I said. "They deserve a choice."

"The security of the Empire sometimes requires that we control other people's choices." Caulin shrugged, as if this were an inconvenience to be tolerated, like a light summer rain. "Choice can be dangerous. You would do well to remember it."

A certain edge in his tone sent prickles down my back. "Dangerous? Surely you aren't threatening me, Lord Caulin."

"You?" He laughed. "Oh, I would never threaten the daughter of La Contessa. No, no. That would be folly. I merely meant that as you make your political moves upon the board, you may wish to consider how they endanger the more vulnerable pieces around you." Caulin's eyes went flat as black glass. "It would be a pity if your friends wound up as casualties of your principles."

I drew in a sharp breath. He still smiled, his demeanor mild and affable except for those eyes full of old death. But I knew whom he meant: Marcello, my Ardentine scholar friends, perhaps even Istrella or Zaira. He could have them killed, if he chose, and no one would ever trace it back to him; that was his job, after all.

I'd known this was coming. It was inevitable, now that I was taking my place on the stage of Raverran politics. My friends would be in danger so long as my enemies saw them as weaknesses.

"Vulnerable?" The voice that came out of me was cold and hard. "Oh, I think not."

"Is that so?" Caulin asked, all innocent curiosity.

Once, he might have successfully intimidated me. But I had made the choice to kill my own cousin to save others, when I held the terrible destructive power of Mount Whitecrown beneath my hand; whatever soft spots remained in me had been blasted away in the volcano's fire.

"You are a fool if you think them unprotected," I said. "It's not my mother's retribution you should worry about. It's mine."

He lifted his eyebrows, affecting an expression of mild concern, and said nothing. But those black eyes analyzed me.

I stepped closer to him. "Let me be absolutely clear, Lord Caulin. I will not bury my meaning in false pleasantries. If you touch my friends, I will destroy you."

The absolute certainty of it hummed angrily in my pulse and resonated in my voice. It didn't matter that Caulin outranked me, or that I was only an heir with little power of my own. I would find a way. And Caulin heard it.

He regarded me awhile, considering, as if I were a difficult passage he was translating from Ancient Ostan.

"I'll bear that in mind, Lady Amalia," he said at last. "But in return, do me the favor of considering the impact your little law could have. I would prefer to be your ally, not your adversary."

I drew in a breath to tell him exactly how much consideration I'd given to the impact this law could have: The nights lying awake wondering if I was going too far, or not nearly far enough. The long discussions with my friends at the Mews over what it might mean for the safety of mage-marked children and the people around them. The hours poring through history books, analyzing the forces at play, the pendulum swing of action and reaction that had rocked the ships of nations since long before the Serene Empire existed.

But before I could utter a word, the echoing patter of running footsteps sounded in the broad marble hall. The ragged urgency of the sound pierced my chest with a thin sliver of alarm; after two months home safe in Raverra, my nerves still expected danger in every sudden motion, every sharp word.

The guard who'd conducted me through the prison halls ran toward us, her eyes wide, gasping for breath.

"Lady Amalia!" she called. "Come quickly! It's your cousin, Lord Ignazio. He's...I think he's dead!"

Chapter Two

Two guards and a physician crowded Ignazio's cell, now awash in glaring light and harsh bands of shadow from a pair of luminary lanterns on the floor. I stopped myself from pushing past them into the tiny stone room; this still could be a trick. But though I could only spy Ignazio's thin, sprawling figure in pieces, between the backlit legs and scabbards moving between us, the absolute stillness upon it gave me little hope this could be anything but death.

The physician rose from her crouch at Ignazio's side with weary gravity, shaking her head. "It's too late to save him."

The guards parted for me, and I saw him at last. Ignazio's body lay facedown on the cold floor, twisted in apparent agony. A moment ago this had been a creature of intricate thoughts and complex misgivings, a living soul I could both hate and still somehow love. Now it was only an empty thing, like dry wood with the sap gone from it. Everything I might have wished to tell him, all his unresolved regrets and unspoken secrets, gone.

"What killed him?" I asked. My voice came out tight as an overstuffed case at risk of springing open.

The physician shook her cloud of iron-gray hair. "I'm not sure yet. I'd guess poison, but—"

Something leggy and iridescent black scuttled out from

beneath Ignazio's sleeve. One of the guards shrieked and jumped back; the physician, with the unruffled calm of a grandmother who's seen worse, brought her boot down on the insect before I could do more than catch a sharp breath.

"There's your answer," she said grimly, lifting her foot to reveal the crumpled remains of something resembling a scorpion. The guard who had shrieked went nearly green and averted his eyes.

"A chimera," I breathed. It had to be. Its legs were too like a spider's, curled up in death, and it had two curving tails instead of one.

Whatever Ignazio had wanted to tell the Council, Ruven had made certain the knowledge died with him.

"I should have realized Ruven wouldn't tell Ignazio something that important unless he was certain he could protect his secrets. *Ignazio* should have realized."

I paced a tight arc in Marcello's cramped office, my hands clasped behind my back to keep them from trembling. Marcello slumped in shock before a writing desk piled high with deployment orders, his eyes wide at the news I'd given him.

"Does the doge know about this?" he asked, pushing the curling black locks of his hair from his face as if he could shove his own thoughts into order.

"Of course. I went to the courier lamps at once to tell my mother." I loosed a shaky breath that wasn't quite a laugh. "She's in a closed Council meeting all day, so I couldn't see her in person. I had to break her the news of her only cousin's death in the courier lamp code."

I couldn't help a certain bittersweet wonder at the strange, cold miracle of magic and imperial bureaucracy that had brought my message to her. A clerk had received and transcribed the brief pulses of light, then handed the scrap of paper to a page to run it through the echoing marble halls of the Imperial Palace to where Ciardha stood waiting outside the Map Room door. Ciardha in turn would have discreetly passed it to my mother without disrupting the meeting. And my mother must have looked down and felt something, some tangle of emotions I could only imagine, before lifting her gaze to the rest of the Council to calmly inform them of this new piece of intelligence.

So I had come here, because Marcello was the only one in all the world whom I could talk to when I was this rattled without fear of the consequences of seeming vulnerable.

"I'm sorry," he said softly.

I shook my head. "There's nothing to be sorry about. He was a traitor, and everything I ever liked about him was a lie."

Marcello rose in front of me, stopping my pacing. We stood so close a strong breeze could have swayed me into him. Face-to-face like this, I couldn't escape the quiet sympathy in his warm green eyes.

"Don't pretend he doesn't matter. He was your family." Marcello's lips twisted into the wry echo of a smile. "You know how my father nearly ruined my life, and I'd still be upset if he died. I understand."

"I'm really fine." I brushed imaginary dust from my lace cuffs, just as an excuse to look away from him. "Seeing him dead so soon after I spoke with him was unnerving, that's all."

"Are you sure?" Marcello hesitated, then laid a gentle hand on my shoulder. "You still haven't talked about Roland, either. It might help to—"

At Roland's name, pain squeezed my chest. I shook Marcello's hand off. "*Anyway,*" I interrupted him, "we need to figure out this plan of Ruven's that Ignazio died to warn us about."

Marcello gave me a long, dubious look. "You're not going to let me help you, are you."

I set my jaw stubbornly. "You can help me stop Ruven all you want."

"All right." He threw up his hands in mock defeat and sank back into his chair. "The wise officer knows when to retreat. In any case, it sounds as if we'll want to watch out for Ruven's control poison."

"It's his most dangerous weapon." I latched eagerly onto the problem; unlike death, it was something I might actually solve. "So long as he has enough alchemists working for him, the sheer mathematics of it are terrifying. All it takes is one controlled person with a vial of potion to bring several under Ruven's control, and then *they* can each spread it to more..." I trailed off, envisioning Ruven's taint spreading across the Empire like spilled ink across a map.

Marcello dragged his fingers through his hair. "And all those people wouldn't be sitting quietly. They'd be sabotaging our infrastructure, killing our leaders, capturing our mages, all right in the heart of the Empire. We need a way to deal with this potion, or to deal with Ruven." He tapped one of the reports on his desk. "Terika's trying to find an antidote—she stole a few samples of the potion when you rescued her from Ruven's castle—but she says it may not be possible to create one. She's determined that we can detect the presence of the potion in a drop of blood, though."

"I'd suggest you start regular testing of everyone in the Mews, then," I said. "Soldiers and staff as well as Falcons and Falconers—anyone who can get in the doors. We should do the same with any other officials Ruven might want to control, from the doge on down."

Marcello nodded. "What about this scorpion chimera? I'm concerned he might use more of them for assassination."

"Ferroli's Tincture of Purity should counteract the venom." I bit my lip, thinking. "I'm not sure how much you have in stock, but it might be wise for key leaders and Falcons to start carrying some."

"I'll put the alchemists on it," Marcello agreed, leaning over his desk to scribble himself a note. "You should keep some in that satchel of yours, too."

"I already do." I patted the satchel's familiar weight on my hip. I'd taken to carrying it with me almost everywhere, since recent events in my life had proven the value of being prepared. "We'll want to raise security on the Falcons as well. Ruven thinks of magic as power, and he's targeted them before."

"You're right, we should." Marcello sighed, rubbing his forehead. "Damn. This is going to mean more arguments."

"Oh?"

He hesitated. "I probably shouldn't talk about it."

"Marcello," I said dryly, "I'm your friend *and* I'm privy to the Empire's most carefully guarded secrets. There is very little on this earth you can't talk to me about."

"I suppose you're right." He flashed me a smile, but weariness lay under it, like brittle gray ice beneath a thin dusting of bright snow. "You know why I joined the Falconers, of course. To help my sister, and people like her."

"Ah." I thought I had an inkling of where this was going. "And not everyone seems to share this perspective, in your talks about security."

"Some of them want to lock the Falcons up like their grandmother's heirloom silver at the first sign of a threat. Or worse." He grimaced. "It's certainly driven home why your law is so important. I didn't notice it as much before my promotion—but when you get past a certain command level, there are no Falcons in the meetings anymore. And the tone of the discussions changes."

"I know what you mean." I shifted uncomfortably. "I've been in those types of meetings myself." The tendency to think of the mage-marked as resources rather than human beings was an obstacle I'd run into disturbingly often in my attempts to garner support for my Falcon reform law.

"I imagine you have. And there's this same ruthless distance when we talk about military strategy—who and how many we can afford to lose." He shook his head. "I can't forget that these are people, not playing pieces. I don't think I'm cut out for command, Amalia. I'm too soft."

My throat tightened. I seized his hand, before I could think better of it.

"Stay soft," I urged him. "The Serene Empire needs more people like you in power. People with compassion."

"I'm worried that over time, I'll start thinking like them, piece by piece, and not even notice." Marcello curled his fingers gently around mine. "I don't know if it's better to quit, and be certain I'll always stay myself, or keep trying to become the colonel's successor, and risk becoming someone I wouldn't recognize."

"You're the most honest man I know," I said. "You'll always be yourself."

"You think so?" Hope warred with doubt in his voice.

"I'm counting on it."

That evening I sat in the drawing room after dinner, writing personal letters to attempt to persuade key Assembly members to vote for my Falcon reform law as I waited for my mother to return home from the Imperial Palace. Finished letters accumulated on the tray as the mantel clock ticked away the hours. My pen hovered over the beginning of the twentieth, hesitating over whether a certain baroness's husband or her consort would hold more sway over her opinion, when at last I heard Old Anzo open the door for my mother. Her voice floated in from the foyer, punctuated by the efficient murmurs of Ciardha, her impeccable aide; she was still working, even at what the clock informed me was an hour past midnight.

I rose, ready to go meet her in the foyer, but she slipped into the drawing room with a swish of midnight-blue velvet and a rustle of lace before I made it to the door. She pulled jeweled pins from her hair as she approached, letting her auburn locks tumble down over her shoulders; she had already cast off the majesty she wore in public like a cloak, probably the moment she walked through our palace doors.

"Mamma," I greeted her, scanning her face for signs of grief.

But she still wore her business mask, enigmatic and aloof. She was either saving her mourning for later, or she'd done it long ago.

"Amalia." She pushed the door shut behind her, never breaking her gaze; the click of the latch sounded grim and final as the seal on Ignazio's prison cell. "Sit down. We have things to talk about."

I settled back into my chair, suddenly feeling as if she'd caught me skipping my oratory lessons to sneak off to the library. Ciardha's voice sounded distant and muffled in the foyer, giving instructions to Old Anzo. "We do?"

La Contessa sank gracefully into a chair opposite me, scattering her pins beside my letter tray. "The Council of Nine is taking your message about Ignazio's warning seriously. We spent much of today coordinating attempts to uncover what Ruven might be up to. Lord Caulin even claims to have already received a tip indicating that Ruven is hiring Raverran alchemists from the Tallows to help spread his poison."

"That was quick," I said, surprised.

"Indeed." Skepticism dripped from my mother's voice. "And thus far, my own people have been unable to corroborate this piece of intelligence."

"You think he's making it up?"

"Caulin has his own sources, and he doesn't always share. It could be good information." She delicately spread her hands. "Or he could be making a mistake, perhaps moving too quickly on an unreliable tip to try to gain cachet as the most newly elected Council member. Or, yes, it could be a fabrication."

"But why would he lie about something like that?"

My mother lifted an eyebrow and waited. Which meant she felt that I was fully capable of arriving at an answer on my own.

It had been rather a long day, and I was no longer feeling particularly clever. But I rubbed my temples and did my best. "People lie when they have something to hide, or when they want to trick someone else into unwise action."

"And what might our dear Lord Caulin have to hide?" La Contessa asked, her eyes gleaming sharply in the fading light of the luminaries.

"Half a Hell full of secrets." I waved a hand as if to swat away a buzzing cloud of them. "He's got to wade through them to get out his door in the morning. But I can't think why he'd want to cover up Ruven's plans—unless he's somehow complicit in them."

"If he is, that's a very grave matter indeed. I don't consider it likely, but neither would I rule it out—unlikely things happen every day. And your second option? Who would he want to trick into unwise action?"

I stared into the evening darkness gathered in my mother's eyes. She waited, sure and cynical as death itself.

"Me," I whispered. "Because my Falcon reform act is gaining ground."

La Contessa nodded slowly. "Step carefully, Amalia. This could be a trap set just for you."

"So your uncle's dead." Zaira took a long swallow from the water flask set out for us, then scowled at it as if annoyed it wasn't wine. "Good riddance to the bastard."

I'd stolen a moment during a break in our morning training session with Jerith and Balos at the Mews to tell her my concerns about Caulin, and about Ignazio's warning and death, to which she'd reacted with this succinct eulogy.

I couldn't quite bring myself to speak in Ignazio's defense. "Yes, well, regardless of what you think of him, you may want to take his warning to heart. You're likely to be one of Ruven's targets. Please be careful."

"Oh, you know me. I'm a model of caution and restraint." She tossed the metal flask onto the heap of our winter coats, discarded on a bench against the training yard wall for being too warm to wear in proximity to balefire. The winter air cut through my light brocade jacket now that we were resting, and I hugged my arms against the chill. "As for Lord Dubious, your mamma's right to give him the dirty eye. That story that Ruven is hiring alchemists from the Tallows is a pile of rat dung."

"I don't doubt it, but what makes you think so?" I asked. "You know the Tallows better than any of us." Zaira had grown up in the Serene City's poorest district, which was populated mostly by honest dockworkers and laborers; but those criminals who stayed beneath the Council's notice—or made themselves useful enough to earn a blind eye—had their enclaves there as well.

"For one thing, you can't make Ruven's potion without the mage mark, so no two-penny Tallows alchemist could mix it up." Zaira wiped her mouth on her sleeve. "For another, there aren't that many mages in the Tallows—even a weak alchemist would do well enough selling pimple cream and impotence cures to gullible rich folk that they could afford to live somewhere nicer. I know the handful who do gray-market jobs out of the Tallows, and none of them would take a job from Vaskandar."

I tugged on a loose lock of hair, thinking. "Then why did Caulin say that? Is he trying to trick us, or did someone trick him?"

Zaira shrugged. "I dunno, but if that worm is trying to pin something on Tallows mages, I'll be damned if I let him get away with it. Come with me later, and I'll ask around and see if any of my old contacts know anything."

Balos strode over to us across the training yard, from where he'd been talking to Jerith in the warded instructor's corner. The thin sunlight picked fleeting gleams from the gold trim on his Falconer's uniform, and his deep brown eyes considered us thoughtfully.

"Are you ready to continue?" he asked.

"If you're still mad enough to want to do this in the middle of the Mews, sure," Zaira said. Her tone was light, but muscles in her face tightened. No one spoke of the reason Jerith and Balos had made the time to prioritize training us during their brief stay in the Mews between border deployments, or of how soon Zaira and I might have to use what we were learning. But it was hard to forget.

"We have faith in your control," Balos said.

"Oh, I don't know, I think loosing balefire inside a populated castle is mad by definition." Jerith strolled over to us, grinning. "But we're only making tiny sparks today. What could possibly go wrong?"

Zaira groaned. "Why did you have to go and say that?"

"What fun is a boring, predictable life?" The mage mark

gleamed silver in Jerith's eyes. "Now give us a tame little fire, the size of your thumb, and let's see how long you can keep it that way."

"*Exsolvo*," I muttered. Even after months of practice, my heart still kicked up when I said it, as if a lion had wandered into the courtyard.

Zaira held out a hand, palm up. A slim, pale flame licked from her fingertips.

It stretched no taller than a candle flame, but its presence was far less gentle. It tugged and twisted in the air as if it yearned to be free, and its eerie blue light cut at my eyes. Zaira stared at it like an old enemy with whom she'd forged an uneasy truce.

"You're fighting it," Jerith observed, as the slip of fire writhed on Zaira's fingers in thwarted hunger.

"Would you rather I let it go?" Zaira snapped. "The Mews might look nicer with a gaping blackened hole in the middle of it."

Zaira's eyes stayed on the wisp of balefire, and despite its hungry snapping at the air, it still hadn't spread or grown. A surge of pride in what she'd accomplished warmed me; with balefire, it was easier to burn down a building than to light a candle. But Jerith's glittering eyes hadn't left her face.

"You don't need to be afraid of it," he said softly.

The flame in Zaira's hand jumped to twice its previous height. "I'm not afraid."

"Mmm. I can see that." Jerith lifted a pale brow. "No bigger than your thumb, remember."

"You're distracting me on purpose, you rat," Zaira complained. But she gritted her teeth, and the flame shrank again. Sweat stood out on her temples, despite the chill air.

"So long as you're afraid, you'll never have true control," Jerith said.

"I'm controlling it just fine. See?" She thrust her hand toward

him, suddenly, and grinned as Jerith jumped back. I sucked
in a breath, but the slim blue flame clung low and tight to her
fingertips.

Jerith's eyes narrowed. "Balos."

"I don't think this is a good idea," Balos warned, his deep
voice dubious.

"Balos."

"All right." Balos shook his head. "*Exsolvo.*"

I glanced at Balos in alarm. He held my gaze and mouthed,
Be ready.

That was far from reassuring.

Zaira eyed Jerith warily. The balefire still licked up from her
fingertips, cruel and hungry, endlessly testing the chain of Zaira's will.

Jerith gave her a broad, sharp-edged smile. "Your control is
a lot better, I'll give you that. But you're not fooling anyone,
Zaira. Not even yourself."

Zaira's hair stirred in a sudden breeze that teased her curly
locks forward into her face and tugged her skirts against the back
of her legs. Where I stood a few feet away, I could barely feel it.
But the bitter blue flame in her hand bent toward Jerith, its top
streaming eagerly in the wind.

"What are you doing?" Zaira stepped away from him, pushing her hair out of her eyes with her free hand. The wind at her
back grew stronger, making a low hissing moan. Jerith's own
spiky blond hair bent before it. "Are you an idiot?"

"Sometimes," Balos murmured.

"If you're not afraid, control it." Jerith's voice went hard and
flat as a knife blade. He stood unflinchingly as his wind stretched
Zaira's flame toward him, streaming with eager fluttering fingers that scrabbled at the air, seeking life to consume.

"You're mad as a sack of ferrets!"

"No bigger than your thumb, Zaira," Jerith said calmly.

Her flames blew a banner long as my forearm, reaching mere inches from Jerith's narrow chest. I stirred uneasily.

"Don't seal her, Lady Amalia," Jerith barked at me. "She has to do this herself."

"Pox rot your smug wretched face!" Zaira snarled, and closed her hand into a fist.

The fire winked out at once. The air grew chill again. Jerith's wind swirled around Zaira, whipping her hair into a tangle, and settled with a skittering of dust along the flagstones.

Zaira's shoulders heaved, her breath quick with effort. She leveled a glare at Jerith that made me wonder his jacket didn't start smoking after all.

Jerith let loose a faint huff of relief or disappointment. "Why did you quench the fire, instead of controlling it?"

"Go kiss a stingroach," Zaira retorted, and stalked off to pick up the water flask again.

Chapter Three

Marcello moved in front of Zaira and me through the dusk-painted, twisting streets of the Tallows, scanning the early-evening crowds warily for any sign of danger among the workers slouching wearily home and the sailors bound merrily for the taverns. Zaira had insisted that no other guards accompany us for fear that the sight of too many soldiers would keep anyone from talking to her, and Marcello took his duty seriously.

This district was too poor for luminaries. Its crumbling façades showed patches of brick through the plaster, and trash bobbed against the walls of the canals. A lamplighter moved across a narrow bridge not far ahead of us, brightening the world one flickering flame at a time. An intoxicating scent of mushrooms cooking in wine teased us from a window above, and a woman's contented humming drifted down with it. Zaira's dog Scoundrel sniffed excitedly at our heels, his tail wagging with a fury of recognition at the smells of his old neighborhood.

As for Zaira herself, perhaps it was the way the gray wash of dusk and the ruddy lamplight mingled on her features, but for a fleeting moment, she looked lost.

"Everything's the same, but it's different," she muttered as we walked. "I haven't been gone half a year, and Pip Gallo's dead and the Six Jays is closed, and the best baker in town's gotten married and moved to Palova."

"It's always strange, coming home after an absence," I said, thinking of my own return from my year in Ardence.

Zaira lifted an eyebrow. "Who said anything about home? Come on. There's a place up ahead that always has information."

We crossed a bridge over a crooked canal slender enough that I doubted the sun ever reached the green water below. On the far side, we had to pause a moment as an old man struggled to right an overturned handcart that nearly blocked the street; Marcello hastened to help him. Zaira crouched down and scratched Scoundrel's rump, but he was too busy sniffing a crumpled bit of oil-stained broadsheet that had probably once wrapped fish to care. A crow eyed the same wrapper from a rooftop; I wondered with an odd pang if it were Kathe's. I might not be able to trust him farther than I could throw him, but I could use his cleverness right now.

"I lived there for a few months," Zaira said in a low voice, jerking her chin across the crooked street.

For a moment I thought she meant a butcher's shop, but then I noticed the spire of a temple rising behind it. I squinted at the green-streaked figure atop it. "The local Temple of Mercy? They took you in?"

Zaira nodded, her eyes dark and shuttered as she rubbed Scoundrel's ears. "After the old woman died. They were nice enough to make your teeth hurt, but they met my eyes way too much, so I had to leave. Then I got to be an expert on floors."

"Floors?" Heat flooded my cheeks. "Oh! You mean sleeping on them."

The look she gave me could have stripped the paint off a wall. "No, I meant licking them, like Scoundrel here. Graces grant me patience, you're dense as year-old cream."

"Sorry." I remembered the tangle of frayed blankets we'd

found in a dark corner of an abandoned laundry, the place Zaira had been living when I'd unwittingly helped capture her for the Falcons. "So you never really had a home."

"Not after the old woman died." Her tone was flat and hard, denying any sympathy. "When you have to keep moving, you don't get attached to places. Or things, or people. Scoundrel was all right, because he could come with me."

"If we can pass this Falcon reform law, you'd be free to live anywhere you wanted," I said softly. "It wouldn't matter if someone noticed your mage mark. You could make a home for yourself at last."

"What makes you think I want one?" Zaira straightened and stretched. "That's Terika. Always talking about getting some little cottage in the mountains, or a town house in the city, and how many cats will I let her have, and do I think luminaries or oil lamps give a more comfortable light, and what do I think about spring green in the bedroom. It's enough to make a person vomit."

Marcello had righted the cart and seen the old man on his way with a cheerful wave. Zaira sighed. "Come on. We're almost there. It's that tavern up ahead—the Laughing Siren." She gave me an assessing glance. "Just keep your valuables close, and don't start any fights you don't want to finish."

The smoke hazing the air of the Laughing Siren tavern bore a heavy scent of sweet herbs, and the lamps and fireplace burned an alchemical oil that made their flames flicker through shades of blue, green, and purple. The cool, shifting light gave the place the appearance of being underwater. An Ostan boy with a cello played dreamy music that wove through the smoke, enhancing the impression. The place was crowded, but the noise remained strangely muted, with patrons huddled in private groups holding murmured conversations I couldn't quite make out even as Zaira led us on a weaving course around tables toward the bar.

A closer glance at the round tables told me why: someone had carefully carved runes into their edges, and cut diagrams into the tops. A muffling enchantment to dampen sound, so no one could overhear you. *Clever.*

More than a few people shot glances our way or even stared openly. I was used to drawing attention as the Cornaro heir, but their eyes slid past me to latch onto Zaira. She ignored them, but her jaw tightened, and Scoundrel pressed close against her legs, his tail tucked.

"Do they know you here?" I whispered.

Zaira grunted. "I used to be in here a lot, but they didn't know I was a fire warlock. Now they do." Her tone was careless, but she wouldn't meet my eyes any more than she would those of the patrons watching her, shades of blue and purple drifting across their carefully neutral faces.

I understood anyway. The Tallows had never been her home, not really, but it was all she'd had. And now everyone she'd known realized she'd always been a stranger here. Even if my law passed, she couldn't go back.

The stinging in my eyes as we approached the bar might have been from more than the smoke. But Zaira showed no hesitation as she leaned on the rune-edged wooden counter and caught the attention of the proprietor, a tiny old woman with a face wrinkled like well-used leather.

"Hey, Rosa."

"Zaira!" the old woman greeted her, in a surprisingly strong voice. "Good to see you, dear, it's been ages. And you've brought friends!" Her sharp black eyes took in Marcello's uniform and lingered on my face. "Showing them the old neighborhood? Or did you come all this way from the Mews for a drink?"

"I'm here for the house special," Zaira said.

Rosa laughed. "Information, eh? It's not the cheapest drink in the Tallows. Can you pay for it?"

"Miss Moneybags here wipes her arse with gold foil," Zaira assured her.

I hoped the blue light hid the burning of my cheeks. "I imagine we could arrange payment as needed, yes."

The old woman assessed me narrowly. "I imagine you could. All right then, what do you want to know, Zaira dear?"

Zaira dropped her voice so low I could barely hear it over the deep liquid strains of the cello. "Heard of any alchemists taking jobs that might have come from Vaskandar?"

"Vaskandar!" Rosa's nostrils flared, and she looked as if she might spit if it weren't her own bar she'd be expectorating upon. "I'd throw anyone dealing with *them* out of the Laughing Siren. I fought those demons in the Three Years' War, you know."

I shifted uncomfortably, wondering if she'd heard about my courtship with Kathe.

Zaira grunted. "I figured as much, but I had to ask. Next question: heard about anyone talking to the Empire in the past day or two?"

Rosa shifted uneasily, giving me a sideways glance. "There are people who pass news to Raverran intelligence from time to time, but I don't give out those names. If this is some test from La Contessa—"

"It's not a test," I assured her hastily. "We're only interested in contact that wasn't through the regular channels. Unusual activity."

"Well…" Rosa drummed her fingers on the bar, frowning. "I suppose given who you are, I can tell you. All right." She dropped her voice until I could barely hear it. "I heard about a gray-market mage crew taking a job that was supposed to be from someone very high up."

"A job, huh?" Zaira kept her tone casual. I tried not to show my own surprise. "Any details?"

"I don't know who or what," Rosa said, glancing at me again. "You probably know more than I do. But if it helps you narrow it down, I know when and where. Some patrician lady's charity ball."

"Lady Aurica's annual dinner dance for the Temple of Bounty?" I asked at once. Her chef's reputation made the event quite popular among the Serene City's rich and powerful, and ensured a crowd at the buffet. It would be a perfect opportunity for Ruven to spread his poison. "Good Graces, that's tomorrow."

"That sounds right," Rosa agreed. "Sorry I don't have more for you, but that's all I know."

"No, that's very helpful. Thank you." I slipped the woman a couple of ducats, which seemed to be far more than she'd expected, given how wide her eyes went and how quickly the gold disappeared.

Once we were out on the street again, Marcello glanced around and muttered, "A job from someone high up. That could be anything. Lady Aurica might have hired them herself, to make the wine glow at her party."

I pulled my coat closer against the winter evening. "I can't imagine Lady Aurica getting her party decorations from the Tallows. And while I can envision scenarios where the imperial government would hire gray-market mages, I haven't heard of anything of the sort planned for her charity dinner." I turned to Zaira. "What sort of jobs do these mage crews do, exactly?"

We'd reached the bridge; Zaira stopped and leaned on the stone rail, scowling down into the murky canal water. Lamps flickered on poles on either side of her, casting light and shadow across her face. "There are only three gray-market mage crews in the Tallows, and I know all of them. They're all right. They do little jobs—harmless stuff, like fraud and smuggling, maybe the occasional heist. This sounds like a setup to me."

I fidgeted with the strap of my satchel, working through the implications. "If Lord Caulin claims to have a tip about Ruven hiring alchemists from the Tallows, but Caulin himself turns out to be the one hiring Tallows mage crews...yes. That only makes sense if he's trying to set up some kind of deception."

"Or if he's working for Ruven," Marcello said grimly, his voice so low the night almost swallowed it.

"I'd like to say that's impossible, but Caulin only has his seat on the Council because his predecessor worked with traitors. And there's Ruven's potion to consider." I gnawed my lip. Caulin should be getting his blood tested regularly, but we would be fools to consider any of our precautions infallible.

"Either way, I'll bet it doesn't end well for the mages." Zaira flicked a chip of loose mortar off the bridge at a passing boat. "As usual. Can't you tell your mamma and get Lord Liar sent to his room?"

"It's not that easy. He's a member of the Council of Nine, and we don't have any proof." I hadn't forgotten my mother's warning; this could be a gambit to get me to make false accusations that would destroy my credibility, or to give him an excuse to move against my friends. "We don't even know that Caulin is the one who hired them. We have to tread very carefully, or risk stepping into a trap."

"I agree we can't confront Lord Caulin with what we have, but we can't just do nothing," Marcello objected. "What if he *is* working for Ruven? What if he poisons half the Council at this party?"

"I'll pass a warning to my mother, and I'm certain she can at least arrange for additional security at the party. But this is happening tomorrow. We don't have time to find out whether

Caulin is truly behind this, and what he might be up to." I took a deep breath. "If we want a chance to unravel this, we'll have to attend Lady Aurica's party ourselves."

I scanned Lady Aurica's party tensely as I danced with Scipio da Morante, the doge's stiff-backed bore of a younger brother and the holder of their family seat on the Council of Nine. Zaira had a much better partner in Terika, who had offered to come along since we might have to deal with a rogue alchemist—but given the warm flush on her cheeks and the glow in her eyes as she danced with Zaira, I rather suspected she'd had a secondary objective. I did my best to appear to listen appreciatively to Scipio's rambling story as we circled each other, in the slim hopes it might help sway him to vote for my Falcon reform act; but my attention was on the party around us, afraid that I'd miss something critical if I so much as blinked.

Lady Aurica had opened up her ballroom and hung it with silk bunting trimmed with grapevines and berries, symbols of the Grace of Bounty; the party was open to anyone who made a donation of a ducat or more to the Temple of Bounty's fund to feed the poor. Hundreds of guests in fancifully embroidered coats and extravagant gowns swirled on the dance floor or frequented the generous buffet, and music and laughter filled the air beneath the soft warm glow of luminaries shaped like apples and pears. The servants wore masks with a vine-and-fruit motif, as a nod to the approaching Festival of Luck and its signature masquerade. The choice muddled the theme somewhat, but I had to admit they looked striking as they passed around trays of wine selected from the Empire's finest vineyards.

The guards stationed discreetly around the ballroom wore the same masks; my mother had taken my warning seriously and made certain to send Lady Aurica additional security. It was all too easy to imagine a hundred kinds of mischief one could hire a mage to accomplish here, ranging from harmless pranks to assassination.

The dance finally ended without any sign of trouble, and I excused myself before Scipio da Morante could launch into another anecdote about his shipping ventures. Perhaps I should take another pass at the buffet, to use my alchemy detection ring to check for Ruven's potion and perhaps sample a little more of the pauldronfish risotto. I claimed a glass of wine from a passing tray and started in that direction.

"Lady Amalia," said a muffled voice, just as I lifted the full-bodied red to my lips.

I turned and nearly spilled it all over my burgundy silk gown. It was one of the masked servants, his head bowed diffidently—except that he spoke with the voice of Lord Caulin.

"Why, Lord Caulin," I greeted him, somewhat breathlessly. "I confess myself surprised to find you here—and in disguise, no less."

"Truly?" His voice might be mild, but his dark eyes shone sharp as knives through the holes in his mask. "Yet I hear you are the one to whom we owe the tip that some incident might occur here tonight. Of course I am deeply concerned, as always, about the security of the Serene City. It's only natural for me to watch over this event in person."

"Of course." I offered him a gracious nod, buying myself a brief moment. I had to think of a way to trick him into revealing some hint of his intent. "One of my associates was fortunate enough to stumble across the information, but I'm afraid it was dreadfully vague."

"What exactly did your contact tell you?" Caulin asked, his tone light and curious, his eyes flicking across the crowd.

"Only that a mage crew might engage in some manner of

illegal activity here tonight." *Let him underestimate me.* I waved vaguely at our surroundings. "I naturally connected it to your own tip about Ruven hiring mages from the Tallows to use against Raverra."

Which was true, so far as it went. Never mind that I suspected the mage crew was working for Caulin himself rather than Ruven.

Caulin's shoulders relaxed visibly. "Just so. I, too, suspect that the two threats may be one and the same. I hope you aren't here with some impetuous notion of catching the criminals in the act?"

I laughed. "I'm here for the buffet, Lord Caulin, like everyone else. I will confess that curiosity as to what may unfold here provides extra spice, but I know my own limitations and am content to leave the catching of criminals to those who have experience in the matter." I neglected to mention that Zaira and I had a certain amount of experience rooting out treachery, ourselves.

"Indeed." I couldn't see much of Caulin's face beneath the mask, but his voice sounded like he was smiling. "Very well then, my lady. I had best get back to watching for these miscreants, so we can stop them before they strike."

"Of course." I dipped him a small curtsy.

As Caulin moved off, I noted which of the guards and servants he nodded to; those ones must be his. It would be much harder to discreetly intercept Zaira's associates with Caulin watching.

"You're stiff as a coffin lid," Zaira greeted me, sweeping up with Terika on her arm in a great rustling of silk skirts. Both of them were flushed from the dance floor and smiling broadly. "Relax and enjoy yourself. It won't kill you."

"It might, if we don't spot your friends and they poison the food," I said, my voice pitched low. "Have you seen any sign of anyone you know?"

"Not yet. But if you scowl around like that, they'll know you're watching for trouble, and we'll never catch them." She squeezed Terika's linked arm close to her side affectionately, while Terika picked glasses of wine off a passing tray for the two of them. "That's why dancing is perfect. Keeps you occupied, leaves your mind free, gives you an excuse to look all around the room. Where's Captain Loverboy? You could dance with him."

All thoughts of finding a way to delicately warn Zaira about Caulin flew out of my head. "Oh! I couldn't."

"Why not? Your crow beau doesn't seem the jealous type."

My cheeks burned. "I think things are confused enough between Marcello and me already." Nonetheless, my eyes drifted over to where Marcello was in conversation with the officer of the imperial guards providing security for Lady Aurica tonight. He was such a splendid dancer.

Zaira snorted. "Stop overthinking it and dance with your soldier boy. Or I'll start telling random star-eyed young partygoers that the Cornaro heir is *right there* and maybe if they dance with you you'll fall in love and make them rich beyond their wildest dreams."

"You wouldn't dare!"

"Oh, it's a dare now, is it?" Zaira's eyes gleamed ominously. "Well, in that case—" She broke off, her gaze going past me. "Hells take it, someone just poisoned the chocolate soup."

Chapter Four

W hat?" I swiveled, but didn't see anything unusual. Zaira was already moving, however, with Terika on her heels; I hurried to catch up, murmuring apologies as we wove past gentry decked out in lace and brocade, brushing against silk and velvet skirts that cleared islands of space in the crowded ballroom.

The chocolate soup stood in its glory at the center of the buffet in a massive shallow bowl, frothy meringue floating atop it like puffs of summer cloud. As we arrived, a stately patrician woman in an ostentatious gold gown was just dipping a ladle with white-gloved fingers to fill her bowl.

"Oops," Zaira said, and with both hands, she heaved the great bowl over onto the floor.

Chocolate flooded everywhere. I scrambled back, snatching my skirts away from the splashing menace; a few partygoers shrieked, and one young man in fluttering lace cuffs frantically waved his fan at it, as if he could blow the spreading spill away from his fine clothes.

Terika threw her hands to her face in horror as if she'd been the one to knock it over and cried out, "Sorry, sorry!" All attention turned to her at once. As Terika rushed about making a great show of fussing over the mess, I almost missed Zaira slipping away through the crowd toward the side corridor to the kitchen—the same one down which she and I had once lurked to overhear the Vaskandran ambassador's private conversation.

I caught up to her in time to see her corner a slim young boy before he could disappear into the kitchen. He was dressed like a servant in one of their masks, but I recognized the cellist from the Laughing Siren.

"Have you poisoned anything else?" Zaira demanded. "Are you working alone? Quick, damn you, before it's too late!"

The boy shook his head, panicked, pressing his back to the wall.

A young woman rounded the corner from the ballroom, resplendent in a lace-trimmed gown of sea-foam green and a spectacular feathered hairpin to match; I would have assumed she was a merchant or perhaps even a patrician lady, but the sharp glare she directed at Zaira was one of personal recognition.

"Now, now, Zaira darling, no need to make a scene," she said, menace beneath the purring surface of her voice. "I thought we were friends! Or have you washed your hands of us common folk now that you're eating off silver plates in the Mews?"

"We were never friends," Zaira snapped. "But I'm here to do you a favor anyway, and stop you from making a demon of a mistake. You're being used, Miranda."

I glanced out at the crowded ballroom. We hadn't drawn any attention yet, but we were bound to, and I definitely didn't want Lord Caulin to see whom we were talking to. "Shall we take this discussion to a private room?" I asked.

Miranda looked back and forth between us, her eyes narrowed. "All right," she said at last. "But if you ever want to show your face in the Tallows again, Zaira, this had better be good."

"First of all, quickly, did you poison anything besides the chocolate soup?" Zaira asked, as soon as the door to Lady Aurica's private conversation room shut behind us.

No one sat in the cozily arranged chairs; Miranda stood with her arms crossed, glaring at Zaira, and the boy stood uneasily beside her, half hiding behind her skirts. Zaira paced, her hands clasped tight behind her back.

"We didn't *poison* anything," Miranda protested. "And you're meddling in things you should leave alone."

"Anything besides the soup," Zaira growled. "Or I go burn the whole buffet to be sure."

"Not yet," Miranda sighed. "And you don't need to be so dramatic. It's just sleep potion."

I blinked. "Sleep potion? Are you sure?"

"I made it myself, so yes," Miranda snapped.

"That doesn't make a damned lick of sense," Zaira said. "You're not even mage-marked—it would last, what, ten minutes?"

"I'll have you know mine is good for a full quarter of an hour." Miranda crossed her arms. "Best you can buy in the Tallows."

"Didn't you ask yourself why in the Nine Hells someone would hire you to put sleep potion in the soup at a fancy party?" Zaira demanded. "You *must* have realized this is a setup."

"That's what I was telling you, Auntie," the boy muttered.

"You're beyond your depth, Zaira," Miranda snarled. "If you had any idea who hired me—"

"Oh, but we do," I said.

Miranda looked ready to spit out a contemptuous retort, but the boy tugged at her sleeve, his eyes wide, and nodded meaningfully toward me. She frowned, then glanced at Zaira's jess, then back to me, and her eyes widened. "Bugger us all. The Cornaro heir." She pulled off a credible curtsy.

"It was Lord Caulin who hired you, was it not?" I asked,

sharpening my voice. We didn't have much time; I couldn't let Caulin figure out we were talking to her.

"I can't tell you the name of my client," Miranda said, with a toss of her long black hair.

"If it's Council business, my mother would know about it." I smiled sweetly. "She's at our palace, just up the Imperial Canal. Do you want me to send a message asking her to come give you permission to talk about it?"

"Grace of Mercy, please don't bring La Contessa into this," the boy said, turning gray. "Yes, yes, it was Lord Caulin!"

"Giram!" Miranda scolded.

"I don't want to die in prison." The boy's eyes stretched wide and bright as luminary crystals. "I told you this job was no good."

"And did he give you a reason why one of the Council would hire a gutter rat like you to put a bunch of rich old goats to sleep for a few minutes?" Zaira asked, crossing her arms.

"To turn the Assembly against the Falcon reform act," I breathed, the realization falling on me like a dropped curtain.

Miranda stared at me blankly. "What?"

"Lord Caulin knows full well the best way to decimate any support for looser restrictions on magic is to make people afraid of mages," I said. "If he creates an incident here that frightens the Assembly, because many of them are personally affected by the attack, and he makes a show of catching the mages behind it, he can more easily convince them that mages are dangerous and need to be contained."

"He's setting you up," Zaira summarized bluntly.

Miranda crossed her arms. "Then it's not a very good plan. I could just tell people the truth: that he's the one who hired me."

"Not if you're dead, you can't," Zaira said.

"I suspect that's why he's here himself tonight," I concluded grimly. "So he can make certain you die in the scuffle to capture you, before anyone else can talk to you."

The boy Giram leaned in close against Miranda's skirts, looking positively ill.

"He's here tonight?" Miranda demanded sharply.

"Yes, in a servant's mask, so no one can spot him. In fact, we'd better finish in here soon, before he notices we're all missing and realizes we're talking to each other."

"But you don't *know* he hired us to create an incident and set us up as scapegoats." Miranda fingered her lacy sleeves; I caught the gleam of metal up one of them.

"It's the only reason for this job that makes any damned sense," Zaira said. "Weren't you even a bit suspicious?"

Miranda drew herself up. "Of course I was. I'm not an idiot. That's why I made him give us a paper." Her hand stirred toward her sleeve again. "So if anyone tried to arrest us, I could show them we had the Council's backing. He didn't want to give it to me, but I told him we wouldn't do the job without it."

Zaira snorted. "You should've known right then that the old stingroach wasn't going to let you live. If it was really Council business, he'd just send his own people, not go looking for a mage in the Tallows who he could throw away like a cheap glove when he was done."

The feathers on Miranda's hairpin drooped. "It was a *lot* of money. I'll admit I got greedy."

"But you still have the paper," Giram reminded her anxiously. "You said they couldn't throw us in prison so long as we had the paper."

"I'll bet he told you to be sure to carry it on you in case of misunderstandings," Zaira said. "Because paper is easy to take off a dead body, and it burns so prettily."

"Of course I have it on me," Miranda said, defeat dragging at her voice. "The whole point is to have it in case someone tries to arrest us. Curse him, he played us for fools."

But my heart had quickened. "Wait. Can I have this writ?"

Miranda and the boy exchanged startled glances. "Why?"

"Because," I said, a bubble of triumph rising in my chest, "paper is easy to take off a dead body, but much harder to retrieve from a live noblewoman. And incriminating evidence makes the *best* insurance."

Miranda eyed me suspiciously. "If I give it to you, what protection do I have against *him*?"

"Mine," I said firmly.

"And he'll have no reason to go after you anymore, if you didn't do the job and Amalia's got the evidence already." Zaira shrugged. "You keep it, you're putting a target on yourself."

"Can I trust her?" Miranda asked Zaira, jerking her chin in my direction.

I tensed, trying not to show how much I cared about the answer.

Zaira didn't so much as glance at me. "Her? She's a terrible liar. She couldn't trick a brat out of their least favorite candy. You can trust her."

"Thanks," I muttered. Zaira flashed me a grin.

Miranda let out a long breath. Then she reached into her sleeve and pulled out a carefully folded paper bearing the imperial seal in blue wax. "Take it, then," she said. "And stick him between the ribs with it for me."

I waited to make sure Miranda and the boy had left the party before confronting Lord Caulin. I had to make certain I was approaching the right masked servant, so Zaira and I watched and picked out the one who was moving restlessly about the ballroom, exchanging murmured words with certain guards. Once he was alone, I approached him, with Zaira and Terika watching from close by.

"Lord Caulin," I called, trying to make my eyes as wide and my voice as innocent as possible. "May I have a word?"

He drew closer, glancing around to see whether anyone had heard his name. I took a moment to relish his annoyance at my apparent disregard for his attempts to keep his presence unknown. For once, I had an unbeatable hand, and knew it before he did, and the feeling was intoxicating.

This must be how my mother felt all the time. I could finally begin to understand why she loved playing this game.

"What is it, Lady Amalia?" Lord Caulin asked, his voice low.

"I've learned something about the criminal deeds planned for tonight," I whispered.

He leaned in close. "What did you learn?" His tone was wary, guarded, but not yet concerned. *Let's see if I can change that.*

"I learned," I said, my voice going deep and deadly serious, "that you're new at this."

Caulin froze.

"Your authority was always secret before," I murmured. "You never had the power to sign anything, to write orders and writs, to put your seal on documents. You never learned how to protect yourself."

I heard the faintest, briefest hiss of air, as if Caulin had sucked his breath in through his teeth.

"It must have seemed so harmless," I went on, with false sympathy. "That document would only be out in the world for a few days, and then you could destroy it. Even if you somehow failed to retrieve it, what harm could it do? You'd already have frightened the Assembly into seeing mages as a threat. You'd have what you wanted."

"And what do *you* want, Lady Amalia?" Caulin asked, grating the words out.

"What do *I* want?" I let my anger come through at last. "I want you to do your job and protect the Serene Empire, Lord

Caulin. You let the Council believe your little scheme was Ruven's plot, distracting us from whatever he's truly planning. You had better find out what that is and stop him, Lord Caulin, or the blood he spills will be on your hands."

Caulin's mask dipped in a wary nod. "I assure you I have been doing my utmost to uncover his plans, and I will continue to do so. If that's all—"

"One more thing," I interrupted him. "If you try anything underhanded like this again—if you do anything to threaten me, my friends, those nice mages you attempted to hire, or the Empire you are sworn to uphold—I will let the whole Assembly know you were willing to poison them to win political points. And I'll show them your writ to prove it."

"Give me the writ, and I'll abide by those terms," Caulin said evenly.

"Oh, no. My mother raised me better than that." I shook my head. "I'm keeping the writ, Lord Caulin. Let it serve as a reminder of a warning you should have taken to heart before this."

"And that is?"

I met his eyes through the holes in his mask. "I told you it wasn't my mother you should be afraid of."

At my mother's advice, I allowed Lord Caulin the grace of telling the doge and the Council that his information about Ruven hiring Raverran alchemists was wrong rather than exposing his scheme to them.

"The doge knows the truth of the matter regardless," La Contessa assured me. "But if you allow Caulin to retain his dignity, he'll have more to lose, and you'll have greater leverage over him." She seemed quite pleased to hear that I had obtained my first blackmail material on a Council member at the young age of nineteen; if I didn't know better, I'd almost think her eyes went somewhat misty.

We were left, however, with one inescapable problem: with Caulin's tip proven false, we had no leads on Ruven's true plans.

Terika's blood test had uncovered a couple of poisoned clerks among a Callamornish general's staff, but no victims of Ruven's potion yet in Raverra, or so Ciardha informed me during my breakfast briefing. Such morning news between sips of warm chocolate had replaced my customary dinners with my mother more often than not of late, as the grim business of preparing for war frequently kept La Contessa at the Imperial Palace overnight.

"The Council may have questions for you about what exactly Lord Ignazio told you before he died." Ciardha laid another paper on top of the pile of intelligence reports and social invitations beside my plate of warm fluffy rolls and almond pastry: a schedule that thoroughly vivisected my day in Ciardha's tidy handwriting. "I've reserved two hours in case they call for you during their meeting this afternoon."

"I need to work on building up support for my Falcon reforms today," I fretted, crushing pastry crumbs between my fingers. "I wanted to speak with Lord Bertali about trading support for his tariff reductions—which I was going to vote for anyway, but he doesn't need to know that. And to persuade the Duchess of Calsida that her city will benefit if Raverra doesn't sweep up all its mage-marked. If I'm sitting around awaiting the pleasure of the Council—"

Ciardha tapped the schedule with one elegant finger. "I've arranged your meetings for this evening, Lady. We haven't forgotten."

"Ah. Of course. Thank you."

I actually looked at the schedule, this time, feeling foolish.

The low golden light streaming through the breakfast room windows caught tiny shadows in every irregularity of the vellum. I drew in a breath to ask whether we'd gotten any useful information from the controlled Callamornish clerks.

But Ciardha lifted a finger, her head tilted to listen, suddenly alert and poised as a cat who hears a mouse in the wainscoting.

"Excuse me, Lady," she murmured. She flowed to the side of one of the breakfast room's tall windows, which let out onto a balcony overlooking the canal. Gauzy curtains obscured the balcony itself; if there was anything out there, I couldn't see it.

She paused a moment, still as a stalking heron. I barely dared breathe.

Then she moved, with lightning speed and fluid grace. Before my eyes could even sort out what had happened, the window was open and she was out on the balcony, the gleaming point of a dagger held beneath the chin of a lean young man who lifted his hands in surprised surrender, an incongruous laugh lighting his familiar face.

Black feathers stirred at his shoulders, and the piercing yellow rings of his mage mark met my eyes through the gap in the blowing curtains. "Hello, Lady Amalia," he said. "I hope I haven't come at an inconvenient time."

Ciardha eased her dagger away from his throat. "You appear to have a visitor, Lady," she announced.

I rose from my chair and offered him a bow, suppressing a flutter of mirth or something more in my chest. "Hello, Kathe."

Chapter Five

In Raverra, we have a quaint custom of arriving at doors when paying visits," I said.

Ciardha whisked the papers off the breakfast table before Kathe might see their contents. "I won't be far if you need me, Lady," she said as she withdrew, with a cool warning glance at my guest. I had no doubt I would find my morning appointments all efficiently rescheduled; with Ruven and his allies poised to attack at our borders, very little took precedence over our alliance with the Crow Lord of Let.

Kathe gazed around the breakfast room, taking in the artifice runes worked into the decorative molding around the tall windows, the fresco of the Nine Graces in their garden set in an oval medallion in the ceiling, and the luminaries in their gilded sconces, crystals dark now in the light of the winter sun. His black cloak with its feathered shoulders seemed jarringly out of place, and his simple gray leather tunic with its asymmetrical Vaskandran embroidery snaking like lightning down one edge was no better. He was a breath of winter setting a candle to gutter, a crow's feather fluttering down onto a silken pillow, a black cat settling with a secret grin among jeweled clockwork mice.

Graces help me, he was beautiful.

"Doors are boring," he said. "Though I should have remembered your bodyguard might not be amused."

"Ciardha isn't my bodyguard. She's . . . my mother's second in command, I suppose."

Kathe lifted an eyebrow. "Shouldn't that be you?"

I laughed. "I'm not qualified." I gestured to a chair, but Kathe prowled around the room, poking curiously at the mantel clock and casting a rather disdainful glance at a potted plant. I supposed they didn't have much need for either in the wild domains of Vaskandar.

I had no idea how to host a guest who wouldn't sit down. Kathe had never visited my home before; in the past two months we'd written back and forth, but only seen each other once, meeting halfway in Callamorne.

"What brings you to the Serene City?" I asked, falling back on ritual pleasantry.

"You, of course. It would be terribly rude to neglect the woman I'm courting."

His circuit of the room brought him to my side. This close, I could feel the barely checked power that shivered the air around him. He offered a hand, a question in his eyes.

I let him lift the backs of my fingers to his lips. He placed a slow, deliberate kiss on my knuckles; I held his gaze, focusing all my will on not flushing. With Kathe, I never wanted to relinquish a crumb of control, or Hells only knew where we'd end up.

A discreet cough sounded at the door, and Old Anzo entered the room, bearing a fresh tray of chocolate and pastries for me and my unexpected visitor. I snatched my hand back, avoiding the old man's eyes. He'd worked for my mother since long before I was born, and for her father before that; I tried not to wonder what he must think of the family heir courting a Witch Lord.

Though to be fair, Old Anzo had probably seen things I

couldn't dream of, working for the Cornaro family for half a century. And indeed, he exuded nothing but professional calm as he laid out new dishes, gathered my old ones onto his tray, and left the room.

"Of course, I wouldn't arrive without a gift," Kathe said once Old Anzo was gone, his eyes gleaming. "And we all know information is the best present of all. Tell me what you have for me, and I'll tell you what I've got for you."

"What makes you think I have anything for you?" I asked, keeping my tone light and teasing despite the quickening of my pulse.

Kathe lifted an eyebrow. "You are a Cornaro, my lady. You always have cards in your hand."

"Very well." I took a sip of chocolate to buy myself time to organize my thoughts, which was difficult under Kathe's watchful, yellow-ringed gaze. We'd been trading simple messages by letter, often carried by Kathe's crows, but having him here in the flesh staring at me was an entirely different experience. "We've managed to infiltrate the court of the Lady of Thorns' daughter, such as it is. She's desperate, with the Lady of Lynxes carving off pieces of her domain and no confidence in Ruven's continued alliance, and would take almost any bargain that will leave her with enough of a domain to survive. There's advantage to be had there one way or another, as her neighbor."

"Interesting." Kathe tapped his chin. "Perhaps I can broker a peace deal between her and the Lady of Lynxes, and wind up with everyone owing me favors."

"Do you have any information on Ruven?" I asked. "I've heard some intelligence that he might be planning a move against the Empire." I tried to sound casual; with Kathe, it wouldn't do to seem to want something too much. I doubted he could resist dangling it out of reach, no matter how sincere his promises to assist the Serene Empire in fighting Ruven.

"Heh. He's likely planning *several* moves against the Empire. My crows can barely keep up with him." He dragged a chair at a confidential angle to mine and settled in it with a swirl of dark feathers. "What do you want to hear about first? Subterfuge or war?"

"It's not a war until he invades us." I perched next to Kathe, entirely unable to relax in his presence, clutching my fresh cup of chocolate in both hands. "Which the doge is certain won't happen until the spring, given that the border passes are buried deep in snow."

Kathe's eyes danced. "But you know better, don't you?"

"I know that this is a man who, when he wanted to take out a fortress, decided that the best way was to erupt a volcano." I leaned in toward Kathe. "I don't think a bit of snow will stop him."

"It wouldn't stop any sufficiently determined Witch Lord willing to take some losses. The reason you haven't been invaded in winter before is because most of us have more care for the lives in our domains, even if only as a source of power." Kathe's mouth twisted as if he'd tasted something bitter. "Ruven, bastion of compassion that he is, has no such reservations. His reserves are marching to the border. He's getting ready to make a move."

I let out a long breath. "That's very good to know." Our forces were concentrated in the heavily fortified river valleys and the Loreician hills; we'd need to reinforce the high passes as quickly as possible if they weren't as safe as we'd thought.

"I've got more for you, but it's your turn." Kathe sniffed his chocolate and took an experimental sip, and his brows lifted. "This isn't coffee."

"No, it's chocolate. I like it much better." I sipped from my own cup. "I'll make this one quick: Terika has come up with a blood test to identify people who've fallen under the control of Ruven's potion. I can get you the recipe, if you've got any alchemists."

"Oh, that *is* useful. I'd know if he tampered with my own people, of course, but it's wearisome not being able to trust anyone visiting Let." Kathe's grin faded. "I wish I had good news to give you in return, but mine is grimmer, I'm afraid. Ruven is making human chimeras."

My guts knotted, remembering the creatures I'd seen in Vaskandar—three-eyed hounds armored in bristling thorns, half-feline reptiles with venomous fangs—and the crushed thing that was not a scorpion on the floor of Ignazio's cell. "He's doing that to *humans*?"

"He's a charming fellow, isn't he?" Kathe's lip curled in disgust. "There isn't much that's forbidden to Witch Lords in Vaskandar. But every rule we have, he breaks, no matter how old and sacred. He's earned a lot of enemies, and even his few allies are starting to distance themselves from him."

"Maybe we can use that." I frowned. "The Lady of Bears and the Serpent Lord still have armies poised to attack us across the Loreician border, and it's forcing us to split our defenses. If we can put pressure on them to back off for fear of being associated with Ruven, we'd be able to bring more of our strength against him. Are any of the more influential Witch Lords taking a stand against Ruven?"

"Your esteemed ancestor the Lady of Eagles is already annoyed with him. It wouldn't take much to convince her to let it be known that anyone continuing to work with him will earn her displeasure, and that's probably all it would take to get Ruven's allies to abandon him." Kathe rubbed his hands. "Nothing quite like sowing a little discord among your enemies. I'll talk to her when I get back to Vaskandar."

I smiled. "Thank you."

Kathe shrugged my gratitude off. "I have a long debt to work off before you owe me any thanks."

An awkward silence fell between us. It was far too easy to forget that he'd betrayed me, but not so easy to forgive. I traced the rim of my chocolate cup.

"I suppose you do," I said at last. "It's difficult to entirely trust you after that, Kathe. I want to, but I can't."

"Trust is such a broad concept, my lady. I have friends I would trust with my life, but not my secrets. Others I would trust with my secrets, but not with the last slice of cake."

I raised an eyebrow. "So with what can I trust *you*?"

A glitter came into his eyes. "I'll bet you can guess how I'm going to answer you."

"I'll wager I can, too." I couldn't stop a smile. "'Let's play a game.'"

"You are an oracle, my lady." He drew a leg up onto his chair, as if sitting still was too much for him and he might launch into action at any moment. "Now, one could argue that trust is nothing more than knowing how a person will reliably choose when faced with conflicting principles. For instance, in a case of honesty versus politeness, I daresay you can trust your friend Zaira to always choose honesty."

I laughed. "Yes, even when most decent people might disagree with her."

"Then shall we take turns presenting each other with such quandaries?" He spread a hand, as if offering me something marvelous. "We can both answer each one."

"Very well." I couldn't resist the chance for a glimpse into Kathe's inner workings. "Who should go first?"

"How about we start with my example?" He cocked his head. "Honesty or politeness?"

"Politeness," I said firmly. "Unless it's a matter of grave importance. And you?"

"Truth, always." He grinned. "But I admit that I do sometimes exploit the difference between truth and honesty."

I raised an eyebrow. "Sometimes?"

"Often." He nodded graciously. "Your turn to ask."

"All right." I thought a moment. "How about this one: friends or country?"

Kathe's face went solemn. "As the Witch Lord of Let, I must always put the domain I rule above my personal attachments. And my friends wouldn't want me to sacrifice the good of my domain for them. But it's hard, I admit, because I treasure my friends."

I nodded. "I wouldn't value blind patriotism over my friends. When you hold power in a great empire, there are times when you must be willing to stand up to it, to keep it from crushing its own people because it's too vast to see them. But if it came down to a matter of survival, between my friends or my whole country, of course I would choose my country."

"You say 'of course,' but I have one or two in my Heartguard who would choose the opposite." Kathe smiled fondly, gazing past my shoulder at someone hundreds of miles away—and for all I knew, he might truly be looking at them, after a fashion, with his magical sense of his own domain. "And there is something to be said for such profound loyalty, even when it flies in the face of reason."

Zaira might let the Empire burn to save Terika, now that I thought of it. And Bree would try to save everyone, rejecting the choice entirely. "I suppose you're right," I said. "Your turn, I believe."

"Let's see." He tapped his lips a moment in thought, then lifted a finger. "Aha! A classic: your life, or your honor?"

"It depends," I said slowly. "I wouldn't throw my life away just for pride's sake. But there are some matters of honor worth dying for. I'd die before bending the knee to Ruven, for example."

Kathe let out a gentle breath, like the ghost of a sigh. "Perhaps it comes of being a vivomancer, but I put life before honor. Honor is a thing you can fix later if you break it. Life, once destroyed, can't be mended."

"I suppose you have a point. But there are times when you need to make a stand. Things more important than one person's life." I shrugged, feeling a bit foolish. "Maybe it's my Callamornish side talking."

"Most likely." Kathe smiled. "Callamornes are a fine people. And stubborn as rocks. Your turn, then."

I couldn't help thinking of Marcello and Zaira. I had no doubt the former would choose honor, and the latter life. "Hmm, let me think..." *Marcello*. Hells, why not? A game needed stakes. I met Kathe's eyes. "Love or duty?"

He hesitated. "Do you mean romantic love, or love in general?"

"Romantic love." I had put this card on the table; I had to play out my hand.

"Ah." A strange sadness came into Kathe's voice, with the suddenness of summer rain. "I don't... well. One must be very careful about who one loves, as a Witch Lord. For one thing, unless something goes wrong, you're going to outlive nearly anyone you might fall in love with."

I hadn't thought of that. "I can see where that might dampen matters."

"I might have loved Jathan," he said quietly, after a silence. "But he was part of my domain, so I couldn't let myself think of him that way."

The name eluded my recall for a moment. But then I remembered: Kathe's friend whom the Lady of Thorns had murdered. "Oh! Oh," I said.

"I suppose that means I already chose duty, doesn't it? Or I'd have figured out I loved him while he was still alive." He took my hand in his slim cold one, an odd, sad smile pulling at his lips. "I have to admit the romantic life of a Witch Lord sometimes seems hopeless. But I think I could come to love you, Amalia, if you allowed it."

Words caught in my throat. *Honesty over politeness, indeed.* I'd always thought the term *falling in love* was a ridiculous one; love was something that grew like a nurtured seed, and anything you could stumble into like a hole in bad pavement was infatuation at best. But every time I caught an elusive flicker of the true soul behind the mischief in Kathe's eyes, I felt myself sliding inexorably closer to a dizzying abyss.

He is a Witch Lord, I reminded myself firmly. *He was willing to get you badly hurt and possibly killed to have his vengeance.* If he was fascinating, so what? Sharks were fascinating, too.

"How about you?" he asked, cheerful again. "Love or duty?"

The question hit me like spilled wine. "Duty," I said. "Like you, I've already made that choice." I'd said as much to Marcello, when I told him not to wait for me.

Kathe winced, and I realized how harsh that sounded, after what he'd said. His hand still clasped mine, and I squeezed it and quickly added, "But I don't believe the two need to be mutually exclusive."

His lips quirked. "Does Raverran romance always sound like contract negotiations?"

"Probably," I laughed.

A discreet knock came at the door.

"Enter," I called. I didn't release Kathe's hand; we were courting, after all, and holding hands was well within the bounds of correct behavior even in public.

Ciardha appeared, bowing with elegant precision. No doubt it was the exact degree appropriate for a visiting Witch Lord. "Your pardon, Lady, but before I leave to attend to La Contessa, there is one more small matter you might wish to attend to. If you were to select a mask for the Festival of Luck, you would alleviate a great deal of Rica's anxiety about ensuring you have a gown to match, and it occurs to me that Lord Kathe might enjoy the opportunity to learn more about Raverran culture."

Kathe blinked. "You have a mask festival?"

"You don't celebrate the Night of Masks in Vaskandar?" I asked.

He shook his head. "We celebrate the seasons of the earth, rather than the gifts of your Graces. But I like masks, and I like learning."

I stood, drawing him to his feet with me, a grin of anticipation spreading across my face. "Well then, I have a treat for you."

Madame Nicola's mask shop was one of the best in the Serene City, and as such, it was abominably crowded with the Night of Masks only days away. But if one were a Cornaro, and especially a Cornaro with a Witch Lord on her arm, one need not even set foot in the packed storefront with its shelves of staring painted faces adorned with bright beads and feathers. For that matter, I could easily have had a servant arrange for me to peruse any number of masks at my palace, but I was glad for the excuse to show Kathe the city—and besides, there were political advantages for both of us to be seen together in public and remind the world of our alliance.

Madame Nicola herself spotted us before we could attempt to insinuate ourselves into the elbow-rubbing masses spilling out her door. In mere moments she had us ensconced in a private back room, draped in burgundy crushed velvet to block the sunlight and illuminated with warm festival lanterns to mimic the lighting the masks would be seen in during the festival. We sipped wine in comfortable chairs while her assistants brought us an assortment of her best masks, laying them out on a luxurious spill of deep black velvet on a long table.

And then Madame Nicola apologized for the busyness of her shop, encouraged us to call for her if we had any questions, and left us alone to peruse the masks with nothing but a mirror for company, shooing her assistants out with a backward glance and nod in my direction. That was one of the things I liked about Madame Nicola's; she understood that not everyone wanted someone hovering at their elbow trying to sell them something when they were attempting to make a decision.

It also left me alone once more with Kathe. In the close atmosphere of the mask shop, the prickling energy of his proximity was inescapable.

He bent over the assortment of masks with great interest. "This is lovely," he said, handing me a delicate confection of glass beads strung on complex swirls of golden wire, "but is it truly wise to put an artifice device on your face?"

"That depends on what it does. This one is harmless." I held it up to show him, the cold wire pressing into my nose and cheekbones. My vision immediately went hazy and green, then began fading slowly into blue. "See, it just cycles the color of your eyes."

Kathe blinked, then lifted his long fingers to the mask, running them delicately along one edge. "How strange. It does make you look like an entirely different person."

"That's the point. It's a game."

As the room warmed through dusky purple toward rose, Kathe's fingertips trailed down my cheek. "You know how I love games."

My skin shivered pleasantly in the wake of his touch. I swallowed. "You can help me choose, then." I set the mask aside, and full color rushed back into the room. The warm lamplight gilded the lines of Kathe's face. "That one's a bit distracting, I must admit."

"How about this one?" He took up a fantastical creation of cunningly shaped and painted leather: a visage of the Demon of Nightmares, with eight twisting black horns and sharp glaring brow ridges. "You could terrify small children."

"That one might look better on you." I took it from him, then held it up to his face instead of my own. His hair tickled my fingers, surprisingly soft. "There, now you're the classic Raverran idea of a Witch Lord."

The mask made his face cruel and fierce, the piercing yellow rings of his mage mark blazing out from dark shadows. But he ruined the effect with a mischievous smile. "It's not very practical, though. You'd poke someone in the eye if you tried to kiss them."

"We can't have that." I lowered the mask, a stray lock of his hair sliding briefly through my fingers. It was somewhat longer than when I'd met him, with more white-blond showing above the black-stained tips. I wondered who dyed it for him, or if he did it himself. "Let's find a more functional mask, then."

We took turns trying on a grand peacock feather masterpiece, which Kathe posed with rather dramatically, and a gold filigree sun mask that spread rays far enough that I feared I'd spear innocent bystanders every time I turned my head. A silk-lined mask of cunningly detailed papier-mâché caught my eye, with deep, rich shades of lagoon green and ocean blue around the eyes. It swept to one side in a shape like a wave, with delicately curled spray tipped in gold. The jewel-hued paint had depth and complexity to it, like the sea itself, and as I held it in my hands I picked out shapes of clouds and ships and faces, holding each briefly in my mind like a dream before it merged back into abstract washes of swirling color. From a distance, the mask would not impress as the others might, but up close, it was gorgeous.

"Try it on," Kathe suggested, and I held it up to my face. It fit comfortably enough, flexing to accommodate my features rather than forcing them into its own shape.

"What do you think?" I asked.

"It's beautiful." Kathe laid a gentle hand along my chin, tilting my face toward the light; the warmth of his touch spread through my whole body. "But does it pass the most important test?"

"Only one way to tell," I whispered, sliding my hand around the back of his neck and up into that down-soft hair as I pulled him toward me.

Our lips met, slow and soft and teasing, the barest brush like falling snow.

A sliver of air slipped between us, enough to take a sharp breath as lightning seemed to slide down my throat and into my belly. I'd closed my eyes, but I felt his mouth shape a smile.

"Better try another angle to be sure," I murmured.

I tipped my head slightly and tried for another quick, light kiss. But somehow it turned warm and melting, and lingered longer than I'd intended. And then there was a rustle of feathers, and his arms went around me, and my own hands slid up beneath his cloak to feel the wiry muscles of his back through the soft leather of his tunic.

"I think this one is good," Kathe said when we came up for air, a husky catch in his voice.

Businesslike footsteps approached the door, and we separated, my fingertips still carrying the warm tingle of his power in them after we slid apart. I smoothed back my hair and struggled to slow my quickened breath. Grace of Love help me, I needed to go splash ice water in my face and stare at some artifice diagrams until the world became rational again.

"Did you find anything you liked, my lady?" Madame Nicola asked, opening the door.

"Quite, yes," I said, removing the mask and hoping she wouldn't notice the flushed cheeks it revealed in the lamplight. "I'll take this one."

Chapter Six

As we stepped out of the mask shop into the sun-drenched square, I struggled to collect myself. I wished I had any real sense of whether this was all just another game to Kathe—or rather, since everything seemed to be a game to him, whether it was a political game or a personal one.

It might be nice to be certain my own motives remained entirely political, for that matter. With Kathe's arm through mine and the tingling energy of his presence all along my side, my heart refused to return to an altogether sedate pace.

"Back at my palace, you mentioned having news of subterfuge," I reminded him as we crossed the square, striving to force my mind back to matters of business.

"Ah, yes. Our game completely distracted me." He grinned slyly, as if daring me to ask which game. "My crows spotted several of Ruven's people sneaking across the border into the Empire, including some of his human chimeras. They were traveling at night and avoiding the roads, heading south toward Raverra."

I didn't like the sound of that at all. "Why would he use chimeras for infiltration? Unless they look human."

"Not at all." Kathe grimaced. "They'd have trouble blending in. But they'll have other abilities. They might be able to see in the dark, climb up walls, move quickly as a cat or fight with the strength of a bear."

"Assassins," I guessed, the winter air chill in my lungs. "Or kidnappers."

"As you say. You'd have a better idea than I who or what their targets might be."

"It could be anything. He could be trying to capture Falcons again, or kill our warlocks, or steal more books of magic from our libraries." I already knew he was seeking a way to make his potion permanent; he could be after the recipe for Demon's Tears, or an expert on poisons. "We need to find out more. Some further hint of what he's up to."

Kathe seemed to hesitate a moment, then sighed. "Alas, much as I would enjoy helping you try to flush Ruven out and block whatever move he's making here, I'm afraid I need to head home already."

"So soon?" I stopped and turned to face him, unable to hide my disappointment. "Surely you'll at least stay for dinner."

"I can't be away from Let for long." Kathe's pale brows drew together. "Not with Ruven testing my borders. It's harder to defend my domain from afar. I'll leave some crows with you, so you can send me a message if something happens."

I closed my lips on all the protests I could have made. What kind of courtship was this, if we only saw each other for half a day once a month? How could he come all this way and only stay a few hours?

But this was only a political courtship, after all, to cement an alliance. And even so, he had come hundreds of miles to see me for those few hours, at a time when his domain faced a dangerous enemy.

"Thank you," I said.

I couldn't kiss him, not with the crowd of mask shoppers outside Madame Nicola's all staring at us sideways and whispering.

I supposed they'd love the show, a juicy piece of gossip to take home: how they'd seen the Cornaro Heir and her Witch Lord suitor kissing in broad daylight beneath the laughing stone eyes of the Grace of Bounty. If I were bolder, perhaps I'd have given it to them. But my first kiss with Kathe had been for show, and circumstances might call for more of its like in the future; for now, I'd hoard the private kisses we'd shared in the mask shop, a secret between the two of us that might have nothing to do with politics.

"I expect we'll see each other soon enough." Kathe sighed. "It's a shame I can't stay for your mask festival. It sounds like great fun."

"Next year, then," I suggested. Perhaps it was just as well; Raverran society probably wasn't ready for the havoc Kathe could unleash at a masquerade.

Except that Kathe wasn't the Witch Lord whose potential for havoc I needed to worry about right now.

"The Night of Masks." I struck my thigh. "Hells. I'd bet half my fortune that's when Ruven is planning to strike."

"That's when I'd do it," Kathe agreed cheerily. "If you're going to all the trouble to hold a festival themed around disguise and deception, it would seem churlish not to take advantage of it. And it would have a certain dramatic flair."

"You sound altogether too excited at the idea."

"On the contrary, I'm even sadder that I'll miss it. Trying to find Ruven's agents in a citywide masked ball sounds like an excellent game."

"Challenging, though." I lifted a hand to my temple, feeling nearly faint at the sheer magnitude of the task. "And the stakes if we lose could be dauntingly high."

Kathe fixed his yellow-ringed eyes on me with sudden solemnity. "They always are, when you play against a Witch Lord," he said. "But Ruven has a personal grudge against you, so it'll be even worse. Make sure you win, Amalia."

Legends told that in the Dark Days, when the Graces walked the earth and inspired humanity to rise up and fight back against the Demons who ruled over them, the Grace of Luck would sometimes appear at people's doors in disguise—be their homes ever so humble or ever so proud—and beg for food or shelter. Those who offered hospitality were rewarded with Her blessing, and received great fortune; and as such, on the Night of Masks, every household must offer hospitality to any masked reveler who showed up at their door.

This custom had, naturally, evolved in Raverra to the throwing of lavish masquerades, made all the more exciting by the possibility that *anyone* could turn up at one's party, from the doge himself to a notorious jewel thief. So long as they wore an acceptable mask, they could join the festivities. Most Raverrans flitted from ball to ball throughout the night, and the revelry poured out into the streets and canals. It was a day of mysteries and surprises, of charity and cunning, of terrible mistakes to be regretted the next morning and wondrous coincidences to transform one's life. A night of intrigue and enchantment, of romance and adventure.

For me, this year, it was a night of waiting for something terrible to happen.

It was also a security nightmare. The Council of Nine had tripled the usual presence of watch officers in the city, as well as circulating disguised agents through the festivities to watch for any signs of Ruven's plans moving into action, but we still had no real clues as to what those plans might be. The city had to be on guard against everything, everywhere, all the time; and that simply wasn't possible.

Given how tense my back felt after just a couple of hours of bracing for assassination, poison, or mayhem to shatter the night like stained glass, my muscles were trying to make up for every relaxed and oblivious reveler in the Serene City.

Zaira and Terika, however, appeared to be having no such difficulties.

"I'm glad we moved on to this party," Terika pronounced as the two of them swept up to the wine table in Lord Errardi's ballroom, where I lingered to keep a watchful eye out for poisoners. They looked fantastic together, with complementary masks—Zaira's a more tastefully restrained sun mask than the one I'd tried on with Kathe, and Terika's the moon; Zaira's gown was all in layers of fiery gold, and Terika's in waves of silver.

Zaira grunted agreement. "The last one was full of boring old bankers. This one is much better."

"But the food was best at the first one, before that," Terika added.

Lord Errardi's fashionable grandchildren had taken over arranging the elderly Council member's annual Night of Masks festivities, and it was rather evident in the age of many of the attendees; the clutches of older aristocrats shook their heads in the corners at the boisterous antics of the young on the dance floor. I scanned young and old alike, searching for the pale hair common in southern Vaskandar, my attempts to identify people frustrated by the masks that transformed them to twisted gargoyles or flower princes or creepily expressionless dolls.

"They're all equally dangerous," I muttered.

Zaira rolled her eyes. "Come on, Cornaro. It's the Night of Masks. Unclench your arse and have some fun."

"We can't have fun," I said. "Ruven could be getting away

with something horrible as we speak. We have to keep moving from party to party until we figure out what Ignazio was trying to warn us about and stop him."

"You're as bad as Dett," Zaira said, waving disgustedly at where Terika's new Falconer, a gangly Callamornish man with hair like straw, sat reading a book against the far wall. Terika had picked him because he didn't mind her frequent trips to their shared homeland to visit her grandmother; he was an affable, quiet man, generally content to trail along wherever Terika wished to go so long as she let him read. "He wouldn't know a good time if it bit him on the privates, either."

"Besides," Terika said, "we don't even know for certain that Ruven's plan goes into action tonight. And your mother's already doing everything that can be done."

The gnawing unease in my belly wouldn't let go so easily. I couldn't forget Ignazio's voice, floating from the shadows that shrouded his face, telling me the Serene City was in danger. I'd be a fool to ignore a warning that had come at such a high price.

"You know Ruven as well as anyone, Terika," I said. "And you're an alchemist. If you were him, looking to attack the Empire with that potion on the Night of Masks, what would you do?"

Terika pursed her lips a moment, thinking. "I'd try to slip my command potion to people at parties, of course." She lifted a finger. "But I wouldn't try for the Council or the colonel of the Falcons or anyone so high up as that. I'd go to parties in the middle-class districts and look for clerks, house servants, cooks, oarsmen, and the like. Not the people in power, but the ones who lock their doors and make their food and lay out their clothing." She grinned with unnerving cheer. "Then it would be simplicity itself to wait until everyone's guard was down after the festival and spread some poison around to kill or control all my *real* targets!"

Zaira whistled. "We're damned lucky Ruven doesn't have you working for him anymore. You're twisty as a weasel."

"Are you calling me a weasel, my love?" Terika put her hands on her hips, but she was laughing.

Zaira gestured grandly with her wineglass. "Cunning of a weasel, grace of a swan, heart of a lion, breasts of a—"

"Thank you," I interrupted, grateful for the mask that hid at least some of the scarlet I knew was warming my face. "That's an excellent point, if a terrifying one. We'll have to dispatch alchemists to test anyone with any sort of access to key people and places tomorrow morning. There's no way we can watch over every single party in the city."

Zaira shrugged. "Then we talk to everyone who looks interesting about the parties they've been to. Never underestimate gossip as a source of information." She nudged Terika. "Come on, you're the charming one."

Terika slipped her arm through Zaira's. "Very well, then. For Raverra!" she cried dramatically, and they moved off through the crowd, skirts swirling together in waves of silver and gold.

I watched them go with a strange, soft, dropping feeling. I recalled with vivid clarity sitting with my cousin Roland and commiserating together over the ease with which his sister Bree flung herself into the midst of a crowd and made immediate friends with everyone in it. I could almost feel him at my side, shaking his head and smiling, a bittersweet yearning on his face.

"I don't know how they do it either, Roland," I whispered.

My eyes stung, and I lifted my mask to wipe them. Not here. Of all the places for his memory to haunt me, not here, with a hundred people watching.

"Are you all right, Amalia?"

It was Marcello, his simple domino mask doing nothing to hide the concern in his eyes. I'd rarely seen him out of uniform, but his well-cut forest-green coat over a burnished gold brocade waistcoat flattered his figure and looked quite fine on him. I could have mistaken him for the idle young patrician gentleman his father's rank entitled him to be, if not for the straight-backed attentiveness he couldn't shed with his uniform. I settled my mask in place and managed a smile.

"I'm fine."

Marcello simply waited, face serious, as the crowd moved past us in all its color and laughter and excitement. My throat ached. He was the one person, I reminded myself, with whom I never had to pretend.

"You caught me at a melancholy moment, that's all," I added. "Thinking of Roland."

"Ah." The single syllable held a world of understanding. "Do you want to talk about it?"

"No." I drew myself up, gathering my resolve. "No, I want to dance with you."

Beneath his mask, his mouth formed the wistful smile I knew so well. The smile, I realized at last, of a man who knew he could never have what he wanted, but enjoyed dreaming about it anyway.

He held out his hand, and I took it, his sword calluses forming a pattern of firm spots in his otherwise gentle grasp.

"Let's dance, then," he said softly.

We danced without words, letting the music enfold us, swirling apart and then together. It was a complex Loreician dance I didn't know well, but when my steps faltered, he guided me by the tilt of his head and the pressure of his hand, always patient, always graceful. Our eyes stayed locked together, at first with a bittersweet intensity that threatened to bring back my tears; but then a grin started to creep onto his face, and mine, too, and as the pace of the music picked up soon we were both laughing. Once, I stumbled as I twirled, but he caught me with a steady hand on my waist.

We left the floor at the end of the dance arm in arm, and I felt giddy and light as if the past several months had never happened, and we'd just danced together for the first time.

"Thank you," I told him, and his eyes crinkled through the holes in his domino mask.

"We're both always on duty," he murmured. "Even when we're technically not. But you make me forget it, sometimes."

"Oh? That's ironic, because you make me remember why I'm doing all this in the first place." Grace of Love, I wished I could touch his face. "What it is I'm trying to protect."

"*You're* trying to protect *me*?" he chuckled. "It's supposed to be the other way around, you realize."

"Not at all. My job is to protect the whole Empire—or it will be someday, at any rate, in the unlikely event my mother ever takes it into her head to retire." I poked him gently in the chest. "You're part of the Empire."

"Your logic is flawless, as always." His voice softened. "Besides, that's what people do when they care about each other, isn't it? They protect each other. From sorrow and pain, however they can."

"And make each other happy, too. Don't forget that." We stopped by one of the tall windows that lined the outer wall of the salon, looking out over the Imperial Canal. Hundreds of colored festival lanterns reflected in scattered motes upon the water, and luminaries turned the elaborate façades flanking the canal into shining palaces of light and shadow against the velvet-black sky.

"What gives you joy, Marcello?" I asked, watching the festival lights reflected in his eyes as he stared out at the evening's magic.

He let out a gentle breath, closer to a wordless prayer than a sigh. "Istrella," he said, without hesitation. "Always, with every brilliant discovery and odd little habit. Also, teaching the children at the Mews—seeing their faces light up with understanding. And the feeling of mastering a new skill, when something that never made sense before suddenly falls into place." His eyes flicked to mine then, the reflected light still shining in them. "And you. The way your thoughts play out across your face. The turnings of your mind, like one of Istrella's devices, complicated and unexpected."

Time seemed to slow until it flowed like molten glass, precious and glowing, too bright to touch. A silent understanding connected us, as if I could see into the clear depths of his soul.

"The light in your eyes gives *me* joy," I said softly. "And the way you frown when you're thinking. You're the one honest, true man in this city of illusion, Marcello. I can't see the future, but I want you in mine, one way or another, always." The strains of dance music ended, and the eddying crowd burst into applause. For a moment, we'd been alone, as if the frame of the window created a private room around us; now the party, with all its noise and splendor, came rushing back, flooding my senses. I swallowed. "Because I'll always be your friend."

I couldn't say more. Not when it could well be a decade or more before I knew whether I'd have to make a political marriage in service to the Empire. I'd already decided it would be cruel to string Marcello along until then; every endearment I uttered could only hurt both of us.

"Amalia..." Marcello hesitated, then shook his head, smiling. "Never mind."

I took his hand and squeezed it. "Come on," I said. "Ruven's people are out there somewhere, and like you said, we're both always on duty. We've got a long night ahead of us."

We followed the flow of the evening from masquerade to masquerade, walking mazy streets bright with festival lanterns, the chill air around us warmed by crowds of merrymakers in outlandish masks and accompanying finery. We glided down canals shivering with a thousand reflected lights like multicolored balefire dancing on the water, the city full of fanciful strangers, faces woven of golden wire or black lace or artfully sculpted papier-mâché. Laughter floated on the air like a haze of smoke, and the night was alive and breathing, watching us, ready to speak a secret through the teeth of its vanishing smile. Far above, the moon kept her sails trim, cold and distant, aloof from all the lesser lights that crowded below.

I couldn't help but think how much Kathe would have loved this night. And how much I would have loved to show it to him, and see the delight kindling in his eyes.

The watch was out in force, and I recognized my mother's agents and imperial guards at every party, alert and ready for trouble. But nothing disrupted the wild swirl of celebration pulsing through the Serene City. Clock bells chimed later and later hours, from mantelpieces and towers alike, as we followed a wandering course through a city entirely undisturbed by calamity. But I couldn't relax. If I hadn't seen Ruven's plan unfolding, that only meant he was getting away with it undetected.

By two hours past midnight, several locks of my hair straggled down from the jeweled pins with which my maid Rica had tried to tame it, the gold-embroidered hem of my sea-colored gown had a rip from being stepped on, and my lip paint was long gone. Zaira and Terika had gone back to the Mews, to spend time with their Falcon friends at the festivities there, but I didn't dare go home to rest. Not with Ruven's intent still coiled and waiting, hidden somewhere in the color and music of the celebration like a serpent in a field of flowers.

I checked the secret pocket sewn into a fold of my extravagantly full skirts to make sure my one-dose elixir bottle was still in place as Marcello handed me out of my boat at the entrance to Lady Hortensia's palace; I'd taken my evening dose long ago, but at this rate there was a good chance I'd need my morning one before I made it home. A sleepy-looking crow regarded me from Lady Hortensia's roof, its hooded eyes seeming doubtful of our sanity for being awake at this hour.

"You look exhausted," Marcello murmured, as servants wearing leaf masks bowed us in through Lady Hortensia's vine-carved doors. She had a great passion for gardening, and while the air held too much winter chill for her masquerade to be held outdoors in her famous walled gardens, she had decorated her ballroom in an exuberant horticultural theme. Silk flowers and vines draped everywhere, and hothouse plants graced every available surface where one might otherwise hope to put down a drink. More leaf-masked servants circulated with trays, and stood alertly by the doors leading deeper into the palace; by the discreet pistols at their hips and the deceptively decorative staves some of them held, they doubled as security, which was not unusual for the Night of Masks, even without the Council watching for trouble from Vaskandar. No one wanted an assassination or robbery to ruin their party and spoil the year's luck.

"Thanks," I replied dryly, tucking a dangling strand of hair back behind my ear. "*You* look unspeakably handsome."

He did, but I shouldn't have said it; all the wine I'd accepted at one party after another had loosened my tongue.

Marcello bit his lip. "I didn't mean it that way. You're beautiful, as always. Only I hope you manage to get some rest soon. You've been working so hard."

"You too," I said softly. The preparations for war had been wearing at him. Even through the mask, I could glimpse the shadows under his eyes.

Before I could say something tender that I might regret,

Lady Hortensia herself greeted me, resplendent in a gown and mask covered with spring-green silk leaves and exquisite pink silk flowers. I soon found myself towed around the room and introduced to dozens of Lady Hortensia's friends, half of whom I already knew; Marcello trailed along at first, but eventually I lost him. I spotted him across the room, talking to a fellow Falcon and Falconer by the dessert table, and stared longingly after them as Lady Hortensia sent me off to the dance floor with her nephew, an influential banker who insisted on talking about nothing but finance. I made appropriate noises and kept my eye out for trouble, but all seemed as peaceful and orderly as one could reasonably expect this late into a night when nearly everyone had been drinking.

Three dances later, I headed for the wine table, hoping for something watered down to soothe a throat dry from uttering the same phrases over and over. I had lost sight of Marcello and his friends; after a quick drink, I should find him and move on to the next party. Nothing seemed amiss here.

I had almost reached the wine when a gentle tap on my shoulder requested my attention.

I turned to find not Marcello, as I'd half expected, but a stranger in an elaborate silver mask. Patterns like frost crystals climbed up the face of it, turning into reaching winter branches and forming a spiky crown at his brow. His matching silver and white coat sparkled with thick embroidery and thousands of crystals, mirroring the wintry theme to striking effect. Two companions by his side wore the black hooded cloaks and long bird skull masks of the Demon of Death.

"Yes?" I asked politely. "Is there something…" My voice trailed off as I met his eyes through the mask.

Violet circles ringed his dead black pupils.

Hell of Nightmares. It was Ruven.

Chapter Seven

$\mathcal{I}$ drew in a breath sharp with sudden fear. But before I could release it, Ruven lifted a cautionary finger to my lips.

"Shh," he said, and my voice was gone.

Hells have mercy. I'd let him touch me.

I reached in desperation for my flare locket, but Ruven clasped my bare arm, a benign smile spreading beneath his mask. His power crawled under my skin, and my fingertips froze before they reached my locket. Every inch of me itched to tear away from him, to scramble back from the venomous cloud of his presence as if he were some loathsome insect, but I couldn't move.

"Let's have a private conversation, you and I," he murmured. "That's all I want; just a little talk, out in the garden."

The crowd flowed around us: women in elaborate gowns swirling past on their way to the dance floor, men with laughing mouths stretched wide beneath their masks, a leaf-masked servant balancing a tray of full wineglasses. No one cast us a second glance; we were just having a private conversation, and nothing about our postures conveyed any hint that something was wrong. I'd made a mistake, one terrible mistake, and dropped my guard, and now I was trapped in a nightmare.

"You must surely be curious what I have to say to you, here in your place of power," Ruven inquired. "Yes?"

I couldn't reply. But damn him, he wasn't wrong, and he could read it in my eyes.

"When I release you, you could make a great outcry, I suppose, and I might have to kill some number of guests here and then leave." Ruven sighed, as if this alternative bored him. "But would it not be far more productive, my lady, for you to hear me out? I could have killed you a dozen times over where you stand, if I wished you harm. What say you?"

My mouth went dry and coppery with fear. Hundreds of revelers milled around us, laughing and gossiping in their carefully chosen masks and finery, completely heedless of the danger they were in. Any of them could be seconds from death. All Ruven had to do was reach out and touch them with a careless hand.

These were my people. Some of them were family friends I'd known since I was a child; others were workers from the Tallows who'd saved up for good cloaks and made their masks themselves, giddy with the excitement of the one night no one could distinguish them from royalty. I had to protect them, somehow, from this predator in their midst who would snuff out their lives simply to laugh at the anguish on my face.

Ruven relaxed his magical hold on my voice enough for me to scrape out a raw whisper. I couldn't show him how much he'd rattled me. "There are politer ways to request someone's attention."

He laughed, throwing back his head. "Indeed, my lady! A fine point." He swept into a half bow, never releasing my arm even as he flourished his other hand. "Well, then, will you do me the honor of accompanying me to the garden? You might learn something of interest, and besides, I am certain things will go much better for everyone here if you do."

An angry refusal leaped to my lips, but I stopped it before it could escape. I needed to keep Ruven in the mood to play games rather than to unleash violence. And besides, this might be my only chance to find out what he was up to.

He could have tipped some of his command potion into my paralyzed mouth before anyone knew what was happening. He could have killed me where I stood, or put me to sleep and dragged me with him. He didn't need my permission. Which meant he truly wanted to talk—and if my enemy wished to speak about his plans, I would be a fool not to listen.

I didn't dare cede him complete control of the situation, however. "Take your hand off me," I growled, forcing the words out past the sluggishness still laid upon my tongue.

"Do I have your answer, my lady?" he asked, tilting his head so the crystals in his mask caught the light.

"Hand. Off. First."

His cool, hard fingers lifted from my arm. The numbing current of his magic faded from my bones, and I could move again. Ruven watched me warily, poised and ready. I had no doubt he would lash out and begin killing at the slightest provocation, just to punish me for embarrassing him.

"Fine," I said, my voice still husky from whatever he'd done to my throat. "I'll grant you a moment of conversation. But if you threaten my people again, our talk is over, and I'll rouse the Empire to hound you all the way back to Vaskandar."

A smile curved Ruven's lips, and he offered me his arm. "Of course, my lady."

I ignored the gesture and headed for the glass doors that ran the length of the ballroom wall, from which steps descended to Lady Hortensia's famous gardens. In the daytime, the wall of glass provided a glorious view; now it looked out into a darkness barely alleviated by the festival lanterns strung from the branches of the winter-bare trees. I brushed past fellow guests who had blurred to a rush of sound and color, a nightmarish swirl of empty-eyed false faces and silk that rustled like demons' wings. Ruven paced at my side, too close, too pleased with himself.

I didn't know whether I was the hostage, or everyone else at the ball was. But either way, by the Graces, I'd find out what I could from him while he was willing to talk. If Ignazio had gotten him to share his plans, perhaps I could, too.

I tried not to think about how that had ended for Ignazio.

We stepped out into the night. Chill air hit me like a plunge into water. Ruven started down the steps at once, wandering past ornamental trees and trellises, into the winding series of sheltered nooks and shrub-walled rooms that formed Lady Hortensia's cunningly designed gardens. I glimpsed one or two couples who had clearly come to the gardens for privacy, their passion or drunkenness inuring them to the cold; as I caught up to Ruven, we looked like just another couple, save for the two black-cloaked companions trailing after us, whose presence prickled the back of my scalp.

I stopped before Ruven could lead us too far from the blazing wall of glass and light. "This is private enough," I declared.

He looked about and gestured to a stone bench in a quiet nook flanked by twin lines of narrow cypresses. It stood in full view of the windows, but the trees cut it off from the rest of the garden and gave it a sense of seclusion.

"What do you think?" he asked, sounding delighted as if he'd designed the garden himself. "Perfect, is it not?"

I stalked to the bench and settled on it, spreading my skirts around me to claim the entire space for myself. Icy cold seeped immediately through my legs from the stone, and I regretted my choice, but now I was stuck with it.

"Talk, then," I said shortly. My throat still ached, and I couldn't manage to speak much louder than a whisper; it didn't help my mood.

"My, my, so blunt! Very well, Lady Amalia, to the point." I'd left him with nowhere to sit, so Ruven stood squarely in front of my bench, crossing his arms. "I am here to offer you an alliance."

"An alliance." I lifted an eyebrow. "Forgive me, Lord Ruven, but that's a strange offer coming from the one who declared war upon us."

"You misunderstand me, Lady Amalia. My offer isn't for the Serene Empire, though certainly it could mean peace between our domains. I want an alliance with *you*."

With the light behind him, I couldn't read his face. "I am uncertain what you would hope to gain from such an alliance," I said carefully.

"That's simple," Ruven said. "I wish, my lady, to survive."

"And you think I can help you with that?" I forbore from mentioning that I had every reason to desire the opposite. The longer I could keep him talking, the more he would reveal.

"You've left me in a precarious position, Lady Amalia." An edge came into his voice. "Once, I had hoped to forge an alliance in Vaskandar strong enough to bury your Empire like an avalanche. But after your interference at the Conclave, my tradition-bound peers among the Witch Lords have balked at my innovative methods, and some of them seem to have taken the notion into their heads that I'm too dangerous to live." He gave a short laugh, but there was no humor in it. "Now I need to acquire enough power that they don't dare challenge me, and quickly. For a Witch Lord, power means land, and the lives within it."

"So you seek to seize territory from the Empire." I shook my head. "It's difficult to comprehend how you could expect me to help you with such plans."

"But, you see, the land doesn't have to come from the Empire." Ruven spread his arms, the diffuse light of the festival lanterns catching in the silver of his mask and the crystals on his coat. "You have enemies in Vaskandar, do you not? The Lady of Bears, the Serpent Lord, the Lady of Thorns' daughter..."

"Your allies," I pointed out.

"Hardly." Ruven flicked a dismissive hand. His two Demons of Death loomed behind him, silent as shadows. "I owe them nothing. Their land will serve as well as yours to fuel my power. The only reason I turn against your Empire instead is because my fellow Witch Lords' domains are already claimed, blooded and bound by stone, and therefore too difficult to conquer."

"And you think an alliance with the Serene Empire would let you defeat your fellow Witch Lords?" I kept my voice neutral, as if this were an entirely reasonable proposal.

"No." Ruven stepped closer; the power of his presence pressed against me like a sickening miasma. "I think you can help me steal their domains out from under them without needing to fight a single battle."

The chill of the winter air settled deep into my bones. "Because I hold the lineage of the Lady of Eagles." The waters of Vaskandar threaded her magical mark through all the land, seeping upstream from the great lake at the heart of her domain. "But her claim on other Witch Lords' domains through the rivers is passive. Secondary. It can't overpower the claim of the reigning Witch Lord. Can it?"

"Oh, she took my half of Mount Whitecrown from me easily enough." Ruven's voice held a bitter note. "That was your doing, as well, if you recall. If two vivomancers have a valid blood claim on the same land, and both choose to contest it, it's the stronger that wins."

"But I'm no vivomancer," I pointed out. "And you have no blood claim."

"You are a lady of scholarship and vision. Surely you can see how it could be done."

Ruven reached out to one of the cypresses flanking my bench; at a flick of his fingertips, half its branches bowed before him, splitting and twining rapid as slithering snakes to form a seat for him, closer to mine than I'd like. He settled on it, leaning toward me, the crown of his mask forming a pattern like bones against the light from the ballroom windows.

"Your blood is the key to unlock every domain in Vaskandar," he whispered, excitement quivering in his voice. "You've read the same texts I have. You've seen the boundary stones, the Truce Stones, even the circles I carved into the volcano. When you blend the patterns of artifice with the power of a Witch Lord, you can etch new laws into the land in a way you never could with vivomancy alone."

"I've seen this, yes," I admitted cautiously.

He flung an arm wide. "You can help me design enchantments to carve my mark into my rivals' domains and steal their hoarded land and lives out from under them. To make new boundaries that will override theirs and swallow up their domains a piece at a time. I am a Skinwitch; I could merge your blood and mine to mark the circles, feed the rivers, blood the stones. Your claim and my power, fused together. You are the one person in all Eruvia who has both the knowledge and the blood to do it."

Hearing Ruven speak so avidly about my blood set my nerves crawling. I slid a few inches away from him on my bench. "I can see how that might work."

"Of course you do. You are a scholar. It's why I admire and, yes, covet you, Lady Amalia." Ruven reached out, offering me his hand, his eyes gleaming behind his mask. "If you help me seize the power I require from my neighbors, I will have no need of your Empire. I can turn my attention away from Raverra and toward our mutual foes."

He must take me for a fool, if he thought I believed that. The Serene Empire could give him much more than land; with its Falcons and its navy, its artificers and warlocks, its courier lamps and wealth and logistical efficiency, it excelled in many areas where Vaskandar lacked. Ruven, unlike his peers, could assert the dominion of his magic over humans as well as plants and animals; if he claimed a piece of the Empire, he could claim all the powers its people wielded as well. If what Ruven truly wished was an edge his neighbors couldn't counter, the Empire would give him that in spades. And having my cooperation would only make it easier for him to get his fingers into all that imperial power.

But I tilted my head, as if listening intently. "Go on," I murmured.

"Expanding my domain would only be the beginning." Ruven's fingers flexed, beckoning, entreating. "Magic runs through everything like blood in the veins of the world, Lady Amalia. You've studied the magical sciences enough to know this, yes? But together, we can tap those veins in ways no one has before. To drain them, to shape them, to scribe our names upon the blank page of Eruvia." He drew a breath that shivered with anticipation. I couldn't keep myself from recoiling from the sickening presence of his power hanging in the air. "Ally with me. Work with me. Together, there is no limit to what we can do."

I stared at his extended hand. And then I lifted my eyes to meet his, unable to hide my revulsion any longer.

"Forgive me, Lord Ruven," I said coolly, "but I see insufficient benefit to myself or the Empire in this arrangement."

Ruven's mouth twisted through a brief flash of genuine disappointment to something crueler. "I was afraid you might feel that way."

His offering hand closed into a fist.

Hells. I'd made an error, rejecting him too plainly, and now the night air came alive with icy menace. The ballroom suddenly seemed impossibly far away.

"You realize of course, my lady, that I don't need to ask." Ruven smiled, his voice silky, and drew a flask from his coat. "You know what's in here, don't you?"

His command potion. The chill from the stone bench beneath me seemed to penetrate my bones. More than being shot or drowned or burned alive, that was the stuff of my nightmares.

"I would hope you've learned by now not to threaten me within my own domain," I said, trying to keep my voice hard and strong. "I don't need vivomancy to raise the Empire against you."

"Threaten *you*? Don't be silly. Besides, you showed me the limits of this potion when you last visited my castle." Ruven sighed with an air of great disappointment and tucked the flask away. "It would place you under my dominion, yes; you would be compelled to obey my commands. But your mind would remain free, and where my commands ended, you could do what you wished against me. It's a flawed tool, no?"

"It's evil," I said stiffly.

Ruven laughed. "Oh, Lady Amalia, you jest! You are not so simple a creature as to believe in evil. But you see how this potion is imperfect for when I wish to bring someone such as you to my side, who I value for the workings of your mind. I need you to serve me of your own will, do you understand? I need you to have *motivation*."

He turned a satisfied smile toward me, his lips curling in pure pleasure. A foreboding like the whispering of the Demon of Despair curled through the cold air around me.

"Don't you dare," I whispered.

Ruven rose gracefully, spreading his arms as if to embrace the night sky. "If I am not mistaken, your motivation should be arriving any moment now."

Marcello. The surety of it struck through me with the leaden agony of a musket ball. He meant Marcello.

I surged to my feet, trying to cry a warning; my voice cracked, still hoarse from Ruven's magic, and came out no louder than a whisper. I reached for my flare locket, but my panicked fingers tangled instead in Kathe's necklace of black claws hanging on a string around my throat.

One of Ruven's demon-masked comrades darted behind me in a swirl of black cloak and seized my arms before I could flip open my locket. His gloved fingers bit into my flesh, sharp as talons, wrenching my arms behind my back. I tried to twist away, the raw energy of fear jolting through me, but he was too strong.

I had to get away somehow, or call enough guards that Ruven wouldn't want to fight them, or talk him into leaving—anything, so long as I did it quickly, before Marcello noticed I was gone and came looking for me.

The unmistakable sound of a pistol hammer cocking back shattered my hopes.

"Release Lady Amalia," Marcello commanded, his voice hard as steel.

Ruven closed his eyes, as if savoring the bliss of the moment, and turned to face him.

Marcello stood in the open space between the rows of cypresses, silhouetted by the light of the ballroom doors behind him. He held a pistol leveled at Ruven in one hand, and pointed his rapier toward one of his cloaked companions with the other. He had torn off his mask, and pure determination shone from his green eyes.

"Marcello, *run!*" I rasped. "Please!"

But, of course, he didn't run. He stood taking aim between Ruven's eyes, with no sensible fear in his bearing.

"If I blow a hole in your face, I can't imagine that will be pleasant for you, even if your powers will let you survive it," Marcello said. "Leave now, and spare yourself the indignity."

"My, such strong words." Ruven clicked his tongue. "I was just conversing with the Lady Amalia. I assure you, I have no intention of doing *her* any harm."

He reached out to casually brush the branch of a cypress,

and the trees leaned together behind Marcello, weaving a rapid screen of branches to block us from sight. My guts twisted with apprehension as I strained to wrench free from the man who held me; Ruven was closing his trap.

One of Ruven's skull-masked companions moved, a blur too fast to track. In a swirl of black cloak, Marcello's pistol went spinning from his hand. He swore and countered with a slash of his rapier up and across his attacker's chest; its tip caught the man's mask, which went flying off into the night.

I tried to scream when I saw his face, but my throat could produce no more than a strangled whimper. Marcello staggered back from the sight as if he'd been struck.

The man's skin was dead pale, with a strange shiny cast like polished bone. His head stretched into an elongated, lipless snout like a lizard's, and his wide grin revealed razor-sharp teeth. Above the human eyes that had peered through his mask sat six more, round and black, gleaming wetly in the festival lights.

Chimeras. A burst of pure, nauseous terror drove me to strain and writhe against the one that held me, but its claws dug into my arms like iron, and I couldn't escape or reach any kind of weapon. *Both of them.*

Marcello had recovered from his shock enough to lunge at his chimera, spearing its shoulder. It recoiled, cloak billowing, but one clawed hand shot out and grabbed Marcello's rapier blade before he could pull it back, closing heedlessly around the sharp steel edges. Marcello tried to yank it back and dragged a few bloody inches of blade free, but the creature only tightened its grasp.

Ruven reached out with casual ease and tapped two fingers to the back of Marcello's neck.

"No!" I cried in anguish, but the lingering effects of Ruven's magic still hoarsened my voice. Applause from the ballroom drowned me out as the musicians finished a dance.

Marcello froze in midmotion, his muscles locked, fear straining his face.

"There," Ruven sighed softly. "Now, my lady, we can negotiate."

He wrapped his hand around Marcello's throat. As his fingers settled like pale spider legs around Marcello's rigid neck, something tore loose in my chest; a fear like nothing I'd ever felt for myself lit every nerve in my body with wild, furious energy.

I stomped on the foot of the chimera who held me, then slammed my head back into its chin. I might as well have attacked a statue. I twisted my arms against its grip, but its talons only tightened on me. It emitted a rattling, annoyed hiss.

Ruven hauled Marcello over in front of me; the trees shrugged together to close off all lines of sight and muffle the sound of music and laughter from Lady Hortensia's palace. He had sealed us into a private box of nightmares, with the city full of revelers all around us, and neither Marcello nor I could make enough noise to let anyone know we needed help. Only the slim sickle moon above could look down on this terrible moment.

"Let's see, how shall we begin?" Ruven eyed Marcello appraisingly. A trickle of blood ran down from beneath his fingers where they gripped Marcello's throat. "This one thinks himself a fighter; perhaps I'd best prevent him from attempting anything foolish."

Marcello stared at me, pleading a message with his eyes, since he couldn't move anything else. I knew what he wanted: *Run, get out of here, get away from him somehow, don't worry about me.* But even if I'd been able to break free of the chimera who held me, I'd seen the lightning speed with which they moved; I had no chance of getting away. Until something happened to interrupt or distract them, we were Ruven's.

I had to stop panicking and reacting, force back the fear shivering like sleet in every nerve, and think of a plan. Somehow.

But then Ruven seized Marcello's shoulder with his free

hand, and his fingers pierced through green velvet and the muscle beneath it as if steel claws tipped them. Marcello flinched as blood seeped into his lace cravat.

All coherent thought scattered from my mind in a fresh wave of rage. "Leave him alone!"

An audible *snap* sounded from Marcello's collarbone, and he went pale as paper.

"That's his sword arm, yes?" Ruven glanced at the rapier that lay on the ground, then at the sheath on Marcello's left hip. "Good, good. Some ribs next, I think, to warm up."

Crack. Crack. Marcello jerked against the magic that held him still, his eyes squeezed shut, teeth clenched against the cry he couldn't utter.

"What do you want?" Desperation shredded the words on their way out of my mouth. "Stop hurting him, and tell me what you want!"

Ruven pulled bloody fingers from Marcello's shoulder and shook one at me, grinning. "Now, you don't expect me to believe you've broken so easily, do you? No, no, you are tougher than that, Lady Amalia. I know we'll have to do far greater damage to this plaything of yours before you are truly ready to serve my will." He sighed. "This may take a while, I fear."

Despair unfolded black sails in my chest. He would unmake Marcello in front of me, one agonizing piece at a time. He was enjoying this, relishing my anguish; anything I did to try to make him stop would only make it worse.

All because I wouldn't take his offer. First Roland had died because I deemed his life a worthy sacrifice to protect the Empire; now Marcello paid the price for another of my choices. The red staining Marcello's shoulder blurred into his pain-lined face as tears flooded my eyes.

"I'll make you regret this, Ruven," I warned through my teeth.

"My lady, I never regret anything."

Then a sudden rushing darkness fell from the sky, screaming, and fluttered over my head.

The chimera released me, reeling, its claws raised to shield its face. It hissed in alarm as a black, feathery shape stabbed again and again at its eyes, cawing raucously.

The crow I'd seen napping on Lady Hortensia's roof. Kathe had been watching over me. Hope gave an uneven leap in my heart; my arms were free at last.

I closed my eyes at once and flipped open my flare locket.

Blinding light blazed red through my eyelids. The eight-eyed chimera shrieked in agony; Ruven cried out as well, cursing the Crow Lord, and branches thrashed. I started running before the glare faded, opening my lids to a slit in time to grab Marcello's hand as he staggered free from Ruven's grip; the Witch Lord had thrown up his arms to block the light.

Marcello let out a strangled groan of pain, but ran with me. We shoved our way through cypress trees that clutched blindly at us, then sprinted between trellises twined by withered brown vines and bushes cloaked with the rattling husks of leaves, toward the blazing wall of light and music that was the ballroom.

I scrabbled at the door and hurled it open hard enough to shatter one of the glass panels, bursting through into the brilliant light and warmth of the crowded party.

A hundred masked faces turned to stare at us. The music screeched and wailed to a confused halt.

Marcello slumped to his knees by my side, blood from his shoulder spattering the floor.

Chapter Eight

I held Marcello's hand in both of mine as my oarsman rowed us through the canals glowing with festival lights toward the Mews, and I didn't care who saw. We had propped him up with silk pillows as best we could, but blood still dripped from his shoulder, staining his golden waistcoat and soaking his cravat. His face gleamed with sweat, and his jaw clenched against the pain.

"Please let me try to stop the bleeding." I pitched my voice low, to carry beneath the laughter and music that drifted over our heads. The next boat over was full of demon masks; it all blended into the dreamlike horror of the evening.

"Don't touch it," Marcello said through his teeth. "I can feel the bone shards grating whenever I take a breath. Let them set it at the Mews, or it'll never heal right."

Worry for Marcello clenched my belly into a tight lump. Ruven could have done anything to him—melted his insides to jelly, twisted his bones in knots. He could be slowly dying without even knowing it, right now. But I nodded stiff assent.

And Marcello wasn't the only matter for concern. "Ruven can't have come all the way here just to make me that offer," I said, both to distract Marcello from his pain and because it was true.

"Did you tell someone he's here?" Marcello's hand tightened urgently on mine.

"I sent word to my mother. They're combing the city for him even now. But I'm sure he wasn't just out for a night of dancing in all the long hours before he revealed himself. Graces only know whether we can figure out what else he's done in time to undo it."

Marcello's green eyes clouded with misery. "I don't know how we can fight him, Amalia. He walked into the Serene City, the heart of the Empire, and did whatever he wanted. If we sent an army after him, they couldn't kill him. He's immortal. What can we do to him?"

"Bah. He's nothing more than a magical theory problem for me to solve." I flexed my jaw. "And when I do, Zaira can roast him till his bones turn to glass."

Marcello managed a weak laugh. "Well, then, he'd better start running. I've never seen a magical theory problem escape you."

"That's right." I squeezed his hand. "So you rest, and let me handle it."

He forced a smile and squeezed back. But rest eluded him all the way back to the Mews, where he dripped a trail of blood up to the gates.

The soldiers stationed there rushed to meet us with a flurry of consternation, and soon we had Marcello settled on a bench in the great entry hall as someone went for a physician. Masked revelers spilled in from the Mews party to see what was happening, glittering like bright birds in their finery, Zaira and Terika among them.

"Holy Hells, what happened to *him*?" Zaira asked, pushing her mask up onto her forehead.

"Ruven happened," I told her, keeping my voice low.

Zaira's breath hissed through her teeth. "I leave, and the party gets interesting, huh?"

"I need to get on the courier lamps," I said, clasping her shoulder. My knees trembled beneath my gown with a saw-edge combination of relief, exhaustion, and worry, but I had to stay collected; there was too much to do. "Can you do me a favor? Can you make sure Marcello is all right, and that Istrella..." I swallowed. "Well, that she at least doesn't hear some stupid rumor and get more upset than she needs to about this?"

Zaira exchanged glances with Terika, who nodded. "That's not a favor, idiot," she said. "That's just common sense. Go do what you need to do."

"Thank you," I said with feeling. There were enough people clustered around Marcello now that I couldn't see him; it made it easier to turn away and head off alone toward the courier lamp tower. But it was a cold and lonely walk through the courtyard garden, with fears lurking in every shadow.

An hour later, I found they had taken Marcello to his room. Zaira met me at the door, still in her golden gown, her mask gone and her hair half down from its pins. I could hear Istrella chattering away inside.

"They've got him bandaged up and gave him about fourteen different potions," Zaira told me, yawning. "Terika says he'll be fine, the physicians say he'll be fine, Marcello says he *is* fine—but I'm pretty sure he doesn't know his own name anymore, so I wouldn't put much trust in that."

My shoulders eased as if stones had fallen off them. "Oh, good. I was worried that Ruven had... Well, you know the things he does."

"Ugh." Zaira made a face. "No, none of that, so far as the physician could tell. He's all right. You can kiss him good night and go to sleep."

"I'm not going to do that," I protested.

"Well, *I* am. Going to go to sleep, that is." She stretched. "You might want to see if you can get Istrella to do the same. She's talking his ear off in there, and I think it's keeping him awake."

Sure enough, I found Istrella sitting in a chair by Marcello's bedside, describing an idea she'd had for a luminary that drew on lunar power rather than solar. Marcello lay staring blearily at her from his bed, his brow furrowed in a desperate but doomed attempt to focus on her words. Perhaps it was for the best that he was too drugged to hear the strain under her enthusiasm.

I heard it all too clearly; the roughness in her voice raked me with guilt. Ruven had hurt Marcello to get at me. It was my regard that had put him in danger, and it was on my behalf that he lay there with finger-shaped holes in his shoulder and several broken bones. Istrella would be well within her rights to blame me for what had happened to him.

Graces knew I blamed myself.

"I'm here now, Istrella, if you want to go to bed," I greeted her gently.

She turned, her eyes wide even without her artifice glasses accentuating them, her hair forming an unruly cloud around her face. I realized she was in her nightdress; she must have gone to bed already when we returned to the Mews.

"They gave him a potion to help him sleep," she said seriously, "but it doesn't seem to be working."

"Maybe he needs quiet," I suggested.

"Ah." She considered that, and then nodded. "You're probably right. I'm not good at silence unless I'm working, and I have a strict rule not to work on projects after midnight ever since the explosion."

I blinked. "Perhaps you should go to bed, then."

"Yes, I think so." She got up, and then wrapped me in a fierce and sudden hug, driving the wind from me. "Take care of him, Amalia."

"I will," I promised, and swallowed a painful knot in my throat. *Better than I did tonight*, I added silently.

When she'd left, I settled down by him at last, taking the weight off my aching feet. The copious skirts of my ball gown rustled around me.

"'Malia," Marcello slurred, the sense glazing from his eyes as the pale gray light of dawn kissed the sky through his window.

"Do you want me to go?" I asked him softly. "So you can sleep?"

"No," he mumbled. "Stay, please."

So I sat by his bed and held his limp, warm hand, rubbing my thumb gently across the back of it, until my chin dropped on my chest and only the boning of my corset held me upright.

"Amalia, wake up. It's past time for your elixir."

I jerked awake. Aches from sleeping in a corset flooded in as I blinked back the bright morning light. My head swam dizzily, and for a moment I couldn't pull my eyes away from Marcello, who still slept, his brows slightly furrowed. His hand had slipped from mine while I dozed. Somehow, in my worry, I had failed to notice last night that his shoulders and chest were naked under the bandages; now the sun dripped gold across his smooth bronze skin.

But that voice—my mind was fuzzy from sleep and from the first gentle warning symptoms of being late with my elixir. It couldn't be.

I turned to find my mother sitting beside me in all her glory: La Contessa Lissandra Cornaro, still in the imposing burgundy silk gown she'd worn when she set out for her own Night of Masks festivities last night, her auburn hair pinned up with gold and jewels. She looked as out of place in Marcello's simple, spare bedroom as a ruby brooch on a piece of scrap linen. Her piercing dark eyes sat in pools of exhaustion, and she offered me an elixir bottle with the air of one sharing a stiff drink after a long, difficult day.

I blinked, but this strange vision didn't dissipate. I took the bottle and downed a couple of anise-flavored swallows, then set it on Marcello's bedside table beside the burned-out oil lamp.

"I do have a bottle with me," I said. I might have made some mistakes last night, but that wasn't one of them; I'd had enough brushes with death not to trifle with the potion that kept me alive. "I didn't stay out overnight without a plan. I just—"

My mother leaned forward and pulled me into a tight hug. "I'm glad you're all right," she whispered.

I pressed my stinging eyes against her silk-encased shoulder. "Mamma, Ruven hurt him to get to me." My voice wobbled as if I were a child again, confessing in tears that I'd spilled chocolate on my favorite book. "He could have killed him if Kathe's crow hadn't shown up, all because of me. Now he's broken and bleeding, just because I care about him. I don't—" The words hitched in my throat, and I had to struggle against some heavy, terrible, nameless thing in my chest to force out more of them. "I can't make this better," I whispered.

My mother held me out at arm's length, then, gazing at me fiercely. "I know," she said, with a conviction in her voice deep enough to shake me. "Believe me, Amalia, I know."

I stared back at her for a moment, amazed at the pain showing clear and bright in her eyes. But then the lingering scent of anise teased my senses, and I realized with a start that she meant me. All those years ago, when I'd been poisoned, and the other times I'd been threatened or kidnapped or people tried to kill me as a child, all in an attempt to get at my mother. I'd never thought before of what she must have felt; she'd treated it as simply the way things were, and lectured me on safety even as she arranged the executions of the people responsible, and it had never occurred to me that every single time had hurt her more than I could imagine.

"What do I do?" I asked her helplessly. "How can I have friends, if I know people will target them?"

La Contessa squeezed my shoulders and stared into my eyes. "You must teach them what happens when they hurt the people you love," she said, in a voice that would set the Demon of Nightmares to trembling.

I nodded, and dragged a sleeve across my eyes. "I'll try." I took a deep breath, and took a moment to attempt to arrange my gown. "Did they ever find Ruven?"

"My sources tell me he's left the city and seems to be returning north." She leaned back in her chair, rubbing her temples. "He did what he came here to do, and now he's going home."

"What he came here to do?" I asked sharply. Even Ruven wouldn't travel all the way to Raverra simply to torment an adversary.

"So I must assume." My mother rose and began pacing, her skirts sweeping the floor. "He sprinkled his poison about, for certain. We've found two parties he attended where we detected alchemy in the food; we're attempting to track down all the guests to quarantine them, but it's a logistical nightmare, and it's frankly going to be impossible to catch everyone. And we've pulled two bodies out of the canal, one of them a soldier. We're working to identify them." She sighed. "It's been a busy night."

"And we can't know what more there may be to his plans." I rubbed my temples, pressing at a headache building there.

"I assure you, we're expending considerable resources to find out." She paused. "Speaking of which. The doge wishes to talk to you at the Imperial Palace, once you've had a chance to get cleaned up."

I glanced down at my bedraggled ball gown. Marcello's blood spattered the ocean-blue silk in places. My insides clenched, and I couldn't help a quick look at his sleeping face to reassure myself he was all right.

"I'd like to wait for Marcello to wake up," I said, my voice dwindling to something small and uncertain. "He asked me to stay."

La Contessa raised one elegant brow, and with it all the objections I knew too well. I was courting someone else; I couldn't keep the doge waiting for a mere captain of the Falconers; it was nothing but silly sentimentality, with Marcello drugged into a sleep too deep to know I was here.

"So long as he doesn't sleep into the afternoon," she sighed. And she came and planted a light kiss on the top of my head. "The serenity of the Empire is in danger, and you are a Cornaro. You have work to do."

"Believe me, I know," I said, bunching handfuls of blood-stained skirts in my fists.

"But remember, Amalia." She gripped my shoulders, holding my gaze. "When you do that work, it will strip things from you, one by one. Force you to cross line after line."

I thought of Roland, with a sharp twist like a knife in my lungs, and wished I could look away. "It's already started," I whispered.

"I know. And that's why you need to decide now, when you're still at the beginning of your journey, what lines you will not cross. What things you will never let go." Her fingers flexed on my shoulders, as if she could squeeze the importance of her words into me. Memories I couldn't begin to guess at crowded like shadows in the backs of her eyes.

She had been La Contessa for my entire life, powerful and inexorable as the tide, standing in the doge's shadow, holding up the Empire and subtly molding it all the while. I had never really thought about what she might have been before she became such a potent and terrible being, or what choices and sacrifices she might have made in the course of her transformation.

I nodded slowly, with the ominous feeling I was sealing a pact whose price I did not yet understand. "I'll remember."

"Good." She released me. "Especially remember it when you're talking to the doge. Niro da Morante has walked a long road. He's walked it for the good of the Empire, but he's left many things behind along the way." A strange smile pulled at her lips. "Sometimes those of us who've been traveling this path too long need the people coming behind us to pick up what we've abandoned and remind us of its value."

Chapter Nine

I had barely stepped onto the dock at my palace, ruined skirts bunched unceremoniously in one hand and the other steadying myself on a post striped in Raverran blue and gold, when a crow fluttered down off the roof and landed on my shoulder. Its sudden, impossibly light, feathery presence at my cheek held all the warmth of a comforting hand, and as it cocked a shiny black eye at me, I could almost imagine the bright yellow rings of Kathe's mage mark flashing curiously within them.

"Hello," I murmured to it, as it shifted its scaly feet to more comfortably arrange the message cylinder tied to its ankle, tilting its head the other way. "Please convey my thanks to whichever of you saved us last night."

The crow blinked, a pale lid flashing across its eye. I had no idea whether it understood.

I must have presented quite an image to the occupants of the boats gliding along the broad waters of the Imperial Canal in the late morning light: the Cornaro heir, in a rumpled and blood-soaked ball gown, disheveled hair spilling half loose down my back, muttering to a crow perched on my shoulder like some dark familiar. Perhaps the gossip sheets would print that I'd gone mad. But then, it was the morning after the Night of Masks; the city was full of strange, bedraggled spectacles as the last of the revelers staggered home trailing the broken bits of night-worn dreams.

I untied the message cylinder and had the slim scrap of paper unrolled before I stepped through the door that Old Anzo held open for me into the warmth of our artifice-heated foyer. The crow still rode on my shoulder, surveying the place with the beady gaze of a dubious dowager.

"I'll get your guest a bit of raw meat from the kitchens, then, my lady," Anzo said, but I was too busy scanning the message to do more than mumble vague thanks.

Returned home to find a weed problem at the south edge of my garden, it said. *Pulled everything up for now. I did stop to peek into that nest we were talking about, and there are indeed eggs in it! Something may hatch soon. Thinking of our shopping expedition and hoping to see you again after I've dealt with this weed issue.*

That line about the shopping expedition stopped me in the middle of the marble-clad foyer, cheeks burning. But this was exciting news, if I read it right; it seemed that the Lady of Eagles had been receptive to the idea of pressuring Ruven's allies to withdraw from his war. Kathe insisted we veil our messages in allusion or code in case his birds were intercepted—though given that he did so even for the most harmless information, I rather suspected it was half an excuse for another game.

Graces knew I could use some good news right now. A rush of gratitude and affection for Kathe washed over me. I lifted a hand to the bird on my shoulder, thinking to pet it, and received a warning nip on my finger.

Anzo returned with writing materials for me and a small tray of tidbits for the bird; he set the latter on the table that normally accepted notes and cards from those who called while we were out. The crow made a fluttering hop onto the silver platter and began unceremoniously snatching up morsels at once.

I sank right down onto the cold marble floor in a puddle of

skirts, clutching my quill and ink bottle and paper, hands trembling with the urge to tell Kathe everything that had happened in Lady Hortensia's garden. He knew too well what it was to have your enemies hurt your friend in order to hurt you. If he were here, he would understand at once, and then ask some convoluted, odd, witty question that would somehow both cut to the heart of the matter and banish its power with laughter.

But I couldn't commit anything so personal to a letter. I closed my eyes a moment, composing the scattered pieces of my thoughts, and then began to write.

Excellent news about the nest. We unfortunately found a rather poisonous snake in our own garden, and it bit a friend. Hopefully he will be well. Thank you for your associate's assistance in dealing with the snake. We are thoroughly looking over the garden for signs of any other damage it may have left behind. I hesitated, then added, *I find myself missing your company already. Wish you were here.*

There. That would have to do. I didn't have time for more; Old Anzo was already pointedly mentioning that Rica had laid out fresh clothes for me in my room.

I had to meet with the doge, after all. And with Niro da Morante, it was best to prepare for even the friendliest meeting as if it were a battle.

"Come in, Lady Amalia. Sit down."

Niro da Morante, doge of Raverra and the Serene Empire, beckoned me wearily into his personal study. I'd heard it said that he preferred the warm light of flame to the cold radiance of luminaries, and indeed, half a dozen oil lamps drew gleams of gold from the ornately embellished ceiling, the walls, and the elegant scrollwork on his desk. Someone had pinned a map of the northern border up over the dark oil portraits on one wall, and his desktop drowned in papers; an aide hustled out past me as I entered, her arms full of more paperwork and her fingers hooked through the handles of several empty coffee cups.

I eased into the room, giving my entire attention to the man before me. The doge held the power of life and death, fortune or ruin, in his every word; it wouldn't do to miss a single one of them. The scents of book leather, coffee, and ink enveloped me as I settled into a delicate antique chair opposite him.

His deep-set black eyes analyzed my face, drifting briefly to the falcon's-head brooch on my shoulder. "You spoke with Lord Ruven last night," he said without preamble.

I nodded, my stomach flipping over at the memory. "He wished to enlist my assistance in magically attacking his neighbors. I turned him down, of course."

"Did he give you any sense whatsoever of what his purpose was in Raverra, what his plans might be, or what else he was doing in the Serene City last night?"

I racked my memory for any detail that might prove useful. It was hard to focus with the doge's eyes on me; ever since I was a child, I'd always felt whenever I was in his presence that I must be in trouble. "He had a flask of his command potion on him," I recalled. "It sounded about half-full. So he must have used some of it."

The doge rolled a quill between his fingers, the feather making a fluttering circle. "We've discovered at least two instances where he did. But my understanding is that it takes very little of this potion to have an effect; the Mews informs me that a cupful in an ale barrel would be enough to place anyone who had even a sip of that ale under his control."

"There were probably more," I agreed grimly. "For that matter, he could have had half a dozen more flasks, for all we know. But I think the potion might be a distraction in this case, Your Serenity."

"A distraction." The doge's pen stilled. "The Council has been working late into the night for months to try to prevent or counter the seemingly infinite types of havoc Lord Ruven could cause with this potion. He could use it to sabotage our border defenses, assassinate our leadership, plant forces behind our lines, spy on our military councils, set up magical traps, control local or even imperial leadership...There are too many possibilities to defend against them all, and any one of them could prove catastrophic. And you're telling me you think it may be a mere distraction?"

"Not in the broader picture, no." I lifted my hands hastily. "But last night, perhaps. Why would Ruven come all the way to Raverra to spread his poison personally? He could send someone to do it for him, with far less chance of discovery."

The doge frowned. Shadows flickered across his face, pooling in his eyes and around his mouth. "You have a point. Very well, then; you know Ruven better than anyone in the Serene Empire. What manner of task would he travel hundreds of miles to accomplish himself?"

I bit my lip. Kathe had made the journey to Raverra for a few hours of conversation with me, but I rather doubted that Ruven shared his consideration. "It has to be something only he could do. Either something he wouldn't trust to an underling, or a task that required his powers as a Witch Lord." I set my hands to my brow to block out the shifting light of the candles and the doge's intent stare, thinking. "Check the major libraries for missing books on magical theory. The personal collections of scholars whose homes were open for the Night of Masks, too. He's definitely still researching magical means to extend his powers, and he wouldn't trust someone else to get the right books." What else? If I were Ruven, what would I want with Raverra? "Graces preserve us. Make sure he didn't do anything to physically undermine the city. If he used roots or water plants to attack Raverra's support structures, he could tumble half our buildings into the lagoon."

I heard the scratching of a quill, but I kept my eyes covered. "Anything else?" the doge asked.

"I'd have alchemists examine the water supply for tampering on general principle. And it's still certainly worth checking for his potion, but I'd focus more on specific people whom he might have wanted to interrogate or to give complex orders he could relay best in person. Sprinkling it randomly around in buffets might let him coordinate some manner of sabotage or mayhem, but wouldn't let him accomplish a specific goal, since he couldn't know who he would get." I lowered my hands at last. "That's what leaps to mind. I'll keep thinking, and let you know if I come up with anything else."

"This is very helpful." The doge rubbed his brow with his fingertips. "Thank you, my lady. Even if I now have more concerns to keep me awake at night. I will have all these looked into at once."

I shifted to the edge of my chair, ready to rise. "Is there anything else, Your Serenity?"

"One thing."

Something about his tone froze me as surely as Ruven's magic.

The doge reached into a cabinet beside his desk and took out a bottle of such a deep red wine that it looked black in the lamplight. He poured a glass, never taking his eyes off mine. The rising music of the flowing wine should have been a soothing sound, but it scraped my nerves raw.

He handed the glass across his desk to me. I took it, but didn't drink.

"You are young, Lady Amalia," he said dryly.

I swallowed, my throat like parchment. "I suppose I am, Your Serenity."

"But even so, you must understand the danger facing our

Empire. The Witch Lords may not have the power to conquer us, but they could shatter this time of peace and prosperity we have built, and cast us into an age of decline and suffering."

I wasn't at all convinced they couldn't conquer us. The doge had never stood before the Conclave of all seventeen Witch Lords, feeling their power crushing the very air with the sheer weight of their magical presence. But I nodded. "I am aware of the gravity of the situation, Your Serenity."

"Then surely you see that now, at this critical moment, we can't afford to make a move that could weaken the Empire and tip the balance into ruin." His black eyes glittered in the lamplight, waiting, watching.

Hells. He was talking about my Falcon reform law. We had a mad Skinwitch with absolute power over every living thing in a domain the size of a country planning to invade our borders with magical powers we could barely begin to comprehend, and he was worried about whether he'd continue to be able to conscript mage-marked children into his army.

But then, I was worried about that, too.

"Now more than ever is the time to uphold the principles that make the Empire civilized," I said softly.

The doge let out a quiet sigh, as if I'd said something predictably disappointing. "Your mother tells me that you are no fool, my lady. She tells me that you believe what you're doing will actually strengthen the Serene Empire, by giving the Falcons more reason to be loyal patriots and less to secretly sympathize with our enemy. And it is not impossible that in the long run, you may have a point." Deep, skeptical lines graven into his face allowed no softening of hope to accommodate any point I might have; the concession was to my mother, a matter of politeness, and not to my ideas. "But you're burning down the bridge we're standing on. This is not the time to talk about whether we need to build a new one."

"And yet—"

"I am not debating you, my lady. I am instructing you."

I stiffened as if he'd slapped me.

This was the moment when, if I were my mother, I might redirect him with a laugh, as if of course he were joking, and find some way to reword what he'd said to seem to be an endorsement of my law, in a way he'd find it difficult to refute. Or back off, for the moment, seeming to agree with his wisdom, and find a new angle from which to make my next move.

But I was not my mother. She had grace and subtlety I never would. All I had was an idea, and a sense of honor I was not willing to bend even for the doge of Raverra. Not when hundreds of Falcons and their families were counting on me.

"With all respect, Your Serenity," I said carefully, "I am a full member of the Assembly, and I have the right and the power to put forth this legislation for a proper vote."

The doge steepled his fingers and stared at me over them for a long time. "You do," he said at last. "And I have so many ways, my lady, to ensure that your legislation fails. Some of them may damage your career, which would upset your mother. Do not make me use them."

It occurred to me, looking into his lined and cynical face, that he might have known about Caulin's gambit to stir up fear against mages at Lady Aurica's party. Hells, he might have ordered it.

My mother's words to me this morning took on a whole new context. *Sometimes those of us who've been traveling this path too long need the people coming behind us to pick up what we've abandoned and remind us of its value.*

She wanted me to save her friend from himself.

The idea that I could somehow restore the idealism of the doge of Raverra was so preposterous that I couldn't quite suppress a smile. Who did she think I was, the Grace of Mercy, to restore compassion to his withered old heart?

No, not compassion. And I couldn't defeat him with reason, either, because he was too skilled with that tool himself. Strangely enough, in this moment it wasn't my mother's tactics or my own I instinctively wanted to reach for; it was Kathe's.

"Your Serenity." I kept my smile on, despite the flicker of annoyance that crossed the doge's face. "You have served the Empire for longer than I've been alive. I've seen how hard you work, and you don't seem to relish the glory one might argue is your reward. Why do you do it?"

The doge's eyes narrowed. "I'm uncertain where you're going with this, Lady Amalia."

It's a game. I leaned forward, searching out some spark of feeling within his glittering black eyes. "You must care very passionately about the Empire," I said, "to dedicate your life to it as you've done. There must be something about it you want to preserve and protect, more than anything. Something you value above yourself."

There was a moment, balanced like the wind-stirred page of an open book, when he might have answered. A moment where I could see the dusty gears of his heart shedding rust and churning back into motion, and words of truth gathering on his tongue. But then he pressed his lips together, and the moment passed.

"Of course there is," he said. "Your point?"

I had to hope that those gears were still turning, even if he chose not to share his thoughts. "Raverra has become great by climbing over the bowed backs of the mage-marked," I said. "Think what heights the Serene Empire could rise to if we let them stand."

He lifted a skeptical brow. "And if, on standing, they put their feet on our necks?"

"You rule the Serene Empire," I said softly. "If you let fear rule you, then you make it the master of us all."

For a moment, there was silence. The light of the oil lamps cast moving shadows across Niro da Morante's face as he regarded me with an expression I couldn't begin to read.

Finally, he blew out a huff of breath and picked up his quill again. "I am more concerned at the moment with Lord Ruven attempting to become the master of us all." Dismissal sounded in his tone. "If you have no further information for me, I have a great deal of work to do, and I imagine you do as well."

I rose and bowed, uncertain whether I had won or lost this game of mine, but suspecting I had at least scored a point or two. "Yes, Your Serenity. That we do."

Chapter Ten

$\mathcal{I}$f the old bastard himself was warning you off, he must think you can win," Zaira said as we crossed the Mews garden together. "Guess I'd better start paying attention to this law of yours after all."

"I agree. Now's the time to move." I'd come back to the Mews with a restless energy coursing through me as if balefire burned in my veins, and had been glad to run into Zaira in the entry hall. I might not have the means to personally thwart Ruven right now, but *this* I could do. "Will you help me draft the final version of the law?"

Zaira laughed. "Because I've got such a way with words. A golden tongue." She held up her hands to frame an imaginary document. "Be it known that any stuffed-codpiece bastard who wants to conscript little mage brats into the army can bugger himself between the eyes from this day forth. By the imperial seal, love Zaira."

"It has a certain ring to it." I hesitated then, not sure if she'd like what I had to say next. "I was more hoping you could help me decide what compromises we can and cannot make to help this pass into law."

She eyed me skeptically. "You're considering some demon's bargain, aren't you."

"Maybe." I slowed my stride and stopped beneath an olive tree, its oily leaves one of the few spots of green in the winter-bare garden. "If we abolish mandatory conscription, we need to regulate magic some other way. As just one example, we need some way to ensure that no one could hire or kidnap their own private mage army."

Zaira grunted. "Can't let the Empire lose its grip on the magic, huh?"

"I'm personally more concerned with avoiding a civil war. History suggests that when military power becomes decentralized, it can lead to—"

Zaira interrupted me with a dramatic yawn. "Save the lecture. I get it." She jabbed a finger at my chest. "If you're so worried, keep the jesses. Then the Empire can still snuff our magic out the instant we do something it doesn't like."

I blinked. "You wouldn't mind still wearing a jess?"

"I didn't say that." Intense cynicism hooded Zaira's dark eyes. "Of course I'd mind. But it's better than having a thousand stupid rules dictating every damned thing about my life because the Empire is scared of what I'll do if they let me out of my cage."

"It would be easier to get the Assembly to pass a law that kept the jesses," I admitted, turning the idea over in my mind. "It kills nearly all of the objections about safety my opponents keep raising. I could probably triple our support."

Zaira snorted. "That's because they're a bunch of cowards. The jesses are there to make you numb-brains feel safe. If we didn't have them, you'd just start killing us."

I wished I could disagree. But there were places in Eruvia where they'd hanged mages or stoned them, before the Serene Empire came in and made them stop. It was the same paradox I'd struggled with all along: freedom had never been safe for the mage-marked.

"Do you think the other Falcons would find that acceptable?"

I asked. "I don't want to trade away something that's not mine to give."

Zaira jerked her thumb toward the dining hall. "I was about to head to dinner anyway. Let's go ask them."

We found a table full of our Falcon friends in the dining hall—and best of all, Marcello was among them, out of bed and clear-eyed, his right arm bound up in a sling. Relief surged through me like clear water. He'd still gotten hurt on my account, but it seemed Ruven hadn't done any permanent damage.

"How are you feeling?" I asked him as Terika slid down the bench to make room for us.

"Not bad," he said, abandoning an awkward attempt to eat soup left-handed. "A bit groggy from all the potions, though."

"You could let me help you instead," Istrella said brightly from beside him. "I have an idea for stimulating bone growth. We'd have to insert artifice wire into your shoulder, though."

Marcello shuddered. "No, thank you."

Istrella sighed and took a spoonful of her own soup. "Everyone always says that."

Down the table, my Ardentine friend Foss was attempting to convince his small mage-marked son Aleki to eat his dinner rather than simply mashing it together with his fingers. The boy's jess had collected a certain amount of food in its intricate swirls of wirework.

"Where's Venasha?" I asked him. Usually the two of them brought Aleki to meals together.

"She's back in Ardence again, at the Ducal Library." He smiled shyly. "She's really hoping you can get your law passed soon, so she won't have to keep traveling back and forth in order to keep her post."

"About that." I raised my voice slightly, pitching it so everyone at the table could hear. "I'm hoping to submit the final version of my Falcon reform act to the Assembly tomorrow, to put it forward for a vote within the week. I was hoping you all might be willing to give me some advice."

Silence fell across the table. Everyone turned to look at me. Jerith whistled appreciatively, exchanging glances with Balos.

Marcello frowned. "Now? With war about to break out?"

"Absolutely. *Because* war is about to break out, and the Falcons deserve a choice about how and whether they'll fight it. Especially the children."

Foss drew Aleki a bit closer to him, failing to notice as the boy dipped his fingers into his milk cup. "We're listening."

"Zaira had an idea for a compromise that I think would vastly increase our chances of getting this law passed." I licked my lips, suddenly nervous. It was hard to look a table full of my friends in their mage-marked eyes and ask them if they were willing to trade away control of their own magic for a greater slice of freedom. "I think I can get a large portion of the Assembly to agree to end unwilling conscription if—and, unfortunately, perhaps only if—we keep the jesses."

"I'm not surprised," Jerith said dryly. "No one will vote to let us out of our kennel if they can't still keep us on a leash."

"Much as I might wish otherwise, that's an accurate assessment." I grimaced. "In particular, we need the backing of the military—this law won't pass without them. Fortunately, most of the military leaders I've talked to like the idea; they'd greatly prefer to have their plans and the safety of their troops hinge on willing volunteers rather than unwilling conscripts." I took a deep breath. "But they want a means to shut down the powers of mages who lose control, are coerced, or voluntarily turn against Raverra."

Terika frowned. "If they still want jesses, what reforms are they backing, exactly?"

"No mandatory conscription into the military," I said. "No forcing mage-marked children to come to the Mews."

"Those are the important things," Foss said, sounding relieved.

"So how would it work, then?" Terika asked, brows lifting. "You'd get a jess, and they'd just let you go on your way, wherever you liked?"

"Essentially." I hesitated. "One idea I had was to call it a civilian reserve. That way, you'd still technically be part of the Falcons, which would mean we wouldn't have to alter the Serene Accords. That means an easier vote, with a lower threshold to pass."

Foss paused in the act of offering Aleki a forkful of polenta. "A reserve sounds like it could be called up."

Jerith shrugged. "The Empire has the power to demand military service from any citizen during wartime. No matter what they call it, if they want mages badly enough, they can take us. Nothing's going to change that." He shared a glance with Zaira, and I knew what they were thinking: the Empire would never let go of such a rare and potent advantage as a warlock.

"That's part of why I think I can get so much more support for this version of the law," I admitted, leaning my elbows on the table. "Because if the mage-marked still have jesses, the Serene City still controls the magic."

Marcello looked around at the expressions on the Falcons at the table: cautious, thoughtful, wearing a mixture of skepticism and hope. "If it doesn't really change anything," he asked, "what's the point?"

"It changes nothing, but it changes everything," Foss said immediately. "My family could go home. Aleki wouldn't have to be a soldier. He could grow up like any other child."

"I wouldn't have to live in the Mews," Terika said. "I could make my own home, and travel, and live how I wanted."

Zaira jabbed her fork at Marcello. "If you're not knocking people out and locking them up like a gang of stinking kidnappers, that sounds different to me."

An odd expression crossed Marcello's face. "Do you think..." He swallowed. "Do you think we'll lose a lot of active-duty Falcons if this law passes?"

Jerith shrugged. "Anyone who'd back out of the fight now, knowing Vaskandar is going to come raging across the border as soon as the snow melts and start murdering civilians, isn't someone I want at my side on the battlefield anyway."

"You'll lose the little brats," Zaira pointed out, nodding toward Foss, who put a protective arm around Aleki's shoulders. "If their parents have any sense, that is."

"I'd hope the colonel wouldn't send children into battle regardless," Balos said, his brows lowering.

"And I'd hope no one would stick a knife in me and steal my purse, but sometimes people don't live up to our expectations," Zaira shot back.

"It's not as simple a question as I wish it were." I turned to Foss and met his worried gaze. "What would you do, if you had the freedom to go back to Ardence with Aleki, but they told you he could save lives by staying in the Mews a little longer to mix up simple healing potions for the soldiers?"

Foss frowned. "Healing potions sound like a good thing, I suppose."

"And then what if they switched him to mixing poisons to coat musket balls, and didn't tell you?" Foss winced, but I pressed on. "They might not even mean any harm by it. He'd be under the direction of fellow alchemists, and some of them can get lost in their work and, ah, lose perspective."

Foss didn't reply, but stroked Aleki's hair, his brow furrowed.

"Children shouldn't make instruments of death," Terika said sharply. Zaira put a hand on her back, and I remembered with a pang that Terika had been forced to make poisons when she'd been abducted by criminals as a child; I could have chosen a better example.

"Oh, I don't know," Istrella put in cheerfully. "I rather like making weapons."

Marcello caught my eyes and shook his head in affectionate despair. Balos and Terika traded uncomfortable looks.

"Honestly, if they know we can choose to leave active duty, they're less likely to order us to do reprehensible things in the first place," Jerith said. "If they want to keep us, they have to avoid putting us in positions where we'd resign in protest. Even if every one of us chose to stay, it would make a difference."

I felt as if I'd finally slid the right key into a stubborn lock. "That's exactly why I have to try to get this passed now. So that the Empire will fight this war in a way we can live with afterward."

Terika nodded firmly. "Submit the version you think you can get passed, then. You can always propose more laws later, right?"

"I can, and I will," I promised.

"When is the vote?" Jerith asked, in an unusually subdued voice.

"If I submit it to the Assembly tomorrow, the vote will be in a few days." I swallowed. "I have to admit, I'm a bit nervous."

"Grace of Luck go with you," Foss said, hugging Aleki tight.

The words settled an ominous weight over my shoulders, like a damp cloak. If what had transpired during her festival was any sign, the Grace of Luck held me in precious little favor.

After dinner, Marcello and I lingered at the table after the others had left. He adjusted his sling, wincing, his face pale and shadowed with stubble.

"How are you feeling?" I asked, guilt gnawing at my rib cage like a sullen animal.

"I've been better," he admitted. "It mostly only hurts when I move, but it's impossible not to move my ribs. I have to breathe."

"I'm sorry. This would never have happened if—"

"If you didn't care about me? You have to care about people, Amalia. If you don't, you wind up like Ruven." Marcello's face went somber. "Honestly, don't worry about me. I'm more concerned about who else Ruven attacked last night."

I set my head in my hands. "Yes, there's that to keep me up all night, too. Has the Mews tested for Ruven's potion?"

"Everyone down to the most junior scullery boy. All clear. I hear that a few bodies have turned up in the city, though, and we had a bit of a scare when one of our soldiers didn't show up for duty this morning." His expression lightened, then. "But he arrived late, with no potion in his veins and what looks like a brutal hangover. So far as I can tell, the Mews is secure."

"That just means Ruven has some other plan we haven't uncovered." I pulled on a loose lock of hair. "Why couldn't this have happened *after* the vote?"

"Focus on your law for now. It's something only you can do, and it's important."

"I can't let the Falcons down." I dug my fingers into my legs. "They're all counting on me to do this, Marcello, and I'm not sure I can. I may not have enough votes."

"You won't let them down." His voice dropped, then, and he lowered his gaze to the table. "Though I'm afraid that I already have."

"You? Let down the Falcons?" I asked incredulously. "You've dedicated your entire *life* to the Falcons."

"Have I?" He spread his hand on a tabletop rough with old burns and knife cuts; a couple of pale scars marked his knuckles and the back of his wrist, too. I'd never asked where they came from, assuming they were part of the wages one paid for being a soldier. "I became a Falconer for two reasons. I've worked hard to rise through the ranks for those same two reasons."

"To protect Istrella, and people like her," I supplied without hesitation. "To keep the mage-marked safe, and to ensure that the Mews always treats them well."

"That's one," he agreed. "But there's always been another." He lifted his eyes to mine, green and honest as always. But this time, that honesty was clouded with pain. "To prove my father wrong."

"Ah." I let the sound out on a long breath. "I do understand how family can prove to be, shall we say, a complex motivational force."

"There's nothing complicated about it in my case. I don't want his approval or his love. Not anymore." Marcello's fingers curled into a fist. "Not after all the years he told me I was worthless and would never amount to anything. No, I just want him to look at me and know he was wrong. I want it to bother him every time he looks across the lagoon and sees the Mews, and knows that I'm in command of the most powerful military force in Eruvia." Marcello shook his head. "That's my second reason. And it's entirely selfish."

I laid my hand over his, gentling his bone-hard knuckles with a touch. "It's all right to have the occasional uncharitable feeling. Especially if it drives you to do something good."

"But that's the problem." Marcello started to sigh, then cut it short and flinched at his broken ribs. "Having that personal ambition only helps the Falcons if I'm actually the best possible commander for them. And I'm not."

"There's no one in all the Falconers who cares more about the welfare of the Falcons than you," I objected.

"Maybe not. But we don't need a Falconer in command of the Mews." He squeezed my hand and leaned across the table, his face intent. "We need a Falcon."

"Ah! Yes, I can see that."

"I tried everything I could to make the Falcons safe and happy. And I thought I'd succeeded. But now I've seen that the Falcons aren't going to tell *me* if they're unhappy." A wistful note entered Marcello's voice. "I still want the job, I admit it. But that doesn't matter. It's long past time the Falcons had one of their own in charge."

"I don't think there's any law against it." I searched my memory. "Falcons can't have noble titles or sit in the Assembly, but they can hold military rank."

"It's only custom that keeps them out of high posts, and that's been fading with time." Marcello's eyes shone with excitement. "There's no reason we couldn't prepare a Falcon to succeed Colonel Vasante."

There was the small matter that the colonel had been grooming Marcello to take her place, and that it had been his dearest ambition since he was fourteen years old. But if that didn't concern Marcello, I supposed it shouldn't concern me. "I can help you garner political support for that."

His smile kindled a small warmth in my chest. "Pass your law, first. I think you have enough on your plate for now."

I thought of everything I had to do over the next few days: finishing the law, submitting it to the Assembly, and the ensuing grand, mad scramble to secure votes. I doubted I'd get much sleep this week.

"Yes," I sighed. "Yes, I do."

The next few days were a blur of meetings and social events as I strove to sway as many Assembly members as possible before the vote on my Falcon law. I choked down coffee with admirals, hosted influential family heads for wine and crostini at the

Cornaro palace, and debated ethics and logic in the salons of the intellectuals. One thousand Assembly members could vote on this law, and by the Graces, I would try to personally convince as many of them as I could in the short time I had.

An unexpected boon to my cause came when news arrived over the courier lamps that the Lady of Bears and the Serpent Lord appeared to be withdrawing their forces from the Loreician border. I found myself suddenly in high favor, with generals lifting gleeful toasts to my name, Assembly members congratulating me on my diplomatic success when we passed in the halls of the Imperial Palace, and even the doge sending me a note of stiff gratitude.

My crow message to Kathe that day was simple: *Thank you for the delicious eggs.* I pictured him chuckling as he read it, and smiled.

The efforts to discover what Ruven had done on the Night of Masks kept my mother busy late into the night. When she came home exhausted from the Imperial Palace with her hair straggling down from its pins, she always took the time to give me some small handful of carefully gleaned jewels of advice on whose support to seek for my law or how to win over this or that influential lord. But the one thing I wanted to know most, she never so much as hinted at.

I gathered up my courage to ask Ciardha, when she'd finished giving me my breakfast briefing and was laying out my schedule on the third morning since my meeting with the doge.

"Ciardha, do you know..." My question caught in my throat. It wasn't the sort of thing I'd usually ask her. But I had never known Ciardha to tell me anything but the truth.

"Yes, Lady?" she prompted gently, as she laid a neat bundle of letters beside my cup of chocolate.

"Do you know what my mother thinks of my Falcon law?"

More words tumbled out, my face growing warmer all the while. "She's given me so much advice on how to pass it, but she never says whether she thinks it's a good idea in the first place, or talks about it when other Assembly members are around. I don't even know if she's planning to vote for it."

Ciardha's brown eyes lost their customary cool distance, their focus sharpening. "I have never known La Contessa to vote against justice, Lady," she said, with quiet conviction.

I let out a tremulous sigh. "She has so much influence. I wish she were more willing to show public support."

"One of the pillars of La Contessa's power is that she has the doge's confidence," Ciardha said. "His Serenity has made it plain that he does not favor your law. So La Contessa must step carefully in public, lest she seem to stand against him."

I ground two pieces of roll together until they shed crumbs like snow. "I suppose she must do her dance. But still, it would be nice to see her make a stand on a moral issue like this."

"If you think she is doing nothing to help you, then you need to look closer. Who is La Contessa's closest ally in the Council of Nine?"

"The Marquise of Palova," I responded automatically. "And *she* declared open support for some of my ideas, so...oh." My cheeks burned.

Ciardha nodded. "La Contessa prefers to keep her hand hidden when she pulls the strings, Lady. And besides, she wants this to be *your* law, and your victory. Not hers."

I frowned. "This isn't some power play to secure my future. It's about the Falcons' freedom."

A small smile pulled at Ciardha's lips. She offered me a slight bow. "Of course, Lady. But you may have noticed that La Contessa rarely does anything for only one purpose. There is no reason it cannot be both."

The morning of the vote, I woke at the first gray murmuring of twilight. I lay awake, staring up at the silk canopy above my bed, running lists of names who might or might not support my law through my head like a string of beads through nervous fingers. It was impossible to know who would truly vote for reform and who had merely made polite noises of agreement to avoid alienating La Contessa's daughter. Graces, what if when the votes were counted, only a handful had taken me seriously? How could I cross the lagoon to the Mews and tell Zaira and Foss and the others that we'd never had a chance?

Slowly, the light in my room grew; at first I could barely pick out the colors in my bedcurtains, or the gleams of gold from artifice devices perched on top of my wardrobe, but soon enough I could read the titles of the volumes on the bookshelf across from me. I wished I could sleep a little longer, to be refreshed and sharp-witted when I faced the Assembly, but the endless clamor in my mind kept me awake. *This is the day. The day you either let down all your friends, or change history.*

I wasn't entirely certain which outcome terrified me more.

At last, I rose, took my elixir, and opened my wardrobe, staring in blank horror at the acres of silk and velvet and lace within.

A firm knock barely preceded my mother through my door. She glided up beside me, already perfect in a gown of midnight velvet, her auburn hair loose about her shoulders.

"I'll pick something out for you myself," she said. "We can't have you showing up in some mismatched coat and breeches you happen to think are comfortable to read in."

"I wouldn't do that," I objected.

"No, I suppose you wouldn't. Not anymore." She ran her fingers through my hair, pulling out tangles. "But I'll pick your outfit for you today anyway."

I turned to her, panic beginning to bubble up in my chest. "I can't do this, Mamma. They're going to laugh me off the Assembly floor."

"Of course you can do it." Her stern tone left no room for argument. "Good Graces, child, you've spoken before the Conclave of Witch Lords. I think you can handle an assortment of tedious windbags like the Serene Imperial Assembly."

"I suppose you're right." I took a deep breath and shook out my hands, trying to cast off the prickling in my nerves. "It's easier, somehow, when everyone is a potential enemy, rather than a potential ally I could be alienating forever."

"You'll do fine."

"That's nice of you to say, but, forgive me, you *are* my mother."

"Yes, I am." She turned me to face her with firm hands, staring into my eyes. "And you may have noticed that in all your life, I have never once given you praise when you hadn't earned it."

My ears warmed at the haze of a hundred commingled memories of criticism and disappointment. "That's certainly true."

"Then believe me when I tell you that I have every confidence in you. I'm proud of you, Amalia. You'll do fine."

My throat thickened as if I'd swallowed a cup of almond paste. *I'm proud of you, Amalia.*

I straightened my spine and turned to face the wardrobe, so my mother wouldn't see me blinking furiously.

"All right, then," I said. "What do I wear to change history?"

Chapter Eleven

When it was empty, the Imperial Assembly Hall held a profound hush, like a theater or a temple. I'd walked through it when the Assembly wasn't in session, and the vastness of the space with the hundreds of blue-cushioned chairs all cleared away made me feel tiny, my footfalls sounding with brash impunity in a room that cherished the echoes of three hundred years of history. The Nine Graces looked down from the vast central ceiling mural, painted dancing on luminous clouds in the starry night sky, surrounded by gold medallions framing more frescoes of proud moments in Raverran history. Their stares always seemed more accusing to me than benevolent, as if perhaps I hadn't been using their gifts well enough.

Now the hall was far from empty, and a thousand murmuring conversations rose up to the ceiling like a flock of fluttering pigeons. Rows of hundreds of chairs for Assembly members filled much of the floor, most of them occupied, and the balcony gallery above was full of spectators. I'd seen votes taken with less than a third of the Assembly in attendance, and no audience at all, but it seemed my attempts to tamper with the fundamental order of Raverran power were ambitious enough to attract a crowd. I paused inside the great oak doors, among other milling Assembly members who had not yet taken their seats. I tried to breathe calm into my lungs and still my hands, which wanted to fret at the fabric of the crimson-and-gold gown my mother had selected for me. To evoke the colors of the Falcons, she'd said.

"This is your last chance to reconsider, my lady."

It was Lord Caulin, and there was no forgiveness in his eyes for my victory over him at Lady Aurica's party. He bowed, necessitating that I bow lower; he was, after all, on the Council of Nine now.

"I assure you, Lord Caulin, I have given it a great deal of consideration already. You should know by now that I am not a feckless girl acting on some impulse of sentiment."

He permitted himself a small, humorless smile. "You are a student of history, are you not, Lady Amalia?"

"I have studied history, yes." More than he had, I'd wager.

"Then you must know that the Falcons once were kept under much tighter control than they are now. Every time the Empire has experimented with giving them more freedoms, it has later found it difficult or impossible to take those freedoms away." He shook his head. "What you do could have consequences lasting a thousand years."

"If *you* have studied history," I said, with some heat, "then you must realize that these additional freedoms for the Falcons do not appear to have in any way hampered the Empire's growth, power, or security. And indeed, if you are so fond of history, I challenge you to show me one society that has ever existed in Eruvia that has gained any enduring benefit from the oppression of its people."

Lord Caulin lifted a cautionary finger. "We are speaking of individuals with the power to destroy entire cities, my lady. You cannot consider them simply as people."

"On that, Lord Caulin, I fear we fundamentally disagree." I gave him a short bow. "Now if you'll excuse me, I have some legislation to introduce."

I felt his eyes on my back as I walked up the long aisle between the rows of chairs toward the front of the hall. He wasn't the only one; conversations fell to whispers as I passed, and heads turned to watch me. A few Assembly members gave me supportive nods or friendly waves, which I returned with what grace and enthusiasm I could muster.

At the far end of the hall, Doge Niro da Morante sat in his gold brocade state robes upon the imperial throne. His black eyes gleamed at me from beneath iron-gray brows as I approached. His face betrayed nothing. What he said here today could have a considerable impact on my law's chances of passing; there were many who looked to him for guidance on how to vote. I could only guess whether my efforts to persuade him not to block me had had any effect whatsoever.

The rows of chairs ended before a square of open floor large enough to accommodate dancing, had the Assembly decided to give up on governance of the Empire in favor of a festive gala. An imperial seal inlaid in rare woods centered this space, fifteen feet across and ringed by a rune-scribed amplification circle so that anyone who spoke before the Assembly could be heard throughout the hall. A row of ten chairs lined the end wall: the doge's throne stood at the center, with the Council of Nine flanking him. My mother caught my eyes from her seat at the doge's left hand and gave me a minute nod.

Rows of gold-cushioned benches flanked the speaking floor, parallel to the right and left walls, for Assembly members with special status or official positions in the imperial court. I headed to my usual seat in the back corner of one of these, smiling a greeting to the elderly lord next to me.

More Assembly members kept arriving, and conversation filled the hall, but I couldn't bring myself to talk to anyone. Caulin took his seat among the Council of Nine, and not long after, the doge called the Assembly to order. I sat through the initial proceedings without hearing a word of them. In the coming moment, I couldn't be nervous or flustered; too much depended on my ability to convince the Assembly. I closed my eyes, slowed my breath, and dug deep within for what I needed: serenity.

My time came, and I was called to the floor at last.

I rose, and a thousand eyes turned to me. I walked toward the great seal inlaid in the floor; when I crossed the border of runes around it, my footsteps echoed unnaturally loud across the hall. I strode to the exact center, standing on the wing joint of the flying horse rearing in the imperial crest, and turned to face the room.

This was it. I took in a deep breath.

"I put forth before this august and serene Assembly the Falcon Reserve Act, making active military duty elective for mage-marked citizens of the Serene Empire and updating some of the more archaic regulations governing Falcons." They all should have received copies of the law, and I could only hope they'd read it; all that remained was to take the brief moment granted me to convince them to vote for it. "We are a civilized society, and it is time to end the practice of conscripting children and taking them from their homes against their will and that of their families. Let us entice the mage-marked into active service rather than compelling them, and thereby earn a far greater share of their loyalty by showing them basic human respect."

Murmurs of reaction grew in the crowd, and I saw some in the front rows shift in their seats. I wished I knew if that was good or bad. "This law does not discontinue the requirement that every mage-marked child born in the Empire must have a jess and a Falconer, though the Falconer no longer need attend their Falcon at all times," I added. "After some basic training, to be completed anytime at the mage's leisure, it will be up to the discretion of the Falconers whether each individual Falcon in the civilian reserve should have their power sealed or unsealed by default." I'd worked out that compromise with Colonel Vasante and her officers, since what might be safe for, say, a well-trained adult artificer might not be for a mage with poor control, a warlock, or a child. "By allowing mage-marked people to decline active military duty, we simply weed out those who are unwilling or unsuited, either of which makes for a poor soldier. By giving them the basic freedom to choose where and with whom they live, we allow our mage-marked citizens to have homes and families, which can only increase their desire to protect the serenity of the Empire."

I saw some nods in the watching crowd, but also some scowls and shaking heads. I couldn't let my resolve weaken now. I summoned a clear passion to fill my voice, letting it ring to every corner of the hall. "Mages without the mark are already part of our society: they make our luminaries and symphonic shells, mix the cures for our daily ailments, and grow us fruits and flowers out of season." I spread my arms. "How is a mage-marked artificer who can make a courier lamp more of a threat than an unmarked one who can make a luminary? How is a mage-marked alchemist who can cure the wasting sickness more dangerous than an unmarked one who can cure a cold? These are our friends and family and neighbors, our fellow citizens! They are not criminals, to be locked up behind warded walls."

By my count, my time was nearly up. I reached out to the sea of faces before me, imploring them. "I urge you to end the injustice of taking innocent children from their homes, and restore the honor of the Serene City. Let our mage-marked brethren show us what they can do for the Empire if their service is freely given, rather than compelled. If we trust the Falcons to protect our borders from invaders, we can trust them to live beside us. If we ask them to risk their lives to defend the Empire, the least we can do is make that Empire not their prison, but their home."

I bowed to the Assembly, and then, more deeply, to the doge and the Council of Nine. My hands trembled at my sides. My mother gave me a slight smile; Lord Caulin's face was flat as a drawn knife, and the doge regarded me with heavy deliberation, as if I were a troubling puzzle.

"Thank you," I said, my throat gone suddenly dry at last, after holding up fine through my speech.

A strange sound, like spring rain, rose up as I walked to my seat. I recognized it with wonder: applause.

"Very good," the old lord murmured as I sat down beside him, smiling encouragingly. "We're all so impressed, by the way, at what you did at the Conclave in Vaskandar, and how you got those demons off our border in Loreice."

I smiled back, uncertainly. Was that why they were clapping? Not because they supported my law, but because I'd helped avert disaster from the Empire? Or perhaps he was merely expressing wonder that I'd managed to survive negotiations with the Witch Lords at all. If I'd heard a year ago of someone attending a meeting of all seventeen Witch Lords and even going so far as to court one, I'd have assumed they had nerves of pure steel and were perhaps a bit mad.

The doge called for any who would speak for or against the proposed law to do so, and I turned my attention to the floor, my hands clenched on my knees.

An old woman with a small grandson in the Falcons spoke passionately in favor of the Falcon Reserve Act, tears standing in her eyes as she told her story of wanting her grandson to spend his childhood at home. A middle-aged woman spoke vehemently against it, claiming it spat on three hundred years of proud Raverran history and would destroy the military power of the Empire. One man warned it would inevitably lead to the rise of mage-marked overlords like they had in Vaskandar; a rotund, bearded fellow declared that he didn't see that it much mattered where the mage-marked lived, and the Empire could still order them to do whatever it wanted, so what was the fuss about, anyway? His speech drew laughs; but then a scholar from the Imperial University delivered a stinging assessment that the mage-marked would be in too much danger outside the Mews, without Falconers to protect them from kidnappers and the violence of the ignorant, and my insides plunged.

And so it went on. I watched the faces in the crowd anxiously, but I heard murmurs of approval and grumbles of dissent alike in response to arguments for both sides. Eloquence and passion seemed equally matched, more or less, in arguments for and against. Applause after each speech varied, from none at all to a polite scattering to enthusiastic cheers, but didn't seem to favor one side over the other. This vote would be close.

After hours of debate that left my muscles sore from sheer tension, at last there were no more from the general Assembly who wished to speak. Tradition held that the Council of Nine and the doge had the last word, and all eyes turned toward the row of thronelike chairs that faced the Assembly. I held my breath; the Council had immense influence, and if they came out largely against my act, it was doomed before the vote started.

Lord Caulin rose to speak first, and delivered a series of dire warnings about the consequences of giving up military power when we needed it most. He gentled his stark pronouncements outlining the terrible threat we faced with assurances that, of course, we could consider such compassionate measures later, once we faced no imminent threat from Vaskandar. His speech garnered more than its share of applause, and I saw a lot of nodding heads; my insides twisted queasily as he returned to his chair.

The Marquise of Palova marched to the speaking circle next. Many in the audience sat up straighter; she was the Council member responsible for the military, a retired general, and a hero of the Three Years' War. Her opinion would hold great sway with many.

She swept the Assembly with her gaze, planted her fists on her hips, and began speaking in a voice strong enough it didn't need amplification to fill the vast hall.

"Lord Caulin is right about one thing," she said. "We face a serious threat now from Vaskandar. And one of our key advantages in this battle is that we have alchemists, artificers, and warlocks, while they, for the most part, don't."

I edged forward on my seat. I thought I saw where this was going, and hope quickened my breath.

"Do you know why I say 'for the most part'?" the marquise demanded. "The potential for alchemy is uncommon in Vaskandran bloodlines, and artificers are almost unheard of there. Do you know where they get their artificers from?" Scattered mutters met her question, but she cut her arm across the air like a sword stroke to silence them. "From the Empire. Mage-marked who flee to Vaskandar not because they think it's a better place to live, but because at least in Vaskandar they can be free. We try our damnedest to make the Mews a place anyone would love to live, lords and ladies of the Assembly, but you could open the gates straight to the garden of the Graces and people still wouldn't thank you for shoving them through by force. I sure as Hells wouldn't. I have too much to do here on earth."

A few people laughed. The marquise's eyes flashed as she gazed out over the hall. "If we force them into the Mews when they don't want to go, they have nowhere else to run but to Vaskandar. We are *handing weapons to our enemies*. And if we drag them to the Mews unwilling, we are not only putting the hilts in our enemies' hands, we're cradling the blades to our bosoms." She shook her head. "We learned this in the Three Years' War. I can't tell you the details, because they're secrets of the state. But there were suborned Falcons who acted against us in the war, and mage-marked from the Serene Empire who were recruited by the Witch Lords to fight on the other side. And even in peacetime, every year there are rogue mages who hide their mark and then wind up losing control, committing crimes, causing havoc—all because they didn't want to go to the Mews, so they don't have a jess. None of that would have happened—battles lost, people killed, lives ruined—if we had passed a law like this one. Let the damned mages stay home, if they want to so badly that they'll turn down a life of luxury. If I somehow find myself running short of Falcons, at least with this law the mage-marked won't be in hiding, and I'll know where to go looking to recruit more of them."

She stalked back to her chair and dropped into it. The room burst into applause. I wanted to run up and hug her.

Then the applause died down. The doge swept the remaining Council members with his gaze. "Would any other members of the Council speak?" he asked.

I tried to catch my mother's eyes. *Please. I'm your daughter. They'll listen to you. Say something.*

But she looked at the doge, not me, and gave a tiny shake of her head.

The weight of that small motion crushed the breath from me. All she needed to do was stand up and say a few words to show she supported me. This moment was too important for her political games—important for the mage-marked, for the Empire, and for me.

But then her eyes flicked to mine, fierce and proud. And they crinkled in a smile.

A tendril of hope unfurled in my heart. Perhaps she thought I didn't need her help, and kept her silence because I'd done well enough on my own.

All eyes turned, then, to Niro da Morante. It was his turn to speak, if he wished. The ambient whispering and rustling in the hall settled to a breathless quiet; a single cough cut through the air, loud as a cannon.

The doge swept his gaze across the Assembly. His eyes flicked briefly to me, then away again, so quickly I almost thought I'd imagined it.

"I have nothing to say on this matter at this time," he announced. "The debate is closed."

A wave of murmuring conversation broke over the hall, and I had to grip the edges of my chair to guard against a flush of giddy dizziness. It had been too much to hope that the doge might speak in favor of my law, but he hadn't come out against it, at least—whether because I'd shaken his convictions or because he didn't want a record of his stance inked in the pages of history until he'd seen it succeed or fail. Either way, I'd take it.

Two acolytes of the Grace of Majesty brought out the great gilded urn used in Assembly legislative votes, placing it in front of the imperial seal graven in the floor. Another pair brought out the blue velvet bags holding the ballot balls, and the head shrinekeeper of the Temple of Majesty stood by, overseeing the proceedings. Soon, Assembly members lined up to each take two marble-sized wooden balls from an acolyte—one black, and one white—and drop one of them down the urn's small round mouth.

The first ballots dropped with a resounding clatter, but the sound became softer as the urn filled. My palms grew damp as I waited my turn in line. I had to wipe them on my skirts before taking my ballots from the hand of the solemn-eyed girl holding them out to me. I separated them, then stared at the wooden orb in my hand a long time, to make absolutely certain that it was white and I didn't wind up voting against my own law through some trick of light or fleeting madness.

At last, I dropped it through the dark round opening. It hit the other balls below with a final-sounding clink. Another acolyte took the ball I hadn't used and dropped it without looking into a black velvet bag, to be saved in case of a close or contested vote.

Then there was nothing to do but sit in my chair and stare at the long line of grave, purposeful Assembly members, telling myself that I wasn't going to try to see how they were voting, finding my eyes drawn to their hands as they dropped in their ballots anyway. *Clink.* Another vote, for or against. *Clink.* One small wooden ball closer to deciding the fate of the Falcons, and perhaps the Empire. *Clink.* I didn't want to think of how I would face Zaira and Terika and, Graces help me, poor Venasha and Foss if the act failed. It was easy enough for me to say we could try again; they were the ones who had to keep living a life without choices in the meantime.

Finally, an ancient woman leaning on a cane cast the last ballot. The acolytes hauled the urn off to count the results under the auspices of the shrinekeeper, without interference. Representatives from the temples of Wisdom, Luck, and Victory would also be there, to make certain no corruption of the vote occurred, and the Council of Nine would verify the results.

I wanted a drink. A nice, sweet dessert wine, perhaps, to relax with. Or something stronger.

Often the crowd dispersed after a vote in the Assembly, content to let the shrinekeepers count the ballots and find out whether we had a new law in the morning. But this time, very few left. The clamor of conversation was no quiet rustle; people argued with each other, gesturing passionately. I glanced to my mother and saw her chatting with the Marquise of Palova, both of them seeming entirely relaxed. Lord Caulin's chair was empty; he was up and about, circulating and talking. After perhaps a quarter of an hour, the Council filed out of the room to join the shrinekeepers and verify the vote.

It felt as if they were gone for a thousand years. When they filed back in, I searched their faces for any hint of the results, but they remained carefully neutral, still and impassive.

My mother wasn't meeting my eyes. That couldn't be good. My heart seemed to descend into my stomach, which squirmed with the effort to digest it.

It was too late to persuade anyone else, too late to make another speech. Zaira's fate, and Aleki's and Terika's and all the rest, were decided. If I had failed them, it was already done.

The doge lifted a hand, and the room fell silent. I braided my fingers together in my lap.

Niro da Morante stepped forward, his stern face unreadable, to announce the results.

Chapter Twelve

The doge moved to the center of the imperial seal and stood facing the Assembly. He cleared his throat; the sound boomed off the walls. Most of the room stared at him, but a disquieting proportion of them watched me. Waiting to see my reaction. I struggled to school my face into a mask, but my anxiety must have shown clear as a printed page.

"The results have been tallied," the doge said, his voice heavy with the gravity of history. "The Falcon Reserve Act is passed into law."

A wave of wild cheering broke over the room. I blinked for a moment, certain I had misheard.

And then suddenly I was on my feet, people were pounding my back, and the most undignified squealing sounds were issuing from my mouth. A portly woman I didn't know hugged me. A narrow-faced man scowled at me, and a faint chorus of boos came from somewhere in the gallery. The old woman with the grandson in the Falcons was crying. And across the room, my mother narrowed her eyes in satisfaction, as if this had all transpired exactly as she had planned.

The cloud of euphoria around me was so great that even Lord Caulin couldn't pierce it, when he came and shook my hand in congratulations, a regretful sort of smile on his lips, his eyes dead and cold.

"This isn't over," he said softly, in a voice pitched to cut under the noise of the crowd.

"Of course not." I grinned at him. "It's only beginning."

"If the Empire falls," he warned, "it will be your fault."

"Come now, Lord Caulin. Neither you nor I will allow that to happen," I said.

He regarded me for a long moment—assessing an enemy, or an ally, or an uncomfortable mix of both.

"No," he agreed at last. "We won't."

All I wanted was to get out of the Imperial Palace and row across the lagoon to the Mews, to spread the word to my friends. But it seemed half the Assembly wanted to talk to me, and I could hardly brush them off when they had helped me pass this law. So I smiled and shook hands and accepted congratulations and offered thanks, with someone else always waiting to fill the gap as soon as I finished a conversation. It took me well over an hour just to work my way across the hall to the doors. They would have heard the news at the Mews by now, but it didn't matter; I'd tell them again myself, just for the joy of seeing their faces.

When I finally emerged under the marble portico that ran the length of the palace courtyard, I still floated on a cloud of giddy relief and the euphoria of victory. The thin winter sunlight beyond the row of delicate columns seemed brighter, and the chill air bracing rather than draining. I turned from the stream of dignitaries leaving the Assembly hall and prepared to cross the sea of white marble that sheathed the palace courtyard.

A strange whooping sound was my only warning before

something slammed into me. Panic flashed through me—but this was a hug, not a grappling attack. And I knew the honey-brown curls tickling my nose. I wasn't being assassinated; it was just Terika.

Or rather, not *just* Terika. Over her shoulder more familiar faces greeted me: Marcello, smiling broadly despite the sling binding his arm against his chest; Istrella, bouncing up and down at his side, her bicolored artifice glasses pushed up to hold back her hair; and Zaira, grinning and shaking her head.

"What are you doing here?" I asked wonderingly, when Terika released me.

"Taking you out for drinks to celebrate, of course!" Terika said, grabbing my hand. "And then we can head back to the Mews and join the party. But we wanted to get to you first."

"They're preparing something for you at the Mews and need us to buy time," Istrella said happily. Terika elbowed her in the ribs.

I stared back and forth between them. "But wait, you're out without your Falconers—oh!"

"Some crazy lady passed a law to get rid of that stupid rule," Zaira said. "About damned time, too. I take back at least four or five of the mean things I've said about you." She slapped my shoulder, hard enough to make my eyes smart, which from her was better than Terika's hug. "Anyway, never fear, your one-winged father goose there insisted we bring half the army with us."

Marcello shrugged his good shoulder. "Just to get us here safely. Once you're with Amalia so she can release you, you're worth half an army by yourself."

"Ha! *Half* an army? You're undervaluing me." Zaira, to my great surprise, linked her arm through mine. "Come on, Amalia. Let's find the best bottle of wine in the city. Your treat."

I rather doubted the best bottle of wine in Raverra was to be found at the modest establishment at which we eventually settled ourselves, with its warm, wood-paneled interior and a fireplace flanked by a pair of inexplicable brass roosters. However, it was quiet enough for conversation, and the servers seemed content to bring us a perfectly decent dry white wine and crostini and allow us our privacy. We toasted the future and watched the sun set over the small fountain plaza outside, the luminaries waking at dusk to rescue the faces of the buildings from the black shadows attempting to swallow them.

"So, are any of you going to leave the Mews and join the reserve?" I asked, tipping my glass respectfully toward Terika and Zaira.

"Not me," Istrella said at once, idly tracing runes on the table with her finger. "I love my tower. It'll be nice to be able to take any old guard and go looking for artifice supplies in the city without having to wait for Marcello to be available, though."

Zaira leaned an elbow on the table. "I'm staying until we take care of Ruven. I've got unfinished business with his face."

"Does it involve balefire?" I asked, pretending surprise.

"Why, yes, it does! However did you guess?" Her grin faded to a thoughtful frown. "After the war, Hells yes, I'll join the reserve. If they let me."

"They'll have to," I said.

Zaira lifted a skeptical eyebrow. "Oh, they'll try to stop me, one way or another. I guarantee it."

"But we won't let them," I replied firmly. "Where will you go?" I tried to ask the question casually, as if of course I didn't mind if one of my few friends in the world decided to move to the opposite end of the Empire.

Zaira and Terika exchanged glances. "Well," Terika said, "I want to travel, but this grump here is skeptical."

"I'm tired of people trying to kill me all the time." Zaira scowled.

"People don't normally try to kill travelers," Terika protested, exasperated. "You've just had bad luck."

"Right, the bad luck of being born a fire warlock."

"You could finally have a home, if you wanted," I pointed out. "You won't have to run or hide anymore."

Zaira snorted. "Yes, I'm sure the world will leave me alone just because of some piece of paper."

"It's true." Terika sighed dramatically, her eyes twinkling with humor. "The Empire is far from the only thing Zaira has been running from."

"Like what?" Zaira mock-scowled at her. "You? I can't run far enough to hide from *you*. You're like a plague; you'd always find me."

"How romantic." Terika kissed her and patted her cheek. "But no, you're running from something even more terrifying than me." She dropped her voice to a spooky register. "Yourself."

Everyone laughed, but I couldn't help privately feeling that Terika was, as usual, onto something.

"And you, Terika?" I asked, when the laughter quieted down. "Will you join the reserve?"

She hesitated, casting a glance at Zaira. "Well, I don't plan to live in the Mews, since I'd like to have my own place, especially if I had someone to share it with me." Zaira took a long swallow of wine. "But I also don't mind continuing to make potions for the Serene Empire, and I'd love to not have to worry about finding a means to support myself. I'm hoping to make some kind of deal where I can work in the Mews but live in the city, and visit my grandmother often."

Marcello nodded. "I'm certain we can. Most of the work the

Empire needs done doesn't require the mage doing it to be an active-duty soldier. Colonel Vasante likes this act because it gives a lot of control and flexibility back to the Mews, allowing Falcons and Falconers to work out solutions with their superior officers rather than having to jump over legal hurdles all the time."

"That's good." Terika sounded relieved. "I think you'll get more people to stay, that way."

"I confess, I'm nervous about how many Falcons will choose to leave active duty." Marcello rubbed the back of his neck, wincing. "I've worked for my entire adult life to try to make the Mews a good place for the mage-marked. If half of them leave, I'll know I've failed."

"Graces grant me patience. It's not about you." Zaira poked a finger at him. "If half of them leave, it's because they want to see what else is out there. When they find out what a festering cesspool the world is, never fear, plenty of them will come back. You raised them from tiny brats to be spoiled lapdogs, and they'll miss the Mews the first winter they have to survive without artifice heating, or when they get the flux because no one's alchemically purifying their water."

"You say the most uplifting things," I murmured.

"You're right," Marcello said quietly. "That it's not about me, that is, not about the world being a cesspool. I'm tired of lying awake at nights thinking how to make people happy who don't want to be there. It'll be nice to teach Falcons who came to the Mews by choice."

"It may be a while yet before you see much real change," Terika said, her round face going serious. "Most of us are planning to stay on active duty through the war. Even setting aside that it's not nice to turn your back on people who are counting on you to protect them, no one wants to try to build a new life in the middle of an invasion. And the last war took three years, so..." She shrugged.

"Let's hope this one is shorter." Marcello gave a strained sort of smile. The falseness of it alarmed me; I took a closer look and realized his whole face was stiff with tension, his lips pale.

"Are you all right?" I reached for his good hand and found it cold and clammy. "Did you forget one of your potions or something?"

"Just a wave of pain." He shook his head, and some of the color returned to his face. "The physicians told me it's normal, with the potions speeding the knitting of my bones. I keep getting this horrid swarming sensation, like I can feel the healing happening—which you would think would be pleasant, but it's really not."

I winced in sympathy. "Let's go back to the Mews and get you some rest. Besides," I winked at Istrella, "I hear there's a party there."

The Mews didn't look as if it were hosting a party.

As our boat glided up to the dock through the moon-painted lagoon water, its hulking, jagged shape loomed black above us. I'd never seen it with so few lights at night. But the chilly radiance of luminaries gleamed from the high, narrow windows of the dining hall, so perhaps everyone was gathered together there in celebration.

Still, our laughing conversation fell silent as the oarsman brought our overloaded boat to bump gently against the pilings. I could tell by the gleam of white at the edges of everyone's eyes as we climbed out that I wasn't the only one feeling uneasy.

Marcello frowned at the great arch of the Mews gates. "Where are the guards?"

He was right. I'd never seen the doors without at least a handful of alert soldiers stationed before them, but tonight they were gone. The rows of piers bobbed with the usual complement of boats of all shapes and sizes, but there was not a single person in sight.

"That's strange," Terika said, drawing closer to Zaira.

"It's not just strange. It should never happen." Marcello strode toward the gate with the air of someone ready to hand down discipline.

Zaira and I exchanged a meaningful glance and followed after him. There were more reasons than laziness or bad planning for the guards to be missing. Terika followed, moving with a wary alertness that reminded me she had been raised as a soldier; Istrella alone seemed oblivious, and came along humming quietly, her eyes already drifting up toward her tower.

The outer doors stood open, as they did during the day when traffic was heavy. I kept my hand on my flare locket as the yawning dark mouth stretched over us, ready to swallow us into the Mews.

"This isn't right," Terika breathed. "This wasn't the plan."

"Plan?" I asked sharply.

"For the party. They were going to meet us at the gate when we got back. They might have had another idea, I suppose, but..." She trailed off and shook her head.

"This doesn't feel like walking into a party," I agreed, my voice nearly a whisper.

Zaira grunted agreement. "This feels like walking into a trap."

Marcello's stern pace didn't slow, and we passed through the dark gullet of the gate and into the cavernous Mews entry hall. The ceiling with its frescoes of Falcon military victories was utterly lost in darkness. Our footsteps echoed off the marble walls.

Then another set of steps approached, pattering quickly, and a young soldier in Raverran blue hurried into the hall. He froze when he saw us.

"Oh!" He saluted hastily. "Captain Verdi! You're back."

"I am," Marcello said, sounding dangerous despite the sling binding his arm against his chest as he advanced on the soldier. "Why are there no guards on the doors? Where is the officer who should be in charge of the gate?"

"Ah..." The soldier glanced around wildly, as if hoping someone might come to his aid. Then his face twisted in apparent anguish. "Oh, Hells. I'm sorry about this, Captain."

He drew a pistol and pointed it straight at Marcello's chest. "You shouldn't have come home."

Chapter Thirteen

The moment froze in crystalline clarity, precise and fragile as a skin of paper-thin ice. Tiny details burned agonizingly into my senses, even as I lost precious grains of falling time to sucking in a sharp, shocked breath. The pink wetness of the soldier's eyes, as if he'd been crying. The veins standing out in his hand as he fought against the compulsion to pull the trigger. The small reddish stain on his cuff, of wine or blood. The surprise on Marcello's face twisting into anguish as he realized what must have happened. All of this tipped toward disaster, and I knew what had to happen next—the bright flash and stink of gunpowder, the cry of pain—but I couldn't move quickly enough, couldn't shake off the half second's paralysis of shock that was more than enough to make the difference between life and death.

But Marcello, thank the Graces, reacted faster. Before the soldier could pull back the hammer, he lunged in and grabbed his wrist, forcing the gun down to point at the floor. In the same motion, he slammed his good shoulder into the young man, shoving him up against a marble column.

My own time unfroze, and I rushed in to help, the copious skirts of the gown I'd worn to the Assembly vote flowing around me. I wrested the pistol from the guard's sweat-slick hand and flung it away, while Zaira and Terika pounced on him and twisted his arms behind him. Istrella stayed back, staring with wide eyes, her hands over her mouth, as the four of us immobilized the squirming, straining, trembling wreck of a soldier.

The scuffle was not quiet, with sharp shouts and thuds and grunts, and I expected reinforcements to arrive for one side or another. But no one came.

"Where is everyone?" Marcello demanded, his voice rough with emotion. He raised his own pistol to point its trembling barrel at the young man's face while Zaira and Terika held him still. "What's going on?"

The soldier's eyes stretched wide and frightened. "Don't kill me, Captain! I didn't want to do it! None of us did!"

"Do what?" Terika asked tautly.

"Ruven's potion," I breathed. "He's controlled." And if one door guard was suborned and the rest missing, that was an ominous sign indeed of what might have befallen the rest of the Mews.

At that moment, an orange light flooded the entrance hall. Around every window and the great arched doors, runes blazed to life, flaring with power.

"The emergency wards!" Istrella flipped down her artifice glasses over her eyes and stared up at the runes avidly. "I've never seen them activated before."

Marcello swore. The soldier's face went pale; he looked deeply, profoundly afraid.

"What does that mean?" Zaira asked warily.

"It means," Marcello said, "no one can get in or out."

"It means they're starting," the guard whispered, looking as if he might be ill.

"Starting what?" Sweat beaded on Marcello's brow; I could only imagine how much the scuffle must have hurt his broken ribs and shoulder.

But the soldier only shook his head, lips pressed tight, his eyes desperate and pleading.

"Are there others who are controlled as well?" I asked sharply. "Where are all the Falcons and Falconers?"

"I can't tell you anything," he whispered miserably. "But please, hurry, you've got to stop them."

"This must be Ruven's plan. The one he killed Ignazio to keep us from learning." Dread uncoiled in my belly. Now we were right in the middle of it, and we still knew nothing. "He's targeting the Mews."

The soldier pulled against Zaira and Terika's grip. He drew in a breath, as if he would shout for help, and Zaira stuffed a fist into his mouth to stop him.

"Let's stick him in a closet or something, shall we?" she growled. "And let's get the Hells out of here. This room is too exposed."

We locked the struggling soldier in a guardroom and followed Marcello up a dim stone stairwell to a second-floor clerk's office, to get out of the exposed entrance hall. The office had windows looking down into the Mews' expansive courtyard garden, and we clustered around them, peering down at the deserted lawn. Only a few of the hundreds of windows surrounding the courtyard showed light, but the wards blazed orange around every door and window, turning the familiar lines of the buildings sinister and strange. An eerie silence smothered the place. The wind rustling through dry branches in the garden below was the only sound.

"This is like a nightmare," Terika breathed, her eyes wide.

"All the tiny little Falcon brats had better be all right," Zaira muttered. I thought of Aleki with a pang of deep, searing anguish. Whatever had happened here to plunge the Mews into this silent, ominous darkness, I prayed to the Graces that he and the other children were safe.

"That soldier talked about others, and he was about to call for help," I said slowly. "He wouldn't have done that if he was worried about getting caught. There's a good chance Ruven controls the Mews right now."

"That can't be true." Marcello's denial held a ragged edge of desperation. "We've been watching *so closely* for any sign of Ruven's potion. Maybe one or two people might have slipped through, but not dozens or hundreds. And that's what it would take to seize control of the Mews within a few hours. They could still all just be gathered together for the party, or..." He trailed off, staring miserably at the lines of orange light burning around each window, well aware that the lack of commotion over the activation of the wards told a different story.

"The party," Istrella said suddenly. She was staring at the dining hall windows, her artifice glasses turning her eyes to round silvery disks in the reflected moonlight. "When we left, they were putting out the food and drink, remember? And everyone in the castle who wasn't on duty was there."

Terika groaned and put a hand to her forehead. "That's right. Someone had broken a few forty-year-old bottles of Loreician white out of the cellars, and they were about to have a toast to the new law. And to think I was sad to miss it."

My stomach flopped over. A toast. Most of the Mews drinking tainted wine at the same exact moment. "That would do it." Ruven couldn't have known this would happen; he must have planted a spy here, controlled or otherwise, and the spy had seen the opportunity.

"So we have to assume the entire Mews is under Ruven's control." Marcello put his back to the wall and slid down it, looking as if he might faint.

I closed my eyes. This was worse than my most dire nightmare scenario. The Mews lay at the heart of the Serene Empire; no enemy was ever supposed to make it this far in the first place. If they did, the mighty Imperial Navy would stop them, and if that somehow failed, the Falcons themselves were more than powerful enough to destroy any army that came against the Mews. It had the best wards in the world, and other magical defenses I could only guess at. No one seriously considered the Mews vulnerable.

But now all that power was turned against us.

"So what about the secret protocols you have in place to kill us all if we rebel?" Zaira asked, cynicism bleeding from her every word. "Don't tell me you don't have them."

Everyone looked at Marcello.

He winced. "The builders of the Mews did take steps in case of a Falcon uprising. But much as I won't blame you if you don't believe me, they're not actually designed to kill you all."

"No, I suppose the Falcons are too valuable." Zaira snorted. "So much the better. What have you got?"

Istrella pointed to the runes that ringed the windows, still faintly glowing orange. "It's a lovely piece of work, actually. They wove additional capabilities into the wards. It's so subtle that it took me years of staring at them to figure it out. There's a thread you can activate to put everyone in the Mews to sleep."

"Or everyone in a particular section of it," Marcello agreed, but no spark of hope lit his weary face. "But if they've activated the wards, that means they've seized the colonel's office, which is where all the controls are. They could knock us out, if they knew we were here, but we'd have to take Colonel Vasante's office back to do it to them."

"Or the doge can do it," Istrella added.

Marcello stiffened. "What?"

"Of course he can," Zaira said dryly.

Istrella shrugged, turning her gleaming spectacles on her brother. "Didn't they tell you? The Master Artificer told me, when he was teaching me about the wards. The doge can also put the whole Mews to sleep from the Imperial Palace."

It was a strange feeling, being so intensely grateful to hear such a sinister piece of news. "Then we just need to get to the courier lamps, and send a message to the doge."

"There's one problem with that," Zaira said, jerking her head toward the window. "They're getting organized."

A large group of soldiers, Falcons, and Falconers had entered the courtyard from the dining hall. They spread out in twos and threes, moving to take up guard positions by certain doors: the ones leading to the entrance hall, the armory, the alchemy and artifice workshops, and the courier lamps. The moonlight caught on the faces of a Falcon and Falconer pair walking past, and they looked absolutely miserable.

"At least they're alive," Terika murmured. "No one looks hurt."

Then a rustling noise came from a bush someone more skilled than I could have hit with a rock from our window. A little girl perhaps ten years old bolted from it, hair flying, a jess gleaming on her wrist.

"Grace of Mercy," I whispered. "No, no, stay hidden."

A few curses sprang up from the people guarding the courtyard, and a cry of "Run!" immediately contradicted someone else's "Stay down!" A handful of guards broke off and ran after her, closing quickly from multiple angles.

Marcello gripped the windowsill. "We have to help her."

"How?" Terika asked, her voice breaking.

I clutched my flare locket, desperately trying to think of some way we could distract the guards and let the girl escape. But a flash of light would only give away our location. I had never felt so utterly helpless.

A Falconer tackled the girl to the ground, rolling to take the impact on her own shoulders, cradling the girl protectively against her chest. The girl kicked and hit, wailing, but the Falconer kept her arms wrapped tightly around her, saying "I'm sorry, I'm sorry," over and over. Her Falcon helped her up, and the two of them started carrying the squirming girl toward the dining hall, apologizing the whole way. A sick feeling settled in my stomach.

"They're going to give her the potion." Terika shuddered. "I take back what I said before. This is *worse* than a nightmare."

"The courier lamps," I said firmly. "We'll just have to deal with anyone who tries to stop us, without hurting them."

Zaira put her fists on her hips. "And how will we do that? We have a fire warlock, three noncombatants, and Captain Armless here with a sword and pistol. We can either flail at people ineffectively or murder them."

"My darling, you should know better than to underestimate an alchemist," Teirka said sweetly, and drew a small glass bottle from her belt purse.

"Sleep potion?" I asked, hope piercing the cloud of dread that had settled over me. A drop in a drink would be enough to knock anyone out, which wasn't much use to us now—but if she shattered that whole bottle, the fumes would be enough to put anyone who breathed a lungful in close quarters to sleep.

"After our adventures in Vaskandar, I carry some around with me, just in case." Terika shook the bottle gently. "I only have three of these on me, though."

"It's certainly better than nothing," I said. "And I have a couple of artifice rings Istrella gave me that might temporarily stop an attacker."

"I have *so many* useful things in my tower," Istrella sighed. "But it's on the other side of the castle."

"I think we'd better hurry straight to the courier lamps." I turned away from the window, taking in my friends' grim, shadowed faces in the harsh orange light of the wards. "Let's go."

We climbed the stairs to the fourth floor, hoping there might be fewer guards on a higher level with no strategically important points to protect, and started making our way through the dark corridors in the direction of the courier lamp tower. This level held mostly the living quarters of common soldiers, interspersed with the occasional storeroom. Stark in their contrast to the more lavish quarters of the Falcons, the simple whitewashed hallways had no luminaries, and no one had lit the lamps. The only light came from the infrequent narrow windows looking down into the courtyard, and the vivid glare of the runes surrounding them.

In the black spaces between the windows, it was hard not to think of terrible things. Of what might have happened to people I cared about, or what Ruven might be planning to do with the Mews in his power, or how little chance we had of stopping him. Most terrifying of all was the thought that as soon as he was certain he had every Falcon under his control, he might put them all in boats and make them leave the Mews, at which point we'd have no way to stop them at all.

A bitter wind had picked up outside, and it howled tunefully across the window slits, as if the Mews were now populated by ghosts. Istrella shivered at one particularly loud gust, and I patted her shoulder.

Then an awful thought struck me. *The wind.*

I dashed to the nearest window, bumping Terika in passing, who let out a startled squeak. The bare trees below swayed, even in the sheltered courtyard; the banners on the roof snapped taut, edges quivering frantically. Clouds scudded across the moon, plunging the castle into light, then shadow, then light again, with alarming rapidity.

"What is it, Amalia?" Marcello asked, coming to my side to peer out into the night.

I scanned the rooftops and balconies, my lip caught between my teeth. It didn't take long to find what I most feared to see.

A lone, slim figure stood atop a watchtower halfway across

the Mews, the moon gleaming in his pale hair. He lifted his arms to the sky, back arched, coat flying on the wind.

Marcello saw him, too, and let out a soft curse.

The others came and clustered around the window; Istrella strained on tiptoe to see. "What? What is it?"

"Jerith," I said heavily, forcing the name out from the sucking black despair in my chest. "He's raising a storm to destroy the Serene City."

Chapter Fourteen

Raverra had stood for hundreds of years, built first on a clutch of tiny islands in a sheltered lagoon, then expanded beyond and between those islands by brilliant engineers: a miracle city of solid stone built upon the water. But none of us who lived there had any illusions that the sea we lived upon was tame. When bad storms came, parts of the city washed inches deep in murky water, and fine lords and ladies wore shoes with great blocky heels and toes to keep them up above it, like circus performers on miniature stilts. The marks of a great flood from my grandparents' day, and from an even greater flood over a hundred years ago, still stained the walls of some buildings; the Temple of Wisdom called out the high-water marks with lines of golden embellishment and a solemn stone plaque commemorating the disasters.

But the Serene City had been sheltered from those storms by the barrier islands that protected the lagoon. Jerith could create a hurricane right over the Mews and unleash forces of destruction upon Raverra such as the Tranquil Sea had never seen.

He could drown my city, wash it away, and rain down lightning like the vengeance of demons on anything that remained. And standing on the tower top, he was outside the wards; the sleep enchantment wouldn't touch him, even if we could trigger it.

"Sweet Hell of Death," Zaira breathed.

"How long will it take him to raise the storm?" I asked, clutching the wall as if the Mews itself could slip away beneath my fingers if I didn't hold on to it.

"That depends on how much he wants to build it up before he lets it go," Marcello replied grimly. "If he only wants to flood Raverra, a quarter of an hour might be enough. If he wants to obliterate it completely...I don't know."

"I doubt Ruven would order him to stop at a mere flood." I gripped the claws around my neck, trying not to think of all the people I loved who were in that city right now.

"It's a gamble," Istrella said.

"What do you mean?" Marcello asked, turning to her from the window. He'd made the mistake of ignoring Istrella's odd statements once; I could see the determination in his eyes never to do it again.

Istrella cocked her head. "When I was under Ruven's control, he would want me to do something, and I wouldn't have a choice. I had to do it, sure as I needed to breathe. But *how* I did it was up to me, so long as I truly thought it would work."

"That's right." Terika snapped her fingers. "You have to do your best, but if there are multiple ways that would work, you have a choice how to do it."

"So Jerith has to decide whether to release his storm early, and hope the city survives, or keep building it up to the point where the destruction will be absolute, and hope someone stops him before he can let it go." I bit a knuckle. I couldn't imagine the desperate courage it took to roll those dice.

"He'll keep building it up," Zaira said, her voice rough. "I know Jerith. He'll take the long chance."

For an interminable moment, we stared out the window at the thin, wind-whipped figure. The clouds thickened as we watched, beginning a ponderous swirl over his head.

"Can you..." The words jammed in my throat. I could only force them out in a hoarse whisper. "Could you make the shot from here, Marcello? If you had to?"

Zaira's fingers dug into my shoulder, sharp and merciless. "Oh, Hells, no. We're not going to do that." She glared at Marcello. "You try it and I'll break your other arm. No killing friends. You don't *do* that."

I'd done it. Shame flooded me like the foulest canal water, dark with pollution.

I'd lost count of the nights I'd lain awake telling myself that it was what Roland would have wanted, and that he'd have given his life gladly and without hesitation to save countless others, had the choice been his. But it hadn't been. *I* was the one who carefully and deliberately traced the rune that killed him, in the blood we shared. And I knew that it made me a monster. But it still hurt like the touch of balefire to hear Zaira say as much.

I doubted Jerith would rather we spared him if it meant letting him sink Raverra and the tens of thousands of people living there beneath the waves. But the cold, logical argument proofing out the mathematics of human lives failed in my throat. I knew too well it was a demon's bargain.

"We don't dare chance it, anyway," Marcello said. Strain and worry carved deep, troubled lines into his brow. "If we attack Jerith, he'll strike us down instantly with lightning. Right now we may be the only chance Raverra has, and we can't throw our lives away trying to shoot him when he can kill us fast as blinking if we miss. We'll have to get close and use Terika's sleep potion."

Zaira's hand relaxed on my shoulder. It occurred to me that if shooting him wouldn't work, our best fallback option was balefire—if Zaira could be convinced to use it.

What in the Nine Hells is wrong with me? Here I was, clinically planning how to get one friend to kill another if circumstances demanded it. I shook my head as if I could clear the dark thoughts from it like cobwebs. My mother had said to choose which lines I wouldn't cross, and that surely must be one of them.

"The courier lamp room is on the way to the watchtower," I said, trying not to show how much my own thoughts had rattled me. "Let's go."

As we crept through the dark corridor, Zaira fell back by my side. "I can't believe you wanted to shoot Jerith," she muttered.

"I didn't want to," I said softly.

"But you were ready to do it."

Yes. I was. Because sometimes, that was what needed to be done, and the integrity of my own soul was a currency I had to be willing to spend when the survival of the Serene City was at stake. But that wasn't an argument I was ready to have with Zaira. Not now, with all of our nerves sharp as blade's edges in the hostile darkness.

"What would *you* want me to do, if you were under Ruven's control and about to destroy the city with balefire?" I asked instead.

"Not assume I wanted to be shot without asking me first!"

"That's what I'm doing now."

We passed another window, and in the narrow rectangle of orange-rimmed light it cast across the corridor, I caught her dark eyes. Pain flickered across her face; she was all too familiar with the potential for her power to hurt people she cared about.

Then we were in shadow again, her face hidden. "That's easy," she said, sounding confident as always. "I'd want you to kill Ruven."

"But if there wasn't time—"

"You really need to make this night more depressing than it already is, don't you?" Zaira snapped. "Of course I don't want to murder thousands of people. But I'm going to have to do that soon enough anyway, when they send us against Ruven's army, so I'd be a damned liar if I said I'd rather die than do it, wouldn't I?"

Terika dropped back to join us, and squeezed Zaira's hand. "Shh," she whispered. "Someone will hear you."

"Then they'll be sorry they did," Zaira grumbled.

"Do you want me to release you?" I asked uncertainly.

"Hells, no. Not unless Ruven shows up in person. There are dozens of little brats like Aleki in this place. I'm not letting balefire loose in here." She let out a frustrated sigh. "Unless we need a lock picked, I'm useless."

We came at last to the stairwell that led up to the courier lamp room, which was housed in a wide, squat tower. We'd heard two more scuffles through the windows, both ending in some poor holdout getting caught and dragged off to the dining hall to be force-fed Ruven's potion. The wind had picked up to a constant keening, but we'd seen no one on the fourth floor. It would seem too easy if I didn't know that the controlled Falcons and Falconers and soldiers were trying as hard as they could *not* to catch people.

Still, I was surprised at first to find no guards at the entrance to the courier lamp tower. Communications were too important to leave unsecured. But then I noticed the artifice seal on the door, and the bubble of suspicion rising within me burst into a murky rain of despair.

Zaira looked at me hopefully. "This is the part where you make some clever scribbles on the circle and unlock the door, right?"

I shook my head, eyeing the perfectly executed seal. The artificer had left no room to tweak the spell away from its intended purpose. "This is good work, from a Mews-trained artificer. I don't see any gaps or mistakes I can work with."

"We'll just have to cancel it, then," Istrella said brightly. She was already rummaging in her satchel of artifice project bits. "I learned this in advanced artifice training last month. It'll take me a little while to inscribe the counter seal around it, so try not to interrupt me. If I drop the magical energy at the wrong moment, there could be explosions!"

She sounded far too cheerful at the idea. The rest of us exchanged glances and took a few generous steps back to give her room.

Istrella pulled out special artificer's paint with ground-in obsidian and started sketching a larger circle around the seal, humming to herself as she daubed on runes. I watched her work with a twinge of envy; it was impossible to study magical theory for years and not wish you could do it yourself.

She wasn't even halfway through when Zaira sucked in a sharp breath. "Visitors," she hissed.

I whirled from watching Istrella to face the corridor, even as Marcello drew his sword and Terika slipped her hand into her belt purse, their faces grim.

A handful of people approached, a dim collection of figures in the dark hallway, moving with wary tension. As they stepped beside a window, the patch of orange-edged light revealed the red and gold uniforms of Falcons and Falconers. Most of them looked vaguely familiar, but I recognized the elegant young man at the forefront immediately: Lamonte Clare, an artificer we'd rescued from Ruven's castle not long ago. He'd chosen to come back to the Mews, staking his chances of freedom on my Falcon reform act when he could have fled into Vaskandar. It twisted my chest painfully to see him here, under Ruven's control once more, on the very day he should have finally been free.

Lamonte hesitated, his assessing glance moving from Marcello's drawn sword to Istrella, who hummed softly as she continued to work on her circle, before lighting on me.

"Hello, Lamonte," Marcello said.

"Evening, Captain Verdi. I'd wish you a good one, but it's

too late for that." Lamonte grimaced and drew a rod twined in beaded wire from his belt. "I don't suppose you'd all like to come with me peacefully for a nice drink?"

"Not if it's got Ruven's potion in it, I'm afraid." Marcello's voice had gone high and strained, and his sword tip wavered. Agony was clearly written on his face. These were the very Falcons he'd dedicated his life to protecting; the idea of hurting them was anathema to him. But all he had to protect his sister and the Serene City was his rapier and pistol, instruments of less than gentle persuasion. "I don't want to fight you, Lamonte. I don't want to fight any of you. There must be some way we can—"

Something small bounced off Lamonte's chest, splashing his uniform with liquid, and glass shattered at his feet with a high, tinkling crash. He sucked in a surprised gasp and fell at once, crumpling to the ground like a dropped handkerchief. The Falconer at his side skittered on broken glass and spilled potion, her eyes growing wide, knees beginning to wobble. The man on Lamonte's other side swayed, his pistol sliding from his hand to clatter on the floor, and sank gracefully to his knees.

We hurried backward a couple of steps, to get away from the whiff of peppermint, as our last standing opponent swore and did the same.

"Terika!" Marcello cried in protest. "I was talking to him!"

"Exactly," Terika said, without a shred of remorse. "Thanks for the distraction."

Lamonte's remaining companion drew a pistol, anguish twisting her face, crying, "Stop me, quick!"

I yanked one of Istrella's rings from my finger and threw it at her, praying to the Graces it would be enough.

It struck the woman in the shoulder and stuck there like a magnet, runes flaring along the band. She went completely still, the muscles in her face relaxing, as if she'd simply forgotten what she was doing—but her eyes remained alert and intent, crying out silently for help.

The Falconer who'd fallen to his knees, meanwhile, started to crawl away from the spilled potion, shaking his head to clear it. Just as he scooped up his pistol, Zaira lunged forward and kicked him in the chin, sending him sprawling across Lamonte's soaked chest. He didn't rise.

I stared at the three collapsed forms and the one standing one, my ribs heaving against the boning of my bodice. The wind wailed outside, but nothing stirred in the hallway; no clamor rose up in response to our scuffle.

Zaira clapped Terika's shoulder. "Nicely done. You're right—never underestimate an alchemist."

"I don't think she's going to be like that forever," I said, waving uneasily at the Falconer I'd hit with Istrella's ring. The effect was similar enough to one Istrella had used on me when she was controlled that I had to conclude it operated on the same principles. Terika and Zaira hurried over to take the Falconer's pistol and haul her into a nearby storeroom, businesslike and efficient as if they disposed of bodies together all the time.

"There!" Istrella said triumphantly behind me. "Stand back!"

Marcello and I scampered to give her space. Light flared from the new circle she'd drawn, and the seal within it sizzled, smoking. Istrella nodded with great satisfaction and opened the door.

Terika held one of her sleep potion vials at the ready as we climbed the stairs; Marcello led the way, his pistol in hand, his mouth set in an unhappy line. He hadn't had to hurt anyone yet, but our capacity to take people out swiftly and painlessly was diminishing rapidly, and he knew it. Still, the courier lamp room waited at the top of these stairs; one quick message would alert the Imperial Palace of the imminent danger to the city, and our work would be half-done.

Then we emerged at the top of the stairs into the courier lamp room, and I saw at once why there were no guards on the stairwell door.

The large, round room normally had the magical, expectant look of a temple, with hundreds of niches rising in rows along the walls, each holding a lamp. Some would flicker like candles, and courier lamp clerks would bend over them as if praying, writing down the messages and signaling back the replies.

But now there were no clerks, no flickering lights. Every niche was dark.

The floor lay two inches deep in shattered crystal. Slashed golden wires hung curling from the ceiling, dangling in tangled bunches from the rune-circled window in the center of the dome that funneled the braid of lamp wires up to the sending spire on the roof. Chunks of wood and brass jutted from the crystal shards that blanketed the floor like boot-churned snow, pieces of lamp bases mixed in with the broken hunks of quartz.

Istrella let out a cry as if we'd found the body of a dear friend and fell to her knees in the doorway, scooping up crystal shards to let them run through her fingers.

"No!" she wailed. "We worked *so hard* on these!"

I had to steady myself against the wall with a shaking hand. This was a staggering loss. Each courier lamp crystal had a twin, many of them hundreds of miles away—hewn from the same rock, magically linked, carefully crafted, and now completely useless. It would take months to replace them all.

And without them, we had no way to tell the outside world what was happening.

Marcello squatted beside his sobbing sister, rubbing her back. "Shh, 'Strella. It's okay. We can make more."

"We don't have time to cry about it," Zaira said grimly. "This means we can't count on anyone to clean up after us if we make a mess of this. We have to stop Jerith ourselves."

I kept my hand on my flare locket as we once again made our way along the fourth-floor corridor. We were quite close to Jerith's watchtower now, and someone had lit the lamps here. I caught my spine curling, hunching down out of some instinctive urge toward stealth, and straightened at once, forcing my shoulders to relax to a more normal posture.

Zaira elbowed me. "Finally, you're learning," she murmured.

A sole guard waited at the door to the watchtower stairs. He sucked in a breath to call for help as we approached, lifting a rapier before him. But Marcello charged him before anyone had a chance to react; he dodged past the soldier's blade and drove a knee into his stomach, knocking the wind out of him. Zaira and Terika piled onto him, and soon they had him down on the ground; one drop of Terika's precious sleep potion forced past his lips was enough to make him go slack and still.

"How long does that last?" Zaira asked, worry in her voice.

"Mine usually lasts an hour, if no one tries to wake them up." Terika shook her head. "I never thought I'd be using it on the soldiers stationed at the Mews to protect us."

Zaira snorted. "Really? I thought about that sort of thing all the time."

Marcello bent nearly in half, panting, his face slick with sweat. He looked as if he might faint or throw up, and wasn't quite sure which. I hurried to his side.

"This fighting can't be good for you." I tentatively laid a hand on his uninjured shoulder; his skin was so hot I could feel it through his shirt, and he flinched from my gentle touch. The pain in his face twisted like a knife in my own side.

"I've felt better," he admitted, on a hoarse wisp of breath. But then he shivered and forced himself straight. "Let's go. The wind is picking up."

That was an understatement. The wind shrieked outside the windows, tearing the banners from the battlements, and the clouds fled across the sky as if they could escape the nightmare that pulled them inexorably into a spiral above the castle. Shouts of alarm and dismay came from the courtyard below. We were running out of time.

No artifice seal locked the watchtower. We hurried up its winding stone steps; narrow windows gave us alternating glimpses of the wind-lashed Mews courtyard and the Serene City—a gathering of a thousand warm lights twinkling like stars, floating above the black waters of the lagoon. Fear crushed my chest at the sight; it was so fragile, and so precious. Jerith could blow out all those lights like festival candles, and drown the warmth and beauty in choking dark water. My invulnerable mother, and Ciardha, and the servants who'd helped raise me— my family, my home. No miracle of the Graces or of their own clever devising could save them from the unanswerable power of the ocean, if it came pouring in to conquer the floating city at last. We were Raverra's only hope.

I wished I felt remotely up to the task. I had my own set of skills, but none of them seemed useful in subduing storm warlocks.

The stairs wound their way to a landing, ending in a stout wooden door. After a glance to make certain we were ready, Marcello threw it open, and we burst into a round guardroom, ringed with slit windows and graced with a handful of chairs and a square table. Steep wooden steps climbed to a trapdoor in the ceiling on the far side of the room.

Between us and the steps stood one man in a Falconer's uniform, tall and broad, the moonlight gleaming off his bare brown scalp and the rock-hard curves of muscular forearms crossed on his chest.

Balos.

Chapter Fifteen

"Captain," Balos greeted Marcello, in his deep, rumbling voice. "I'm sorry, but you know how this has to be."

Marcello nodded and drew his rapier. He turned with slow grace to face Balos left-handed, presenting only the side of his body. With his right arm bound up in its sling, he made a brave, hopeless figure, perfectly poised for a fight he stood no chance of winning. My throat tightened, and I wanted to throw myself between them, to stop either of them from getting hurt.

"Please wait outside, Istrella," he said.

Istrella nodded, paling, and withdrew onto the landing. But she didn't quite close the door, peering through the crack with wide eyes to see what would happen to her brother.

"Are you ready?" Balos asked.

Before Marcello could answer, Terika lunged forward, hurling a tiny glass bottle at Balos with all her might.

He barely glanced away from Marcello. His hand darted out, and the vial smacked into his palm. He held it up, intact, gleaming in the moonlight.

"You'll have to do better than that," he said, with gentle regret. And he threw it back at Terika.

I dove away, holding my breath; glass shattered behind me, and there came a startled yelp and a rustling thud. I scrambled to the far wall and pressed my back against the cool stone before risking a tentative sip of air; it came back clear of peppermint, and I turned, pulse racing painfully, terrified of what I might see.

Terika lay sprawled on the floor, shattered glass glittering like diamonds around her. Zaira stood tense and ready by the opposite wall, eyes fixed on Balos, hands curled into fists; Marcello poised on his toes, panting, as if he'd lunged in and out to try to take advantage of Balos's distraction. But Balos stood unharmed, balanced and ready, his grave eyes gleaming in the moonlight.

"The colonel couldn't stop us, either," Balos said, with careful emphasis. "She took the armory, but we sealed her and the others in there, so you have no help coming."

"Thank you for telling me," Marcello said quietly. "I'll try to get her free after this. And I promise we'll do everything in our power not to hurt Jerith."

Balos nodded. "If you hurt him, Captain, I'll break every bone you've got left." He said it with perfect calm, as if he were discussing the weather. I didn't know how he managed it; every piece of me, from my hair to my toenails, seemed to scream with the urgency to get up those stairs and stop Jerith before he unleashed disaster. The wind outside was howling with enough force to make the tower shudder; we couldn't have much time left.

I knew one way we might get past him.

"Eyes!" I called, and flipped open my flare locket.

My closed lids blazed red. I edged forward, ready to break for the stairs, and peeked the second the light dimmed enough.

Marcello lunged toward Balos, to attack him or slip past him while he couldn't see. But Balos stepped to one side, catching Marcello's arm and twisting to disarm him of his rapier. The blade clattered across the stone.

Marcello leaped back, cursing and shaking out his arm; Balos stood squinting in the fading brilliance, still firmly between

us and the stairs. He had closed his eyes against the blast of
light, too.

"You need another trick, Lady Amalia," he said. "You're getting predictable."

"How about this, then?" I threw the last of Istrella's rings at
him; the runes sparked in the air as it sailed toward his head.

But he leaned to the side, and it missed, striking the wall
behind him. A seal of golden light flashed uselessly into life on
the stones; the ring chimed as it fell to the ground and rolled
away.

"Better," Balos acknowledged. "But you need to practice
your aim, and give less warning."

Hells. We weren't running out of options—just nonlethal
ones. Balos must know it, but he remained serene as ever as
Marcello cursed and drew his pistol.

"Don't make me set you on fire, Balos," Zaira rasped. I caught
her eyes, asking a silent question. She shook her head minutely,
her face pinched and haunted.

"I'm afraid I don't have the option to relent," Balos said. "Do
what you need to, my friends. Just don't hurt Jerith."

My gut twisted. "*Exsolvo*," I whispered.

"No," Zaira snapped, fury in her voice. "Hells, no."

Balos angled to face her. "I don't want Raverra destroyed,
Zaira."

Zaira let out a desperate laugh. "If I burn you, your husband
will kill me."

Balos frowned, as if considering this. "He might, but you still
need to stop me."

While his attention was on Zaira, Marcello hurled himself at
Balos.

He moved quicker than I'd ever seen him, cracking the hilt
of his pistol up into Balos's chin. As Balos's head rocked back,
Marcello kicked a foot around his leg and swept it out from

under him. He crashed into the floor hard enough to rattle the furniture.

Marcello fell on him with both knees, and Zaira and I ran in as well. I threw myself on one of Balos's arms in a billowing of silk skirts, focusing on pinning him down. He heaved beneath the three of us, strong enough that for a moment I thought he would break free; Zaira cursed as his knee connected with her head, but she held on. We managed to wrestle him under control long enough for Istrella to run in, grab the last vial of potion from Terika's bag, and drip a single drop onto Balos's face. He went still at last, and we all scurried out of reach before the scent of peppermint could reach us, too.

Marcello's breath came raggedly, and he slumped against the wall, pale as paper. Istrella awkwardly patted his good shoulder, biting her lip.

"We're going to need to carry you home in pieces in an envelope after this," Zaira said, shaking her head in awe. "Nicely done. I've never seen a man your size move so fast."

Marcello nodded weakly, but couldn't seem to speak at first. After a moment, he managed between gasps, "Couldn't let you have to use your fire."

"Last thing I want is to burn one of the few decent men in the Empire," Zaira agreed gruffly. "Even if he knocked out Terika." Her eyes slid to Terika, then, and she took a step toward her before checking herself, shaking her head. Even from here, I could faintly catch the trace of peppermint in the air.

Zaira held out her hand to Istrella instead, taking Terika's last vial of potion. "Come on. We don't have time to pat ourselves on the back. Let's go keep Jerith from doing something he'll really regret in the morning."

Marcello pulled himself up, still leaning against the wall, and went to retrieve his rapier, favoring his side. Just watching him move hurt.

"Wait," I said. "Jerith can strike us with lightning faster than I can blink. If we go charging up there looking like we're going to attack him, he'll have no choice but to do so. We need to give him an excuse not to kill us."

Zaira frowned. "You're right." Her eyes drifted to Terika, where she lay sprawled on the floor. "Amalia, you go first. Tell him we're here to negotiate. He'll believe it from you, because you're useless in combat and talk too much."

"Thanks," I said dryly.

"I'll come next, to talk to him warlock-to-warlock." She pointed to Marcello. "You stay down here with Istrella."

"I can't let you go face him by yourselves," he objected.

"You wait and see what happens. If we fail, you can shoot him. You're our reserve."

Marcello looked as if he wanted to argue. Istrella laid a finger on his lips. "If you go, I'm going," she said sternly. "You wouldn't want me to stay down here undefended, right?"

He stared at her helplessly. I had to admire her; my mother would have applauded the ruthless manipulation of that move.

Marcello sighed, giving in. "It makes sense. Jerith will never believe I'm not there to take him down."

"He'd probably kill you the moment he saw you," Zaira agreed. "All right, Amalia, let's go face down the man with the lightning before he washes Raverra away like dog crap off the palace steps."

The wind hit me like a slammed door as I climbed up onto the roof. It seized my hair and whipped it to the side, and I clung to the stone floor for a moment, halfway out of the trapdoor, not certain I dared stand up and take its full force when I was a hundred feet off the ground. A great moaning rose up all around the castle, and the mottled sky hung so low and roiling overhead that it seemed as if it might crush us.

Jerith stood at the exact center of the tower top, his hands spread palm up before him, tiny purple sparks crackling at his fingertips. The silver rings of his mage mark blazed in his eyes, and a purple-white gleam flared within them. The wind played in his hair and tugged at his jacket like a mischievous lover.

"Took you long enough," he greeted us.

Zaira and I climbed up onto the roof to face him. We staggered as the wind hit us; I had to seize Zaira's arm to keep her from getting blown to the parapet. The heavy skirts of the gown I'd worn to the Assembly dragged at me, caught in the wind, and I shivered in the biting cold.

Zaira steadied herself, then laughed harshly. "How was I to know you'd start the party without me?"

"Sorry about that. Something unexpected came up, and I couldn't wait for you."

I'd heard them both clearly, as though the wind that raged around us parted for their words. Even more than the gathering clouds above us or the lightning waiting in Jerith's fingers, this kindled awe in my heart—that he could stir the clouds like a kettle with one hand while mincing the wind fine enough to hear us with the other. And even clothed in all the power and majesty of the storm, he was still *himself*; the times I'd seen Zaira unleash on this scale, she'd become a creature of flame, divine and humorless, seeing with the fire's eyes and speaking with its tongue.

Zaira was clearly thinking the same thing. She shook her head. "Your control is too damned good. How do you do it? I'd be lost to the fire by now."

"If we both live through this, I'll teach you." Jerith rotated one hand palm-out and lifted a warning finger. "I know you're likely here to stop me. If I think you have any chance of actually doing so—if I see one spark of balefire, or a weapon, or if you reach for your flare locket or make any kind of sudden motion—I have no choice but to strike you dead where you stand. So please, by all means, don't let me see you make any threatening moves."

I hadn't missed the particulars of his wording. I licked my dry lips, suddenly afraid even to pull back the hair that stung my face. If I staggered the wrong way as the wind shoved at me, or made some gesture Jerith interpreted the wrong way, I would be dead before I knew what happened. The Serene City glittered in the night, full of glowing life across the water; the Mews below lay hushed beneath the cry of the wind, as if it were watching us.

"I know you don't want to do this, Jerith," I began.

"You're stalling," he said. "What are you stalling for?"

To keep him focused on me. To give Zaira a chance to act. "Surely you don't think I'm going to tell you." I glanced deliberately toward the trapdoor we'd emerged from, as if I might be hoping for reinforcements from below. "What about you? Do you pretend you're not stalling as well?"

"Me?" He let out a bark of a laugh. "I'm gathering my storm, and waiting for the tide to rise a bit more. I've thought this through, you see." His gaze shifted to Zaira, who stood quite still, braced against the storm. "Don't tell me you haven't done it, too—thought about how you would destroy Raverra, if you ever took it into your head to do so."

Zaira's tangled curls danced in the wind like flames, partially obscuring her face. "Of course I have. You can't hold the Hell of Disaster inside you and not think about what would happen if you unleashed it."

"Sometimes it's a nightmare," Jerith said softly. "Sometimes it's a fantasy. There are days when you can't help but want to burn it all down."

Zaira nodded, her eyes dark, wide pools. "That's how it always begins," she whispered.

I had to get his attention back to me. "Jerith. What does Ruven want? If we accede to his demands, will he spare the city?"

"Damned if I know." Jerith spread his arms wide; the clouds above him began a slow, ponderous churn. "I have one instruction: destroy Raverra. He hasn't done me the courtesy of showing up in person so I can question him further." The sparks on his fingers leaped in agitation, as if they yearned to find Ruven and ask certain unanswerable questions of their own.

"Isn't there any way to stop this?" I pleaded.

"I only know one way," Jerith said grimly. "Now if you don't have anything more substantive to say, I have to ask you to let me concentrate. I don't have much excuse for holding off any longer from my task."

Jerith reached toward the clouds. The glow in his eyes grew until they seemed to be pools of liquid lightning. The tower shuddered in the wind, and my claw necklace rattled on my chest. I needed to distract him somehow, and quickly.

"Balos is safe," I blurted. "We only knocked him out. We didn't hurt him."

Jerith's shoulders sagged, and for a second, his eyes closed in relief.

In that instant, Zaira leaped forward and splashed a spray of sleep potion into his face.

Jerith reeled, his eyes glazing. He threw up his hands, and my breath froze, certain lightning would rip through us both before my heart could beat again.

But the sparks on his fingers flickered out, and he collapsed like an empty sail.

The wind died immediately; I staggered, leaning into a gale that was no longer there. The silence fell around us so suddenly that I worried for half a second that I had gone deaf.

Zaira fell to her knees beside Jerith, trembling all over. "Sweet Grace of Mercy," she gasped, "I thought I was going to die."

I went to help her up, and somehow, for a brief moment, we were hugging each other on our knees on the cold stone of the tower top, salt-damp hair in our faces. Then Zaira got to her feet by herself, shaking her arms out as if she could cast off the same jittering energy that still surged through my veins.

"Right," she said. "We're not done yet. That bought us an hour. Let's go take back the Mews."

The four of us wrangled Jerith's limp, unconscious body down the steep stairs as best we could. With Marcello down to one arm, Zaira and I had to do most of the lifting, putting him down every few feet and taking deep breaths of clean, peppermint-free air before hoisting him again. I could feel precious minutes sliding away, but we didn't dare leave him outside the wards.

After we'd laid Jerith next to Balos in as comfortable a position as we could, Zaira tore down a curtain from one of the windows to fold it into a pillow and slip it tenderly under Terika's head. She stared for a moment at her face; a worried divot punctuated the alchemist's brows even in sleep, though her chest rose and fell with gentle regularity.

"I don't like leaving her here," Zaira muttered.

"No one will hurt her," I assured her. "Ruven wants the Falcons alive. The worst that will happen is they'll give her his potion."

"She *hated* being under that stingroach's control. She still has nightmares about it." Zaira drew in a breath, bent to squeeze Terika's hand, and then stood, determination in her dark eyes. "But we can't exactly drag her along with us. So we'll just have to do this as quickly as possible. Come on."

We'd barely started down the spiral stairs when a great clatter and commotion came from below, as if a large group of people were thundering up the tower with no semblance of caution. We froze in the shadowed stairwell; orange gleams of ward light reflected from Zaira's eyes as she flicked me an alarmed glance.

But Marcello broke into a broad smile. "That's Colonel Vasante," he said. "She's broken free of the armory!"

Sure enough, it was Colonel Vasante who rounded the curving stairs at the head of some twenty grim-faced Falcons, Falconers, and soldiers. Her eyes went flat and ready when she saw us; one Falcon behind her exclaimed, "Hells take us, it's Zaira!"

"Wait!" Marcello frantically held up his good hand as they all reached for weapons. "We're not controlled! We weren't even in the Mews during the toast, remember?"

There came a tense pause. My pulse pounded in the silence as Colonel Vasante swept her assessing gaze over the four of us. Istrella, oblivious to the danger that prickled in the air, gave her a cheery wave.

The colonel's shoulders sagged. "Fantastic," she said sharply. "I thought our situation couldn't get any worse, but now on top of everything else, I have to play bodyguard to the Cornaro heir."

Chapter Sixteen

The colonel's group moved with professional precision. We jogged in a tight pack, two abreast in the narrow dormitory corridors, with the most experienced soldiers in the front and the rear; a pair of Falconers checked every intersecting corridor we crossed. Everyone was heavily armed with nonlethal weapons, potions, and artifice devices from the armory where they'd been trapped, and the two Falconers in front bore small round shields marked with artifice circles that could neutralize some common magical attacks or slow down a musket ball. At the center of the formation with Istrella and Zaira, I felt very much out of place in my crimson Assembly gown, a soft rustle of silk surrounded by the hard clink and jingle of military gear. It was no wonder the colonel thought me a liability; but I resolved not to become one, keeping up with our pace and staying alert for any sign of danger.

For a few brief minutes I thought we might make it to the colonel's office unopposed. But the colonel's breakout from the armory hadn't gone unnoticed. Shouts rang out both ahead of us and behind, mingled with the tramp of feet rushing to meet us.

A Falconer swore, hefting a club with a wire-wrapped crystal bound to its tip. An artificer wound a coil of rune-marked rope nervously about her hand, and an alchemist thumbed the cork on a potion bottle. I had no tricks left; my flare locket was expended, my rings gone. I had my dagger, but the last thing I wanted to do was stab a controlled Falcon. I met Zaira's eyes and found them as wide as mine. She curled her empty hands into fists, shaking her head.

"No stopping!" the colonel barked. "No matter what, keep pressing forward!"

Then the approaching forces rounded the corners before and behind us, closing in to catch us between them.

I couldn't look away from their faces. A soldier lifted his pistol, despair scrunching his features. A Falcon shook her head frantically, mouthing *No, no, no,* as anguished recognition of her friends flickered in her eyes. A kitchen boy sobbed as he came up behind us, lost and frightened, a vegetable knife clutched in his white-knuckled hand.

"Oh, Hells, that's my wife," the Falcon with the rope moaned, staring at another Falcon in the group behind us. "I can't fight her."

She pushed abruptly past our rear guard and flung her rope across the corridor, without taking her eyes off her wife. The rope's painted runes blazed with light—a ward. It wouldn't last long, but the attackers coming up behind us surged to an uneven halt for now.

There was no time for relief. I whipped back around to face the front, where a group twice our size braced unwillingly to meet our advance. Between the shielding legs of the soldiers and Falconers they'd put in their vanguard, I glimpsed a little girl with a jess on her wrist who couldn't be more than seven, tears streaming down from eyes wide with fear.

"Not the brats, too," Zaira whispered. "Hells, no."

The two Falconers in our front line lifted their shields; behind them, more readied weapons. *Grace of Mercy, this is really going to happen. We really have to fight them.*

"I'm sorry," one of the soldiers facing us cried. "I'm so sorry."

And with a deafening crack, he discharged his pistol.

I barely swallowed a shriek. The shot struck a bell-like note from one of the shields, splitting it down the middle; the Falconer carrying it swore and dropped it, shaking out her arm. Another gunshot sounded, loud as the end of the world in the cramped quarters, and she dropped to one knee, crying out in pain. The orange light of the wards caught eerily in the haze of gunsmoke floating in the air.

"Keep going!" the colonel shouted, and our front lines pressed forward around the wounded Falconer as she gripped her bleeding leg and let out a stream of curses.

I crouched down beside her, desperate to do *something* to help, unwilling to walk past the pain constricting her face. "Do you have any bandages? I can—"

"Keep moving, Cornaro!" Colonel Vasante snapped. "Let the controlled ones treat her. They've been taking care of the fallen on both sides. You!" She swiveled in front of me to jab an imperative finger back at the group blocked by the rope ward, rising on her toes to call out over the heads of her troops. "Treat the wounded! Go get some alchemical salves if you don't have them already!"

One of the Falcons behind the ward saluted. "Yes, Colonel!"

Then our front rank slammed into the forces standing against us, and our column compressed with the impact. Shouts of fear and pain rose up as the Falcon with the crystal-tipped club laid about her, delivering stunning shocks with every strike. At her side, the remaining shield blocked some kind of hurled artifice device, its runes flaring. The stink of sweat mingled with the sharp scent of gunsmoke. A Falcon in our second rank cast a net wound with artifice wire at the controlled soldier with the pistol; he fell in a tangle of coppery strands that tightened around him, with a strangled whoop.

Suddenly, I had to step over fallen bodies. My heart slammed repeatedly into the back of my throat as I tiptoed over the sprawled and twitching form of a woman who'd been stunned by the crystal club, then lurched into Zaira in my attempt not to step on the netted soldier. Violence still thrashed a few paces ahead of me; half the shouts and cries seemed to be apologies or denials, and it wrenched my heart to hear people begging a man who wasn't even here to stop making them hurt their friends.

A soldier staggered back into me, clutching his throat, choking from some powder an alchemist had cast into his face. I caught him as he fell, looking around in a panic for someone who could help as he struggled for breath. A Falcon behind me pulled a bottle from one of dozens of small pouches ringing her waist and tipped some purple liquid into his mouth, her face blank with focus, and he gasped in a lungful of air. I helped steady him, then looked up to find that we'd fallen behind as our vanguard pressed forward, leaving a trail of incapacitated comrades in their wake.

I hurried past a couple of unconscious soldiers who reeked of peppermint and several more weakly stirring victims of the shock club. A Falconer with both legs tangled in artifice wire had dragged herself to help a soldier who clutched a horribly burned hand, tears streaming down his face. A sickening crunch and a wet scream sounded from the surging mass of combatants ahead, and I could only hope to the Graces it was nothing worse than a broken nose or some lost teeth. My stomach turned at the acrid smell of scorched hair.

These were the same dormitory halls I'd walked down chatting idly with Zaira and Marcello countless times, my shoulder brushing the warm wood paneling now scarred with burn marks and streaked with blood. It was as if when the orange light of the wards flared up in the darkness, the whole Mews had been plunged straight into the Hell of Nightmares.

As I caught up with the back of our embattled group, I found Istrella with both hands over her ears, her face pale, clinging close to her brother. My heart twisted at the lost look in her eyes. Marcello, with one good arm and only lethal weapons, was helping triage the fallen, quickly checking each body to make certain they were in no immediate danger.

Zaira emerged from the press of bodies before us, struggling out between the back line of packed-in soldiers like a dog weaseling under a fence, with a bloody streak on her face and the little girl Falcon struggling in her arms.

"Get a door open, quickly!" she snapped, averting her eyes as the crying girl gouged at her face with small fingers.

I threw a door open on someone's untidy bedroom full of dying potted plants. Zaira all but tossed the little girl into it and slammed the door.

"Stay in there and stay safe!" she shouted, holding the door closed as the girl thudded into it, still crying. "Damn it, I can't lock this from the outside. Not with her banging on it like that—she'd break my picks, and it'd take too much time."

Istrella ran up to us, determination in her eyes and a charcoal stick in her hand. She scrawled a quick runic circle on the door and jabbed an obsidian-headed pin from her satchel into the center of the design. It took her mere seconds. "That won't hold more than ten minutes," she warned us.

"Good enough," Zaira said roughly. "Let's go." And we turned back to the fight.

After that, the four of us made a team, dealing with any less than fully incapacitated opponents who fell behind our lines. Zaira and I threw open doors and hauled bodies, Marcello checked for injuries, and Istrella sealed the doors. It was sweaty work, and we picked up bruises from flying fists and knees; Zaira took a light slash on her arm when she reached for a ten-year-old boy who wasn't quite done fighting. My corset dug painfully into my waist whenever I bent over, and the others had the same grim, haunted expression I knew must be on my face. But we were doing something that got innocent people out of harm's way, and that gave us an excuse not to look at the terrible and desperate shouting mess of violence a few feet up the corridor.

Then we broke through the opposition at last and ran down the hallway, free and clear. More shouts and footfalls approached; it sounded like someone was rallying another group together to try to stop us, but with everyone fighting the compulsion any way they could, they were slow to get organized. My pulse pounded with bitter insistence in my head, and my dry throat craved a cool drink of water.

Hells. I was probably overdue for my elixir. The last thing I needed now was to collapse from poison symptoms. As we thundered down a staircase, I worked a vial out of the secret pocket in my skirt and downed it; the swallow of anise-scented liquid barely dampened my tongue, but I managed not to spill any. I wished I could drink more just for the water in it.

Then we were sprinting across the dark cavern of a first-floor dormitory entrance hall, with cold marble floors and a vaulted ceiling; a shadowy doorway on the far side led to the wing that housed the officers' quarters and, eventually, the colonel's private office. Our footfalls echoed like the pattering of hail on a tile roof. More shouts and running steps came after us, but we were going to make it.

But a line of glowing runes sprang to life across the threshold of the doorway, illuminating a terrified teenage boy crouching behind them in a glare of harsh blue light. *A ward.* We scrambled to a halt in front of the doorway as the boy fled, his work done. Zaira let out a string of curses.

"Istrella Verdi!" Colonel Vasante barked. "Get up here and cancel this ward!"

Istrella, pale but determined, hurried to the front; Marcello went with her, hovering protectively. I felt a strange surge of pride; when two artificers pitted their work directly against each other like this, a combination of skill, precision, and raw power would determine whose enchantment prevailed. The fact that the colonel hadn't hesitated before calling for Istrella spoke volumes for her abilities.

Echoing shouts and the clattering rumble of footsteps and gear broke into the hall. I swung around to face the arriving forces as the sixteen or so remaining in our party formed an arc to protect Istrella.

Some twenty people poured through the main door into the gloomy hall, fanning out as they approached us. My heart dropped; we were outnumbered. The soldier in the lead bore a saber and a more determined expression than the others, who moved with hesitant reluctance, seeking with each step to find a way around their compulsion.

But I had no eyes for him. All I saw were two figures near the back of the group, miserable and tear-streaked. Foss, desperation hollowing his face, clutched a fireplace iron in one hand—and Aleki's tiny hand in the other.

Despair squeezed my chest. *Hell of Nightmares.* Not Aleki. He wasn't even three years old.

Aleki cried and clung to his father, who put himself in front of his boy as much as he could. But Aleki kept walking toward us with the rest, terror on his small, helpless face, compelled by Ruven's command the same as the others. Angry cries of protest rose up from more than one person around me when they saw him.

"Oh, bring that piss bucket here," Zaira growled. I had no doubt she was talking about Ruven. "I'll burn him slowly, so he can feel himself dying one piece at a time."

"We've got to help Aleki." I could barely stop myself from pushing past the Falconer with the last remaining shield, who stood in front of me, and rushing to grab Aleki and get him out of here.

"Please don't do anything rash, Lady Amalia," the Falconer with the shield said. "We'll get him to safety. Never fear."

Marcello stepped forward from Istrella's side, staring hard at the soldier leading the opposing force. "That's the one who came in late with the hangover this morning," he muttered. "Except..." He raised his voice. "You're not Bertram."

The soldier spread his arms, holding his saber wide. An unsettling mix of bright silver moonlight from the open door and sullen orange glow from the runes around it lit his face. "Of course I am! I'm controlled, the same as the rest. Sorry to have to fight you."

Marcello drew his pistol. "Bertram is left-handed. You're holding your sword in your right. And your walk is all wrong. Who are you? How are you wearing Bertram's face?"

I tore my eyes from Aleki to look at Marcello, startled, and then at the soldier. The man who wasn't Bertram hesitated. Then he sighed, lowering his arms. "You caught me, Captain Verdi. But it doesn't matter anymore. The Mews already belongs to my Lord Ruven."

"Like Hells it does," Colonel Vasante snapped. "Even if you take us down, you can't hold the Mews forever." Her eyes flicked back toward Istrella, so quickly I doubted Not-Bertram noticed. She had no interest in this conversation, and knew perfectly well it would all come down to fighting; she was stalling to buy time for us to get through that doorway.

Not-Bertram's eyes narrowed. "Oh? Bold words, Colonel. What do you say to *this?*" To my horror, he lunged sideways and seized Aleki's arm, yanking him away from his father. "This one's too small to be of use to my lord. Surrender now, or I'll kill him."

"No!"

The scream had formed in my own throat, but someone else released it first: Foss.

He threw himself on the soldier's sword arm, knocking him away from Aleki. And at the same time, Zaira dashed forward, leaving a streak of sizzling obscenities behind her.

I lurched a step after her without thinking, fear for her and Foss and Aleki shoving me forward.

"Back her up!" Colonel Vasante roared, frustration and fury clear in her voice, and our careful defensive arc broke as most of us ran after Zaira to protect her. I charged a few steps behind the rest, pulling out my dagger, with no clear idea what I would do when I caught up.

All around Foss and the struggling soldier, the line of controlled Falcons and Falconers turned to face our onrushing attack with wrenching slowness, forced to raise weapons against their will. Not-Bertram must have fallen outside the compass of their orders, as no one seemed compelled to help him; but he was more than a match for shy, scholarly Foss. He shook him off his arm like a wet rag.

Artifice devices and potions flying past her, Zaira hurled herself at Aleki. She scooped the squirming, crying bundle of him up in her arms.

And the soldier with Bertram's face whirled, saber flashing, and struck her in the back.

The air rippled as if his sword had hit water, sounding a piercing chime. The blade rebounded in his hand, wrenched out of his grasp to skitter across the floor, while Zaira curled protectively around Aleki.

Relief shattered the lance of icy fear that pierced my lungs. She was still wearing her enchanted corset from when she'd gone out into the city to meet me. Thank the Graces.

One of the soldiers who'd charged with Zaira drove a sword into Not-Bertram's chest. Bertram staggered back, taking the sword with him, stuck in his ribs; a Falcon caught the now-weaponless soldier in the face with a splash of vitriol, wailing an apology, and he dropped to his knees, screaming.

And then our charge crashed into their faltering line, and chaos erupted in shouts and clamor all around us.

I caught up to Zaira even as Foss pulled Aleki from her arms, his eyes stark with horror. He hugged his son tight to his chest, but Ruven's compulsion made him launch a kick at Zaira even as he did, his face drawn with misery.

"Come on!" I shouted to Zaira, ducking something that sailed over my head. She leaped back from a knife that a frightened clerk swung at her even as the Falconer with the shield stepped up to cover her and help form a line. "We've got no business in the front lines, and we can't leave Istrella undefended!"

Zaira nodded, her lips pressed tight together, and the two of us ran back to where Marcello, Colonel Vasante, and a couple of others still formed a broken arc around Istrella as she crouched over the threshold, painting runes to counter each one of the sigils on the warding rope laid across the doorway.

But someone else was running at the protective knot, too: a controlled Falconer, pistol in hand. She stopped several paces away, feet braced wide, and screamed "Look out!" as she lifted her weapon.

Marcello lunged at her, desperation in his eyes. Zaira tried to fling herself in the way, arms spread, ready to take the ball on her corset. But neither of them were fast enough.

The pistol's muzzle flashed, and its retort echoed painfully loud in the marble-sheathed entrance hall, its echo ricocheting around the room.

Istrella shrieked in pain, and her paintbrush clattered to the floor.

Chapter Seventeen

Istrella!" I threw myself to my knees at her side, dimly aware of the battle continuing behind me, of Zaira and Marcello struggling with the soldier who'd shot her. In the clashing blue and orange glow of the wards, all I could see—all I cared about—was the blood that seeped between her fingers as she clutched her left arm.

"I'm fine," she said through her teeth, rocking back and forth with the pain. "I'm fine. I've got to finish this. *Ow.*"

"Let me take a look," I urged her.

She shook her head, her artifice glasses flashing, and peeled her bloodstained fingers away from the small, round hole in her sleeve. And then she picked up her brush, hand trembling, and resumed painting.

Marcello dropped to his knees by my side, his face drained of color. "Is she—"

I gripped his good arm. "Let her finish," I whispered, tears standing unshed in my eyes.

Marcello crushed my hand in his, staring at the blood on his sister's arm in anguish. I glanced behind us, nerves singing, ready to throw myself into the fray to protect them both with my dagger if I had to.

But the fight was already over. Bodies lay strewn across the floor like fallen leaves; I had to hope they were all only uncon-scious or otherwise incapacitated. Someone had backed Foss, Aleki, and a handful of others into a corner and warded them there with another rune-scribed rope. Several of our people hurried from one downed opponent to the next, making cer-tain everyone was both all right and unlikely to get up again soon.

"There," Istrella gasped, and a flash of light and the scent of scorched stone came from the doorway. She swayed against Marcello, who put his good arm around her; an alchemist came rushing over, clutching a satchel full of supplies, roll of bandages already in hand.

Colonel Vasante whirled on Zaira, all the fury of the Demon of Carnage in her face. "What in the Nine Hells was that?"

Zaira rose from the side of the fallen Falconer who'd shot Istrella and turned to face the colonel, tense and wary.

Vasante slammed a fist into her palm, striding toward Zaira. "It's not your job to break ranks and fling yourself at the enemy. It's your job to stay out of the way until we need something set on fire." She flung an arm at the bodies littering the marble floor. "You could have gotten good people killed."

"I don't give a plague-infested rat carcass for what you think my job is," Zaira retorted hotly. "And I never asked anyone to protect me."

"You are too damned valuable for us to risk losing, and you know it." The colonel jabbed a finger at Zaira. "We only won because they were trying not to fight back. Istrella wouldn't have been shot if it weren't for your idiocy."

"What? She got hit?" Zaira whipped around, dark eyes wide, to stare at Istrella. The alchemist was tying off a bandage on her arm, having removed the ball and applied a healing salve. Istrella bit her lip, tears standing in her eyes.

"Hells, Istrella." Zaira's voice was hoarse. "I'm sorry."

Istrella managed a brave smile. "Oh, it's all right. Only we'd better hurry. I think I hear more people coming."

Sure enough, the sound of running boots thundered outside. I helped Marcello haul Istrella to her feet between us, and we ran through the shadowy maw of the doorway, deeper into the Mews.

At long last, we burst into Colonel Vasante's office. As our rear guard still struggled to hold back the controlled people rushing to stop us, the colonel strode without hesitation to a small room that had been hidden behind a bookcase now pushed aside. I couldn't see what she did in there, but the wards that had glowed orange all through the long bloody corridors flared all at once with an intense blue light.

In the hallway past her door, the din of battle cut suddenly short in a cascade of rustling thuds as everyone collapsed, defenders and attackers alike. Through the window I saw every guard in the courtyard fall, too, limp as a dropped handkerchief.

A terrible silence fell over the Mews, broken only by the harsh breathing of the dozen of us crammed into the office. Everyone else was asleep.

Then someone swore, and someone else laughed, and a soldier burst out crying. Zaira breathed Terika's name and passed a hand over her face. Istrella reached out shakily to Marcello, who gathered her into a one-armed hug. He met my gaze over her head with haunted eyes.

My red and gold Assembly gown was stained and torn, and beneath it my legs trembled. But there was no room and no time to sit down. We were far from done with this night's work.

Colonel Vasante knew it. She took a deep breath and straightened her spine.

"Right," she said, her voice clipped and commanding. "That

should have knocked out everyone outside this office. We need to round up every single inhabitant of the Mews and confine them in the shielded training rooms until this damned potion wears off. We can sort out who's controlled and who isn't later. And we need to get a message to the Imperial Palace at once."

"I'll go," I said, my voice wavering despite my best attempt to keep it steady. "They'll let me through to talk to the doge and the Council without question, so I can deliver the message most quickly."

Colonel Vasante nodded brusquely. "Take Verdi and your Falcon with you, Lady Amalia. Then you'll have plenty of protection in case something goes wrong. We don't know what else Ruven might have set in motion."

Marcello cast an anguished glance between me and Istrella. Zaira protested, "I need to make sure Terika is all right."

"Take five minutes and two guards," Colonel Vasante said curtly. "But I want you out of here. If something goes wrong and the Mews falls back under Ruven's control, I don't want to give him *two* warlocks."

I expected some retort, but Zaira made no reply. I took a closer look, alarmed. Surely a silent Zaira must mean she was bleeding to death—but aside from an assortment of minor cuts and bruises too insignificant to have triggered the magical protection of her enchanted corset, she seemed unhurt. But strain showed on her face—in her temples and her jaw, well hidden enough that I doubt anyone else but Terika would have noticed.

"'Strella—" Marcello murmured.

Istrella pushed gently at his chest. "Go with Amalia. I'm fine. If you stay here, you'll just stare at me and look sad the whole time, and it'll be creepy."

I lifted a hand to cover a smile.

"Make sure you have a physician look at that wound," Marcello fretted.

"I will," Istrella promised. "And we should have one look at your shoulder, too, when you get back. You used it too much tonight."

A strange expression passed over Marcello's face. "It's not as bad as I expected it to be," he said, with a one-sided shrug. "I feel fine."

"You may now," I said dubiously, "but we still need to warn the Council and the doge. I have a feeling this is going to be a long night."

It was odd, gliding down the Imperial Canal with its splendid façades and glimmering luminaries, surrounded by the usual evening traffic: half-drunken revelers, their voices echoing loudly over the water; finely dressed patricians on evening visits, decked out in lace and velvet; and the last round of weary merchants and artisans heading home after stopping in a hostelry for dinner. The night air was alive with chatter and laughter and the lap of water against wood and stone, with the occasional swelling of song. I overheard a comment or two about how the breeze had quite picked up for a while there, or how strange the clouds had looked for a minute, but no one had any idea that the entire city had been in danger of obliteration.

My oarsman had seen and suspected more as he waited faithfully for us at the Mews docks. His face looked a bit pale and ragged, but his hands stayed steady on his oar as he guided us toward the Imperial Palace. I made a mental note to slip him a ducat and a word of thanks when we disembarked.

"Well, that was awful," Zaira said, wrapping her arms around her knees.

I nodded emphatically. "I'm not sure which was worse. Having to fight friends, or knowing what would happen if we failed."

"Or watching the place I've dedicated my life to protecting get taken by the enemy and my beloved little sister *shot*." Marcello put his hand over a face still pale and glassy with shock.

Zaira gave us both a sidelong look. "Or watching everyone drop like puppets with cut strings at the end, and realizing the Empire asked past Falcons to work their fingers raw building a trap to keep their own people from ever rebelling. That wasn't fun, either."

"No, it wasn't." I grimaced.

"And damn me to the Nine Hells, but I hate that I have to be glad they did it." Zaira shook her head. "That was too cursed close."

"It could have been a lot worse." I drank in the lights and voices around me that meant the city was alive and safe. "Jerith wasn't the only Falcon at the Mews who could have destroyed Raverra; he was just the one who could do it most quickly."

"Thank the Graces you weren't there for the toast, Zaira." Pain roughened Marcello's voice, and he held himself with care on his cushioned seat in front of Zaira and me. "I shudder to think what would have happened."

"Thank you very much. I've been trying hard *not* to think about that," Zaira snapped.

"Sorry." Marcello glanced around the boat, as if he might find a change of subject lying in the bottom. "I hope the colonel has someone looking after the children," he said finally. "They're going to be frightened when they wake up. It's going to take us a long time to recover from this, in more ways than one—days of quarantine for the whole Mews, our courier lamps gone, wounded soldiers, bad memories."

"Those poor little brats who got controlled." Zaira's knuckles were white on her knees, and her fingers dug into her skirts. "I keep thinking of Aleki's face. I keep thinking..." She broke off.

I reached out, tentatively, and touched her shoulder. "It's all right. Everyone's safe now."

Zaira shook her head. "That Jerith is such a bastard," she said abruptly.

I blinked. "What?"

"He knew just what to say to rattle me. Do you know how many times I've had nightmares about my fire getting out of control and raging through the city?" Her lips pressed tight together.

I remembered something she'd said to Jerith on the tower top, which hadn't made any sense to me at the time: *That's how it always begins.*

"It won't happen," I assured her. "I won't let it."

"I suppose that's what I keep you around for." She let out a long breath, as if she could expel her feelings into the shining Raverran night.

"I'm worried about Bertram," Marcello said abruptly, shifting the strap of his sling on his shoulder. "He's been posted at the Mews for years. But that man wasn't him. It was his face, but he had too much muscle on him, and not enough freckles, and he held himself all wrong."

"Ruven," I said, my stomach contracting with the terrible surety of it. "*That's* what he was doing in Raverra on the Night of Masks. Finding someone who could get into the Mews and replacing him with one of his own people. That's why he had to come himself—so he could use his vivomancy to sculpt the face to match."

Marcello shivered. Zaira swore, touching her own cheeks. "I'll bet that hurt."

The more I thought about it, the more disturbing it became. "This is bad. If he can hide his own people among us with faces we trust, we can't catch them with Terika's blood test like we can someone controlled by the potion. He has two different ways to infiltrate us, both of them devastatingly effective."

Zaira snorted. "The face trick won't be too hard to catch, now that we know about it."

"Oh?" I asked.

"Watch this." She turned to Marcello. "Hey, Captain Lefty, whose fault is it the Mews got taken?"

Marcello grimaced. "Mine. I should have had Bertram questioned when he came in late. I should have—"

"I don't actually care," Zaira interrupted. "I'm just making a point. And Amalia, what changes would you make to the Mews wards after today?"

"Well, I'd update them to automatically signal the Imperial Palace when they were activated, using bridge runes so no one could alter the enchantment to bypass the signal, and—"

"Don't care about that, either. But you see my point. If you know someone, it's not hard to tell if they're acting right." She nodded at Marcello. "Even Captain Oblivious here noticed that guard wasn't who he looked like right away, from across the room, once we knew something was wrong."

"I wonder what he did with the real Bertram?" Marcello asked. But by the heaviness in his voice, I suspected he could guess the answer as well as I could.

"The bodies that turned up after the Night of Masks," I said grimly. "There might be more face-shifted people out there. That's another warning we need to give the doge right away."

"Well, you're about to get your chance," Zaira said.

The Imperial Palace reared before us, ablaze with lights, rising in sugar-spun glory above its wavering reflection. At this hour, most of the staff who didn't live there would have gone home, but I'd lay odds my mother was still working, and half the rest of the Council besides.

"And the Empire endures," I murmured.

Zaira followed my gaze. "They don't even know what almost hit them." She uncurled somewhat, then, chuckling. "I suppose that's one upside to all this. I can't wait to see the doge's face."

I had been to the Imperial Palace after hours many times, to meet my mother when she worked there late into the night. It was a different place after midnight, its glorious gilded halls empty of officials and pages, petitioners and courtiers and hangers-on. The guards remained, of course, and an occasional servant or clerk hurried past in the grand, airy spaces designed to accommodate hundreds. But with the glow of the luminaries not quite reaching the ceiling frescoes and the portraits watching us with night-dark eyes and studious frowns, it felt as if we were intruding on some sacred and secret place, trespassers in the halls of the Graces.

The guards all recognized me and let me through, bowing to the urgency in my stride, eyes widening at our ragged appearance. Every time we crossed a threshold, I laid my hand on the center of an artifice seal worked discreetly into the elaborately carved molding around the great arched doorways, feeling the tingle of magic in my palm. My mother had never told me what would happen if I didn't, but I could spy the artifice runes and wirework hidden away in the swirling vines and leaves of the decorations on every portal, so I wasn't about to chance it, even if it slowed down our pace as we hurried to get to the doge and any of the Council still in the palace.

We soon arrived at the end of the public spaces, a great set of closed gold-chased doors. Six guards with pikes and pistols stood at attention before them, and an official in a blue-and-gold jacket rose from the chair he'd been reading in beside the door as we approached.

"Lady Amalia," the official greeted me with a bow. "La Contessa is still in the Map Room, in a military strategy meeting. Do you wish me to find out if you can join her?"

"We have urgent news for the doge and the Council." I didn't bother to hide my shortness of breath. "I need to speak to them at once."

The official's face grew serious, and he gave a sharp nod. "I believe you will find His Serenity at the courier lamps." He waved to the guards, who opened the golden doors.

We hurried through into the Thinking Room, a long corridor designed by an early doge who wanted a place to pace while working through difficult problems. Windows lined one wall, overlooking the sparkling lights of the Imperial Canal, and paintings depicting great discoveries and accomplishments in imperial history now hung opposite them.

"The doge first," I decided. "Especially since he's at the courier lamps. He can spread the word."

At the end of the Thinking Room, we veered away from the gallery that led to the Map Room and the other chambers of the Council of Nine, and toward the ducal apartments and the courier lamp room. But before we reached the elegant curve of marble steps that ascended to the lamp tower, it became apparent the climb wouldn't be necessary; the doge was striding toward us, his golden robes flowing, a pair of guards trailing after.

His glare fell on me. "You! I knew I shouldn't have listened to you. You pass your cursed law, and mere hours later the Mews apparently has such an inflated sense of independence I can't even raise them on the courier lamps. What have you done?"

"Funny you should mention that," Zaira muttered.

I bowed. "Your Serenity, there's an emergency. Lord Ruven has made his move."

"I'm well aware of that, which is why I need to contact the Mews." He made as if to move past me, then spotted Marcello and stopped. "Captain Verdi! Why is no one manning the courier lamps?"

A cold spear of understanding pierced through the net of confusion his words had cast over me. "Your Serenity," I said slowly, "I think we may be talking about different emergencies."

The doge went still, the flush of anger draining from his face. "You aren't referring to the border fortress?"

"Border fortress?" I asked. "Ruven's invading?" Beside me, Marcello sucked in a soft gasp. I couldn't blame him; I wanted a chair to sink into. "Good Graces, not now. This is terrible."

And, of course, he'd planned it that way. It didn't matter that we'd saved the Mews; with half the Empire's Falcons in quarantine, our magical might was crippled when we needed it most.

"What's *your* emergency?" The doge's black eyes flicked between us. "You've come from the Mews. Tell me what's wrong."

"Your Serenity," I began, "Ruven has—"

But before I could finish, Marcello doubled over as if he'd been punched in the stomach, letting out a muffled cry. There was a lost note in it that wrenched at my heart, as if something vital had torn away inside him.

I spun and reached to catch him in case he fell, sickeningly sure a broken rib had pierced his lungs in all the fighting and now he was dying.

"Is he injured?" the doge asked sharply. One of his guards started forward.

My hands closed on Marcello's good arm. I could feel the heat coming off him even through his uniform jacket. And not only heat—the faint tingle of magic.

A shiver ran across his shoulders, brief as a gust of wind stroking a flash of silver from a sheet of falling rain. His breathing went from ragged to calm in an instant.

Something is very wrong. The surety of it hit my gut as if I'd swallowed a burned-out coal. It was the sensation of having just dropped something priceless and fragile out a window, watching it fall sickeningly away in the instant it was too late to recover it.

Marcello's head snapped up, and he met my eyes.

His were the cold green of a dark and ancient forest, all warmth and light gone from them. His mouth curved slightly in a secret, wicked smile.

The world slipped askew. *That's not Marcello.*

He burst into motion, too fast to follow. His sling fluttered down in the air where he had been, discarded; my fingers clutched at nothing.

The doge's first guard fell with a knife in his belly. The second got his pistol half drawn before Marcello's sword sliced across his throat.

The doge reached for his heavy necklace of jeweled artifice medallions, his eyes widening, but Marcello slashed a cut across his chest that snapped the chain. Gems in rune-graven settings and twists of golden wire scattered everywhere, skittering across the marble floor.

The doge staggered back, gasping with pain and shock. Blood spread across the gold brocade of his robes. The impossible, terrible splash of scarlet shocked time back into motion, breath back into my lungs.

"Stop!" I screamed, and threw myself in front of the doge, even as Zaira jumped on Marcello from behind, grappling for a hold on him.

He twisted out of her grip, whirled, and threw her against the wall with vicious force. She sank down it, stunned.

"Marcello!" I cried.

This was a dream, sent by the Demon of Nightmares. It couldn't be real. The man before me was Marcello, unquestionably—the way he moved, the way he'd spoken and acted all the way up until he attacked, even his scent; I knew him too well to be wrong. So it had to be reality itself that was wrong, broken like a mirror, and I would wake up any minute.

He turned to face me. The luminaries cast his features into

a harsh map of light and shadow, pulling hard gleams from his narrowed eyes. Behind me, the doge slumped against the wall, his breathing ragged.

"You must be controlled," I said quickly, my hands up and empty between us, my heart ready to shatter with each merciless racing beat. I'd already discharged my flare locket against Balos, and it had to absorb a day's worth of sunlight before it would work again; I had nothing to protect myself with save my dagger and my words. "I know you don't want to do this. There has to be a way out of his command."

Marcello's rapier tip drooped. A familiar furrow appeared between his brows. My heart spasmed at the sight of it.

But then he drew his pistol and pointed it straight at me, drawing back the hammer.

"I'll shoot through you if I have to, Amalia." His voice broke on my name, changing from distant and clinical to human and aching. "Step out of the way. Please."

"No." I spread my arms, blocking as much of the doge as possible. I could hear shouting back the way we'd come; all I had to do was stall him until reinforcements arrived. "Marcello, he's hurt, he's probably dying, you did what Ruven wanted. Put the pistol down."

Behind him, Zaira stirred, lifting a hand to her head. The distant clamor of shouting guards grew louder.

Marcello's face twisted in anguish. He raised his pistol, his hand rock-steady despite the horror haunting his eyes.

"Don't," I whispered.

His finger moved on the trigger.

The night cracked open with a sound like thunder.

Chapter Eighteen

Pain kissed my cheek in a hot, bitter line. An inarticulate cry sounded behind me.

I whirled in time to see the doge collapse, his bloody robes billowing about him, red blooming on his forehead like a terrible new eye.

"No!" I reached out toward him, but my hand dropped halfway, trembling. There was no arguing with the blank, flat glazing of his eyes, or the dark wet hole Marcello's pistol had made.

Niro da Morante, doge of Raverra and the Serene Empire, was dead. An era was over. And Marcello had murdered him.

"Hells, now you've done it," Zaira groaned, lurching to her feet.

Marcello dropped to his knees, the pistol clattering on the floor. "Grace of Mercy, forgive me."

More guards came running at last—not from the direction I'd heard shouting, but from the corridor that led to the ducal apartments.

"What happened?"

"*Oh!* His Serenity!"

They froze, horror on their faces. Not one of us could take the moment back, no matter how desperately we strained to roll time in reverse like a great stone wheel. It was done, we had all failed, and the doge was dead.

And I was a Cornaro. Which meant I had to take up this awful moment in my hands and command it.

I drew in a shuddering breath. "Captain Verdi is under the effects of Lord Ruven's control potion. Seize and disarm him, but don't hurt him," I ordered.

Marcello looked so broken, kneeling there, his hands raised to his face. All I wanted was to drop down beside him and hold him. To tell him it wasn't his fault, and it would be all right. But he was still controlled, and I didn't know what more Ruven might compel him to do.

The shaken guards seemed glad for orders. Marcello didn't resist as they took his knife away, checked him for other weapons, and raised him up between them with a firm grip on his arms. He stared down at the floor, moving with the numb looseness of a man still dreaming. The black waves of his hair hung in his face.

Oh, Marcello. I'm so sorry. My throat ached for him.

But then his head lifted suddenly. "Amalia," he gasped. "Hurry. He's going after the Council, too."

A thousand shards of ice pierced my heart. *My mother.*

That shouting we'd heard hadn't been guards running to help the doge. The palace was under attack.

All logic left my mind in one blank instant, and I started running toward the Map Room.

Zaira caught up to me swiftly and growled as we ran, "I've had enough of this. Release me."

"*Exsolvo,*" I panted grimly, trying not to think about what a fire warlock could do to the Imperial Palace.

We whipped past the Thinking Room, and my heel skidded on a puddle of water. A damp, dripping trail led from the long line of windows, as if something had crawled out of the canal itself.

The first body came almost immediately after, sprawled in her blood in the blue and gold uniform of the imperial guard. I leaped over her without pausing, then sidestepped another, fear clawing inside me like a terrible beast shredding its way through my rib cage from within.

The trail of water led past three more dead guards, picking up smears of blood. Zaira swore, with feeling, but I couldn't speak. *Not my mother. Not my mother.* I refused to let this nightmare end that way.

The door to the Map Room stood ajar, one final dead guard crumpled before it, his throat slashed open by something that couldn't have been human.

"Wait," Zaira called, "you're not even armed, don't—"

I drew my dagger without slowing, threw the door open, and burst through.

Broken, still bodies lay strewn across the floor. For an instant, my chest seemed ready to tear in half like wet paper.

But the bodies had sharklike faces, curving talons, and skin that shone like a beetle's armor—human chimeras, sickeningly unnatural even in death. As I stood frozen in the doorway, Ciardha smoothly pulled her daggers out of the last of them, letting the body drop to the floor with the rest.

Most of the Council of Nine pressed against the back wall, as far away from Ciardha as possible, staring at her as if she were the Demon of Death. Old Lord Errardi sat on the floor, clutching a wounded arm; Lord Caulin appeared to be treating him, despite the slash marks of claws across his own face. The Marquise of Palova stood protectively in front of them, reloading her pistol.

My mother leaned against the wall, her face pale, arm clamped against her side. A dark stain marked the emerald green velvet of her bodice.

"*Mamma!*" I cried, like a child, and ran to her. The lines of pain on her face were like cracks in the world. She should have been safe—here, in the most secure room in the most secure building in the Empire, protected by the best bodyguard in Eruvia—but that was blood spreading slowly from beneath her arm.

"Amalia, what are you doing here?" she demanded, her voice rough with pain. "Are you all right?"

"I'm fine. But you're hurt!"

"Excuse me, Lady Amalia." Ciardha spared me a quick, graceful nod as she stepped up to La Contessa's side; I gave way, shocked to spy a bloody tear in Ciardha's own sleeve. I'd never seen her so much as scratched before. Worry tightened her usually imperturbable face as she flipped open one of the discreet pouches on her hips and began pulling out tiny vials and handing them to my mother, murmuring the purpose of each. "To stop the bleeding. For the pain. In case of poison. To prevent infection. To keep you alert." My mother downed each as she received it with the grim efficiency of someone who has, at some time I could not begin to imagine, done this before.

I was dimly aware of commotion in the rest of the room, and of Zaira nearby, but I couldn't take my eyes off my mother's strained face. All I wanted was for Ciardha to turn to me and say she would be all right. After everything that had happened tonight, by all the Graces, I wanted this one thing.

"You should let me tend to the wound, Contessa," Ciardha said, her voice so low I almost didn't catch it.

"If it won't kill me to wait, I'll tend to the Empire first," my mother said, wiping the traces of bitter potion from her mouth.

"It won't, Contessa, so long as you're quick." Disapproval flattened Ciardha's voice, but her words sounded like the blessing song of the Graces to me.

My mother's eyes flicked back to mine, sharp and assessing.

"What's wrong, Amalia? There's more bad news; I can see it in your face. Out with it, quick."

I stared at my mother, still clutching my dagger, a lump of mingled relief and horror blocking my throat. The room had fallen quiet, with the Council tending to each other's wounds, and I felt wary and curious eyes on me. They'd been fighting for their lives, watching their guards slaughtered—they could have no idea of anything that had happened outside this room. There was too much awful, heavy truth bottled up inside me to shape words to it.

Zaira stepped up beside me. "Colonel Vasante has the entire Mews locked up because they all fell under that wretch Ruven's control and came within a rat's whisker of sinking this city like a sixth-hand rowboat," she offered, her harsh voice cutting across the room. "And the doge is dead."

Gasps rose from the rest of the Council. Scipio da Morante, the doge's brother, let out a choked noise.

My mother went nearly gray. She didn't make a sound, but I had never before seen shock show so plainly on her face.

It flickered there a moment; then, like shuttering a window, it was gone.

"I see," La Contessa said.

My mother wasted no more than a second in mourning her friend. Whatever she felt for that one brief instant when emotion had broken through her mask, it was gone now, corked in a bottle and dropped in a dark well to deal with later. She heard my fuller explanation as the rest of the Council gathered around, grim-faced. Scipio da Morante stood unnervingly close to me, devouring every word, his dark eyes bright with unshed tears.

Whenever I faltered, Zaira stepped in, supplying the bluntest possible word to continue my dangling sentence.

Ciardha, meanwhile, gracefully fielded the guards and other palace denizens beginning to arrive at the door in varying states of panic and consternation. By the time I was halfway through my clipped description of the terrible events of the evening, she had guards set up defending the Map Room, pages running to fetch physicians and more guards, and servants removing the dead chimeras. Ruven might have struck at the very heart of the Empire; but with Ciardha at work, if we could no longer be sure of safety, we could at least restore serenity.

When I finished my account, La Contessa gave a sharp nod, turned to her fellows on the Council, and immediately began issuing commands, her arm still pressed tight against her wounded side.

"Lord Caulin, would you secure the palace? Marquise, we should reinforce the Mews..." None of them were precisely phrased as orders, but they had the same results, as each person she spoke to sprang into immediate action. Even Lord Caulin, though he hesitated for a bitter second, his face bleeding sluggishly through the alchemical powder dusting it.

My mother had the magic of seeing immediately what needed to be done, and the sheer sense of her requests made them impossible to quarrel with; the blood staining her side was a rebuke to anyone who might consider refusing her. This was what she was born to do: to take the shattered pieces of the Empire, swiftly gather them up, and begin fitting them calmly and logically back together.

"What about my brother's killer?" Scipio demanded, his hands in fists at his sides.

I sucked in a sharp breath. *Marcello.* Surely they wouldn't blame him—he'd been under Ruven's control.

La Contessa didn't so much as glance in my direction, but a subtle shift of her stance warned me to stay quiet. "An excellent point, Scipio," she said. "Ciardha, make certain the controlled officer is safely quarantined, and begin an investigation into how he was poisoned, not to mention who let those chimeras in through the palace wards."

Ciardha bowed. "It shall be done, Contessa."

Scipio seemed satisfied, at least for now. My mother tasked him with attending to the courier lamps and spreading word to other key people and locations of the danger, and he left with a sizable escort and the desperately purposeful stride of a man seeking something to do to help ward off grief.

In his wake, there was the briefest lull, like an indrawn breath, with no one within my mother's immediate range to send on another task. She swayed on her feet, ever so slightly; Ciardha touched her shoulder as if merely seeking her attention, subtly steadying her.

"Now, Contessa, let's see to your wound," she said firmly.

I leaned against the Map Room table, hands trembling. My mother wasn't going to die. She had taken control of the situation, and my duty was done. I could no longer stave off the memory of Marcello's eyes utterly bereft of warmth, as if a stranger stared out of them. And the doge sliding down the wall, his eyes glassy and blank, his robes soaked with blood.

Anxious for any kind of distraction, I turned to Zaira. "Are you all right?" I asked. "You hit that wall hard enough I was worried about whether you'd get up again."

Zaira rubbed the back of her head ruefully. "I won't lie, it hurt. But nothing seems broken, and I'm thinking straight." She dropped her voice, then, her dark gaze holding mine. "Straight enough to know he shouldn't have been able to throw me like that. Not with a broken collarbone, anyway."

"Ruven must have healed him." I tried to pretend it was just another magical theory problem, set by one of my cleverer professors. "His command potion makes people temporarily part of his domain, which allows him to use his vivomancy on them from afar. That's why he was in pain first—his bones knitting so quickly hurt him."

"When in the Nine Hells did he manage to get poisoned?" Zaira asked. "He wasn't there for the toast."

I shook my head. "I don't know. We need to find out. It's entirely possible that Ruven's agent poisoned more than just the toast, and he took a tainted drink right before we left the Mews, for instance. Or he could have gotten poisoned near the end of the fight, if someone figured out a way to put the potion on a blade."

But that still didn't explain the look he'd given me, right before he attacked the doge.

It had only been there for an instant. He could have been grimacing, not smiling. Or the luminary light cast strange shadows across his face. I must have imagined it.

"My mother will be busy restoring order for hours," I said. "She doesn't need us. Will you come with me to check on Marcello?"

Zaira slapped my shoulder, so gently it barely stung. "Of course."

Whoever had designed the antechamber to the Room of Judgment had entertained certain assumptions as to the guilt of the accused. The Grace of Majesty glared sternly down from a medallion in the ceiling, and the frescoes on all four walls depicted busy and detailed scenes of torment in the Nine Hells.

But I had eyes only for Marcello, who sat slumped on one of the bare wooden benches that ringed the walls, his head cradled in his hands. He looked up when we entered, and the Hell in his eyes twisted at my heart far more than any of the painted ones around us.

I didn't care, in that moment, that he was still under Ruven's control, and still dangerous. As he rose to meet us, I threw my arms around him.

He stiffened, sucking in a little gasp as if I'd hurt him. But then the muscles in his back relaxed under my hands, and his arms went around me, too, with exaggerated care, as if he'd forgotten how to use them.

"I'm so sorry I had to leave you," I whispered, as Zaira muttered something to the guard and the door closed on the three of us.

"No, it was good you left." His voice came out rough and raw. "You shouldn't be here now. I'm not safe to be near."

"He has a point," Zaira cut in. "I told the guard I'd keep him from murdering you, but that's hard to do if you're cozying up inside his uniform."

I spun toward Zaira, blushing. "You never miss a chance, do you?"

She shrugged from her position near the door. "Who wants to live a life full of missed chances?" Her eyes stayed on Marcello, wary and sharp.

He settled back down on his bench, still moving with an oddly exaggerated control, as if he had to repress some other movement before shifting each limb. Unease tightened my scalp, and I opened a step or two between us.

"I don't know how anyone stands this," he said, rubbing his

shoulder. "I feel like I'm rotting from the inside out. Like he's scooping me hollow and smiling."

"I'm going to burn that wretch's *skull* hollow and use it as a pisspot," Zaira growled, and I knew she must be thinking about Terika. But my unease only deepened; neither Terika nor Istrella had ever described the potion's effects that way.

"I'll help you do it." Marcello's lips pulled back in a snarl. "If they don't execute me first."

I couldn't help staring. I'd never seen such animosity in his face before. "They're not going to execute you."

"I killed the doge, Amalia."

"You were magically compelled." I started pacing, to use up the unpleasant energy coursing through me. "I won't let them punish you. This was Ruven's act, not yours."

"Was it?" Marcello's gaze went vague, as if he stared at something miles away.

"Of course it was," I said sharply.

"Part of me wanted to do it." A shudder traveled across his shoulders. "I was…When I shot him, I felt…satisfied." He savored the last word, something like wonder entering his voice.

My pacing stilled, as if an invisible hand had reached out in silence to stop me. *That smile, curving his lips, of wicked anticipation.*

"And now, when I think of it, I should be horrified. And I am." He shook his head, with fierce vehemence, as if trying to dislodge something clinging to his hair. "But mixed through it, there's this…this…Oh, Amalia, it was *glorious*."

His green eyes lit with an unholy rapture. I shuddered.

"That's not you," I said sharply. "Marcello, that's not you. Do you hear me? Those aren't your feelings. They're Ruven's, leaking through somehow, while you're magically linked."

But the words felt false in my mouth. There had never been any such leakage with Terika or Istrella, or any of the others who'd been controlled. They had remained themselves, hating

Ruven's orders and fighting them—never reveling in them. *Graces help us both.*

Marcello blinked, focusing on my face, and the terrible delight faded from his eyes. The familiar, worried divot appeared between his brows in its place, and my shoulders sagged with relief.

"I can't believe I shot at you," he said huskily. He reached a trembling hand to my cheek; I winced as he brushed the bloody line where the pistol ball had grazed me, despite the gentle warmth of his touch. "I never wanted to hurt you, Amalia."

"I know," I said, my heart aching.

"Never." His eyes went suddenly hard and narrow. "Even when you hurt me."

His voice had changed, taking on a cutting edge. His fingertips dug sharply into my face.

Horror trickled down my core, as if I'd swallowed poison. "Marcello, what are you doing?"

"What I should have done a long time ago," he hissed. His nails caught the cut on my face, and I jerked away.

"All right, enough." Zaira smacked his reaching hand away and pushed me back, stepping between us. "You can have this talk once the potion wears off."

But the potion didn't change people like this. It didn't make them cruel.

I stared at Marcello over Zaira's head, unsure who was looking back at me. He turned his face away, flinching as if I were suddenly too bright to look at. His temples shone with sweat.

"She's right," he said. "I'm sorry. I told you—I'm not safe for you right now."

The pain in his voice pulled at me, but I wouldn't have stepped close to him again even if Zaira hadn't remained firmly between us. I felt as if I'd reached for a friend's hand and found a scorpion cupped in it.

"Come on," Zaira said gruffly, tugging at my arm. "We can come back later. You're only poking each other's burns now."

Marcello still wouldn't look at me. He jerked his head in a nod of agreement. But as I turned to go, a bare whisper slipped out of him:

"Please don't go."

I stopped, halfway to the door. Zaira gave me a warning glance and shook her head.

I dreaded what I would see if I turned around. Marcello's honest face, warm green eyes full of embarrassed desperation— or a mocking smile, and a stranger watching me with distant malice. I wasn't sure which would hurt more.

"What will you do if I stay?" I asked.

"I don't know," he said softly, his voice catching. "But I'm afraid of what will happen if you leave."

Zaira's hand tightened on my arm. "Don't," she muttered. "I don't know what in the Ninth Hell is wrong with him, but you need to get out of this room. You're not making him better."

I didn't dare turn around and see his face. "The Marcello I know wouldn't ask me to put myself in danger for him," I said at last.

"No," he said bitterly. "The Marcello you know would suffer in silence until he bled to death inside, and you would never notice."

I started to spin, but Zaira stopped me, grabbing my other arm as well, her hands strong as iron. "Don't be stupid," she hissed.

The door swung open. Two guards peered in warily, flanking an out-of-breath page.

"Lady Amalia," the page panted, "La Contessa calls for you."

"I have to go," I said, a confused wave of anguish, relief, and shame sweeping over me. "I'll be back, Marcello. I promise."

I couldn't help casting a glance over my shoulder at him as I followed the page out of the room, Zaira still maintaining a hold on my arm.

The last thing I saw before the door closed between us was Marcello staring after me like a drowning man watching his ship sail out of sight.

Chapter Nineteen

My mother had moved to a small audience chamber in the public area of the palace, rather than trying to impose order on chaos from the cloistered Map Room. The doge's throne stood empty; someone had brought my mother a chair, which she ignored, still on her feet in the same bloodstained gown she'd worn to vote on my Falcon Reserve Act a hundred years ago that afternoon. The stars had begun to fade in the sky outside, but La Contessa's eyes remained bright and sharp despite the coming dawn.

To nearly anyone else, she must have seemed unaffected by death, chaos, and injury, a radiant beacon of imperial serenity, indomitable and immortal. But a myriad subtle signs told me otherwise. She stood slightly off-kilter, favoring her side. She kept her hands busy, handling maps or cups, or bracing them on a table, so they wouldn't tremble. Her face was too pale. I wanted to beg her to lie down and rest, to recover from her wound, or to at least sit down—but I knew exactly what she was doing, and why. The Empire needed her to be immortal now. Never mind that her daughter was all but shaking with the realization that she wasn't.

"*Someone* opened the ward on that window to let those chimeras in, whether they were controlled or an impostor," she was saying to the captain of the Imperial Guard, her voice strong and clear as ever, if perhaps a shade more cross than it would have been under other circumstances. "If you can't figure out who, quarantine everyone who could have done it."

"That includes me," the captain objected.

"Place the good captain under quarantine," La Contessa commanded one of the officers standing guard at the door, before returning her gaze to the shocked captain. "Make a list of everyone who could have done it. Ciardha, get me a corroborating list from other sources."

Ciardha nodded. "It shall be done, Contessa."

As apologetic guards led the unresisting captain away, my mother turned to face Zaira and me. Someone who knew her less well might not notice the deep shadows of exhaustion beneath her eyes, but I did. "Amalia. And Zaira, too. Good. Come here."

For all that sometimes they had their differences, Niro da Morante had been her friend for twenty years, but she hadn't let his murder shake her. I needed to be as strong. With a huge effort, I shoved Marcello's face from my mind, ready to focus on whatever the Empire needed from me. "You called for us, Mamma?"

"You will probably not be shocked to learn that Ruven combined this assault on our leadership and our Falcons with a military attack." She gestured toward a clerk's scriptorium on which someone had spread a map. "We don't have the full details yet, but we've lost communication with one of the border fortresses north of Ardence. We need more intelligence on what's happening on his side of the border. Can you send a message to the Crow Lord?"

"If I can chase down one of his crows from the roof of our palace, yes," I said.

"Do it." She looked me up and down, then, as if assessing my condition; a faint frown creased her brow, and her voice softened slightly. "And prepare for travel."

"Thought that might be coming," Zaira said.

"The entire Mews is under quarantine for at least three days." La Contessa's disapproval of this situation stiffened her spine. "I hate to send you away from Raverra now, but if this is a full-scale invasion and not some petty skirmish, we need to send magical reinforcements to the border. And you're very nearly all we've got."

Zaira shrugged. "I'm a light packer. I can be ready in a few hours, if you want."

"Not quite that soon." My mother passed a hand through her auburn hair, brushing it back from her face; for a moment, her weariness showed through. "I need you here tomorrow for the vote, Amalia."

"The vote?" I stared uncomprehendingly. The vote I had poured so much of my soul into had already happened. Surely the Assembly wouldn't conduct normal business tomorrow, with the Empire under attack.

"To elect a new doge." La Contessa's voice dropped low enough that no one standing farther away than Ciardha would hear her. "Ruven has struck us a heavy blow. We can't allow it to be a crippling one. I'm insisting we hold the election tomorrow, and I'm putting forward the Marquise of Palova. She'll be perfect in wartime, and she takes my advice in peace."

"I'm not certain the Marquise of Palova wants to be doge," I said.

"That's why we're speaking quietly. It's a surprise." My mother's mouth quirked in a tired smile. "I shall have to think of some way to make it up to her. But I need to nominate a strong candidate before anyone thinks to nominate me; the last thing I need is to be bogged down in ceremony and politicking now. And I'm also concerned that Scipio will make a play for the crown."

I tried to wrestle my brain around to think of politics, but after everything that had happened today, it balked like a horse that only wanted to go back to the barn. "Scipio da Morante? Would he be so bad?"

Zaira grunted. "I met him at a party. He's a wet fish."

My mother nodded, appreciation gleaming in her eyes. "Precisely," she said. "He always just backed his brother and parroted whatever Niro said. We need a real leader now, and Scipio means well enough, but he doesn't have the mind or the charisma for it. But the da Morante family will fall in behind him, and they have a lot of influence. I'm afraid my good friend the marquise is the only one with the clout to challenge him." She hesitated. Then her voice dropped even further. "Speaking of Scipio. You should know he's been calling for your friend's head."

That got my attention. A chill settled in my gut. "Marcello was controlled," I protested. "You know he'd never—"

"Of course I know." La Contessa lifted a cautionary finger. "But you would do well to step back from the matter. Don't make a fuss over Captain Verdi, for his own sake. If his life becomes a point of contention in this election, it will not end well for him. Better to keep him quietly confined and put off the da Morantes with vague assurances until we have a new doge; so long as it's not Scipio or Caulin, it shouldn't be an issue. None of the others who were under Ruven's control are being held accountable, after all."

I nodded. "All right. I'll try not to draw attention to him."

My mother resumed a more normal volume. "In the meantime, when you return Lady Zaira to the Mews, make sure they're doing everything they can to get a courier lamp working so I can talk to them from the palace."

"I can do that."

She laid a hand on my shoulder, giving it a gentle squeeze. "And then get some sleep, Amalia. You've had a long day."

"All right. But Mamma—" I dropped my voice almost to a whisper. "What about you? You're hurt. You need rest." Impatience flickered in her eyes; I quickly added, "You need to be in top form for the election tomorrow, after all."

Ciardha cast my mother a meaningful look. "Lady Amalia has a point, Contessa."

My mother sighed and closed her eyes. "Fine. I'll get some sleep myself as soon as I've got things stable here. Now go home and rest. I'll send someone to get you when it's time for the vote."

As we crossed the lagoon in the pale cold light of dawn, I said quietly to Zaira, "Thank you."

She gave me a sidelong glance. "For stopping you from making stupid decisions? There was no way I was letting you stay with Captain Crazy Eyes any longer."

"I don't..." I swallowed down a ragged surge of emotion and tried again. "I've been thinking about the alchemical side of this. I'm not imagining things, am I? He wasn't acting like Terika and Istrella did, when they were under Ruven's control."

"You weren't imagining it." Zaira hunched her shoulders. "They acted like dogs straining against a leash. For a couple minutes there he looked like he was holding the leash in his own teeth, still attached to a bloody severed hand."

"Thanks," I said, shuddering. "You're always so reassuring."

"Not my job." She waved the idea off like an annoying fly.

I pulled my jacket closer around myself. I was far too exhausted to make enough heat to fight off the chill in the air. "I'm worried that it's not the potion." I forced the words out, past the fear that speaking them would make them true. "I think Ruven might have...done something to him, when he attacked us at Lady Hortensia's party. With vivomancy."

"Done something?" Zaira eyed me warily. "Like what?"

"I don't know." I shook my head helplessly. "I don't know much about what Skinwitches can do. And if it's not the potion, I have no idea how to undo it."

Zaira blew out a lungful of breath, frowning out over the lagoon toward the Mews. "Damn. He can be an ass sometimes, but he doesn't deserve that."

"He begged me not to go." His pleading voice, and that final anguished look, kept haunting every moment my mind wasn't occupied with my mother's injury, or some other terrible aspect of the various emergencies that faced us. "I need to help him somehow, Zaira."

She poked my arm with a sharp finger. "You're not thinking of going back there, are you?"

"Well..."

"No." She jabbed again, harder; I winced. "Don't visit him again without me, you understand? Or bring your mother's shadow, the one who took out all those chimeras."

"Ciardha." I nodded. "She'd keep matters under control."

Zaira snorted. "She'd keep the Hell of Discord under control. You can visit him if you take her, or me. Otherwise, stay away. Promise?"

I hesitated. "I don't think he should be left alone for long. If I can't get either of you—"

Zaira sighed. "Look. Istrella's bound to want to visit him, and I'm not going to let *her* go alone, either. If you promise me, and *only* if you promise me, I will make sure he gets friends visiting him from the Mews so you can get some sleep, and elect a doge, and whatever else your mamma needs you to do without fretting about how poor little Captain Murderface might be lonely."

Some portion of the tension drained from my shoulders. "All right. I promise. And thank you."

"Good." Zaira hunkered down in her seat, seeming satisfied.

"Now you drop me off and go get some sleep. You're a wreck. Last thing I need is you half off your hinges when we're getting sent off to war."

That night I slept in such dreamless oblivion that it seemed only seconds had passed when my maid Rica shook me awake, urging me to get dressed and hurry to the Imperial Palace; the vote for a new doge was imminent, and my mother had called for me.

After the initial relief that she was well enough to be holding the vote, I realized with a wrench that I wouldn't have time to visit Marcello beforehand. Had they left him locked overnight in that bare antechamber with its scenes of torment? But if they'd moved him, that might be worse; I was less confident of my ability to protect him if they whisked him off to some prison cell. What was going through his mind, abandoned and alone, with Ruven twisting at him somehow and nothing but the knowledge he'd committed regicide for companionship?

But no, I reminded myself as I got dressed and gulped down a cup of chocolate, Zaira had promised to see that he had company. And my mother was right; if I showed too much concern for him before the vote, I made him a piece in the Council's political games, to be traded or sacrificed. I would have to trust Zaira and Istrella and the others at the Mews to take care of him, and focus on my duty to the Empire until after the election. No matter how much that last look from his pleading eyes haunted me.

Besides, my mother was hurt, too, and she needed me. After living nineteen years in her protective shadow, by all the Hells and Graces, when she finally needed me I would be there for her.

Soon enough, I stepped back into the Assembly Hall of the Imperial Palace, one endless day after I'd walked in full of nervous hope to try to shift history in the direction of justice. I'd never seen it packed so full; every seat on the floor was filled by the time the officials closed the doors. An electric tension hung in the air, of fear and excitement, and whispers rustled around the hall like wind riffling the waters of the lagoon. Even the Graces in the ceiling fresco seemed to stare down with avid interest.

The doge's throne stood starkly empty. The Council, seated around it, couldn't seem to bring themselves to look at it, and I found myself averting my eyes as well. Niro da Morante had sat there since before I was born. It was his seat. It seemed wrong, somehow, to elect someone else to fill it.

The Council themselves showed a stark and chilling reminder of the toll of last night's attack. Exhaustion hollowed every face, and discreet bandages flashed white beneath cuffs and collars here and there. There was no hiding the claw marks raking Lord Caulin's face; alchemical salves had closed the wounds, but the angry red lines would still take days to fully heal, and might well leave scars. My mother sat stiffly, paler than usual, but her own wound was hidden beneath the bodice of her gown, and she would allow it no concessions. She gave me a small, fleeting smile as I settled in my seat. I gauged the shadows beneath her eyes and judged with some relief that Ciardha must have succeeded in getting her to sleep for at least a few hours.

The moment came when the doge would have called proceedings to order. A sort of muted hush fell on the hall, as the realization that he would do no such thing fell over the Assembly one at a time.

Finally, Lord Errardi, as the most senior Council member, cleared his throat and called out, "Your attention, please."

But then he faltered, uncertain where to go from there, grief cutting deep lines into his expression. A thousand silent faces stared at him, waiting.

Into the hush, my mother rose, and strode to the amplification circle. She was never one to let someone else fumble imperial business without picking it up and setting it to rights, with the same instinctive efficiency with which she might straighten my collar or fix my straggling hair.

"Welcome, my friends," she said, her tone stern but stirring. "I stand before you in grief, for we lost an extraordinary man last night. But we can afford no time for mourning. Lord Ruven has struck at the heart of the Serene Empire, and he has dealt us a grievous blow. We need a new doge now—one who can move with decisive strength and our united will to put down this threat to the Empire." She swept an arm behind her, where the rest of the Council of Nine remained seated. "I therefore nominate the Marquise of Palova to the office of doge of Raverra."

The marquise straightened, glaring at my mother; I half expected her to get up and march into the circle to interrupt. But she followed protocol and held her peace, though she looked as if she were chewing old leather.

"The marquise is a hero of the Three Years' War, the best strategic mind in the Empire, and has the universal respect of our military," La Contessa continued. "She already holds authority over our armed forces, and electing her as doge will ensure smooth continuity of command in a time of crisis. I urge the Assembly to put the needs of the Empire above politicking and factions, as the marquise herself has always done, and choose her to lead us in this troubled time."

Enthusiastic applause followed my mother's speech, and she returned to her seat looking satisfied. She had avoided her usual spot to the left of the imperial throne this time, and sat on the end of the row, next to the marquise; I'd wound up in the corner seat nearest her, and she caught my eye and murmured, "That should do it," as she settled back in her chair.

I tended to agree. In one neat move, she'd answered the

unspoken question of whether she would seek to take the crown, removing herself from consideration, and put forward an exemplary candidate nearly everyone could accept before most of the Assembly would even have begun wrapping their minds around the idea that we were electing a new doge today. She'd made the marquise the default choice, the standard any contenders would have to beat; a task that would prove difficult, given her excellent reputation and the Empire's position on the brink of war.

The Marquise of Palova, however, was less appreciative of this display of political acumen. She gave her friend a reproving look. "How could you, Lissandra?"

"The best candidates for doge never want it," my mother said with a wry smile. "I'm sorry, but we must put Raverra first."

"Hmph. I'll get you for this."

More Assembly members came forward to make nominations, one after another. Normally, electing a doge was a complicated process that took at least a week, wherein the Assembly chose electors who in turn chose more electors who selected candidates to put before the Assembly for multiple rounds of voting; but everyone had agreed to streamline the process given the current emergency, and the shrinekeepers took a simple show of hands to determine whether a certain minimum portion of the Assembly considered a nominee a viable candidate before hurriedly preparing a ballot box for them. There were some five or six nominations that received enough support, including Scipio da Morante and Lord Caulin. The former received particularly heartfelt applause, led by the powerful da Morante family, especially on invoking his brother's name; I tensed, worried not only for the fate of the Empire, but for Marcello.

But La Contessa seemed unperturbed. "Look at their faces. They're cheering for Niro, not Scipio. None of them have enough support to beat you," she said to the Marquise of Palova, giving her a sympathetic pat on the hand. "You're stuck with this, I'm afraid."

The marquise grinned wolfishly. "We'll see about that."

"You wouldn't." My mother's voice dropped half an octave.

"Damned right I would."

And the marquise rose and walked to the amplification circle.

"Surely she's not going to..." I whispered. But then the marquise began speaking, her bold voice booming throughout the Assembly Hall.

"My peers of the Assembly, I am honored beyond words that my good friend Lissandra Cornaro put me forth as a candidate. But I must disagree with her that I am the *best* candidate. There is only one possible choice in this election." She spread her arms. "When disaster struck last night, my friends, I am not ashamed to admit that we were shaken. In one swift move, our enemy knocked out two of the supporting pillars of the Empire. I stood staring in the face of the Demon of Death and was sure, for a moment, I would watch the Serene City fall."

The room hushed at her words, staring enraptured at the marquise's lined face and her regal crown of braids. She spoke with the power of a woman who knew how to inspire armies, and the amplification circle set her voice resonating in the bones of every person in that hall. I glanced at my mother and saw her clutching the arms of her chair, her face deliberately impassive, her jaw tight.

"But you and I are here in this room, right now, because one woman did not hesitate," the marquise continued, her voice ringing with passion. "We are here because one woman stepped forward and continued the work she has done for decades, from beside the throne. She saw what needed to be done, my friends, and she did it. La Contessa Lissandra Cornaro is *already* acting as our doge. Let us elect her to continue the work she has always

done, and grant her the honor she has so selflessly offered me."
The marquise managed to keep all irony out of her voice, but
my mother's eyebrow jumped. "I trust you, lords and ladies of
the Assembly, to vote her into the office she has so thoroughly
earned."

The marquise bowed and returned to her seat. Under cover
of the thunderous applause that shook the hall, she turned to my
mother and broke out into a wide, gleeful grin.

"Take *that*, Lissandra," she crowed.

"You're ruining everything I've worked for," La Contessa
hissed.

"A wise woman once said that the best candidates for doge
never want it," the marquise said piously.

"I'm more effective working from the shadows, and you
know it."

"This is what you get for starting a fight with the best strategic mind in the Empire." The twinkle of mischief dimmed in
the marquise's eyes, then, and her tone grew serious. "Besides,
Raverra needs you now. I meant everything I said."

There were no further nominations, so the shrinekeepers
began setting up the ballot urns. I wasn't certain how to feel
as they set a card with my mother's name beside the last one; I
couldn't help a surge of pride, but that plain silver urn threatened to upend my world.

I filed into line to vote with the rest of the Assembly, and
accepted my handful of colored balls: from red for one's most
preferred candidate through black for one's least preferred, they
let the Assembly rank candidates in order to avoid the need for
further rounds of voting. A young acolyte set up a wooden sign
reminding us of the order of the colors. I was far from the only
one fingering my ballots and staring at the names beside the
urns, struggling to decide on an order.

My mother wouldn't see how I voted. If I were completely

honest with myself, I tended to agree with the marquise that in the long term, my mother would make a better doge. But if she won, I had little doubt that it would impact our happiness for the rest of our lives. Being on the Council of Nine was bad enough, but at least now our family still could claim some measure of privacy, walling off some tiny piece of our lives that belonged to ourselves and not to the Empire; if she became doge, we surrendered that hard-won reserve forevermore.

My turn to vote came all too soon. I hesitated over the marquise's urn, then dropped in my red ball, a dutiful daughter. But my conscience forced me to give my white ball, for my second-choice candidate, to my mother. Lord Caulin got my black ball, since the thought of a man with so few firm principles leading the Serene Empire genuinely alarmed me, and Scipio da Morante the gray one for second-least favored. The remaining handful of candidates I ranked as best I could in the middle. And then I was done, my votes cast; my future was out of my hands.

No rule prevented me from leaving now and going to visit Marcello. The vote and the subsequent tally could take hours yet; I had time to relieve the worry gnawing my gut. I wanted to lay eyes on him in daylight, without a night of murder and catastrophe pressing at all our nerves. To find that I had overreacted last night, imagining things in my exhaustion, and that he was still entirely himself.

But I had promised Zaira not to visit him without her or Ciardha along. And if my fears weren't baseless after all, seeing him alone could be foolish indeed. So I watched the elite of the Serene City file up in an orderly fashion and drop balls in urns to decide the future of the Empire—and of my family.

The election of a doge was crucial enough that the shrine-keepers traditionally counted the votes in public. Once the voting was over, nearly everyone in the Assembly stayed to watch as acolytes gradually emptied the ballot urns, sorting the balls by color into groups of tall glass jars, one cluster per candidate. The whole Assembly stared, with tense and waiting quiet, as slowly, slowly, the jars began to fill. One tiny ball at a time, they began to sketch out a vision of the next era of imperial history in growing columns of color.

My mother sat stiffly in her seat, watching the tally with a grim expression. The Marquise of Palova kept casting glances at her and chuckling.

And she had reason. While the marquise, my mother, and Scipio da Morante were all doing well, my mother's jar of red first-choice ballots was filling rapidly, outstripping all the others. A murmur grew and swelled in the hall; the count continued, but it was clear enough how this election would go. Some of the dignitaries seated around me started offering me congratulations, as if this were something I'd wanted.

I'd never wanted this. Nor had my mother. We'd had Cornaro doges enough; it was a complication and a burden we had no desire to take into our lives. But in this, the Assembly had final and ultimate power, and the Assembly's choice was clear.

It was so like my mother that one of the very few times in my life I'd seen her lose, it was by winning.

The marquise made some teasing comment, and my mother turned to her with iron in her eyes and a voice of steel.

"Fine. You insist that I rule this empire, over my objections. Then, by the Grace of Majesty, *I will rule*."

The marquise smiled. "I ask for nothing less, Your Serenity."

As the shrinekeepers declared the official results, the world seemed strangely distant and muffled, as if I were sinking further and further away from the reality I knew. I might as well have watched the proceedings from underwater, with a silent roaring weight in my ears.

My mother accepted her fate graciously enough, thanking the Assembly for their trust and pledging to dedicate her life, as she always had, to the service of the Serene Empire. The sense that this must surely all be a strange dream intensified as the shrinekeepers brought out the ducal crown, which Niro da Morante had worn only for state occasions, for the swift, no-fuss emergency coronation my mother had insisted on before she knew it would be her own head bending to accept the crown. The shrinekeepers invoked the blessings of the Nine Graces, and my mother swore an oath, and the head shrinekeeper of the Temple of Majesty placed the gold-wrought crown upon my mother's auburn hair, and it was done.

My mother was the doge. It was impossible, but there she stood before the Assembly, her face stony and determined.

"There will be time to celebrate, and time to mourn," she said. "For now, you elected me to do a job, and there is work to be done. Will the Council of Nine please attend me in the Map Room."

It was over at last. I started toward the exit, shaking my head to clear it of its surreal haze; I was finally free to see Marcello, and that meant ascertaining where he was and then collecting either Zaira or Ciardha.

"Amalia, where are you going?" It was my mother's voice, pitched sharp and low.

I looked up to find her standing by me at the edge of the Assembly floor, her face regal and remote save for her eyes, which gazed on me with something far too much like pity.

"I...I was going to inquire into a certain matter." I barely stopped myself from saying *Mamma,* here in front of the Assembly. "Your Serenity." The words tasted strange in my mouth; it was like taking a sip of a drink expecting chocolate and finding it to be wine.

"I called the Council of Nine to the Map Room," my mother said.

I stared at her blankly. Of course she had; I'd heard her. What did that have to do with me? My mother was the one on the Council of Nine.

Except that she was the doge now. And she couldn't be both.

Oh, Hells. Panic flooded in like black lagoon water into a leaky boat.

"Yes." My mother's voice softened. "That means you."

Chapter Twenty

Someone had scrubbed the bloodstains from the beautiful map of Eruvia inlaid in the Map Room floor. No sign of last night's violence marred the room's stately gravity as I crossed the threshold, stepping onto the turquoise blue of the Summer Ocean. The incident had been swallowed by the thick layers of history folded invisibly into the shadows, hanging like smoke in the air.

The table was set up for a private Council meeting, with ten chairs drawn up around it. I'd mostly been here for larger strategy sessions, when the Council pulled in outsiders like military leaders, key imperial officials, and the occasional heir in training. More often the doge and Council met alone, behind closed doors, their business swathed in secrecy.

Ten chairs, for the ten most powerful people in the Serene Empire. And one of them was mine.

I paced slowly across the golden-brown coast of Osta, with its elegant temples and ancient walled cities rendered in alabaster and mother-of-pearl. I'd never truly thought this day would come—not until some unimaginably distant future, when my mother retired or passed away. It seemed likely as not that I'd die first, given all the trouble I'd gotten into. The Cornaro Council seat was a doom that had hung over my head since childhood:

When you take your place on the Council of Nine, you won't be able to blurt out any foolish thing that leaps into your head, Amalia. You won't have time to read books all day when you're on the Council. As one of the Council of Nine, you'll have to get used to making sacrifices. My only consolation had been that this grim future remained several decades away.

Now it was here. Once I sat at that table, my freedom was over.

My mother watched me from the head of the table, her eyes grave. I pulled out a chair and sat down.

Lord Caulin cleared his throat, giving my mother a meaningful look. "Your Serenity, is it truly appropriate for your daughter to join us in this meeting?"

My mother lifted an eyebrow. "Lady Amalia was confirmed as my successor in the Cornaro seat when you were still struggling to grow a beard, Lord Caulin."

"Of course." Caulin's smile barely stretched his scars; no humor touched his eyes. "But at that time, the Lady Amalia was not yet a Falconer. It's already a violation of the law for her to retain her seat on the Assembly after putting a jess on a fire warlock; for a Falconer to ascend to a seat on the Council is an even grosser breach of the rules laid down to separate magical and political power. Surely, we cannot blithely accept such a disruption to the balance that has maintained the serenity of the Empire for three hundred years without at least giving the matter some serious consideration."

"Excuse me, Lord Caulin," I said sharply, fighting to keep the heat from rising to my cheeks. I knew one thing for certain: I couldn't let this turn into an argument between my mother and Lord Caulin while I sat here being talked over like a child. "It seems far more disruptive to tamper with the equally hallowed process by which the Empire selects its highest council. Having four inherited and five elected seats has protected us from civil

war more than once. Are you challenging the process by which
not only myself, but several others here ascended to our seats?
Do you question our legitimacy?"

"I should hope not," old Lord Errardi scoffed, drawing himself up. "Rather bold for someone who's only been in his own
seat a few months, Lord Caulin."

Scipio, his eyes still red from what must have been a sleepless
and grief-stricken night, frowned at Caulin. The da Morante
seat was the oldest inherited spot on the Council. "We already
had this discussion, when Lady Amalia first became a Falconer.
We cannot set the precedent that a Council member or confirmed heir can be stripped of their seat by a magical accident,
such as the one that melted the knot of the Lady Zaira's jess and
made it impossible to remove."

"And yet," Caulin said silkily, "such a concentration of power
in the hands of one family—"

"I assure you, neither Lady Amalia nor I asked for the positions of power we currently hold," my mother said tartly. The
Marquise of Palova chuckled, leaning back in her chair with
great apparent satisfaction; it broke the tension, and the more
established members of the Council exchanged knowing smiles.
"Now, the Empire faces a crisis the like of which it has never
seen, and we cannot afford to be distracted by political squab-
bles. Shall we move past the niceties and take care of the business
at hand?"

Nods and murmurs of assent traveled around the table. Lord
Caulin let the matter drop. It seemed impossible that this same
group of people who had met behind our drawing room door
when I was a tiny child, parceling out the future of the Empire
over clinking glasses of wine late into the night when I was supposed to be asleep, had now accepted me as one of them. But the
moment of challenge had passed, and I was still here at the table.

"Let's get straight to the point," my mother said. "Our first priority must be to preserve the Empire. Marquise, what is our latest military intelligence on the invasion?"

The Marquise of Palova shook her head. "I just got an update on the way in here. It's not good. We thwarted attacks in a few locations, but Ruven has taken one of the smaller border fortresses. The pass it guards was ten feet deep in snow and too rough for wagons even in summer; he must have used vivomancy to either clear the snow or march his army over it. Our scouts haven't been able to get close enough to determine how."

Lord Caulin frowned. "If it's too steep for wagons, how is he bringing supplies?"

"He's not," the marquise said bluntly. "Or not nearly what an army needs. He's got some pack mules and what his soldiers can carry. Either he has some way to feed them and keep them warm with magic, or he doesn't care if they die."

My mother glanced inquiringly at me.

"With Ruven, it could be either," I said.

"He's crossed the border with several thousand troops," the marquise continued. "I don't have a reliable count yet, because he's been shattering courier lamp relay mirrors along the way, but it's not his main army. Still, it was enough to overcome the forces we had defending that remote section of the Witchwall Mountains. Since his soldiers don't have baggage slowing them down, they're moving quickly out of the mountains toward Ardence."

My heart lurched unpleasantly. *Ardence.* I had friends in the path of Ruven's army. And since most of our forces were at the border, it lay virtually undefended in the soft interior of the Empire.

My mother frowned at the map spread out on the table. "This seems like a rash move. Ardence is well fortified; even if we can't get significant reinforcements there before Ruven's army arrives, we can cut him off from the border, surround him, and destroy his forces before he can take the city. What am I missing?"

Silence fell. I stared at the little drawing of Ardence on the map, with its stone walls and the River Arden running through it, trying to think what Ruven could be up to. And then it struck me, with a chill like mountain snow.

"He's going to lay his claim upon the city," I said, certain of it. He'd tipped his hand in Lady Hortensia's garden, with his talk of using circles and stones and enchantments to steal land from his enemies. Only in the Empire, he wouldn't need my blood to do it, since there was no competing Witch Lord's claim to overpower. "We can't think of this like our wars with other Witch Lords. He only needs to hold the city long enough to magically claim it as part of his domain." Ardence's walls would make that easier, providing a ready-made boundary for Ruven to mark with his blood. "Once he's done that, the entire population of Ardence—sixty thousand people—will be his."

The Marquise of Palova swore. "How long will it take him to claim it? And how does he do it, exactly? Does he need to control the city, or just surround it?"

I shook my head. "Normally, it takes a couple of months to become a part of a Witch Lord's domain through drinking the water and eating the food. But Ruven has already used enchantments to establish a weak, temporary claim at once, when he set up his circles around Mount Whitecrown. That might well be enough for him to exercise control over the people living in the city, and all he'd have to do is carve symbols into the walls and blood them."

"So we can't let him surround Ardence for any length of time." The Marquise of Palova let out a frustrated puff of breath.

"How long will it take us to get a force to Ardence sizable enough to defend it?" my mother asked.

The marquise frowned at the map spread out on the table. "Normally, we'd reinforce them with Falcons from the Mews, since that's the quickest way to get the most power there. That's always been the imperial strategy for responding to surprise attacks. But that's not an option now. We can pull forces from the border, but that weakens our defense against his main army. The sabotage to our courier lamp relay lines means that only troops deployed on intact lines can respond quickly enough, too, which limits our options—we've lost contact with the major fortress closest to his army."

"We can figure out exactly where we're pulling the troops from later in this discussion. Just answer me this: can we get a force of sufficient size to Ardence before him?"

"No," the marquise said quietly. "Not one big enough to stop his forces without heavy Falcon support from the Mews, especially given that they've got a Witch Lord with them. He'll beat us there by two to three days. Any force we could field before then will just get slaughtered."

Silence fell over the table. I gripped the edges of my chair, thinking of Domenic and Venasha and all my other friends in Ardence. The notion of leaving them to Ruven's mercy for a few days was intolerable.

My mother let out a long breath, heavy with consequences. "With Ruven supporting them, that's more than enough time to take the city. We can't let that happen." She lifted her eyes to me. "Amalia, I would vastly prefer to keep you here fulfilling your duties on the Council, but with the entire Mews in quarantine, I can think of only one way to get Ardence the power it needs to defend itself before Ruven's army arrives."

I nodded, my belly clenching. "Zaira can likely handle a small army. If Ruven is with them, however, I can only guess at what he can do."

My mother's eyes narrowed. "This ability of his to control

people is a problem. He nearly crippled us in one night. We're still catching people in Raverra and across the Empire who seem to be acting under his command. I have reports coming in of farmers damaging bridges and breaking courier lamp relay mirrors, trusted servants murdering leaders, and soldiers caught in the act of trying to open border fortresses to Ruven's chimeras."

"If we're going to stop him, we have to do it soon," the Marquise of Palova said. "He's targeting the sources of Raverran power: the Falcons, the courier lamp network, infrastructure like roads and the chain of command. And his control potion has the potential to expand exponentially; there was an alchemist stationed at that border fortress he took, so he can definitely make more of it now, if he couldn't before. We need to strike back and hurt him badly enough that he can't keep chipping away at our ability to fight him."

"That man needs to die," my mother said bluntly. "I'm normally all for diplomatic solutions, but Lord Ruven is too dangerous and unprincipled to live."

"I can send assassins after him," Lord Caulin offered, "but my understanding is that they would likely prove ineffective."

Every eye around the table turned to me. I shifted uncomfortably, but it was only fair; I was the only imperial citizen alive who'd been directly involved in the deaths of two Witch Lords. "I've been researching the matter. It won't be easy. He can draw on all the lives in his domain to sustain his own." I opened my mouth to explain the particular challenges and my thoughts on how they might be overcome, but then realized that in the unlikely event anyone here cared about those details, there was little chance they'd understand the magical theory involved. "I'll keep working on it," I said instead. "Lord Kathe may be able to help."

"Good. Talk to him. Make this effort your top priority," my mother said. "Use whatever resources you need. No matter what it takes, we need to find a way to kill him. You know Ruven, you've faced him before, and you understand the magic involved; you are the person I most trust to handle this."

I nodded, trying to appear competent and confident and not at all as if the crushing pressure of responsibility had just tumbled down on me like a mountain.

"What about justice for my brother?" Scipio da Morante asked sharply. "That is *my* top priority. After the safety of the Empire, of course."

My back locked as tight as if someone had stuck a fork into my muscles and twisted them like spaghetti. I sealed my lips, knowing full well that leaping to Marcello's defense when no one had even mentioned him by name yet could doom him.

"We've found the individual responsible for the breached ward in the Imperial Palace," Caulin reported. "She appears to be a Vaskandran agent who came somehow into the possession of the face of an officer of the imperial guard who we now believe to be missing. I've turned her over to some of my best people for questioning."

I couldn't help a twinge of sympathy for the woman. If Ruven didn't want her to talk, she would be incapable of talking, no matter how much Caulin's *best people* made her want to.

Scipio gave a grim nod. "And the man who killed my brother?"

I struggled to keep my face impassive, silently willing my mother to find some way to redirect him.

But it was the Marquise of Palova who answered. "Yes, the control potion should wear off in a few days, and then I'm sure he'll be happy to tell us everything he knows with no additional persuasion required. I know the man; he's a good officer."

"I will do everything I can to find a means to destroy Lord Ruven, so we can bring your brother's true murderer to justice," I added, buoyed by a rush of gratitude to the marquise.

Scipio nodded with reluctant acceptance. To my relief, the discussion shifted to moving troops to defend Ardence. The Marquise of Palova argued with Lord Errardi over how many troops we could afford to shift off Ruven's border, and when the Falcons at the Mews would be ready to return to active duty. Ciardha brought my mother a report of a servant caught attempting to smuggle a vial of Ruven's potion into the palace kitchens, and of a mountain town in the path of Ruven's army presumed destroyed.

Graces help us. This was the Empire crumbling at the edges, and now it was my job to fix it.

I straightened in my chair, bending every scrap of focus and spark of imagination I possessed to each problem as it came under discussion. I offered to ask Kathe to send crows to spy on Ruven's army. I suggested putting our quarantined artificers to work making alchemy detection rings and distributing them to the kitchens of key military outposts and civilian command centers. But I knew none of it was going to be enough.

Finally, my mother called a break to get food and attend to other business. As the others left, talking to each other in pairs or striding off to accomplish pressing tasks, she asked me to wait with a flick of her eyes.

"You and Zaira should go at first light," my mother said, once the others were gone. Now that we were alone, she let pain and exhaustion roughen her voice at last. "I'll arrange a military escort, and Ciardha has found you an aide to help you conduct at least some Council business from the road. If you use the imperial post stations and every moment of daylight, you can get to Ardence in less than two days, which should allow you to beat Ruven there."

I nodded, trying not to show the dread churning in my stomach. I couldn't quite make myself speak. *War.* We were going to war at last.

My mother's eyes softened, and she reached out to smooth hair back from my face. "I know this isn't easy for you," she said quietly. "Nothing will be easy for a long time. How are you holding up?"

I remembered someone asking La Contessa that same question at our palace, not long after my father died. *Well enough to serve the Empire*, she had replied.

My mother never asked me questions like that. She expected me to do what needed to be done, no matter how I felt. We had come to a dark time indeed, if she seemed genuinely concerned for my feelings.

But that was unfair. She had always cared how I felt. She'd just never needed to ask.

"Oh, I'm just fantastic," I said, letting irony fill my voice, and holding her eyes. "How about you?"

She laughed. "Also fantastic." And she pulled me into an embrace, still chuckling. I returned it carefully, mindful of the wound in her side. "Everything is simply lovely. Oh, Amalia, how did we get here?"

I breathed in the familiar, comforting scent of her perfume. "I don't know, Mamma. But here we are."

She held me out at arm's length, scanning my face. "Indeed. And never doubt that we're equal to this challenge, Amalia. We are Cornaros. We do not hold ourselves satisfied with merely doing what we can; we do what must be done."

My spine straightened. "You're right. And I'll have Zaira with me. She's an unstoppable force, even with her balefire sealed."

"That she is." My mother squeezed my shoulders. "Now, go home and get some sleep. You'll need to get up before dawn."

"I've got to check on Marcello first." Profound disquiet at the thought of leaving him behind in Raverra in his current condition settled over me like a damp cloak. "Mamma, can you promise to look after him for me? To make certain he's comfortable while he's in quarantine, and that no one tries to blame him for the doge's death?"

"I'm certain we can—" She broke off as Ciardha slipped in through the Map Room door, face grave, and murmured something in her ear. My mother's face went still. My gut tightened with apprehension.

"About that, Amalia," my mother said, her voice slow and grave. "There's some news."

Terrible possibilities rolled down into my stomach as if I'd swallowed a cup of lead shot. "What is it?" I whispered.

"Captain Verdi is missing," she said. "He took down his guards and escaped."

Chapter Twenty-One

Missing?" I breathed. "I've got to—"

"You will do nothing." My mother's voice cracked like a whip. "We don't know what orders Ruven has given him; you could well be his target. Ciardha, is he still in the palace?"

"No, Contessa. He apparently escaped about an hour ago."

"He could be anywhere by now, then." I pressed a hand to my temple. "Hidden in the city, on the mainland and heading toward Vaskandar, or trying to break into the Mews."

"I'll send a messenger over to warn them he's escaped, and set people looking for him," Ciardha said. "Do you wish me to keep this discreet, Serenity?"

"Yes," my mother said. "And find a courier lamp pair from some less important location that we can swap to the Mews. Sending people back and forth in boats takes too much time."

"It shall be done, Serenity."

She left. I stared at the Map Room door as it closed behind her. All I could think of was Marcello begging me not to leave him. And Marcello, out somewhere in the winter evening under the cold moon, doing Ruven's work, with Raverran soldiers hunting for him.

I hadn't visited him all day, swept up in the election and its aftermath. And now my friend, a man I loved, was in dire trouble, knowing I'd abandoned him.

"Amalia." My mother touched my hair, briefly; she had moved up behind me, and I hadn't even noticed. "I know Captain Verdi is your friend. Hopefully, they'll capture him soon."

I swallowed. "Mamma, are they going to . . . Will they have orders to . . ."

"To capture him alive." My mother paused. "Unless, of course," she added slowly, "you would recommend otherwise. You know better than I how much damage he could cause."

Hell of Nightmares. Marcello knew everything about the Falcons, from their combat tactics to the personal weaknesses of every resident of the Mews. The idea of that knowledge in Ruven's hands was chilling.

My stomach twisted in rebellion at the idea of essentially sending assassins to murder him. By all the Graces, he was my friend, a man I loved; we'd both risked our lives for each other more than once. I couldn't let that happen to him. Surely this was one line I couldn't cross.

But I had killed my cousin to spare innocent lives. I'd already crossed that line months ago. Hadn't I?

"I . . ." I drew in a shaky breath. "We should try to capture him alive if at all possible."

My words fell into the silence like rocks into a deep well: heavy and hard and plummeting into a dark place. My whole body burned with shame at that *if at all possible.* If someone had asked Marcello the same question about me, I knew it would have been *at any cost.* What kind of demon had I become?

The kind who sat on the Council of Nine. Like my mother.

She squeezed my shoulder. "I understand," she said softly.

I stepped out of the Map Room half-blind with unshed tears. I had to believe Marcello would be captured unharmed, that was all. Or at least alive. We would find him, and bring him back, and the alchemists and vivomancers at the Mews would figure out what was wrong with him and fix it. The thought of not having his warm, honest, dependable presence in my life was too terrible to contemplate.

I had to focus on finding a way to defeat Ruven. He was the source of all the problems besetting the Empire and the people I loved, Marcello included, and my mother had made him my responsibility. I needed to unravel the problem of his immortality as if it were simply another complex magical theory challenge put before me by the professors at the University of Ardence.

Please don't go.

"Hells take it," I muttered, wiping at my eyes.

"Excuse me, Lady Amalia. Reporting for duty."

I turned, well aware I must be flushing bright red, to find a rangy young woman with a strong jaw and dark hair pulled back in a tight braid at my side. Her combination of sleekly tailored coat, twin knife belts, and an air of almost painful earnestness left me completely at a loss to determine whether she was a soldier, a clerk, or some minor courtier. On a closer look, she couldn't be older than me; I'd guess seventeen.

"And you are . . . ?"

She bowed. "Lucia of Calsida, my lady. Your new aide."

I blinked. "Right. My aide." My mother had said something about that. By all the Graces, I couldn't deal with this now—but I had to. The wheels of the Empire didn't stop turning for anyone's tears.

"And your bodyguard, my lady. Ciardha assigned me." Her eyes lit up, sparkling as if with tiny internal festival lights. "Of course," she added breathily, "I've got a long way to go before I can be anywhere near as good as *Ciardha*. She's a legend. Did you know—" She swallowed and bowed again. "But yes, um. Reporting for duty."

I stared at her for a long moment, wondering how this had become my life. But then I nodded. "All right, well, I'm heading back to the Cornaro palace to prepare for my departure tomorrow."

Lucia rocked eagerly onto her toes. "Yes, my lady. I'll have word sent ahead to commence packing. Do you wish to select your own books, my lady, or do you want to dictate a list?"

"I'll, ah, pack my own, thank you." I tentatively started walking; Lucia marched briskly along at my side. "I need to figure out what will be most useful in researching ways to overcome Ruven's regenerative abilities."

"Do you want any volumes from the Imperial library?" Lucia asked, quivering and ready like a drawn arrow.

"No. Wait—maybe Crespi's *Theory of Magical Energies*."

"Yes, my lady." Lucia waylaid a passing page, muttered a few quick words, and returned to my side. "Anything else?"

I couldn't help a stab of annoyance. All I wanted now was to be alone with my thoughts; the last thing I needed was someone hovering eagerly at my shoulder, like a gull waiting for handouts. I had a hundred worries balled up in my chest, and a great deal to do.

"No," I said. "I've got to get home and catch a few hours of sleep, but I also need to prepare to leave at first light, make sure Zaira has everything she needs for our departure, find out if Istrella is all right—"

"I'll send someone to the Mews at once to coordinate with Lady Zaira and inquire discreetly after Istrella Verdi, my lady," Lucia said immediately, procuring a small leather-bound notebook and a charcoal pencil from an inner pocket and making a note. "What else?"

I slowed my stride for a moment, staring at her. She gave me a tentative grin.

"All right." I picked my pace back up, a strange energy surging through me at the giddy realization that I could simply declare things and expect them to be done. "I want overview reports on all incoming intelligence about Ruven's movements and activities. And a briefing on Ardence's current defense capabilities, and any special concerns we may want to be aware of before we arrive."

"Naturally, my lady." Lucia scribbled more notes. She couldn't quite constrain herself from giving a small sort of skip as we walked. "And?"

"Send thank-you gifts to the major supporters of my Falcon Reserve Act." Graces, I could get used to this. "I also want to keep a watchful eye on its reception, both in the city and throughout the Empire. How people are reacting to the law, what the mage-marked are doing with their new freedoms, that sort of thing. Can you arrange that?"

"Of course, my lady. Anything more?"

Yes. Something that sat in my stomach like a swallowed stone. I dropped my voice, glancing at a clerk scurrying past with an armload of documents. "Quietly watch the effort to find Captain Verdi for me. I want reports on any progress or sightings."

"Yes, my lady." She hesitated, her voice losing its certainty. "If there's news during the night, should I wake you?"

"Please." I cleared my throat of a sudden huskiness. "No matter the hour."

Lucia might not have quite Ciardha's level of delicacy, but she possessed enough to leave me to my thoughts after that. It was strange, having her stick close as my shadow through the palace halls and all the way home in my boat along the Imperial Canal in the chill and sparkling evening. I was used to having servants and guards around, but there was something proprietary about the way Lucia hovered, as if I were her sole and overriding concern. I wasn't certain I liked the idea that she might become my Ciardha, following me wherever I went and efficiently transforming my will into reality. The very need for such an aide implied that my chances for those wishes to be "leave me alone to read in the library for the next six hours" would be distressingly small.

I didn't want to be effective right now. I wanted to be alone—no, I wanted someone to whom I could pour out all my fear and grief and worry. Someone who could listen without judging, without wanting anything from me, and maybe hold me for a little while, so I could fool myself into believing that I was safe. That anything could be safe again, if the Mews and the Imperial Palace and even my mother were vulnerable.

I wanted Marcello. Graces help us both.

I had barely stepped inside my palace door, Old Anzo taking my jacket and exchanging assessing looks with Lucia, when our courier lamp clerk burst into the foyer, her eyes wide with agitation. "Lady Amalia! Come quickly! There's a message for you."

My heart dropped through the marble floor. "From the Imperial Palace?" Horrifying possibilities burst through my mind, hot and painful as fireworks: my mother had succumbed to her wound, or Marcello was dead, or some other new catastrophe I could never have anticipated.

But the clerk shook her head. "No. From a border outpost. It's..." She licked her lips. "My lady, the clerk there says there's a strange man there who just *appeared* inside the fort. No one knows how he got in. And he claims to be the Crow Lord, and he's asking to speak to you."

Ragged wings fluttered in my chest. *Kathe.*

I took the clerk's hard wooden chair before the one courier lamp in the hushed, round chamber that glowed with a patient inner light. I barely breathed as I pressed two fingers hesitantly to the crystal.

It's Amalia, I tapped, the crystal winking on and off beneath my touch. Far, far away, I knew another crystal flashed, casting warm pulses of light across the smooth contours of Kathe's face.

The lamp stuttered with the rapid, skilled flashes of a trained courier lamp clerk. *Lady Cornaro, this is Ensign Hamis. The Crow Lord is here and we are all concerned for our safety. Please advise.*

I put my face in my hand, letting out a shaky laugh. Of course, Kathe had terrified them. He probably thought it was funny.

He won't hurt you, I promised. *Just give me his message.*

Yes, Lady Cornaro. I will relay his words. A pause. Then, *Hello, Amalia. I gather you've been busy.*

I snorted at the lamp as if it could hear me. *That's an understatement. Why are you scaring innocent courier lamp clerks, Kathe?*

For a moment, the lamp remained dark. I could imagine the clerk flushing red as he translated for Kathe, and Kathe laughing.

My crows gave me some reports strange enough that I wondered if they'd been in Raverra too long and learned to drink wine. A storm over the Mews, chimeras climbing out of the lagoon, murder at the Imperial Palace. With no message from you, I thought I should check to make sure you weren't dying, controlled, or otherwise indisposed.

I was so surprised my fingers slipped on the crystal. *You were worried.*

I was not. A pause. *I just like to know what's going on.*

I leaned against the hard wooden back of the chair, smiling. He was worried, all right. But the grin slipped off my face as I tapped out a curt summary of everything that had befallen the Serene City in the past terrible day and a half.

There came another long pause when I was done. A knot formed in my chest, and I almost wondered if Kathe had wandered off, with the conversation having become so unamusing.

The lamp flickered to life again at last. *And here I thought my crows were exaggerating. But you're well?*

No. How could I be well when my mother was badly injured, Marcello was taken by my enemy, and my world lay in shattered pieces at my feet? But he knew that. Kathe wasn't one to talk about feelings, any more than I was—at least, not directly.

Well enough, I said.

Let me ask you this, the lamp flashed, at a more deliberate pace that suggested Kathe was thinking over his words as he spoke them. *Which is more important now: to protect what is yours, or to strike back against him?*

I considered the question. All my instincts pulled inexorably toward defense: to retrieve and cure Marcello, protect Ardence, help and heal my mother. But if we kept merely reacting to Ruven's attacks, he would break us a piece at a time.

To strike back. I jabbed at the crystal hard enough to rock the lamp in its base. *I have to keep him from taking Ardence first, but then I am going to destroy him.*

You'd make a fine Witch Lord. Something tentative about the flashes of the courier lamp expressed the clerk's incredulity or reluctance to find those words passing beneath his fingers, and the compliment didn't sit quite as easily with me as perhaps Kathe intended. *I'll see what I can do to help you. Be bold.*

That startled a short huff out of me. Marcello would have told me to stay safe. But I supposed that for Kathe, personal safety was never a priority. *I'd say the same to you, but I doubt you need the encouragement.* Especially given that he'd broken into an imperial outpost just to say hello.

Ensign Hamis again, my lady, the lamp pulsed, a quick and sub-dued flutter. *He's gone.*

I leaned back in the chair and closed my eyes, letting loose a sigh like a bedraggled bird.

Chapter Twenty-Two

Well, that was odd," I said to the empty courier lamp chamber. Still, I couldn't help but feel inexplicably heartened.

Kathe had wasted no time exclaiming over the horror of the situation. He'd gone straight to what to do next. I needed to do the same.

I hurried to the library, filled with a sense of urgent purpose, and began combing my bookshelves for texts that might help me unravel the Ruven immortality problem. Old Anzo had to remind me gently that I should have dinner and get some sleep. I took a book down to the dining room to peruse while I ate. Kathe was right; I had to strike back. The first step was figuring out how to do it.

I had only gotten a few bites into dinner and a few pages into my book, however, when Lucia bowed her way into the dining room to inform me that I had a visitor.

I frowned. "I'm frankly too busy and too tired for visitors."

She nodded with her customary zeal. "I can tell her to come back another time, my lady, if you wish. But it's Lady Zaira."

"Oh!" I nearly knocked my chair over rising to my feet. "Please, show her in."

"I hear you're really important now," Zaira greeted me as she sauntered into the dining room. "What should I call you? Your Nine-ness? Lady High Mighty Imperial Bilgesucker? Biscuit Cheeks?" She sat down opposite me, and without hesitation pulled my half-eaten dinner in front of her—cuttlefish in a thick black sauce of its own ink—and began consuming it.

"Hello, Zaira. It's good to see you, too. I'm doing as well as can be expected, thank you, and I imagine you'll continue to call me whatever crosses your mind." I eased back in my chair as if letting weariness take me, but it was really a rush of dizzy relief that she was here. "I can't tell you how good it is to see you and know that some things are still the same."

She gave me a strange look, almost pitying. "Don't you know yet that nothing's ever the same?"

My eyes stung unexpectedly. I thought I'd pulled myself together. But everything was changing, slipping through my fingers like sand dragged off by the tide. Marcello gone, my life given over to the Council, the Mews fallen, my mother mortal.

"Let me pretend," I said roughly.

Zaira shrugged. "You can pretend you're the Grace of Bounty for all I care." Her fork paused a moment then, and she sighed. "I came here because I heard the news about Captain Loverboy running off."

It was just as well Zaira was eating my dinner. Any appetite I'd had vanished. "Oh," I said.

"A curse on that pox-faced stingroach," she said helpfully. "Ruven, that is."

I forced myself to keep my voice light, hiding the sickening mix of guilt and worry in my gut. "It's true that every time I think I couldn't possibly hate him more, he finds a way to exceed my expectations." I hesitated, then asked, "Did you see Marcello at all today?"

"I visited him with Istrella. Her arm's doing better, by the way." Zaira swallowed a mouthful of cuttlefish. "I hate to say it, but he was almost as creepy with her as he was with you."

"How did Istrella take that?" The thought of a wounded Istrella facing her brother when something cold and cruel kept glancing out of his eyes twisted a tight knot under my breastbone.

"Well, she didn't notice at first. You know Istrella." Zaira licked jet-black ink off her lips. "But she caught on all at once, gave him a look like he was trying to sell her a batch of bad dream poppies, and said, 'You're not my brother.'"

That didn't help ease the snarl in my chest. Old Anzo came in with a glass of wine for Zaira and more for me. I took a long draft of the citrusy white before he left the room, and he returned without a word and filled my glass again.

"I can't imagine he liked that," I said when Old Anzo was gone.

"No, he didn't," Zaira said shortly. "We took Istrella home not long after that. I nearly punched him in the face for upsetting her, but I held back for you, in case you wanted him to stay pretty."

I leaned my elbows on the table and put my forehead in my hands. Nothing would make Marcello feel worse than upsetting his sister. "I shouldn't have left him there."

"Yeah, I know. I didn't like leaving Terika in Ruven's castle, either." Zaira stabbed her fork viciously into the black mess that remained of my dinner. "But Terika and Istrella were all right after Ruven got his claws into them, and he'll be all right, too. He's not as soft as he likes to think he is."

"I hope so." I had to tell myself I believed it. I had a job to do, and no idea where Marcello was or how to help him. *Focus on the problems you can solve.* Was it my mother who had told me that, long ago?

No, I realized. It had been the Marquise of Palova, of all people, bending over to help me when I'd knocked an entire tray of crostini onto the drawing room floor when my mother had had her over for drinks. My mother had added, lifting her glass, *And then find solutions for the ones you can't.*

"Yes," I said more firmly. "He'll be fine. I'll make sure of it."

"That's the spirit."

"How goes it at the Mews?" I asked, trying to wrench my thoughts away from what Marcello might be doing even now, and whether Ruven's orders would allow him to find a place to sleep.

Zaira grimaced. "It's empty as the Hell of Despair with everyone locked up in quarantine. At least now I can leave whenever I want to—though the colonel did make me bring about a dozen guards." She started counting on her fingers. "Terika's busy as a dockside barkeep trying to brew all the potions for the whole damned Empire while she's one of maybe three alchemists in the Mews not under Ruven's control. Istrella's making courier lamps day and night, with one good arm—that girl is unstoppable. Probably helps distract her from being upset about her brother. Aleki's all right, because at that age, I swear, a brat could get eaten by a lion and coughed up again, and they'd just toddle off causing mayhem like nothing happened. Foss is helping take care of all the brats in quarantine and leading them in little games and it's so sickening you might as well just swallow a cupful of sugar."

"How about you?" I asked, taking a closer look at Zaira. She couldn't have gotten much sleep; her dark eyes sat in hollows of exhaustion.

"Me?" she snorted. "I'm the only Falcon free of Ruven's control with nothing to do. Everyone else is working their arse raw, but I lounge around, waiting for someone to show up who needs to be on fire."

"You won't have to wait much longer," I said softly. "We're

not going to be able to talk our way out of using your fire in Ardence this time."

She let out a long breath, leaning back in her chair. "I know."

I waited, but she didn't say anything more. She didn't look away, either, not bothering to hide the trouble in her deep brown eyes.

"Will you be all right?" I asked quietly. "You don't have to do this, you know. The Falcon Reserve Act passed. You could quit active duty. They can't force you to use your fire—not anymore."

Zaira picked up a table knife and twirled it slowly between her fingers, watching the reflected gleam of the luminaries slide along it as it turned. "I've thought about it," she admitted. "I won't lie, I'm not pulling at the leash to become the monster Vaskandran parents use to keep their brats in line." She let out a humorless bark of a laugh. "Go to bed, or Zaira will burn you up."

I swallowed. "Well, in that case, I'm certain we can—"

"Oh, stow it." Zaira flipped the knife, catching it adeptly. "Of course I'll do it. I'm not going to leave the entire city of Ardence on a wet rock with the tide rising. I'm just..." She trailed off, scowling.

"Afraid?" I supplied quietly.

"Hells take you, Cornaro." She stabbed the knife into the satiny finish of our dinner table, leaving it quivering in front of her.

I winced. "I only meant—"

"Yes," she snapped. "Of course I'm afraid. I've spent my whole life keeping this demon locked in the cellar, while I stand on the trapdoor pretending everything is fine as it claws away beneath me." She shook her head. "And now you want me to let it out. Damned right, I'm scared."

"But you're always yourself again after." I reached out, plucked the knife from the table, and offered it back to her, handle first.

"Yes, when the fire comes upon you, you're like the Grace of Victory crossed with the Demon of Death. But then it fades, and you're Zaira again. The demon goes back in the cellar."

"So far." She stared at the knife for a moment, then took it from me and stabbed it right back into the table, with a grin that said, *What are you going to do about it?*

I tried again. "Suffice to say that if you ever need, well, a listening ear, or…" I trailed off, because Zaira's shoulders were shaking with silent laughter.

"Or what? A hug?" She shook her head. "I've got a dog for that. Come on, Cornaro, we both need sleep. We've got to get up at a rat's arse of an hour tomorrow."

The stars still shone hard and bright in the black velvet sky when my boat stopped at the Mews to collect Zaira and her baggage. Several of the Mews windows glowed with warm light despite the predawn hour, mostly concentrated in one wing where they'd warded the quarantined people. Lucia had brought me reports that with hundreds of Falcons compelled to seek a way to retake the Mews and their Falconers equally compelled to assist them rather than sealing them, the Mews had to be on constant high alert even with all the mages locked up in training rooms specially shielded to contain magic.

Zaira waited for me at the docks, rubbing her eyes and grumbling at the hour; Terika stood at her shoulder, wrapped in a warm shawl against the winter night. But the third person waiting for us surprised me, sitting perched on top of a massive trunk with the moonlight reflected in the artifice glasses pushed back into her hair.

"Istrella?" I asked, as Lucia handed me out of the boat. "What are you doing here?"

"I'm coming with you," she said, lifting her chin. "I volunteered to help defend Ardence, and the colonel agreed."

I stared at her in horror. "But we're going to *war*, Istrella. People are going to get killed."

"And Ardence needs better wards and weaponry." She started to cross her arms, the picture of determination, but then winced in pain and dropped the gesture. "It's not as if I'm going into battle. I'll stay in the garrison, away from any fighting. They need an artificer badly, and I'm one of the only ones available. And I even have experience with Ardence's defenses and have some ideas already about how to improve them."

I glanced at Zaira and Terika for support; Terika shook her head. "Don't look at me. I tried arguing with the colonel, but she says that we have to send *someone* to reinforce Ardence's defenses, and if Istrella wants to go..."

"I do." The stubbornness in Istrella's voice reminded me painfully of her brother. And that, in turn, made me suspicious.

"Istrella," I said slowly, "this decision to come with us wouldn't have anything to do with Marcello, would it?"

"No!" She grimaced. "Maybe. All right, yes." She held up the jess on her wrist, leaning forward so eagerly that I feared she'd fall off the trunk. "I can track him if I get close enough, because we're linked. And he's not in Raverra. I improvised a device to give me a longer range, and when I lost him, he was moving north."

"Toward Ardence." I chewed my lip. "I still don't think you should come with us, but I suppose I can't stop you."

"Hooray!" Istrella slid down off the trunk. "All right, let me get my things loaded." She waved some of the soldiers standing nearby to help her.

"Speaking of coming with you," Terika said, taking Zaira's hand.

"Oh, no." Zaira shook her head, curls flying. "Not a chance. You stay here this time."

"You're going to need me," Terika said quietly.

"No. Hells, no. I know what I'm going to have to do there, and I don't want you to see it."

Terika laid a tender hand on Zaira's cheek. "You know I don't care about that. I'm not going to stop loving you because you do what you must to protect a city full of innocent civilians."

Zaira didn't flinch away from her touch, as I half expected her to. She took up Terika's other hand in both of hers, staring intently into her eyes, mage mark to mage mark.

"I know," she said. "But you're the only person in the world who doesn't give a dry rat turd that I'm a fire warlock. The only damned soul who looks at me and never sees balefire."

"I'll always see you as yourself. Always."

"You don't know that," Zaira cut in, her voice intense. "You've never been around when I've let my fire all the way out, Terika. I become someone else, and I don't want you to ever meet that bitch. Even if you're deranged enough to still love me anyway."

Terika met her gaze for a long time. Then, finally, she laughed. "Nothing says romance quite like calling the woman you're courting deranged. All right, Zaira. I'll stay." She poked a finger at me. "But that means *you* have to take care of her. Do you hear me?"

"I'll do my best," I promised, not without some trepidation. Zaira snorted her contempt for the idea.

Terika ignored her. "Good." She pulled a small glass vial out of her pouch and handed it to me. "This is an experimental new reinvigoration elixir. It's meant to wake people up from sleep potion, but there's a chance it might work to temporarily revive a fire warlock who's collapsed from overexertion, as well. I've been thinking about that problem ever since your little jaunt into Vaskandar. If you find yourself in a situation where having to drag Zaira around unconscious could get you killed, it's worth a try."

"Thank you." My hand closed over the cool glass.

"Don't use it unless you have to," Terika warned. "If she's collapsed, it's because she's got no strength left. If you use this, it'll take her longer to recover." She patted Zaira's curls. "And you'll probably have a headache fit for the Nine Hells."

"Beats dying," Zaira said.

"That it does." I tucked the vial carefully into one of the compartments in my satchel.

Terika faced Zaira, hands on her hips. "Now, if I can't come with you," she said sternly, "you have to give me a decent good-bye."

"I think even a lout like me can manage that," Zaira said, her voice rougher than usual.

I turned to oversee the loading of the baggage into our boat before I caught more than the very beginning of their enthusiastic kiss, my face warming against the chilly air.

By the time everything was ready to go, a faint gray glow stained the edge of the eastern sky. Zaira and Terika still held each other close, as if even the light couldn't part them.

"Unfortunately, we've lost courier lamp communication with Greymarch, the major border fortress best situated to send forces to intercept Ruven's army," Lucia reported, referring to her little notebook as our coach shuddered along at a terrifying speed on the road to Ardence. "We've got a rider on the way there, but they won't be able to send help in time."

I tried to give her my focus as I clung white-knuckled to the bench, my bones jarring and rattling. I was sure our coachman was part demon. Outside, our horseback escort rode before and alongside us, clearing the way; even the orderly columns of troops and supplies making their slower journey to reinforce Ardence had to clear the way for the coach that carried Zaira's fire to the city's rescue.

"What forces can we get to Ardence before Ruven arrives?" I asked.

"There's some Callamornish cavalry that could beat him there, but other than that it looks as if we'll have little more than the six hundred soldiers and three Falcons already stationed at the Ardentine garrison."

"While Ruven's invading army numbers about four thousand, according to Kathe. And he has a far greater army poised at the border."

I touched the crinkly spot in my jacket where Kathe's most recent note rode, over my heart. The crow bearing it must have left Let before our conversation on the courier lamps. He'd sketched a tiny crow at the bottom, and it had lifted my spirits far more than it had any right to.

"Where's that stingroach getting all these people?" Zaira asked, frowning. "His domain didn't exactly look crowded to me. Unless you're counting angry trees in those numbers."

"Only a small fraction of the Empire's citizens are soldiers," I said, lurching sideways into Lucia as the carriage wheels slammed through a pothole. "Ruven's conscripted almost every able-bodied person in his domain into his army, because he doesn't care about maintaining a functioning society. And he can use his vivomancy to ensure they don't starve."

"Of course, that's not sustainable long term," Lucia said, and then flushed. "Er, if my lady wishes my opinion."

I straightened in my seat as if I'd heard distant horns. I knew that language. "No, that's quite all right. Are you a scholar, Lucia?"

"I studied briefly at the University of Calsida." Pride shone in her eyes.

Well, that would make this partnership a bit more interesting. "How did you wind up becoming my aide, if I might ask? I know Ciardha picked you, but what made you interested in the first place, if you started as a scholar?"

"My mentor encouraged me to go into politics, since I seemed set on changing the world." Lucia shrugged, grinning apologetically. "I like making things run more smoothly. But I can't get a seat on the Assembly; my parents are fisherfolk, not patricians. My mentor told me that there are plenty of government positions I could get on merit, but if I truly had the ambition to rise to the top level of imperial government as quickly as possible—well, she said it's personal aides like Ciardha who really run the Serene Empire." When she said Ciardha's name, her eyes went almost misty with worship. I exchanged glances with Zaira and bit back a laugh; after all, Ciardha was as nearly perfect a being as I had ever had the privilege to meet, so I could hardly criticize.

"Your mentor is wise," I said instead. "I'm glad to have you on my side, Lucia."

She beamed. "Thank you, my lady."

Zaira grunted agreement. "Damned right, we're glad. If we're outnumbered that badly, we're going to need all the help we can get."

That night, I woke in the darkness with the sure knowledge I wasn't alone.

Fear jolted through me like Jerith's lightning. For a moment of utter confusion, I forgot I was at an inn in Palova and not at home, and I couldn't understand why the moonlight wasn't hitting the walls in the right places. I groped under my pillow, grabbed my dagger, and lurched out of bed, half tangled in the bedclothes. I blinked the rest of the way awake, the room taking shape and sense around me, half expecting to find I'd startled myself with a coat draped over a chair back.

But no. Hells have mercy, there was someone there in the darkness, standing in front of my inn room window.

I drew in a breath to yell for my guards. But then I registered the achingly familiar silhouette framed by my starlit square of open window. The line of those shoulders, the curl of that hair.

Marcello.

Chapter Twenty-Three

Marcello?" I breathed.

He lifted a finger to his lips. With the light behind him, I couldn't see his face.

"Ruven doesn't know I'm here," he said.

I stood motionless except for the painful thunder of my heart, my nightdress swishing around my ankles. He backed up a step, the window curtains stirring in an icy breeze to briefly enfold him.

"Don't come any closer, and don't call for help." His voice carried a low, raw urgency. "I'm only barely keeping control. It gets worse if I'm startled or agitated."

I wanted to grab him and hang on to him, so he couldn't disappear again. But I didn't have the skills to subdue him. He was right there, *right there*, and I was going to lose him again in a minute. If he didn't kill me or kidnap me first.

"What did he do to you?" I demanded.

"I don't know." He shook his head vehemently, as if struggling to clear it. "Sometimes, I'm almost myself, like now. But then my thoughts twist up, and I get these horrible impulses, and it's like I'm someone else."

"Ruven?" I asked sharply. Anger and revulsion pulsed through me at the thought that he could be using Marcello like a puppet, as if this man I loved were nothing more than a convenient tool.

"No." He pushed his hair back from his forehead with both hands. It was a heartbreakingly familiar gesture; that was pure Marcello, when he was anxious or overwhelmed. "It's not someone else stepping in and taking over from outside. That's the worst part. It's me."

I'd heard of alchemical potions that could affect one's feelings and behavior, inducing rage or calm or trust. But I'd never heard of vivomancy having an effect like this. "We'll find a way to cure you," I said desperately. "We need to get you back to the Mews."

But Marcello shook his head. "Don't. That's why I came here—to warn you. Please don't try to save me, Amalia."

The words sent a chill of foreboding down my spine. "Of course I'm going to save you."

"He wants to use me against you." Marcello shuddered, half turning away. "That's why he did this to me. To kill the doge, yes, but also to get a hold over you. He wants your blood so badly."

My skin crawled as if a thousand invisible ants marched across it. Ruven had said it himself, in Lady Hortensia's garden: Marcello would be my motivation.

"That's why you have to forget me, Amalia." His voice dropped to a hoarse whisper. "I'm a trap."

"A trap that won't work." I took a step toward him, barely stopping myself from reaching out. I had to remember that he was dangerous, no matter how much habit and instinct told me he was the one and only person I could always and completely trust. "Ruven should know I'm not going to give in just because he threatens my friends. I've already shown I'll make sacrifices when I must." Like Roland.

Marcello went still. "Yes." He spoke carefully, exploring his words. "Yes, you have."

His voice had gone distant, almost cold, with an alien anger beneath it. A thrill of horror trickled down my back like winter rain off a palace roof. "Marcello..."

"Like you sacrificed me."

The words cut me like a whip. I flinched. But no—this wasn't him. My Marcello never lashed out at his friends in anger; he wouldn't say that.

Even if it was true.

"Marcello, stay with me," I urged him, seeking out the lines of his face in the darkness for some sign of the good man I knew. But the window behind him made his face a flat shadow, haloed by silver where the moonlight graced the waves of his hair.

"Oh, I'm not going anywhere." He stepped forward, narrowing the distance between us. "Like the loyal dog I've always been to you. I'll follow you wherever you go."

I was losing him to whatever Ruven had put inside him, watching him slip away.

"Don't you dare let him win like this," I urged. "Whatever is happening, you have to *fight* it, Marcello."

"I lost that fight already."

"No! You can still—"

"You should remember." His voice became almost caressing. "It was when you abandoned me when I needed you most."

His words blew through me like winter itself. "I..."

"When you left me alone as I could feel my own soul dying, something dark clawing its way into my mind, and I begged you to stay." He advanced another step toward me. "But you shut the door in my face. And I fought alone. And I *lost*, Amalia. Because you weren't there."

"I'm sorry." Tears stung my eyes. "I'm so sorry, Marcello."

"Then come with me," he said softly, and reached out his hand. "If you're truly sorry, you can prove it by staying with me now. I need you. Will you abandon me again?"

"No," I whispered.

"Then come." His hand hovered in the air, the same warm hand whose calluses I knew by touch.

Grief ripped through me in a flood tide. I couldn't make myself fool enough to take it, even when I yearned to. I shook my head, my throat burning too much to speak.

He grabbed my arm, yanking me toward him. "Come," he repeated. His fingers dug into my flesh, cold and strong as iron.

"No!" I shouted.

Down the hall, a door slammed.

Marcello hissed, releasing me. "She's here. I can feel her— *Istrella.*" His voice broke on her name, becoming human and familiar again, full of anguish. He turned and bolted for the window, quick as a shadow receding before a sudden light. My arm still tingled from his fierce grip.

The door flew open. Lucia stood there, daggers in both hands, her face cold and blank as death itself.

"Wait!" I blurted. "Don't kill him!"

Marcello leaped up into the window, framed in it for an instant like a crouching cat, and then he jumped down out of sight.

I ran to the window, my chest squeezing with dread at what I'd see; my room was on the second floor, and it was a long drop. But the street below was empty save for moon-washed cobblestones. He was gone.

"He's moving that way." Istrella pointed through the inn walls, still bleary-eyed in her nightgown. She'd come into my room shortly after Lucia, with Zaira close on her heels. "Very fast. He's fading—let me get my device." She ran from my room, bare feet pattering on the floorboards.

I stared off through the window into the smoky night air of Palova, as if my straining eyes could see through the buildings clustered over the cobbled streets and pick Marcello out of the myriad slinking shadows of the city. "Lucia, send searchers after him."

Lucia hesitated. "My lady, I don't want to leave you. I should have been here when he attacked—"

"It wasn't an attack." I struggled to slow my breathing to a more sedate pace. At the very least, it didn't start as an attack. I had to believe that. "I've got Zaira with me. I'll be fine. Send a search party."

"Yes, my lady." Lucia bowed and left. She wasn't good yet at keeping her doubts out of her voice when she disagreed with me; I supposed that was something it took time to learn.

Zaira peered out the window. "He jumped down from here? And he didn't break his legs?"

"It seems strange to me, too," I admitted. "Not to mention that he shouldn't have been able to get here by now on foot, even with a head start through the night. Ruven must be helping him somehow."

Zaira shook her head. "If Ruven can whisk him off like a gull with a stolen biscuit, your knife girl won't catch him. He's gone."

I leaned on the windowsill to ease my trembling legs. "He was here, Zaira. And I didn't save him." And now he was out in the night once more, alone with whatever demon Ruven had put inside him. "I can't abandon him again. I have to—"

"You have to leave this to other people," Zaira said bluntly. "You're on the Council now, remember? You don't get to go haring off into the night after the most obvious bait I've ever seen."

"But they're not going to find him. You just said as much."

Zaira nodded, her dark eyes somber in the starlight. "I did.

And he'd let *you* find him. And that's the whole pox-cursed problem."

All the rest of the night I paced before my window while my searchers combed the city of Palova, straining at every night sound like a dog hearing distant barking. Istrella had rushed back into my room with a disk a bit like a sound amplification circle pressed to her wrist over her jess, but could give us no better information than that he was still moving north at a fairly quick pace. I finally convinced her to go back to sleep, but couldn't do the same myself.

Ruven's words in the garden reverberated in my memory: *I need you to have motivation.* I felt extremely motivated. Motivated to find a way for Zaira to burn him to death, then jump up and down on his ashes before they blew away.

Marcello eluded my guards, just as Zaira had said he would. And come the first thin light of dawn, we were back in the coach, jarring along at our breakneck pace farther and farther from any hope of finding him. I couldn't bring myself to talk, and buried my face in a book even though I found it impossible to focus on the words. Istrella somehow managed to work on creating new courier lamps despite all the bumping and rattling and a wounded arm, her face set with grim concentration as she twisted wire around large chunks of quartz crystal. Zaira appointed herself the important task of testing out Lucia's capacity for off-color jokes; Lucia appeared well-equipped to handle incoming fire that left my own cheeks burning, but had few arrows in her own quiver to return—a lack Zaira was all too happy to remedy.

At our first post station stop to switch horses, however, Zaira pulled me aside and marched me to the lacy shade of a bare-branched tree, scowling as if she'd caught me pilfering her favorite sweets.

"What is it?" I asked, at a loss as to how I might have offended her.

"What did he say to you?" she demanded. "You've been mopey as a lovesick farm boy all morning. I was in fine scandalous form there—you should have been redder than a radish, and you couldn't even manage a decent shade of pink."

I opened my mouth to make some retort, then snapped it shut. She wasn't mocking me, for once; her dark eyes were clouded, not bright with laughter.

"The truth," I said reluctantly.

"Oh, that narrows it down." She put her hands on her hips. "I need you to be reliable on this trip, Cornaro. If that means talking about your feelings, I can suffer through it this once. Confess. What did he say?"

"That I abandoned him." I looked down at the scuffed toes of my boots—my most comfortable pair, for traveling, not the fashionable ones I wore around the city. "That I sacrificed him."

"And you believe that?"

"Yes." I met the fierce black rings of the mage mark in her eyes. "While my friend was struggling against a terrible enemy, I left him to his fate for the sake of politics and a good night's sleep."

Zaira blew air through her lips. "No, you stayed away because he was dangerous as a dog with the foaming sickness."

"I left him when he needed me." My voice had sharpened to a hair short of shouting. I took a deep breath and gentled it; Zaira deserved better. "And you know he would *never* have left me if our situations had been reversed. He was right. Whatever you call my reasons—for my own safety, for the Empire—I sacrificed him. Just like I did Ro . . ." My throat squeezed shut on Roland's name. Zaira watched me, frowning, and offered no help as I swallowed and tried again. "I can tell myself it's in the service of the Empire, or that it's my duty as one of the Council, but it's still my choice. This is what I'm becoming, Zaira. I don't think I would have done this a year ago." I wound my fingers in my hair and pulled as if I could somehow rein in the wild grief bubbling up in my chest. "I keep losing little pieces of myself. I'm afraid of what'll be left at the end."

"No," Zaira said flatly, "you're not losing pieces of yourself. You're throwing them away."

I stared at her, miserably unable to argue.

She jabbed my sternum with a sharp finger. "Ever since you erupted that volcano on your cousin, I've seen you wrap yourself in duty like a beggar's shroud. First the Falcon law—and I'm glad you passed it! But it's no excuse for not living your own damned life. Then the election, and now it'll be Council business. If you put on your duty like a mask, eventually that mask is going to become your face."

Her words slid between my ribs like an assassin's knife. I lifted my hands to my temples, almost surprised to find them soft and warm. "I don't want to forget how to be a person," I whispered.

"Then be one. People make mistakes." She shrugged. "They make a plague-rotten mess of things. Maybe you could have saved him, and maybe you couldn't have, but either way, it's done. All you can do now is try not to ruin everything next time."

I almost snapped at her that it was easy for her to say, since she'd never killed someone she loved. But then I remembered in a guilty rush that she had.

Up until less than a year ago, she'd killed *everyone* she'd ever loved, with the exception of her dog. And she was still the most human person I knew.

I let out a long, shaky breath. "Very well. You're right."

Zaira grinned. "As usual. Say it."

"Fine. As usual." I pulled my spine straight. "I suppose the Council of Nine could use another human on it, mistakes and all."

"Another?" Zaira snorted. "You give them too much credit." She glanced over toward our coach; they'd finished switching out our horses, and even changed a wheel. "Looks like they're waiting for us. Come on, High Lady Moodybritches, let's go."

After a long, miserable day's journey, at last we crested a hill and Ardence came into view.

The city embraced the river that ran through its heart, a thick sprawl of cheery red roofs and soaring temple spires standing out from the winter-brown fields around it. Snow dusted the hilltops surrounding the city, frosting the trees like sugar on a pastry, but the valley remained untouched. Smoke rose up from hundreds of chimneys, reaching toward the gray sky before dissipating into a thin haze. It should have been a cozy sight, a promise of mulled wine and well-stocked libraries and warm comfortable beds, with friends' smiling faces to greet us.

But far in the distance, up the river and over the hills, toward where the mountains lay invisible beyond the smothering clouds, hundreds of dark birds wheeled in the sky. From this distance, they were no more than tiny black specks, but to be visible at all from this far away they must be vultures and ravens, gathering for a great feast.

Ruven's army was coming. And it left a wake of death behind it.

By the number of chimneys still merrily puffing away, plenty of people remained in Ardence. Whether they'd stayed out of determination to fight or blithe unconcern about the army bearing down on them, now they were in harm's way. It was our task to make certain they didn't all become Ruven's puppets, and Ardence the newest outpost of his domain. I shivered to imagine the city grown through with twisting dark trees, chimeras and wolves roaming its streets.

"You know what would be nice?" Zaira said, staring out the window. "Visiting Ardence without worrying about setting thousands of people on fire."

"Perhaps in the spring," I suggested.

"It'll be good to see Domenic, though." She made an appreciative sound. "He's a fine piece of landscape."

"Does he know you're courting Terika now?" I asked.

"Sure. I've talked to him on the Mews courier lamps once or twice." She made a face. "Back when the Mews *had* courier lamps. Last I heard, he was entertaining some potential courtships, himself. He's got to make an heir, after all." Zaira waggled her eyebrows suggestively.

"Ah." My ears warmed. "I suppose he does."

Zaira grinned. "Don't you need to make one, too? Now that your mamma is the doge, you need a wee Cornaro lined up to take your precious council seat if someone pushes you into the lagoon."

I sank into my coat collar, wishing I could disappear. I could tell Istrella and Lucia were listening, though the former was pretending to focus on her courier lamp and the latter kept her gaze riveted out the window. "I'm certain if I perished tomorrow my mother would adopt whatever distant cousin she found most promising, to ensure a clear succession." Adopted heirs were common enough for patrician couples who couldn't otherwise have children, and my mother was too canny to allow a succession struggle in her own house. "But yes, certainly it would be more ideal for the Cornaro family and the serenity of the Empire if I, ah, produced an heir of my own." Which meant marriage. Which meant I had to think more seriously about where exactly I planned to take this courtship with Kathe.

"You can suck the fun out of *anything*, can't you?" Zaira observed dryly.

Lucia shot me a sympathetic but amused glance, then pointed out the window. "Look! The garrison."

As I leaned close enough to the window that I could feel the cold air pouring off the glass onto my burning face, I'd never liked Lucia more.

A black mourning flag flew over the imperial garrison, a sprawling fortress that perched on the last hill looming above Ardence. The full complement of the castle's officers turned out to meet us in the stable yard, rigid at attention, with black mourning bands on their uniform sleeves as well. I was startled to see such a formal welcome—it hadn't been like this when I visited last year—but then I remembered that receiving a member of the Council of Nine was an entirely different matter than receiving the Cornaro heir.

Once the initial formal reception relaxed, the garrison commander and a couple of his most senior officers lingered to speak with me as soldiers efficiently unloaded Istrella's belongings and cared for our horses. Istrella was already staring up at the runes warding the castle walls, hands on her hips and artifice glasses down over her eyes, clearly ready to make improvements.

"We're still not able to reach the Mews directly," the commander began delicately. "Should we expect more Falcons to reinforce us soon, or..."

"Not for a few days." I dropped my voice. "The entire Mews is still under quarantine."

The commander looked vaguely ill. "I see." He glanced over at Zaira, who was enthusiastically greeting a dog who'd gotten loose in the stable yard. "I've heard the stories about what fire warlocks can do, of course, but does Colonel Vasante truly think one warlock will be sufficient against an army?"

In theory, Zaira should be more than sufficient. Balefire grew and spread with every life it consumed, so the greater the numbers of the enemy she faced, the more powerful she became. But even killing a handful of opponents wrought a change in her, as the fire filled up her soul with a pitiless and terrible majesty, and left her shaken after. I had no idea what unleashing her balefire against an entire army would do to her, and seeing her unguarded grin as she scratched the dog's ruff pierced my heart.

"You won't ask that question again after you've seen balefire," I said quietly. "I just wish we didn't have to use it."

We couldn't stay at the garrison for long; the sun was already hanging low over the hills, and we needed to make it down to Ardence before dusk. After a brief discussion of strategy with the garrison commander, and a promise to communicate further via courier lamps, I pulled Istrella aside to say good-bye while Lucia traded information and discussed logistical details with the garrison officers.

"Will you be all right?" I asked, scanning her face anxiously. "I hate to leave you here alone."

"Oh, I won't be alone." Istrella gestured vaguely around the fortress, which swarmed with soldiers busily preparing for the approaching army. "Besides, they have a brand-new artificer! A family came here with their little girl this morning, after they heard about the new Falcon law. I think she's nine. Apparently they'd been hiding her, but now that they know she won't have to go to the Mews, they want to get her some training. She's adorable. I'm going to let her watch me work and answer questions!" Istrella bounced on her toes. "And I'm also going to go out tomorrow and lay down some trap circles in the fields north of the city, since they've evacuated those farms. I've never done those before!"

It was disconcerting to hear a fourteen-year-old girl so enthused at the idea of creating death traps that could kill or mangle dozens or hundreds of people. But I forced a smile. "Well, if you're sure you'll be fine."

She nodded enthusiastically. "I've got so much to do. It should be fun!" Her smile faded. "Assuming my brother doesn't remember he left my power unsealed and shut down my magic."

The wavering note in her voice went straight through my heart. I clasped Istrella's shoulders, trying to catch her eyes through the round red-and-green lenses of her artifice glasses. "Istrella, listen to me. Marcello may try to seek you out. If you see him—if he talks to you—well, while he's under Ruven's control, he's not himself. He's not safe."

"I know that." Her brows contracted. "I'm not stupid. I was controlled, too, remember? And you both kept trusting me, like idiots."

"I suppose we did."

"If I do the same thing, I forfeit the right to make fun of him about it forever." Istrella shook her head. The light caught her glasses just right, sparkling in a drop of moisture at the corner of her eye. "I'd never do something to risk that. Don't worry about me. You stay out of trouble yourself."

"I'll try, Istrella," I promised.

The edges of her smile trembled. "I hope he can come home soon."

I swallowed a sudden hard lump in my throat. Marcello should be here with his sister, to be her moral anchor while she was making these deadly weapons, and to be with her when she saw them in use for the first time.

"I hope he can, too."

Chapter Twenty-Four

A heavy complement of soldiers manned Ardence's gates, and cannons lined the walls. Its suddenly militant appearance made the familiar city strange to my eyes, but it was all the people leaving through the gates that tore at my heart. Families on foot carried belongings and children. Wagons overflowed with too many people trying to bring too much of their lives with them; a little boy perched on a pile of trunks dropped his doll in the gate and wailed anxiously until a guard ran after his wagon to hand it up to him. The sun would be setting soon, and it was too late to be only starting out; these people likely had nowhere to go. The soldiers asked everyone leaving if they had food and water, and gave them a loaf of bread or filled their flask for them if they didn't; I suspected that was Domenic's order.

"Not enough people are leaving," I murmured to Zaira as the soldiers cleared the departing crowd to the side so our carriage could pass through.

She stared at me. "What are you talking about? Hundreds of people are leaving."

"Ardence has a population of about sixty thousand," I said. "Hundreds are leaving, yes. But more are staying."

Zaira's chin jutted out. "We'll just have to make sure they're safe, then."

I'd known the people of Ardence were bold and resilient, but I was still shocked as our carriage rolled through the city to see people strolling the streets as if it were a normal day, to hear music and laughter coming out of taverns, and to see lights coming on one after another in window after window as dusk began to fall over the city.

"Do they even know there's an army coming for them?" I wondered, staring at a pair of children playing beneath the statue of the Grace of Victory fighting the gorgon.

"They're too used to being safe." Zaira shook her head. "People like that never believe they're in danger until it's too late. They're trusting the Empire to take care of them, like brats waiting for mamma to wipe their noses."

Right now, Zaira was all the Empire had to give them. I didn't say it aloud, but I could tell by the frown furrowing her brow that she was well aware of that.

"I wish they'd at least gotten all the brats out of the city," she muttered. And a minute later, when a dog trotted by, its nose down and tail up, on some serious canine business, Zaira groaned. "Not the dogs, too. Hells. I can't let Ruven get the dogs."

I refrained from any commentary on her priorities. If knowing there were innocent dogs in the city made it easier for her to do what she needed to do to protect Ardence, I wasn't about to argue.

It was strange, sitting down to drinks with a friend in a room where I'd seen a man murdered.

Domenic Bergandon, Duke of Ardence and my old university friend, had welcomed us into the lavish River Palace with all appropriate pomp and splendor; half the court and most of the ducal guard seemed to have turned out to greet us. But he whisked us off as soon as he could to receive us in his own apartments, where we could have a far friendlier and less formal greeting in private.

But the Hall of Victory was the most intimate audience chamber in ducal apartments too grand to offer such a mundane convenience as a sitting room, and Domenic might well not have asked when moving into his new residence in which room his predecessor had died. Given the effort he was putting into maintaining forced cheer as we sipped a fine full-bodied red wine and caught up on each other's lives, I thought it best not to mention this detail.

Domenic himself had changed in the months since we'd last seen him. Someone had trimmed his dark curls more evenly, and his cheekbones stood out sharply in his face, as if he hadn't quite been eating enough. He'd left off the ducal crown, but his doublet in the Ardentine style was of fine white brocade, with golden silk showing through the slashed sleeves. He wore no jewels save a flare locket and the ducal signet, and the rapier at his hip looked quite serviceable, but it was an outfit that made certain concessions to the sartorial glory expected of the ruler of Ardence.

It was half an hour before he finally mentioned the pressing crisis that brought us here. "...So the construction of the new canal locks on the River Arden has been proceeding marvelously, but I don't know what will happen with Ruven's army coming south alongside the river." He sighed heavily. "Do you think he'd sabotage the work we've done?"

"I doubt he'd take the time," I reassured him. "And if he intends to claim this land, he might want the river navigable, to more easily bring in supplies and reinforcements."

"Well, that's something, I suppose." Domenic took a long swallow of wine. "I've been thinking a lot about what might not survive, if he takes the city."

Zaira snorted. "Besides us, you mean?"

"Oh, believe me, the slaughter of the people who trust me to rule them is my first and foremost nightmare." He grimaced. "But you know Ardence. It's a city of art: sculptures and fountains, paintings and temples, hideously overwrought yet architecturally significant interiors." He lifted his near-empty glass to the dramatic fresco of the Grace of Victory on the ceiling, as if in a toast. "And let us not forget the books. We have two world-class libraries, here and at the university. Venasha will kill me if anything happens to a single volume. Even if I evacuate every single person from this city—and a great number of them wouldn't go, not to mention that we're out of time—what we stand to lose is staggering."

"Ruven wouldn't hurt the books," I said. "Not on purpose." But Domenic had studied history; he knew as well as I did that when a city fell to magic, damage was inevitable.

"I just wish more people would leave," he said. "But that's a hard decision to make so quickly—fleeing from your home, with only what belongings you can carry, without anywhere to go."

"Well, if it's any consolation, Ruven doesn't want to kill your people." I tried a hollow smile. "He wants to magically enslave them."

Domenic blinked at me. "That's not reassuring, Amalia."

"Sorry."

"I'm trying to be a good leader. To think of what needs to be done, and make sure it gets taken care of. It's difficult, because my nobles used to rely on Lady Savony for that sort of thing, and, well..."

"I killed her," Zaira supplied helpfully. "Lit her on fire."

"And she deserved it, mind you." Domenic poured himself more wine. "But I've only been doing this for a few months, and already it looks as if I may be the last Duke of Ardence. It's not the legacy I wanted to leave to history."

"History can take care of itself." Zaira put her boots up on the spotless lacquer of the beautifully inlaid table that held our crostini. "*We'll* take care of Ardence. Your city will be fine. I promise you."

His eyes lit like stars when they rested on her face. "Do you think you can save us, then? I'm told this Vaskandran army will get here before an imperial one can."

Zaira spread her arms. "I *am* an imperial army. And I'm right here, drinking your wine."

"Well, I'm glad it's a good vintage, then." He flashed her a brilliant smile.

As we crossed through the bustling Hall of Beauty on our way out—the glorious crossroads at the heart of the River Palace, connecting each of its grand wings—I heard a familiar voice echoing up to the frescoed ceiling.

"Please, be careful with that crate! It's got the only known copy of Muscati's *Theory of Light* and Kurahm's original handwritten draft of the *Saga of the Dark Days!*"

Lucia stiffened and lifted her head, turning toward the sound like a dog hearing the scrape of leftovers. That's right—she'd been a scholar, too.

"Isn't that Aleki's mamma?" Zaira asked.

"The very same. Venasha!" I spotted her hovering anxiously over a trio of servants carrying crates of books and hurried across the hall to meet her.

She smiled at the sight of me, but didn't lose her harried air. "Amalia! I'm so glad you're here. I'm at my wits' end. Did you see Foss and Aleki back in Raverra? Are they really all right? I've been so worried, but I can't leave—we've got to get the rarest of the books in the Ducal Library safely moved to the warded vault in the University of Ardence library before the army arrives, just in case. *Where do you think you're going?*" She hurried around to dance in front of a servant who hadn't stopped when Venasha did, and was still heading for the door. "Don't take that out of my sight! Look, why don't you put them down for a moment and rest. Gently, *gently!*"

The servants rolled their eyes. Lucia inched closer to the crates, trying to appear vigilant and attentive while also sneaking a quick peek at the books. Yes, I definitely liked her.

"Aleki and his papa are fine," Zaira said. "They're locked up behind a ward until that bastard's potion wears off, but they're fine. Foss told me to tell you not to worry."

Venasha sighed. "Of course he did. He'd say that if his arm was falling off."

Zaira shrugged. "It seemed pretty well attached to me."

"It's been like riding out storm swells in a rowboat for the past few days." Venasha moved her hand vigorously up and down to mime going over steep waves. "First we get news of the Falcon act. Hooray! We get to move back to Ardence as a family!" Her hand plunged over an invisible cliff. "Then rumors start flying around that there's been an attack on the Mews, and the courier lamps aren't working, and I have no idea if my baby is even alive." Her voice took on a strident edge as her hand swept up, then down again. "But then I hear that they're not hurt! But then there's an army marching on Ardence!"

"It's been an excessively interesting week," I agreed.

"I just want it to be over." Venasha tried a smile again, but couldn't quite pull it off. "I want these books to be safe so I can run to see my family. I want my family to be safe so we can be together without worrying. And I want my home to be safe so

I can bring them back here with me, and we can finally go back to simply living our lives again, like we did before Aleki's mage mark showed up."

I hugged her, and Venasha squeezed me so hard I thought she might rebreak the rib the Lady of Thorns had snapped two months ago. "We're working on it," I said, my throat thickening with a sudden swelling of desire to be with my own mother, to make sure she was resting enough to heal from her wound. "I hope to the Graces that soon you can do all of those things."

"You will," Zaira said fiercely. "I worked too hard to not have to burn this city down. I'll be damned if I'll let Ruven do it."

"Well, thank you." Venasha laughed. "And forgive me, but I'd better get these books to safety. There are two dozen more crates, and I have to supervise them very closely, because these manuscripts are irreplaceable."

"Lucia," I said, "can you help Venasha make certain all these books make it safely to the warded vault in the university library?"

Lucia's eyes lit up. But she hesitated. "I shouldn't leave your side, my lady."

"Nonsense," I said firmly. "Ciardha leaves my mother's side all the time, when my mother has important business for her to attend to. And what could be more important than this?"

"But if you're attacked while I'm gone—"

Zaira raised an eyebrow. "If something attacks us on the way to the Serene Envoy's palace that *I* can't handle, we have bigger problems than Amalia getting murdered."

"Consider it an order," I suggested, smiling.

Lucia bowed with even more than her usual enthusiasm. "Yes, my lady!"

I hugged Venasha again; we promised to see each other soon, and Zaira and I left her and Lucia to shepherding their precious charges to safety.

Zaira blew out a long, heartfelt breath as we headed toward the palace doors. "All this is killing me."

I offered her a sympathetic glance, dropping my voice. "Everyone counting on you to save them?"

"Every single person we see." Zaira looked around the hall and made a repulsed face. "I hate responsibility. How in the Nine Hells did this happen?"

I squeezed her hand briefly, her jess pressing cold against my wrist. "I suspect it's my fault. Sorry about that."

"Oh, stow it." She rolled her shoulders, eyes narrowing. "Someone's got to stand up to that bilge scum. And if that means I've got no choice but to be a hero, well, all I can say is they'd better build me a good-looking statue."

No quantity of cloud-light down or softness of silken sheets could lull me to a restful sleep that night. I must have dozed intermittently, but I also spent hours staring at the patterns of moonlight as they moved across the ceiling of my familiar guest room in the Serene Envoy's palace. Tomorrow or the next day, Ruven's army would arrive, and Zaira and I would face the reckoning of flame I'd dreaded since I first became her Falconer.

Worst of all, we'd have to face it without Marcello. I needed him here to pour out all my doubts about whether it was truly just to trade one set of lives for another, and my worries about what this would do to Zaira. I wanted to hear his sensible, heartfelt advice. I'd give so much to hold his hand right now, and draw strength from his quiet presence. But instead he was alone out in the darkness, with Ruven's power sunk deep in his mind, suffering in ways I couldn't begin to comprehend. And here I lay in a comfortable bed, one of the ten most powerful people in the Empire, powerless to save him.

I needed rest, to have the strength of mind to deal with everything I had to do. But with a hundred awful possible futures unfolding in the shadows behind my eyelids every time I closed them, rest eluded me.

It came almost as a relief when a soft knock sounded on my door, in the silent black hour before dawn when only the damned are awake.

"My lady," Lucia called, her voice tense and worried.

I sat up, alarmed. "Yes? What is it?"

"Duke Bergandon is asking for you and Lady Zaira, if you'll come to the north gate of the city. Something is stirring."

Hells. It was already beginning.

A fog lay across the valley, plunging the city streets into ghostly mystery and drowning the barren fields in a sea of cloud. Zaira, Lucia, and I stood at the northern parapets with Domenic in the first gray inklings of predawn, as the sky only began to remember what light was. The valley stretched north before us, hills rearing up on both sides, the River Arden half hidden by its blanket of fog. I could just make out the Raverran garrison on the crest of the closest hill, its blocky towers rising darker black against the deep velvet sky. Our breath misted in the air; I pulled my coat close around me and wished for a scarf.

"There," Domenic said, his voice low and troubled. He pointed across the valley to the far northern end. "His army is just beyond those hills. But that's not why I called you up here."

Domenic could laugh at almost anything; it was one of his finer qualities. But right now, nothing marked his face but worry. His finger drifted down the river to indicate a spot much closer to Ardence, along the riverbank not far from its walls. A line of cypress trees poked through the fog, sentinels marking the edge of a road, and a lonely light shone from the door lamp of a nearby house; a barn hulked behind it, a vague shape like a sleeping monster in the gray light.

"I don't see anything." I whispered, though I couldn't say why.

"Wait for the wind to stir the mist a bit. *There*."

I spotted them: a group of perhaps a dozen figures walking along the road toward the city, indistinct in the lingering darkness. Something about their purposeful tread carried an implicit threat, even at this distance.

"Demon piss," Zaira said, her voice low and troubled. "Only one kind of person walks up to a city like they were going to shove it down in the gutter and break its legs. I ought to know."

"Is that…" I couldn't bring myself to finish.

Domenic wordlessly handed me a spyglass, its brass bands carved with artifice runes. I lifted it to my eye and found that everything was not only closer, but somewhat lighter, and the fog less obscuring.

It was enough to allow me to make out the unmistakable pale features of the man in the lead of the group, his hair slicked back into a long ponytail, his dark coat stirring behind him as he walked.

"Ruven," I breathed. "This can't be good."

Chapter Twenty-Five

So you don't think Ruven is coming to parley?" Domenic asked, his voice stuck between hope and irony.

"If by 'parley' you mean 'spout arrogant bilge at us and make threats,' maybe, if we're lucky," Zaira said. "But I wouldn't count on it. If he wanted to do that, he'd have waited until it was light."

In the round window of the spyglass, Ruven suddenly stopped between a pair of olive trees. He reached out, a smile curving his lips, and laid a hand on each of them, closing his eyes.

"What's he doing?" Domenic asked nervously.

"I'm not sure." I swept the spyglass over the olive trees. They swayed slightly, but didn't seem to be doing anything particularly menacing. I trained it lower, and saw the ground buckling up under Ruven's feet.

I lowered the spyglass, frowning, and blinked in the poor light. Through eddying breaks in the fog, I could see the figures accompanying Ruven spread out, coming closer. The cypresses along the road shivered as if a wind passed through them, blowing toward the city.

But the wind was in the east. The ripple of motion was traveling the wrong way.

Hells. I knew what he was doing. "We need to get everyone down off this wall. Now."

Domenic's eyes widened. "The roots," he breathed. "But that'll take him hours—won't it? Can we drive him off or distract him before he undermines the walls?"

"It would normally take a vivomancer hours, yes. But Ruven is a Witch Lord." He wouldn't have to coax the energy the trees needed for rapid growth up from the soil; he could pour it into them from his own domain, with the power of millions of animal, plant, and human lives to draw on. "Order everyone off this wall, and out from under it!"

Domenic whirled to the officers standing nearby and began relaying commands. I peered over the edge of the wall, where a scattering of red-roofed houses spread out below.

The sign above a tavern door began swinging. A shutter banged. One house visibly dropped half a foot; tiles slid off its roof and smashed on the ground below. A dog started barking, frantically.

"Time to get off this wall now, my lady," Lucia said firmly.

"You're not joking." Zaira grabbed Domenic's hand. "Right, Mr. Important Duke, the view is nice up here, but let's go down. You're much prettier in one piece."

"You have a point," Domenic agreed.

We hurried to the narrow stone steps that descended along the inside of the wall from the parapet. Yelling and clamor rose all around us as the guardhouses above the river and flanking the gate emptied, disgorging musketeers in Ardentine uniforms who also ran for the nearest stairs. Some carried lamps that cast their shadows vast and flaring against the bricks; shouldered muskets waved an alarm against the fading stars.

I galloped down the steps behind Zaira and Domenic, sliding a tingling palm along the wall for balance, sure I was going to pitch headfirst to the bottom at this pace. A shudder passed through the bricks beneath my fingertips, and my heart skipped in my chest.

Then my boots touched the hard cobbles. We ran clear of the steps, all the way to a fountain with a statue of the Grace of Bounty that centered the plaza before the gate. As we heaved cloud-puffed breaths of cold air, soldiers spilled down the stairs and into the streets, their shouts breaking the predawn stillness asunder. Lights glimmered awake through the haze of fog. My nerves jangled like cut lute strings.

"Evacuate any houses built up against the northern wall," Domenic called, his voice ringing out hoarse but commanding across the square. "Check to make sure no one is still sleeping inside." His soldiers saluted and hurried to obey. People began tumbling out into the streets in their nightgowns, some of them clutching crying children.

"Are we far enough back, my lady?" Lucia asked, eyeing the great arch of the northern gate. It stood closed, with new-timbered gates built when the threat from the north became clear; as I hesitated, estimating distances, a faint muffled crash sounded from beyond.

With a groaning creak, the gates shifted on their massive hinges. The paving stones of the plaza buckled up in places, and mortar crumbled down from the wall in a fine rain.

"Maybe not." Domenic's voice came out higher than I'd ever heard it.

"Graces preserve us, it's coming down!" Panic flooded my limbs with wild energy; screams rose up around the square, and we all turned and ran. My heart lurched at the thought of all the soldiers still moving beneath it, knocking on doors, dragging people out of their beds.

A great rumbling shook the ground beneath our feet, jarring up through our legs. Zaira swore. I stumbled, my feet jerked out from under me; Lucia reached to steady me, but staggered.

I caught myself on the cobbles with stinging palms as the rumbling grew to a terrifying, rolling crash, like thunder that didn't end. A cloud of dust blew over us on a sudden wind.

I scrambled to my feet with Lucia's help and turned to stare, horror rising like bile in my throat.

Brick and stone tumbled down in a cascading torrent of rubble. The great gates lay smashed into kindling, buried in a pile of wreckage; pebbles and bricks skittered across the plaza before coming to rest. The fountain we'd stood beside was smashed to pieces, the trunk of the statue sticking up akilter from the rubble. Screams and sobs lifted in the fog and dust that choked the air.

"Oh, Hells," Domenic moaned, bringing his hands to his mouth. "There've got to be people trapped under there. We have to help them." He started unhesitatingly toward the shattered wall, even as shards of brick continued to clatter down the unstable pile. Zaira and I exchanged wide-eyed glances.

"Your Grace..." Lucia began.

A handful of figures came bounding over the ruins, black cloaks flowing behind them, bricks cracking and tumbling under their feet. Even through the fog, I could tell they moved too fast, their limbs bending in not-quite-right ways, their eyes catching the light like a cat's or gleaming in the wrong places.

Holy Hells. Chimeras.

They spotted Domenic's bright white-and-gold doublet and headed directly for him.

"*Exsolvo!*" I cried, even as Zaira grabbed Domenic by the belt and jerked him to a halt.

Lucia stepped in front of me, drawing her daggers. Several Ardentine soldiers threw themselves between us and the chimeras, blocking Zaira's clear line on them. She hissed with frustration. A shot split the air, then another, and puffs of smoke rose from the soldiers' muskets to merge with the fog.

If they hit, the chimeras didn't much care. They tore into the guards like cats onto mice. I recoiled, my stomach turning at the splashes of scarlet and the anguished screams. *No. Not this again. Please.*

Domenic cried out in anger and drew his rapier, but Zaira hadn't let go of his belt.

"Don't be an idiot! It's you they're after," she shouted. "Don't give Ruven what he wants!"

He gave in to her tugging. We ran from the plaza, a few soldiers rallying to us as we fled to guard our rear. Lucia's face had gone pale as cream; whether she'd seen death before or not, this had to be her first experience with chimeras. But she kept her daggers out and ready and ran with graceful efficiency, her mouth in a grim line.

"What kind of duke am I, if I'm fleeing when my people need me?" Domenic demanded on ragged breaths, bitter anguish twisting his face.

"A live one," Zaira replied roughly. "You can't help anyone if you're dead."

The fog muffled everything in shades of gray, making it impossible to see more than fifty feet in front of us; I struggled to recognize the hazy buildings looming around us with darkened windows and night-doused lights. A shape lurched out of the fog, and one of the soldiers almost shot at it before realizing it was an old woman.

"Careful," Domenic warned, as she ducked away, eyes wide.

But then another cloaked shape formed out of the fog, and the nearest soldier hesitated just long enough for it to lunge in like a striking snake and rip her throat out with inch-long claws.

I couldn't stifle a shriek. The young soldier gurgled horribly, her throat a red gaping ruin, and tumbled to the ground as the chimera moved to the next one. The guard got off a clean shot to its chest, but it didn't matter; it knocked her to the ground and pulled back a claw to deliver a fatal blow.

The fog lit up blue. Zaira stood with one hand extended, pale flames fluttering on her fingertips like leaves in the wind, as the entire top half of the chimera burst into fire.

It fell off the downed soldier, writhing, emitting a terrible screeching sound; a tail lashed the paving stones, flailing free from under its cloak. Everyone scrambled away from it except Zaira, who stood staring at the creature impassively as it burned.

"Grace of Mercy," Lucia whispered, her wide eyes reflecting bright blue sparks of balefire.

I watched Zaira's face, tense, waiting for her expression to go remote as a statue and the leaping flames to spread out of control. But only the chimera glowed with the wicked blue light, until in a matter of mere seconds the screaming stopped and the writhing stilled. The sickening scent of burned meat clung to the misty air.

The flames winked out, as if they'd never been. A charred and twisted thing lay on the cobbles, all blackened bones and ashes. Zaira turned her back on it, jaw tight. "Come on."

Domenic stared at her in awe. The two remaining soldiers gave her a certain space as we started forward again.

I was mustering the calm to compliment her on her control when one of our guards stumbled, choking.

Everything seemed to slow down. As I turned, far too slowly, panic rising up in me like an indrawn breath, a dark cloak whipped past my face. Lucia slashed at it, her knife catching nothing. Then the last remaining soldier fell against me, knocking me into Domenic.

A wet warmth soaked my coat as I grappled with the loose weight slumping on me, a scream building and building in the back of my throat. *Dead.* The two soldiers were both dead, or dying, in the space of a few rapid beats of my terrified heart.

An inhuman face loomed before mine, slick white with gaping black eyes like a skull. I couldn't move quickly enough, still grappling with the body in my arms. It was too close, and I was going to die.

Something metallic clinked on the ground. And then the chimera staggered sideways, blood flowing from its mouth, as Lucia pulled her daggers from its chest and kicked it aside.

Domenic and Zaira stepped up beside me, the former with his sword out and the latter with her hands raised and threateningly empty, as the dead soldier slid down out of my grasp to lie in his blood in the street. I gripped my flare locket and drew my dagger, pulse shooting through my veins like lightning. The four of us fell into a loose arc facing the wounded chimera and a second one that emerged, its joints making insectile clicks, from a mist-shrouded alley.

But something was wrong. A faint ruddy light teased my eyes from below, and my balance felt off.

I glanced down and found an artifice circle glowing on the ground around my feet.

How the Hells did that happen? But a rune-marked ring lay on the cobbles beside my shoe, similar to the ones Istrella had made for me.

"My lady?" Lucia asked sharply.

I tried lifting my feet, but they wouldn't budge. "I'm trapped," I said, my voice coming out thin and uneven. Despite the fear trembling in my legs as the chimeras circled us, my mind couldn't stop working. Ruven shouldn't have artifice rings like that. Certainly not enough of them to equip random chimeras, anyway.

"Then we'll have to protect you until it wears off," Lucia said, raising her bloody daggers in a guard position. Zaira's fingertips kindled. Domenic pointed his rapier at the chest of the unwounded chimera; it hissed, forked tongue flicking, and drew a sword of its own to face him.

Then the wounded chimera moved, so quickly I could have

blinked and missed it. Domenic seemed ready for its attack, and slashed a deep cut across its skull-like face with his off-hand dagger. But it still closed with him in a swirl of black cloak and darted out again, blood dripping down its face. Domenic's rapier clattered to the ground; he clutched a bleeding thigh, crying out in pain.

The chimera lunged at him again, bloody claws slashing; I closed my eyes and flipped open my flare locket, pushing it at the creature with enough panicked force that the chain dug sharply into my neck. An intense flash reddened my eyelids, and the chimeras hissed in protest.

I opened my eyes to find them staggering back, clutching at their inhuman black orbs. Domenic and Lucia blinked fiercely, blinded; but Zaira, who knew me well, lowered a protective arm from her face. Her dark eyes gleamed clear and sharp as a spark of fire kindled in them.

Balefire furled out from her fingers like a snapping blue sail, catching both chimeras. They shrieked as flames enfolded them, alien faces stretching in agony. I winced away from the searing heat and the scent of burning flesh. Graces help them, they'd been human once, and I could still hear traces of it in their voices.

Zaira made a slicing motion, and the flames winked out, the harsh blue light gone from the foggy air. It had been enough; the chimeras collapsed, smoke rising from their fire-ravaged bodies. Her breath came quickly, as if she'd been running, and her eyes were strained around the edges, but she stood poised and ready to do it again.

But no more chimeras appeared. Silence fell, save for our uneven breathing and the distant cries of distress still coming from the gate. The fog closed around us in a smothering cloud.

I didn't dare admit the barest spring tendril of relief. I licked dry lips, staring around in the deep gray twilight at the looming shadows of buildings and the damp gleam of cobblestones, surrounded by bodies and the scent of burning. Too many of Ruven's chimeras had already found us; they had to be tracking and targeting Domenic specifically, which meant more would come.

Domenic still clutched his bloody leg, making no move to pick up his sword. "I think," he said, his voice alarmingly vague, "I think I feel a bit strange."

He fell to one knee, listing like a broken ship. Zaira swore and dropped to his side. "Let me see that leg."

I strained against the circle that held me locked to the bloody street. "Grace of Mercy. Its claws could be venomous."

Zaira's breath hissed through her teeth. "Oh, that is *not* a good color. What do I do, Cornaro? Suck this demon's piss out of the wound?"

"No! Don't touch it." I tried to pull my foot from my boot, but it wouldn't budge; the magical force ran through the soles of my feet and up my legs. "Zaira, Lucia, quickly! My satchel is back in my bedroom at the Serene Envoy's palace. I have a vial of Ferroli's Tincture of Purity in there—it's bright blue and smells of lemons. It'll cure him. Just don't give him my elixir by mistake, and hurry! *Go!*"

"Right," Zaira said, and hauled Domenic to his feet, pulling his arm over her shoulder.

Lucia, however, shook her head. "I can't leave you, my lady."

"This should fade in a few minutes." I waved a frustrated hand at the circle around my feet. Zaira wasn't waiting, thank goodness, moving off as quickly as Domenic could limp. "It doesn't have a good power source. I can catch up; Domenic's the one they're after."

"*We* can catch up," Lucia said firmly. "It's my duty to stay by your side in a dangerous situation like this. Lady Zaira, protect His Grace! We'll come after you in a minute."

"Got him," Zaira confirmed, already fading into the fog. "Don't die, Cornaro."

"Grace of Luck be with you!" I called.

Then I was alone with Lucia and a handful of bodies in the gray predawn light. The buildings around us were mostly workshops, their windows black and empty; the street lay cold and deserted as a dream from which the sleeper has awakened, fog softening the angles of the brick and plaster walls around us. My heart began to slow down at last as eerie silence fell over the city.

Lucia let out a trembling breath. "That was a lot different than the bodyguarding I did as an apprentice," she admitted.

"More chimeras?" I asked sympathetically.

"More everything." She rolled her shoulders uncomfortably. "I stopped an assassin, once. He had a knife, like a sensible Raverran. Nobody trained me for—"

A gunshot called sharp echoes from the walls, and Lucia staggered.

"Lucia!" I screamed.

She seized my arm, but there was no strength in her grip. "My lady," she wheezed, blood bubbling on her lips. "Get... down..."

She sagged to the ground beside the dead soldier, her knives clattering on the cobbles. Blood stained the edges of a small round hole in her coat, over her chest.

I dropped to my knees beside her, barely aware that for me to do so the binding circle must have faded. She dragged in desperate, shallow breaths, her eyes glassy and distant. Graces help me, she was dying, and I didn't have my satchel, and it came crashing down on me like the crumbling north wall that I wasn't a physician and had absolutely no idea what to do.

Boots sounded on stone behind me, hard and slow and echoing. And then a sleek, cultured voice, awful in its familiarity.

"Now, that's much better. I do wish to talk privately, after all."

I rose and turned, covered in other people's blood, to face him.

A tall shape emerged from the fog, stepping into the gradually warming light of dawn. His high-collared black coat swirled around his ankles, and his blond ponytail hung over one shoulder. The mage mark gleamed violet in his narrowed eyes.

"Ruven," I growled. "I don't have time to talk to you right now."

"Because of your friend?" He glanced at Lucia and laughed. "She has life in her yet. She'll last through our little chat, I promise."

I lifted a hand to my flare locket. "Why should I talk to you, after you shot my aide?" I forced confidence into my voice. I couldn't show any sign of the frost that spread in lacy crystals through my veins. Ruven was like a vicious dog; if he scented fear, he would attack without mercy.

Ruven's smile broadened. "Why, because I'll only guarantee her survival for as long as we talk. And because when last we met, we never finished our negotiation."

He beckoned toward an alley behind him, without looking.

From it stepped another figure, blurred by the mist. But I would know that shape anywhere. The broad shoulders, the wavy dark hair, the rapier and pistol slung at his side.

Marcello.

He stopped behind Ruven, his head hanging, shoulders hunched, clearly struggling to disobey. Fury swelled in my chest until I felt as if I could unleash balefire myself.

"If you think I'll do your bidding because you shoot and poison my friends—"

"Ah, but I never poisoned Captain Verdi." Ruven spread pale fingers on his chest, all innocence.

"What did you do to him, then?" I demanded, taking a step forward, my hands squeezing into fists.

"Do you wish to know?" Ruven asked, smile broadening.

Of course I did. But my throat locked against the words with sudden dread at the terrible glee in Ruven's eyes.

"Show her, Captain Verdi," Ruven said softly, his eyes never leaving mine. "Don't be shy. Come closer, and let her see."

Dragging as if he struggled against iron chains, Marcello took one step forward, then another.

I didn't want to see, after all. I didn't want to know. But I couldn't help staring anyway, paralyzed with dread, as he advanced toward me, the fog thinning between us.

The growing light picked out the bloodstains that still marked the uniform he'd been wearing when he murdered the doge. One hand clenched his belt, white-knuckled; the other still held the smoking pistol with which he'd shot Lucia. Droplets of mist glimmered in his raven-black hair.

"Look at her," Ruven whispered, his voice a razor's caress.

Marcello lifted his face to me.

One eye was the same as always, green and human and harrowed with pain. The other blazed orange, with a slit pupil like a lizard's. Silvery scales surrounded it, covering half his brow and continuing in a sweeping path down his cheek and neck before disappearing into his uniform collar.

No. Oh, Marcello, no. His name turned to dust in my throat.

Ruven had turned him into a chimera.

Chapter Twenty-Six

Despite the crushing pressure in my chest that drove the breath from me, no trembling shook my legs. The fury that flooded me like hot magma rising in a volcano's heart held me up.

"You…" Words were my primary weapon, but my quiver was empty. No one had created words to express what I needed to say. I stepped forward, not sure if I was advancing to seize Marcello away from him or to attempt to strangle Ruven with my bare hands.

"I'm sorry." Marcello turned his face away, hiding the inhuman side.

"You have nothing to be sorry about." I wanted to touch his cheek, to let him know I meant it, but there was no gentleness in me right now.

"Didn't he turn out beautifully?" Ruven surveyed Marcello proudly. "He's my first attempt at crafting a chimera without being physically present. Well, without more than a tiny piece of me being present, at least."

A tiny piece of me. My stomach twisted as memories connected in a horrifying cascade: Ruven pulling his bloody hand back from Marcello's broken collarbone on the Night of Masks. Marcello claiming he could feel bone shards grating in his shoulder on the boat ride to the Mews. The waves of swarming pain

Marcello had attributed to his healing potions. "You left a fragment of your own bone in his shoulder," I realized with horror. "So you could use your magic on him from afar."

"See, this is why I admire you so, Lady Amalia! It took me weeks to come up with the idea, but you understand it immediately." Ruven beamed at me, as if I were a clever student. "A finger bone, in fact, which I regrew at once. I wasn't certain it would work; even a Witch Lord can't reshape a creature on such a fundamental level without, shall we say, a certain personal touch, requiring us to be physically present. But it was quite effective!" Marcello squeezed his eyes shut as if in pain; Ruven laughed. "But making a chimera takes time, so I had to change him slowly, piece by piece. The subtle things first, to avoid tipping my hand: strength, speed, resilience. I left his personality alone and didn't attempt to give him any commands, so you wouldn't realize what was happening. Your pet here was already halfway a chimera for days before I took control of him, and you didn't even notice."

This was what I had let happen, when I walked out of the room as he begged me to stay. I'd abandoned him to suffer alone as Ruven stripped his very humanity from him. The knowledge burned like a bucket of coals in my stomach.

"We'll fix you," I told Marcello, ignoring Ruven, my voice rough with emotion. "We'll find a way to change you back."

"There is no going back." Marcello turned his fiery orange eye on me. "This is what I am now, Amalia. A monster."

"Indeed." Ruven rubbed his hands. "Shall we illustrate the point? Break something, Captain Verdi. Perhaps her fingers, so she can't use any of her clever little artifice devices."

Oh, Hells.

Marcello hesitated only a fraction of a second before stepping toward me. I backed away from him, stumbling over a soldier's body, panicky energy coursing down my limbs.

Lucia stirred suddenly, hauling herself to her knees as blood trickled from her mouth. "Run...my lady."

"Stay down, Lucia," I called, my heart leaping painfully. Her chances of survival were much lower if she attracted Ruven's attention. "Stay out of this."

Marcello paused, half turning toward Lucia. Ruven's eyes flicked to her, narrowing with annoyance. "How rude you are, to interrupt us."

Lucia's hand dipped into her coat and came out with a slim flint-lock pistol with an engraved silver barrel. "I'll...hold them..."

A resounding crack split the air. Ruven flicked his head as if attempting to avoid an insect; for one brief instant, a red hole appeared in his throat, but it closed almost immediately. By the time the sharp scent of gunpowder reached me, the battered and bloody shot clinked on the cobblestones, and there was no sign Ruven had ever been wounded.

"Now, now. This interference is intolerable." Ruven advanced on Lucia, who dropped her spent pistol and reached, swaying, for a knife.

"You promised she'd live through our talk," I reminded him sharply. *Graces, please, don't let another person die for me.*

Ruven sighed. "You're right, I did."

He reached out and touched Lucia's hair, gentle as a benediction, ignoring the dagger she swung at him; she collapsed limply to the cobbles, the knife clattering free.

"There." He turned back to face me, with all the forced calm of a performer still frustrated after a disruptive heckler has been removed from the theater. "I can't have you distracted, so now she will both sleep *and* survive for at least an hour—so long as you give me your complete attention, Lady Amalia."

He gestured with polite grace to Marcello, his lips curving into a smile. My gaze pulled against my will to the silver scales gleaming down the haunted lines of his face.

"Carry on, Captain Verdi," Ruven said softly.

Marcello took another step closer to me. My pulse raced painfully through my veins. I couldn't read his face; his human expression was guarded, and his slit eye stared with pure animal madness.

"The Marcello I know would never hurt me," I said, trying to sound confident.

His lip curled. "The Marcello you knew is dead."

I shook my head, clutching instinctively at my flare locket; my fingers found Kathe's necklace instead. "I refuse to believe that."

"You're a scholar. You shouldn't let what you want to believe get in the way of what you know to be true." Marcello's voice was raw with anger. "I've learned that lesson now. I was naïve, Amalia. I believed that the Mews was a good place. That the Empire wanted the best for its Falcons. And I believed in you."

There was a glimmer of the real Marcello there, under that pain. I had to reach him, somehow—to draw him out before he slipped away forever. "You see the good in things. That's different than being naïve." The claws at my throat bit into my palm. "It's one of the things I—I admire about you." There was no way in the Nine Hells I was going to tell him I loved him for the first time now, like this, in front of Ruven.

Marcello advanced another step, his orange eye and the green one both fixed on me. "You still can't say it, can you?" He was too close, his words dropping low enough that only I would hear, but I didn't back away. "I can. Fear is another thing he killed in me."

"Marcello," I whispered, my eyes stinging. "Don't do this."

"I love you, Amalia. Even now." He reached out and gently slid his fingers through a dangling lock of my hair. "I don't think I could bring myself to kill you."

Something prickled my neck. His nails formed curved claws,

like a cat's. I jerked my head away in horror, leaving a strand of hair hooked in his grasp.

Marcello's eyes narrowed. "But oh, I think I can hurt you."

He moved so quickly I had no chance to react, seizing both my forearms. I tried to twist away, but his claws pierced deep into my arms, hooking into my flesh. I shrieked, as much in shock as in pain.

Marcello flinched at the sound, but didn't let go. All the gentleness I loved in him was gone from his silver-scribed face. His green eye stared into mine with pleading despair, just as it had before the door closed between us; the slit in his orange eye narrowed to a bare slash. For a moment, I thought the Graces might have mercy on me, and my heart would actually burst from pure anguish, and I would die.

But I was still trapped here, catching my breath in a great ragged gulp like a sob, Marcello's claws hooked into my arms. He gritted his teeth and twisted them deeper, trembling as if he could feel the pain in his own flesh. Ruven watched from a few paces behind his shoulder, smiling with delight.

I had to think of some way out of this, for Marcello and Lucia as much as myself. I tore my eyes away from Marcello's and caught Ruven's instead.

"I thought you wanted to talk," I gasped through the pain. "Are you a liar, then?"

Ruven's eyes narrowed, and he lifted a lazy hand. The claws retracted from my arms. Marcello backed away, his hands bloody and trembling.

"Far from it," Ruven said. "I merely wished to show you what is at stake in our conversation." He rested a hand lightly on Marcello's shoulder, the same one he'd left a bone shard in; Marcello shuddered.

I folded my bleeding forearms tight against my chest in an effort to subtly put pressure on the wounds. I didn't dare look at Marcello's face, or I would fall apart; I couldn't let Ruven see how much he'd gotten to me, or how much it hurt.

"If this is still about your supposed desire for an alliance," I said shakily, "your tactics are far from convincing."

"But I have so much to offer you!" Ruven spread his hands. "I am the only one who can restore Captain Verdi to his former state. Or a close approximation of it, at least; sometimes one does find it difficult to get the small details right."

Marcello's jaw clenched, and the claws in his fingertips flexed and retracted. Whatever changes Ruven had wrought in him, he still held no love for his new master.

"In return for what?" I asked, struggling to keep my voice controlled and neutral.

"You know what I want." He extended a hand. "Come to Kazerath with me. Use your knowledge, your imperial power, and your blood to help me lay down my mark upon the land and claim all of Vaskandar, one piece at a time."

"While you invade my country?"

"Of course not!" Ruven affected shock. "I would withdraw my troops at once. Even with your help, it will take sufficient effort to conquer Vaskandar that the Empire can consider itself safe for quite some time—from not only myself, but *any* Witch Lords. And after that, well, if Raverra does not attack me, what quarrel could I possibly have with it?"

In the gray shroud of fog, with the cold reaching through my bloody coat to pierce my bones—with weeping holes in my arms, and Lucia badly wounded on the ground, and Marcello suffering before me—it was almost tempting. I could almost make myself believe that all I would sacrifice was myself. My own life would be miserable, certainly, living in Ruven's thrall and bleeding for his enchantments, but I could save the Empire and Marcello both.

Ruven saw my hesitation. He stepped forward, his violet-ringed eyes lighting eagerly. "Well? Is it not a fine offer? You can save thousands of lives, and your dear captain, too. I'll even heal your guard here, since you seem concerned for her life."

But it wasn't so simple. My mind was full of the Empire's secrets, which Ruven must not learn. My mother was the doge now, and I was on the Council; power over me meant power over Raverra. And if my blood truly could unlock Vaskandar for him to claim, that would make him so powerful that not all the might of the Serene Empire could stand against him.

"I am a member of the Council of Nine," I said slowly. "My life is not my own to give away. And my service belongs to the Serene Empire alone."

Ruven clicked his tongue reprovingly. "Don't be so hasty, Lady Amalia. If you fail to give my offer due consideration, there will be consequences."

He snapped his fingers, and Marcello doubled over with a muffled cry. His uniform doublet rippled as if impossible movement scurried beneath it.

"Stop," I called sharply, barely catching myself from reaching out to him. *Don't show weakness. Don't let him see it's working.* "I'm merely pointing out the difficulties. Only a fool jumps into an alliance without taking time to think."

Ruven's eyes gleamed with satisfaction. He made a brushing movement in the air with one lazy hand, and Marcello went still, then slowly straightened. I forced myself not to look at him; I had to keep the appearance of control, and if I saw his eyes, I couldn't.

Shouting rose up in the distance, coming nearer—not the panicked cries of earlier, but the more disciplined calls of a trained military force approaching. It sounded as if the Ardentine forces had regained control.

"Take your time to think, then, if you must," Ruven said. He crooked a finger at Marcello, who turned, his shoulders rigid, and began walking away. "In fact, I want you to think about my offer every single day." Ruven relished the words on his tongue, lingering over them. "But don't take *too* long to consider, or I'll change him further and further. He might look nice with spikes growing from his back, don't you think? Or perhaps a few more arms?"

I couldn't keep the twist of revulsion and fury from my face. "Don't you dare."

"But I'll leave the one human eye," Ruven said thoughtfully. "Even when the rest of him is changed beyond all recognition, he'll always keep that one green eye, so you can still know him, and witness the moment his mind is lost to madness."

"You are a vile piece of work," I said, contempt dripping from my voice.

Ruven nodded graciously, as if acknowledging a compliment. "I'll see you again soon, Lady Amalia Cornaro."

And as the shouts and running steps of Ardentine soldiers approached, he turned and disappeared with Marcello into the fog.

Chapter Twenty-Seven

"Curse it, we shouldn't have left you," Domenic grumbled.

He reclined on a gilt-embellished divan in the Blue Room in the Serene Envoy's palace, his leg propped on a velvet cushion. Shadows beneath his eyes and sweat beading his temples suggested that a mere hour hadn't been enough to recover fully from the chimera's venom, but it was good to see him alert and out of danger, at least.

I tried to focus on that. I could feel everything that was terrible waiting like the Demon of Madness, hovering with a thousand claws and teeth to fall on me and rend me to pieces. I had to fix myself on the few good things, with all the vigilance of a traveler in a vast winter wood keeping one spark going to light a fire.

"Nonsense," I said, more curtly than I'd intended. "If you'd stayed with me, you'd be dead."

"I can vouch for that," Zaira agreed from her protective perch on the divan's arm, above Domenic's head. "I thought I was dragging a dead body for a minute there. A heavy dead body." She shook out her wiry arms.

"But Lucia could still die," Domenic said, his face grave. "I don't like the idea of trading her life for mine."

"Neither do I." I rose from my own seat and started pacing,

my bandaged, aching arms crossed on my chest. I couldn't stand being still; I had to be doing something, *anything*. "The physicians seem to feel they can save her, however, and you would certainly have died without the tincture. We can't change the past. The question is what we can do now to salvage the future."

Domenic rubbed his forehead. "I've got people working on a barricade in the huge gap in my city wall, but Ruven's destroyed any chance we may have had of withstanding a siege. We have to stop his army before it reaches the city."

"That's my job," Zaira said, with grim resignation. She met my eyes then, the dark rings of her mage mark piercing mercilessly through whatever fragile shell of armor I might have erected between myself and the memory of everything that had happened this terrible morning. "So he's a chimera," she said. "What are you going to do about it?"

I released a long breath, flexing my fingers. The motion sent jabs of pain up my arms, but I didn't care. "I'm going to hit Ruven back where it will hurt him most."

Zaira snorted. "I'd like to kick him in the bollocks as much as anyone, but I'd just break my toe, and he'd make some stupid remark about the magical omnipotence in his trousers."

Whether from blood loss or simple inurement, I didn't even flush. "No, in his true vulnerable point. His domain."

Domenic frowned. "I thought Witch Lords were infinitely more powerful in their domains."

"His domain is the source of his power," I agreed, with a humorless grin. "But he's made a mistake. He's told me himself how to steal it from him."

"With the special magic blood you got from your great-grandma?" Zaira lifted a dubious eyebrow. "How? You're no Witch Lord. You're not even a vivomancer."

"No," I agreed, "but I know where to find one who I'll bet is willing to help me." Kathe had no love for Ruven, and I suspected the sheer cheek of snatching pieces of Ruven's domain away would appeal to him. An unexpectedly fierce yearning came over me to have his clever, unpredictable strength at my side right now.

A grin spread across Zaira's face. Before she could reply, however, a servant peeped in the open doorway.

"Lady Cornaro, Your Grace, there's an armed force approaching the city."

Domenic started to struggle to his feet; Zaira held him down with a single well-placed finger on his forehead. "Ruven's army? Are they here already?"

"No, no," the servant said hastily, waving her hands. "A Callamornish cavalry unit, coming to assist us. Perhaps two hundred riders. Lady Cornaro, your cousin, Princess Brisintain Lochaver, appears to be leading them."

If any circumstances existed under which I would truly have been emotionally prepared to face the cousin whose brother I'd killed a scant two months ago, I could state with some certainty that these were not them.

Bree's cavalry made a stirring sight as they rode up to the western gate of Ardence in the golden light of early morning, the hills rising behind them, with their horses' manes tossing and cuirasses gleaming. But I felt nothing but dread as I stood to meet them, my eyes locked on the heroic figure riding in the lead with her hair a windblown tangle and a white cape streaming behind her.

When they approached within yelling distance, all two hundred of them reined to a halt, with admirable coordination. Bree regarded me for a moment from horseback, then slid down and approached on foot. I stepped forward from the welcoming contingent arrayed around me, coming to meet her halfway. I was painfully aware that Lucia should have walked in my shadow, and Marcello should have been there to give my hand an encouraging squeeze. Their absence left me unsupported, as if the ground around me crumbled with each step.

Bree stopped in front of me, looking regal and martial in her gold-chased cuirass with a saber at her side. She reminded me of our grandmother. The morning sun picked out the freckles I knew so well, but also grim lines by Bree's mouth and a hard look in her eyes that were new to me. And, most likely, my fault.

"Hello, Amalia," she said, as the wind in the open valley blew strands of hair across her face.

"Hello, Bree."

We stared at each other with the deep, expressive silence of a connection binding as blood, strong with a lifetime of knowing each other. Words would have only weakened what passed between us.

I'm sorry, I told her in that silence, meaning it with my entire soul.

I know, her grieving eyes replied. *I still don't forgive you.*

Bree's gaze traveled to my bandaged arms, then searched the hollows of my face. "You look like the Ninth Hell," she said bluntly.

"I've had a difficult morning," I admitted.

"Come on." Bree slapped my shoulder with her riding glove. "Let me get my people settled and our horses stabled, and then we can go have a drink."

Two hours later, Bree leaned on the scarred wooden bar before us and stared at me. "Grace of Mercy. That's terrible." She tossed back a swallow of wine without breaking eye contact.

I had told her that there was no way a tavern would be open two hours after dawn in a city that was about to be under attack. She had told me that I understood nothing about taverns. And here we were, in a small, grubby place with a thick layer of dust on most of the bottles behind the bar, working on our second bottle of wine—though Bree was more than half responsible for the first. I'd toasted Lucia's health after a report came that the physicians had pronounced her out of immediate danger, but was trying to indulge only lightly.

"It's been a rough year, by which I mean the past few days, and it's not looking to get any better," Zaira said.

"And Graces preserve me, what am I going to tell Istrella?" I groaned, cradling my forehead in my hands.

"Don't tell her anything," Zaira urged. "Fix him first, then tell her. No point upsetting her."

"Don't I owe her the truth?" Never mind that I wasn't at all certain I could fix him; I couldn't think of that, not now, when I hadn't even tried. "It's my fault this happened to Marcello in the first place."

"It's not your fault," Bree said sharply. "It's that demon Ruven's fault."

That was the same thing I'd tried to tell myself a hundred times, without success, about Roland. I caught her eyes. "But I made choices that caused it to happen," I said. "I bear at least some of the responsibility."

Bree frowned. She'd caught the double layers of what I'd said, and she searched my face as if more might be written there. "What are you going to do about it, then?"

"I don't know yet." My hand tightened on my wineglass. "I have plans and ideas for how to save the Empire, and how to fight Ruven, but none of my research into the magical sciences has ever touched on a method to restore a chimera to their original form." The unsteady surge of emotion that had been trying to force its way up like bile from my stomach rose again, and I swallowed it down with a gulp of wine. "Graces' piss, this is sour," I complained.

Zaira let out a mock gasp. "Such language!"

The proprietress, having heard, turned from chatting with a pair of Bree's soldiers to glare at me. "Well, pardon me, princess! I'm not exactly serving royalty here, you know."

Bree and I blinked at her, and the soldiers exchanged incredulous grins, but the proprietress stalked off to the other end of the bar. Zaira bit the edge of her hand to try to hold back her laughter.

"Should we tell her?" Bree asked, a mischievous smile tweaking the corner of her mouth.

"No." Zaira waved a hand. "It's funnier if she doesn't know. A princess, the doge's daughter, and a fire warlock walked into a tavern... Holy Hells, we're a bad joke."

"But in all seriousness, I've never heard you swear like that," Bree said, clasping my shoulder. "You're upset. Have some more awful wine."

"I need to be able to think clearly." I pushed my glass away. "And I need to find an answer, Bree. I'm going to have to keep making these kinds of choices—weighing lives against each other. We all will."

Marcello had faced similar decisions, as a military officer. But somehow he had retained his mercy and compassion. I wished I had him here, to ask him how he'd done it.

If he could even remember. If Ruven hadn't truly killed the good man he'd been.

"I might not have to after all." Bree grimaced. "Word's gotten out that I'm a vivomancer."

Zaira slapped her shoulder sympathetically. "Not everyone can be a warlock. They'll get over their disappointment eventually."

"You're still the heir to the throne of Callamorne," I said firmly. "You can't get out of it that easily."

"I suppose not," Bree sighed. "But the nobles are having trouble deciding whether their love for the Lochaver family outweighs their distrust of vivomancers. It's not so comfortable at court for me right now. That's why Grandmother let me go out and ride patrols in the hills."

A thought occurred to me. I squinted suspiciously at Bree. "Does the queen know you're here?"

"Ah, well, as to that." Bree took another swallow of wine. "She probably does by now."

"Bree!"

"Oh, hush. So long as I manage not to die here, she'll forgive me." Bree flashed me a grin.

I exchanged glances with Zaira. She shook her head and muttered, "That's another one I have to keep alive. Bugger an ox."

"Anyway," Bree said, lifting her glass to me, "I know what you need, Amalia. You need clarity of purpose."

I frowned. "Clarity of purpose?"

"Grandmother says it's necessary in battle, to achieve victory. But to have clarity, you can't dwell on what you've lost and where you've failed." She poked a finger at me. "You must focus on what you still have to protect, and what you need to do. If you know that, you'll know when you need to make a sacrifice, and when you must fight to the death rather than give something up."

"Well, I still have plenty to protect." I laid my bandaged arms on the counter, staring at the spots of blood that had begun to seep through. "As for what I need to do..." There was so much. See my Falcon law through. Defeat Ruven. Save Marcello. Make sure my mother was all right, and protect the Serene Empire. "I have to figure out a way to fix everything."

"You don't have to fix *everything*." Bree shook her head.

"Wrong. It's her actual job." Zaira cuffed my shoulder. "You fix everything that needs fixing, I break everything that needs breaking."

"That's very nice," Bree said, laughing, "but a bit ambitious. You're not one of the Graces, you know, Amalia."

"No." I pushed on the bar with both hands and levered myself to my feet. "I'm a Cornaro."

A tinkling crash sounded at the far end of the bar. The proprietress stared at me, her mouth hanging open, the glass she'd dropped shattered at her feet.

That afternoon Ruven's army came marching down the river valley at last, spreading wide beyond the road in a dark mass. Domenic and Zaira and I stood once more at the parapet, on a section of undamaged wall some distance from the fallen gate, watching the invading army flow closer like some deadly flood. The fog had burned off, and the winter sun picked out gleams of metal from cuirasses and pikes and muskets. Even from this distance, I could spot chimeras moving among them, irregularities in the weave of humanity.

Domenic handed me his spyglass, shaking his head. I trained it on the chimeras, and found dozens of them, mostly along the flanks of the army: armored weasels big as wolves, nightmarish lizards the size of horses with foaming mouths, bulls with faces like bird skulls full of dagger-length teeth. A few small units of human chimeras marched in the army, too, mixed in with the pikemen and musketeers. I scanned those groups closely, but didn't see Marcello among them.

I passed the spyglass to Zaira, feeling queasy. She took a look and immediately swore. "Half of them aren't even soldiers."

"What, the chimeras?" I asked. "I didn't think there were nearly that many."

"No. The people. Half of them look like I'd expect soldiers to look, trained and disciplined and ready for this. But the other half..." She swept the ranks of the army with the spyglass, her mouth tight. "Some of them are probably grandparents. Grace of Mercy, this one's got to be Istrella's age. And even I know that one's holding his musket wrong."

"We knew Ruven was conscripting everyone able-bodied into the army." I couldn't help thinking of the old Vaskandran innkeeper who'd been taking care of babies while their nursing mothers cut firewood, after their village had been emptied to swell Ruven's forces. "They can do that in Vaskandar, with vivomancers to ensure there's still enough food."

"They're scared." Zaira handed the spyglass back to Domenic, shadows of what she'd seen lingering in her eyes. "Damn that smiling bastard to the Hell of Carnage. Those poor sods have got no business being here, and they know it, but he's forcing them against us anyway."

I tried not to think about how it would feel to be taken from my family and forced to go to war in a strange country, marching beside inhuman monsters against an empire armed with powerful magic. If we didn't kill these people, these desperate and unwilling conscripts, they would murder or enslave the tens of thousands of equally innocent civilians in the city we stood to protect.

I suspected that afforded Zaira only moderate consolation. She hugged her arms as if against the cold as she stared out over the valley—but cold didn't usually affect her.

Vultures circled above the army, patient and waiting. The gates of the Hell of Death were already open. There had to be some way to keep this from turning into a slaughter, surely, to make them turn back and return home to Vaskandar as so many of them clearly wanted to do.

Then a circle of light flared on the grass beneath the feet of one section of the vanguard, and perhaps twenty of Ruven's soldiers dropped to the ground. Another circle flashed farther down their front line, with the same effect. Distant cries of fear reached our ears, thin and faint on the wind, before the breeze shifted and carried them away.

"The first of the trap circles," I breathed.

"What happened to the people who stepped in them?" Zaira asked warily.

I shook my head, feeling no sense of victory, but rather a sick dropping despair. "That type of circle delivers a shock that stops the heart."

Zaira let out a soft curse. "How many more are there?"

"Only a handful. You have to bury great chunks of obsidian beneath the entire ring, so they're difficult to make." When they'd told me the plans, I'd wished we had more. But that was easy enough to wish for when enemy soldiers were faceless numbers rather than frightened people forced from their homes.

Any hopes I might have had that Ruven's army would turn around at the first sign of resistance faded. His lines closed ranks and kept marching, more pristine farmland and fields of winter-brown stubble disappearing beneath the advancing ocean of boots.

"They should be coming in range of the garrison's artifice cannons soon," Domenic muttered.

At my side, Zaira tensed, gripping the stone-capped edge of the parapet over which we watched. She stared at the blocky fortress standing on its hill, then at the army advancing across the valley.

"Everything that happens here is Ruven's fault," I murmured to her. "He's the one doing this. Not us."

"Istrella made those cannons," Zaira said, her voice low and troubled.

Grace of Mercy. She was right. Istrella would be watching as her creations finally unleashed their destructive power, with no one to comfort her as she came face-to-face at last with the death she could cause. And Marcello was out there somewhere. If one of her cannons killed *him*...

But no. He was too valuable as a hostage. Ruven surely wouldn't put him in danger—and besides, Istrella could sense his location well enough at that range to keep them from firing on him.

My hand slipped into the satchel slung over my shoulder, where I carried extra elixir, writing materials, and a few other key supplies. I dug in the bottom, among the grit left over from stuffing half-eaten pastries and alchemical powders in there over the months since I'd last let Rica clean it out, until my fingertips brushed a small nub of cool metal.

I gripped the button Marcello had given me before my unexpected trip to Vaskandar, the familiar ridges and grooves pressing into my skin. Worrying about him would accomplish nothing. I had to believe he would survive this day.

On the battlements of the Raverran fortress, a red light flashed. A hot streak arced through the air, sizzling a mile or more across the valley before descending into the front ranks of the army below. Beside me, Zaira sucked in a breath.

The shot exploded on impact into a great ball of fire, loosing a cloud of black smoke and throwing the lines into a panicked chaos visible even from this distance. A rumbling boom echoed down the valley, the sound broken and repeated by the hills.

"And so it begins," Domenic said sadly.

After a moment, another red flash came from the fortress, and then another. Two more fireballs erupted in the Vaskandran front lines, wreaking utter devastation. The front half of the army compressed, bristling, like a living creature recoiling from an attack.

Domenic lifted the spyglass to his eye. Whatever he saw made him flinch, but he didn't look away. "They're trying to flee," he reported.

"That would be good," Zaira said hopefully.

I shook my head. The sick, empty feeling in my gut knew better. "Ruven will never let them."

Sure enough, the ripple that had run through the army stilled, with an eerie suddenness that should not have been possible for a mass of thousands of panicked people. And their forward march began again, into the cannon fire, splitting neatly around the smoking craters full of corpses each shot left in the ground.

Domenic swore and lowered the spyglass at last. "Those are his own people. He must know they're all going to die. Even if he takes Ardence, when the imperial forces and the Falcons arrive, they'll be wiped out. He's forcing thousands of his own subjects to go terrified to their deaths, and for what?"

"So he can piss on your city to make it his, like a dog marking a tree," Zaira said roughly.

"He sacrifices a few thousand to gain tens of thousands." I shook my head. "If you don't care about human lives except as the coin of power, it's a sensible strategy."

"No it isn't," Zaira said, her voice gone hard. "Because he's not gaining anything. I'm here, and I'm going to stop him."

My stomach dropped. "Now?"

"I'm sure as Hells not waiting for my birthday. Those cannons aren't slowing them down. That army would be knocking on the gates within the hour, if you still had gates to knock on."

Domenic's hand stole over and squeezed hers, briefly. "I have always admired your courage, Lady Zaira. How close do you need to get?"

Zaira shrugged. "The fire starts from me and spreads from

there, so long as it has lives to eat. I don't think you want balefire too close to your city, though, so I'm going to go out there and meet them."

"Do you want me to send some of my ducal guard with you?" he asked.

"No," Zaira said. "They'd just get in my way." She turned to me, her dark eyes unreadable. "You don't have to come, you know. You can seal me from up here."

"Of course I'm coming with you," I said. "I'm not making you do this alone."

She closed her eyes a moment, then opened them again. "Thank you."

"And I'll ask Bree's cavalry to stand ready to get you out if anything goes wrong," Domenic said. "They should be mobile enough to stay out of your way, but to respond quickly if you face any unexpected threats."

"Good thinking," I approved.

"All right." Zaira took in a long, ragged breath. "Let's do this."

A cold wind from the north whipped Zaira's dark curls behind her. I turned up the collar of my coat around my face as we climbed the grassy mound in some farmer's field where Bree and her cavalry had dropped us off. My boots turned in the soft, fog-dampened earth beneath the broken stubble left over from the fall harvest. The sun hung over the hills to the west, throwing their long slopes into shadow and picking out every bump and wrinkle in the valley floor with soft golden light. The River Arden shone bright as a luminary, winding a broad path of liquid mirror down the long throat of the valley.

We crested the low rise in silence, save for my own huffing

breath. Before us spread the valley in all its beauty, and the advancing stain of the army that choked it. I could make out the bristle of pikes and muskets and the pale flecks of faces. Istrella's cannons had ceased their bombardment, their magical reservoirs temporarily dry, and the distant rumble of thousands of footsteps beat at our ears.

There were so many of them. It was madness, for the two of us to stand here alone in the empty stretch of fields before the city. Bree's riders waited a safe distance behind us; it was hard not to lift my arm and give them the signal right now to come and get us, before the soldiers could come within shooting range, since clearly we'd made a terrible mistake.

At my side, Zaira shuddered. "Bugger it all. I don't want to do this."

She was staring at the approaching army with white-rimmed eyes. She reached out sideways, fingers clutching with blind need at the air; it took me a stunned moment to realize what she was looking for and give her my hand.

"I know," I said quietly, as she crushed my fingers.

"I shouldn't have looked through that spyglass," she groaned. "I shouldn't have looked at their faces."

The enemy troops marched closer, the ground trembling beneath our feet with their coming. I tried not to think about how much longer we had before they came into musket range. "Maybe not," I said, keeping my eyes fixed on her face, striving to give her all of my attention as the vultures circled overhead. "But maybe it has to hurt. You wouldn't want this to be easy."

"I can't do it." She tore her gaze away from the advancing army to face me, her dark eyes stretched wide with panic, the wind dragging strands of hair across her face. "Curse it, Amalia, if I slaughter all these people—hundreds of them, thousands of them, with babies and dogs and parents and homes waiting for them—I become a demon. That's not a line you can cross and go back home again like nothing happened."

"I know." I took her other hand, too, and squeezed both of them. "Believe me, *I know*."

My eyes stung. The wind, I told myself, surely the wind, because I couldn't be fool enough to be at the verge of tears here, now, over what I'd done months ago, when I decided that military strategy and the safety of innocents were more important than my cousin's life. Or over what Marcello had said in the grip of the cruelty Ruven had planted in him. But I didn't look away, even as the encroaching tide of Ruven's army grew in the periphery of my vision.

Zaira's eyes narrowed with recognition. "Maybe you do."

"If…" I took a breath, forcing myself to commit to the words I was afraid to speak. "If you don't want to do this, you don't have to. We can call Bree to take us back to the city."

"How in the Hells would I tell Domenic I decided to leave him to fend for himself?" Zaira shook her head fiercely. "There are countless brats in that city who didn't do anything wrong, and some half-decent adults, too. I know what Ruven will do if we don't stop him." She turned, as if fighting a powerful force, to face the army again. "Ardence needs me to be a demon now. So I'd better pack for my trip to the Nine Hells."

"I'll be right there with you," I said quietly.

"Damned right, you will." She'd gone the shade of old vellum, and her hands were clammy in mine. "I'm going to have to lose myself further into the fire than I've ever gone before. I'm counting on you to bring me back."

"I will. I swear to you, I always will."

Zaira nodded, and released my hands. The wind snapped her skirts behind her like a banner as resolve hardened her face.

"*Exsolvo*," I whispered.

Chapter Twenty-Eight

Deep within Zaira's eyes, a blue spark kindled.

A pack of chimeras detached from the oncoming army and bounded toward us, flowing fast as water, their scaly backs gleaming in the sun, fanged maws gaping. Behind them, the front rank of soldiers shifted their muskets from their shoulders to hold them crosswise in their hands, ready to stop and fire as soon as they came into range.

Zaira smacked her fist into her opposing palm, then flung her arms wide. A wall of fire roared up twenty feet in front of us, blue banners streaming hungrily upward, forming a dancing curtain of death. Its ends raced away to the right and left, searing a line across the worn winter grass.

The foremost chimera couldn't stop in time, and careened into it. The creature thrashed, covered in fire, tearing great gouges in the earth and uttering awful screams; the others contorted to avoid the flames and backed off, growling and hissing. Several hundred feet behind them, the front ranks of the army faltered almost to a halt.

Sweat beaded Zaira's temples. "Come on," she urged through her gritted teeth. "Turn around. Go back. You can't win against me, damn you."

Somehow, by the Graces, she was still in control, holding up a line of balefire a quarter mile long. But without lives to feed it, she couldn't keep it up forever. The fire would eat away at her strength and drain her dry and empty.

Through the distorting shimmer of the flames, the army wavered. I squinted against the blistering heat, my eyes drying, desperately hoping that Ruven's attention was elsewhere and he would let them run.

But the lines shifted, and the soldiers changed the angle of their march toward one end of Zaira's line. The pack of chimeras sprinted in the opposite direction, clearly planning to pass the other end and come at us from both sides.

"Oh, no you don't," Zaira growled, and pushed her hands forward. The fire spread and curved inward, cutting them off, racing to flank them.

I stared at her in awe. Her wall of balefire burned razor-thin, a single sheet of twisting pale flames licking up as if from a narrow crack in the earth to some subterranean Hell. The lines of fire swept fast as the wind up the sides of the hills now, surely a mile across and growing, bending to surround the entire front portion of the army in a blazing half circle. Chimeras paced in frustration behind the shifting and rippling curtain of heat and light, snarling, unable to reach us.

Still Zaira held the fire from spreading beyond the bounds she set for it, her teeth bared, her fists clenched, her face straining with the effort.

"You aren't my master," she panted. "I can beat you."

For a confused moment, I thought she meant Ruven, and glanced around in fear of finding him there. But then the cold realization hit: she was talking to the balefire.

She was pushing herself to her limits to save the Vaskandran conscripts. To try to give them a chance for Ruven to see the futility of his attack and allow them to retreat.

Tiny flames began blooming on her skin, like some strangely

beautiful pox—no, as if pieces of her mortal flesh were falling away to reveal the creature of fire beneath. Delicate tendrils of blue flame wound themselves through her hair, and flames licked up around her feet. I backed away a few steps, my breath quickening.

Then beyond the flames, there came a sudden flurry of movement. Three chimeras launched themselves up and over the writhing barrier of fire, springing impossibly high. Their maws full of a hundred teeth opened wide in reptilian faces as they fell toward us; I threw up my arms and ducked instinctively, letting out an unabashed shriek.

A blinding wave of balefire exploded from Zaira, washing over the chimeras. It stripped away flesh and bone in a heartbeat, devouring them in one gulp like a starving thing. Only ash rained down onto the ground before us.

I recoiled from the blast of heat and the sudden stench of burned fur and meat and bone, lifting a sleeve to shield my nose and mouth. My eyes stung, parched, and I blinked the gritty dry air off them.

Zaira stood with her head tipped back, arms stretched wide as if she would embrace the sky. Flames leaped up all along her arms, eerie and delicate, rising from her like steam. Her eyes overflowed with blue fire until it ran in trails down her cheeks.

"Zaira...?" I asked, nervously.

She didn't answer. But like an enormous fist closing, all across the valley, her fire surged forward. The line of ravening blue flame that had been so disciplined, so narrow, roared at the Vaskandran army like the sky itself falling down upon them.

A sound caught in my throat and died there before I knew whether it was a shout or a whimper. The commotion of terror from the army drowned it out, a thousand screams rising like a storm on the wave-tossed ocean. The ranks surged with wild panic, people pushing and collapsing and falling on each other in their frantic animal urge to escape the roaring wave of death that rushed toward them, trailing a veil of smoke that sent the vultures scattering.

And then it was upon them, and the screams changed, twisting to the agony of the dying.

"Let the Grace of Mercy hide her eyes in dread." The voice that came from Zaira was wild as the fire itself. She stepped forward, reaching out in benediction, trailing a cloak of flames. "For mine is the kingdom of death."

Her words resonated with divine majesty of the Graces themselves, but they were from no sacred text I had ever heard of. She was gone, lost utterly to the flames; they spoke through her mouth with a voice of terrible and pitiless power.

I clapped my hands over my ears against the screaming. The devouring fire swept relentlessly on, closing its circle of destruction, clawing higher into the sky. It billowed in great horrible clouds now, swallowing trees and farmhouses, glutted on hundreds of lives and still starving for more. A vast black column of smoke rose above it, a dark omen befouling the sky and dimming the sun.

There was no escape for those who had been trapped between the arms of Zaira's wall. The twin waves of fire met in the middle, turning the valley to a lake of blazing death.

Where a thousand soldiers had moved in a great bristling mass, a thousand lives that breathed and spoke and hoped, the balefire had performed its mad alchemy of agony and terror; now there was only flame. It towered like an infernal mountain, some great beast older than time and more terrible than death, ripping at the world that birthed it in its fury.

The back two-thirds of Ruven's army struggled in a ragged surge away from the fire, trying to flee. The north end of the valley rose toward the steepening hills, and the formerly rear-most stragglers raced up the road, now in front, black dots in the distance running for life and freedom.

But then they slowed and drew up in ranks, an unnatural order falling upon them when they should be most panicked; the rear of the army was re-forming under Ruven's control, away from the fire, ready to try again.

Graces help me. I could end this now, with half the valley drowned in fire and a monster of horror and death unleashed upon them already. I could stop this unnatural killing blaze before it reduced any more lives to ash and bone. But then, unless Ruven actually acknowledged defeat and let his forces withdraw, Ardence would still face an army.

I kept my silence.

Zaira stepped forward to the peak of the low rise on which we stood, wrapped in a column of living flame. I could barely make out her shape through the terrible fire that streamed off her. My skin ached with heat, and every cough to clear ash from my lungs brought a dry pain stabbing through my chest, but not one lick of flame bent in my direction. It was as if a great wind came from Zaira, sweeping it all toward her enemies. For now.

She lifted a hand, palm out, toward the retreating army, and spoke again in that voice of terrible beauty. "All those who would destroy what I protect, I consign to a Hell of fire."

Oh sweet Graces. I cringed from what I knew was coming.

The fire cavorting and roiling where a thousand people had stood began clawing its way up the valley, taking more and more of the screaming souls who tried to flee from it. They were far enough away now that their cries came thin and distant on the wind, wails faint as the damned beyond the gates of the Nine Hells. Blue tendrils of licking flame spread like spilled blood, groping toward the hills with fingers of bright, shining oblivion.

It was impossible to imagine what the valley had looked like before it was made of fire. That it had once been full of life, before Zaira's flame converted that delicate and profound power to raw light and heat, casting the remains as smoke to stain the sky.

I fell to my knees, coughing, and pressed my lace cravat to my face to try to filter out the blowing charred grit from the air. The heat stole my tears before they could leave my eyes. Crows circled and cawed urgently overhead, though all the other birds had fled long ago; I wondered if they were Kathe's.

I know it's madness, I wanted to tell them. *And yes, I know I need to stop it.*

I couldn't look away. I couldn't allow myself to be overcome, and to cower on the ground while the balefire unleashed its fury upon the world. It was my duty to watch, and to speak my word to put an end to this horror as soon as I thought it was safe.

Safe. For every second I waited, dozens of people were dying. I had to weigh their lives against those in Ardence, and make the scales balance somehow. Who in the Graces' names was I to make that judgment?

I was Amalia Cornaro, of the Council of Nine. And I was Zaira's friend, whom she trusted to bring her back.

I staggered to my feet, my breath painful in my raw lungs. The balefire raged in a terrifying inferno, consuming nearly the whole valley and spreading up the hills. It was not a landscape of the mortal world, where life could exist; it was the geography of the Hells, made real and written in fire and death upon the earth.

Zaira paced slowly forward down the gentle incline toward the flames, leaving a wake of fire flickering behind her. I didn't try to follow. I had no illusions of safety if I should step too close or stray in front of her. I glanced back behind me and saw, a hundred yards away, Bree's cavalry fighting to keep their horses from fleeing the mile-long raging inferno and the smoke-throttled air; I supposed we should have thought of that.

It was hard to squint north, across the valley lit up end to end with conquering blue flame. It burned everywhere, on barren earth and charred bone, on rock and grass and the river itself. No trees or houses rose from it, and no movement stirred within its compass save the twisting dance of the flames. Far across the valley, the tail end of the army still fled up the road, a distant and blurry crowd of dots and smudges streaming away from Ardence. But the fire was faster, and it caught them one after another, devouring them. They were too far away now for me to hear their screams.

There had to be fewer than a thousand left. I wasn't in a position to estimate, but by the Graces, we'd killed enough of them. If Ruven insisted on sending them against the city again, Bree and the garrison could handle them.

Enough.

I opened my parched mouth and croaked out, *"Revincio."*

A terrible silence fell. All at once, the flames vanished, their blue glare gone, plunging the valley into ashen twilight.

Where there had been the harsh beauty of fire, now there was boundless devastation. What had been rolling fields and pretty farms marked with wandering lines of cypress trees now was a barren wasteland of blowing ash. Nothing remained of the thousands of men and women who had stood here a mere hour ago save bits of charred bone sticking up from the black fields of ruin.

Zaira collapsed gracefully, almost seeming to float down like a dropped feather, as if the balefire had left her empty as a blown milkweed pod. Ash puffed up where she fell, her curls sprawling on the scorched ground.

Cold descended upon me, with the fire gone. A bitter wind

skated across the valley, blowing clouds of ash. The last of the smoke drifted up into the sky, cut loose from the fire that had tethered it, floating higher and higher to join the thick gray haze that lay upon the air. The River Arden poured fresh clean water between its ash-choked banks, pushing the gray sludge downstream, beginning to wash itself clear again, but it was the only bright thing in a landscape of death and shadows. Zaira had scoured the land of all life, leaving only a terrible blackened scar upon the earth.

I tottered over to her and sank down on the ground at her side, my legs trembling too much to hold me up anymore. I held her head off the ground and brushed ash out of her hair, then turned my head to spit up a grimy mess onto the blackened earth.

She was warm, and her chest rose and fell. *Thank the Graces.* It seemed unnatural that one person could deal so much death and still remain alive.

Hoofbeats thudded behind me, soft on the unburned ground. A single rider. I didn't have to look to know who would be brave enough to approach us, or to know whose boots now crunched through the cinders. If nothing else, only a vivomancer could convince a horse to come this near.

"Graces wept," Bree said, and knelt down beside me. "Will she be all right?"

"I think so." Zaira's face seemed flushed with health, in fact, as if unleashing so much horror had only made her stronger. The jess gleamed on her wrist; the knot that bound us together had blurred further from the raging power of her balefire, more damaged than before. "What are the survivors doing?" I lifted my head, wearily, to peer across the valley.

"Milling about in horror, from the look of it," Bree said. "They haven't got nearly the force they'd need to attack us now. After I get you two safe, I'll join up with the Raverran troops and we can run them off."

I nodded dully. Thousands dead, the valley scourged with fire that would leave its mark for years, and I doubted Ruven cared. His gambit had failed, but he always had another plan. Perhaps he had not understood what Zaira was capable of. Now he knew.

Bree stared out at the devastation, then at Zaira, shaking her head in awe. "She's not human."

"But she is," I said. "She is. And that's the problem."

Chapter Twenty-Nine

Zaira showed no signs of waking. I stayed with her through the last embers of the day and all the long night. They set up a bed for me in her room when I declined to leave, the servants moving quickly and with many terrified glances to where Zaira's dark curls poked out from underneath her coverlet.

Domenic visited twice. The first time, when we brought Zaira in, he hurried to her side and held her hand anxiously, asking me again and again if she would be all right. I told him yes, she would be fine; this was normal after unleashing on such a scale. The second time, he was more somber and quiet, staring at her with a worried frown, then glancing northward as if he could see through the palace wall to the blackened valley.

Bree and Domenic praised my dedication for staying with Zaira, but I had my own reasons. Yes, she was certainly a target more than ever now, and I asked Domenic to post trusted guards at her door. And yes, I wanted to make certain she had a familiar face with her when she woke up, since Graces only knew what she would remember or how she would feel. But more than anything, I needed the silence. No one would bother me when I was waiting by the bed of my fire warlock friend, who had just killed a few thousand people and needed her rest.

So I sat in the dark through half the night, struggling not to sink into the black swamp that threatened to suck me down. Every time I pushed the sound of distant screaming out of my mind, Marcello's face replaced it, orange eye staring from its slit pupil, scales running down to the clean line of his jaw.

The palace had gone still and quiet long ago when I finally curled up and tried to sleep. But still I lay staring into the moon-silvered shadows, listening to Zaira's steady breathing, reminding myself that it was real and the screaming was not. The scent of smoke kept me awake, clinging to my hair, my skin, everything in this room.

A tapping came at the window.

I sat bolt upright in bed, dagger in hand. *Marcello.*

But this time, there was no human silhouette against the paler square of night sky, no presence in the room. It had been a windblown branch, perhaps, bare with winter.

Tap.

Something small moved in the corner of the window. It cocked its head at me and tapped again. A crow.

"Do you have a message for me?" I went to the window, my heart slowing back to a normal pace, and opened the casement.

"You should be more careful. That could have been a trap."

I bit back a shriek and turned my head to find Kathe perched on the next window ledge over, like a crow himself, the feathers on his shoulders fluttering in the winter wind. The starlight caught in his pale, black-tipped hair, and gleamed in his eyes.

"Doors," I reminded him. "There is absolutely nothing wrong with doors. Lots of people use them all the time."

He shrugged. "I didn't want to wake anyone up. Are you going to let me in?"

I glanced back over my shoulder at the lump that was Zaira, still asleep. "Wait there."

I closed the casement and slipped quietly through the door to the small sitting room adjacent to Zaira's bedroom, where

Kathe's window was. The wards on the Serene Envoy's palace required no special key beyond physically unlatching the window from within to allow entry, and Kathe sprang down lightly onto the inlaid wood floor on a breath of winter wind.

"Make yourself comfortable." I gestured vaguely to the furniture in the cramped sitting room, and only then remembered I was wearing my nightdress. Kathe settled on a chair, his legs tucked up under him; if he noticed my flush, he didn't show any sign of it. Well, it might not be the most flattering garment, but it was perfectly modest; I decided to act as if I received visitors in my nightclothes all the time, and arranged myself on a divan opposite him. "I fear the luminaries are out for the night. I could light a lamp, if you wish."

"I saw what happened today," he said. My eyes were well adjusted to the moonlight, and I had no difficulty making out the seriousness of his expression.

"Ah." I let out a long breath. "So now you know what Zaira can do."

"It will have caused Ruven no small discomfort, to have so many lives of his snuffed out at once," Kathe said. "If that's any comfort to you."

I rubbed my forehead, as if I could somehow scrub away the memory of screaming. "I'm not certain it is. But thank you."

Kathe parted his lips as if he would say something, then closed them and watched me for a moment in silence.

"What is it?" I asked warily.

"I also know what happened to Captain Verdi," he said quietly.

I couldn't bear to face his sympathy. I rose abruptly and went to the window, staring out at the chimney smoke rising over city roofs, letting the moonlight slide over my face.

"I don't know what to do," I whispered, my breath misting the glass. "First Marcello, then burning all those people...It's too much. I have to become numb, or I'll go mad."

Feathers rustled. "I don't recommend numbness," Kathe said from behind me. "Some Witch Lords take that path when they can't handle watching all their friends and family die, one by one, while they live on. Or when they can't stand feeling life after life snuffed out in their domain, year after year, eventually including almost every person they've ever met."

"What happens to them?" I asked, tracing an artifice rune in the damp cloud I'd left on the window.

"They become cruel and distant. Their domains are places of nightmare." I turned to face him; he still sat in his chair, watching me. "In Let, we consider this a great danger to the domain, and have a tradition to prevent it from happening."

"Oh?" Curiosity dragged my thoughts up from the dark places to which they had descended. "What is it?"

"The Heartguard. You've heard me speak of them."

"I assumed they were bodyguards."

"That, too. But their most important role is to keep me human." An ironic smile pulled at the corner of his mouth. "And to hold me accountable."

"I didn't think anyone held a Witch Lord accountable," I said, with a trace of bitterness.

"That's precisely why I need them." Kathe hesitated, a strange uncertainty softening his face. "My Heartguard, ah, made it quite clear to me that they felt I did you wrong at the Conclave. That I should have asked permission before using you as bait."

An untidy tangle of feelings rose up in me, twisted together like the roots the Lady of Thorns had used to try to kill me that night. Old anger at Kathe's betrayal—but also an aching recognition. *People make mistakes*, Zaira's voice reminded me. *They make a plague-rotten mess of things. All you can do is keep trying not to ruin everything next time.*

"You should have," I agreed, keeping my tone light to cover

my unsettled thoughts. *I don't want to forget how to be a person*, I'd told Zaira. Apparently, I wasn't the only one.

A possibility occurred to me, and I frowned. "Did you only apologize because they made you?"

"No. I apologized because they were right." He shifted restlessly. "I have no natural talent at compassion. But I can get there. Sometimes I need a little help."

I collapsed back into my seat. "I'm much the same. Maybe I need a Heartguard."

"Maybe you do."

I'd asked Marcello to be essentially that for me. To help make certain I always cared, and didn't grow cold and manipulative. But now the man I had trusted to guard my heart was gone.

I twisted the skirts of my nightdress in my hands. *No*. Not gone. No matter what he'd said when Ruven's poison in his mind drove him to cruelty, I would not give up on him.

"What do you do, then, if you've hurt someone?" I asked.

"You make it right," Kathe said softly. "You find a way to make it right."

The moonlight gleamed in his eyes. I knew what I had to ask him, but I was afraid that I could already see the answer in his grave, steady gaze.

"Once someone has been turned into a chimera," I began, "Is there any way...How would you go about..." I broke off as Kathe closed his eyes.

"I'm sorry," he whispered.

"No." My fingernails dug furrows in my legs. "No. There has to be some way to undo it. Ruven said he could undo it."

"Ruven could," Kathe agreed heavily. "Because he is a Skinwitch."

"Then some other Skinwitch could fix him."

"Perhaps?" Kathe spread his hands wearily. "It would be very difficult, because this theoretical Skinwitch wouldn't know what precisely Ruven did to change him. And it's irrelevant, because Skinwitches are rare to begin with, and are killed if caught in many domains. I don't know of any currently alive other than Ruven."

"There has to be something I can do," I insisted desperately. "I can't just leave him like this. Please, there has to be some way I can save him."

Kathe rose and started pacing. "What would you have me do, Amalia? I can't change how vivomancy works. I can't become a Skinwitch to restore him. I would help you if I could, but this is beyond my power." By the bitterness in his voice, it pained him to admit it.

"What if we kill Ruven?" I asked.

"That wouldn't change him back. When a vivomancer makes a chimera, it's a permanent transformation."

"But his mind," I pressed. "He wouldn't be under Ruven's control and influence anymore. Would he return to the person he was?"

"He might. It depends on what Ruven did to him." Kathe frowned, thinking. "I don't make true chimeras, even animal ones. But sometimes I make minor enhancements to animals that don't harm them—like boosting my crows' intelligence, or giving horses more endurance. And I've also noticed that when I focus my attention on a particular animal, commanding it or guiding it, I influence its behavior, even if that's not my intent. That influence is much stronger if I've altered the animal." He stopped pacing and shrugged helplessly. "If Ruven changed your friend's brain, those changes are permanent. If it's only Ruven's influence that's twisting him, there's a chance that killing Ruven might return him to something like the man you knew."

It wasn't much of a hope, but I seized it. "Then that's what I'll do."

"I don't want to lie to you." Kathe's shoulders slumped, as if the energy driving him had drained out. "It's unlikely that Ruven took care not to damage him. Unless you can somehow get Ruven to undo his work, you'll have to accept that he's never going to be the same."

"Fine. If I can trick Ruven into fixing him, I will. And if not, I'll save whatever I can of him." My voice wavered, despite my determination that it wouldn't. I pressed the heels of my hands into my stinging eyes. "Curse it, I'm not going to cry."

"Everyone with a heart cries." There came a rustle of feathers; I looked up to find Kathe crouching in front of me, his pale brows furrowed. "I may have mentioned I'm not good at compassion. Do you want me to go, or—"

"No." I swallowed. "No, I think I want you to hold me."

He settled down next to me, then, and his cloak folded around me like a wing. I strangled the exhausted sobs that tried to climb up out of my chest, struggling to think of anything but one orange eye blazing with cruelty, and one green one staring at me with the pleading horror of a drowning man slipping under the water for the last time.

"I'm guessing you don't feel like a game," Kathe said tentatively.

A laugh burst out of me, then, with all the ragged strength of the tears I'd been suppressing. "You really *are* bad at this."

"Well, they always cheer *me* up." But he was laughing, too, his chest shaking silently with it.

That only made me laugh harder, tears leaking from the corners of my eyes, the knot of grief loosening in my chest. Kathe's arm tightened briefly around my shoulders, and I leaned into the warmth of him, feeling him breathing against me. It was so strange, that he did something so common as respire, when he carried the power of an entire kingdom in him. But he was warm, and human, and I could feel the pulse beating in him.

He smelled of pine trees and snow and a wild hint of lightning, not smoke and ruin and death. I breathed his scent in deep and closed my eyes, and at last none of the horrors of the day appeared in the warm darkness behind my lids.

When I woke to the clear morning light, hours later, I was curled alone on the divan, Kathe's feathered cloak draped over me.

Zaira woke at last a few hours after I did, as I was poring over magical theory texts, making notes on possible methods to use my blood to claim pieces of Ruven's domain out from under him, as he wanted to do to his neighbors. I was frowning over a passage on directionality in magical flows when a pitiful moan came from her bed.

I laid down my pen on her writing table and hurried over. She collapsed back into the pillows after a failed attempt to sit up, eyes squeezed shut, cradling her head in both hands.

"Headache?" I asked, settling into the chair by her bedside.

"Grace of Mercy, bugger a duck," Zaira groaned.

I poured some of the potion I'd had prepared into the waiting small cup and offered it to her. "This will help."

"Is it poison?" Zaira gulped it down without waiting for an answer, then made a face. "Ugh! No, poison tastes better than that. What is this disgusting...oh." She blinked her eyes open and let out a long sigh. "Oh, that's better."

"I thought you might need some of that. How do you feel?"

"Thirsty as a sailor just arrived in port." I handed her a cup of water, which I also had ready, and she blinked as she took it. "Damn, you've thought of everything."

"I *am* a scholar of the magical sciences." I watched her carefully. It was like waiting for someone who'd cut themself with an extremely sharp knife to realize how badly they'd been hurt. "What's the last thing you remember?"

"What I remember? Wait, we're in Ardence." Zaira set the cup down, frowning. "That's right. Ruven's army. What happened?"

"The city is safe," I said. "You saved it."

"I can see that." She gestured around the room as if the peace of it annoyed her: the bright morning sunlight, the elegant furnishings, the breakfast tray uneaten on the writing table beside my stack of papers. The latter caught her attention. "Hell of Hunger, I'm starving. I must have burned a lot of..." Her voice trailed off. She stared at me, her eyes opening wide into dark pools that gathered more and more shadows.

"What's the last thing you remember?" I asked again, softly.

"The chimeras leaping at us." It came out as a hoarse whisper. "I lost control, didn't I?"

"You protected Ardence," I said. "You saved sixty thousand people."

Zaira's fingers clenched in the covers. "How many did I kill?"

"Zaira, listen to me. You never made a choice to kill anyone." I reached for her hand, half expecting her to snatch it away, but she let me take it. "You did everything you could to spare them. When you were lost to the fire, it was I who made the choice when to stop you. *I* decided how many people would die. Not you. Don't burden yourself with their deaths."

"That's a pretty sentiment," Zaira retorted. "So pretty you can tie it up in a posy and lay it on their graves. I made my choice to kill the moment I let loose my fire. Do you think I don't know what it does?" She shook her head. "I knew what would happen. The best you can say is we did it together."

"Then we did it together," I said.

"Just a nice friendly outing with the two of us. Now tell me. *How many?*"

I closed my eyes. I could still see the valley burning end to end in a lake of blue flames, and hear the wild, high chorus of distant screams. "I don't know the exact numbers."

Zaira sighed. "Hells take the numbers. I'm no good with them anyway. Show me."

I took Zaira up the narrow stairs to the sending spire on the roof of the Serene Envoy's palace. Wind caught us at once as we stepped out onto the square platform, barely bigger than Zaira's guest bed, with the gilded spike of the sending spire towering above us. I was glad for the stone railing that ensured the stiff breeze couldn't stagger us clean off the platform onto the sloping red tile roof below, but wished I'd thought to grab a coat before coming up here. The chill wind cut through to my bones.

I pushed windblown hair out of my face as Zaira stepped forward and gripped the northward banister, leaning on it with both hands.

"Graces wept," she whispered hoarsely.

A sea of red roofs separated us from the city walls and the brief stretch of rolling green-and-gold farmland beyond. The snow-dusted hills reared up soft with distance around us, and the River Arden wove a shining ribbon through it all, appearing and disappearing in bright glimpses.

It would have been a beautiful view if it weren't for the hazy pall of smoke hanging over everything, and the terrible black scar of the valley.

From up here, there was no missing the sheer scope of the charred, ruined wasteland Zaira's flames had created. The blasted swath of blackened stubble and gray ash stretched the width of the valley and much of the length of it, endless acres of scorched earth where there had once been fields and farms, taverns and houses. Low skittering clouds of ash blew streaks across the jumbled mess of sticks and cinders; here and there the thin crumbling spike of a blackened cypress trunk or house beam remained jutting up from the rest.

We were too far away to see the bones, thank the Graces.

I stepped up beside Zaira and gazed out at what we had done.

"It's like the paintings of the Dark Days in the temples. Or the Hell of Death itself." Zaira's knuckles flared white on the railing.

There was no denying it. All the scene needed was demons with whips driving the damned before them. I couldn't think what to say, so I simply stood there at her side.

"All my life, I've had to worry about people treating me like some kind of demon." Zaira's voice wound tight to the point of breaking. "Now it turns out they were right."

I remembered what Bree had said: *She's not human.*

"They're wrong." I squeezed Zaira's shoulder and released it. "I know you, Zaira. You're no less human than I am. Or than my mother, or Kathe, or anyone with power."

"Those are terrible examples. Your mother and the Crow Lord are demons, too." The corner of Zaira's mouth twitched, ever so slightly. "You're bad at this, Cornaro."

Like Kathe. "Ask Terika, next time you see her, then," I urged. "She'll tell you you're human."

"She's biased."

"Well, ask your dog," I said desperately. "I'm sure they can smell monsters. Right?"

Zaira laughed. There was an edge to it, but it was real. "Scoundrel would cuddle up to the Demon of Carnage himself for a bit of leftover beef." She shook her head. "No, let me be a demon. This is worse if I'm human. A human shouldn't do something like this."

I gazed out over the fields of smoking ruin. "I can't do that," I said quietly.

Zaira pulled her eyes from the devastation to look at me. They were deep black wells, bottomless and aching. "Do what?"

"Let you be a demon." I gave a helpless shrug. "You're my friend."

For a while, she stared at me in silence. Then her mouth moved in the ghost of a smile. "You have questionable taste in friends."

A Witch Lord, a chimera, and a killer of thousands. "I suppose I see what you mean," I allowed. "But no. I have to disagree. My taste in friends is excellent."

Her slim warm hand found mine, and we stared out at the plain of death together.

Chapter Thirty

There is one key question we need to answer," I said, scanning the faces gathered around me in a meeting room at the Serene Envoy's palace.

"Where I can get decent beer in this city?" Bree suggested, leaning an elbow on the table.

"How to prevent energy loss over time in a solar artifice circle?" Domenic countered.

"Most satisfying place to stab Ruven," Zaira declared, with finality.

"Zaira's closest," I said grimly.

Kathe let go a sigh as carefully as if he'd cradled it for half a year. "How do you kill an immortal?"

Everyone turned to look at him. He seemed to take up an unequal space somehow as he lounged at the table, like his namesake crow strutting in among a flock of sparrows. I'd given him his cloak back before the meeting; every time my eyes fell on its feathery ruff about his shoulders, I couldn't help but recall its soft, light warmth.

"Since you mention it," I said, "yes. That."

Silence fell over the room in heavy folds. Domenic's eyes sat in shadowy pools of exhaustion—I doubted he'd gotten a full night's sleep in days. Zaira met no one's gaze, strain showing in the taut lines of her face. Bree had left a certain extra distance between her chair and Zaira's—out of instinctive awe rather than on purpose, I suspected, but I had no doubt Zaira had noticed. I'd invited Istrella, but she was late—busy with some project at the garrison probably, but I couldn't help worrying extra significance into the delay even though an accurate sense of the passage of time had never been one of Istrella's signal virtues.

Lucia should be here, too, and I knew it. And Marcello, of course. Their absence ached like missing fingers.

Domenic frowned. "Define immortal."

"There are two problems." I glanced at Kathe, but he'd leaned back in his chair and looked disinclined to talk, so I continued on my own. "First, he's a Witch Lord, which means that the vast power of life in his domain will allow him to survive almost any injury short of completely destroying his body. Second, he's a Skinwitch, which means he can heal himself instantly of any harm we manage to inflict."

"But you've killed Witch Lords before," Bree said, glancing between me and Zaira.

"I tried setting Ruven's face on fire like I did his papa's," Zaira growled. "Sadly, it didn't work so well."

Domenic whistled. "His healing can outpace balefire? That's impressive."

"That's the difficulty," I confirmed. "Zaira was able to kill the Wolf Lord because the lives he consumed for power also fed the balefire, so its strength kept building until it reduced him to ashes, which is too much for even a Witch Lord to survive. As a Skinwitch, Ruven can rebuild his own body faster than even balefire can destroy it—at least while he has a domain to draw on. And I'm certain Ruven would be willing to consume every single life in Kazerath to sustain himself."

Bree eyed Kathe across the table. Neither she nor Domenic had quite dared sit near him, and now she seemed reluctant to meet his eyes, with their vivid yellow mage mark. "I know Witch Lords kill each other from time to time, in fights over domains," she said. "What, ah..." She waved her hands vaguely. "Are there popular methods, or is it a big secret how you do it, or do you have to find the special way to kill each particular one?"

"You understand," Kathe said, lifting an eyebrow, "if I am somewhat reluctant to discuss with a rival power the means by which you might kill me."

"That's fair," Domenic said. He twirled a quill thoughtfully between his fingers. "Would beheading do the trick, perhaps? If it's a matter of killing him too quickly to heal?"

Kathe rocked his chair back on two legs. "Beheading wouldn't kill Ruven. Don't underestimate him. And suffice to say, without getting into detail, that's difficult to make work even with a normal Witch Lord."

Zaira snorted. "'Normal.'"

"We have a story in Callamorne," Bree said slowly. "About a king long ago who lured an enemy Witch Lord into a ravine, then caused an avalanche and buried him under half a mountain's worth of rubble. No idea if it's true, but maybe something like that could work."

Kathe nodded. "Entrapment is a known but dangerous method to attempt to destroy one of us. There's a tomb on a small island off the coast of Vaskandar where the Worm Lord lies bound in slumber, undying, behind great and terrible seals. Every child in that region is warned never to wake him."

Bree and Domenic exchanged horrified glances. Zaira cracked her knuckles. "Buried alive forever. Right. Wouldn't normally wish that on anyone, but Ruven is special."

Kathe rose and stalked to the mantel, examining the clock there as if it were an object of mystery. "The difficulty with live entombment is that it doesn't stop us from controlling our domains. That's bad enough when it means a nation full of angry wildlife seeking to free their master or enact vengeance, but Ruven would still control a large human army as well. He'd be no less dangerous."

I thought of other Witch Lord deaths I knew of. Kathe's mother had drowned in a shipwreck; he'd said she could have remained alive, perhaps indefinitely, but had chosen to let herself die rather than drain the life from her domain to sustain her own in the crushing torment of the deep. I had no doubt that Ruven would never make such a choice.

"I wonder if you could get a jess on him," Domenic mused.

"If someone put a jess on him, he'd just cut off his hand and grow a new one," Zaira said. "If you could even get a jess on that viper without him touching you first and tying you in knots, or bursting your heart."

"A jess would stop his healing, but his domain would still serve and sustain him, since he doesn't need to actively wield magic to use a connection that already exists." Kathe flicked the clock with a fingernail, and it chimed faintly. "You could try to kill him like you did the Wolf Lord at that point, but I gather that took some time."

"I don't think Zaira could kill him quickly enough that he couldn't just murder his would-be Falconer, who'd have to be standing right next to him," I said, thinking it through. "Still, I'll get one from the garrison in case an opportunity arises." Though if it did, we'd have to find someone to put it on him; I couldn't do it myself, since I was already linked to Zaira.

Bree let out an explosive sigh. "There's got to be *some* way to kill the bastard. Drop him in a volcano? Feed him to hungry bears?"

I hesitated, then began slowly, "I do have an idea for weakening him, which I got from Ruven himself. But it's more of a long-term or partial solution."

"If you got the idea from Ruven, it can't be good." Zaira

swung her booted feet up on the table. "His head's full of demon piss and snake venom."

"And knowledge of the magical sciences," I pointed out. "He wanted to use my blood to steal others' domains from them. I see no reason not to turn his own idea against him."

Kathe turned from the mantel to eye me as if I were a dog that could be friendly or dangerous. "Are you talking about trying to claim his domain yourself? You're not a vivomancer."

"No," I said. "But I think I could claim it for the Lady of Eagles."

Kathe started pacing, a restless motion, as if it sat poorly with him to speak of such things within the gilded confines of an imperial dining room rather than in the wild, open forests of Vaskandar. "Yes, that might work. If you blooded his domain, she's strong and skilled enough to use that to claim it from him. You could probably use Ruven's own blooding stones and boundary markers."

"I have no idea what you're talking about," Bree said cheerfully. "But I like the idea of stealing Ruven's kingdom from him and giving it to our great-grandmother."

"So do I," Kathe said reluctantly, "but you're right about it being slow—it could take months to have any effect. It would certainly get his attention, though—I imagine he'd drop everything to come try to kill you the moment you started tampering with his claim."

I tapped the table, thinking. "That could be useful for luring him into a trap."

"Hey." Zaira turned to Kathe. "What about the murder rocks?"

He blinked. "Murder rocks."

"Yeah, you know." Zaira swished her hand in a circle. "The rocks that were in a ring around the Conclave, that you murdered the Lady of Thorns with."

Kathe lifted a hand to his forehead. "The Truce Stones are an ancient and sacred artifact. They aren't..." He sighed. "Well, I suppose you could call them murder rocks. But that's not their purpose. And more to the point, you'd need his blood to activate them, and I doubt you have buckets of it lying conveniently to hand."

"Collecting some would be fun, though." Zaira grinned.

"Wait." I nearly sprang from my seat. "We may not have buckets of Ruven's blood, but we do have vials of it."

Domenic's brows lifted. "You do?"

"The samples of his potion Terika stole to try to research an antidote. His blood is the key ingredient." I turned to Kathe. "It would only be a tiny amount, mixed in with the potion. How much would we need?"

He shrugged. "A few drops suffices."

"Then it could work," I said, excited. "If we activate the stones, lure him into their circle, and trick him into hurting the right person, we could cut him off from his domain and make him vulnerable, just like you did with the Lady of Thorns. And then Zaira could burn him." Realizing how callous that might seem right now, I hastily added, "If you don't mind lending your balefire, that is, Zaira."

She shrugged. "I'm all right with any plan that lets me set Ruven on fire. I admit I'm not much in the mood to burn things at the moment, but I'll make an exception for his face."

Bree leaned her elbows on the table. "So let me get this straight. The plan is to get your hands on these murder rocks..."

Kathe put both hands over his face. "Truce Stones," he murmured through his fingers.

"It's your own fault, murder bird," Zaira cackled.

"...And then lure Ruven into the trap by doing something magical to his territory," Bree continued.

"Pissing on his trees," Zaira supplied helpfully.

"Bleeding on his rocks," I corrected, my ears warming. "And it's a bit more complicated than that, but yes, fundamentally."

"And the stones will temporarily remove his connection to his domain," Domenic concluded, "so Zaira's balefire can overcome his unaugmented healing powers and kill him." He cocked an eyebrow at me. "This plan seems to involve an awful lot of personal risk for one of the Council of Nine. Will they let you do it?"

I felt an odd pang at the question, and gave him a lopsided smile. "Domenic," I said, "I'm 'they' now."

He blinked. "So you are."

"As a member of the Council of Nine, I have almost unlimited authority in dealing with threats to the security of the Serene Empire, and the doge herself tasked me with coming up with a way to destroy Ruven." I faltered over my mother's new title; the words felt wrong on my tongue. "I'll want to coordinate with her and the rest of the Council over the courier lamps, of course—but honestly, between Kathe and Zaira, I'll be safer than I'd be in the Imperial Palace." I winced, then, remembering the context of recent events. "Unfortunately."

"So how do we get ahold of these Truce Stones?" Domenic asked, rubbing his hands together.

"Normally, I'd say there is absolutely no way their guardian would allow you to use them to entrap and kill a Witch Lord." Kathe leaned back against the wall, crossing his arms. "But at this point, with Ruven making human chimeras and attacking his neighbors, most of us agree that he has to die. She might be willing to loan them to you, for a price."

"That sounds promising," I said. "Who's the guardian?"

Kathe grinned. "The Lady of Spiders."

"Grace of Mercy's tits." Zaira's boots clunked from the table to the floor.

I lingered in the room after the others left, hoping for a private moment with Zaira. But mere moments after Kathe left to go talk with his crows—through the door, with a wink as if he did it to humor me, but with the windows heavily warded I had my suspicions his reasons might be more practical—Istrella burst into the room, an overflowing box of artifice scraps under her uninjured arm.

"I'm late, aren't I?" she asked, thumping her box on the table with a sigh. "I knew I took too long gathering up something to work on in case the meeting was boring."

"That's smart, though," Zaira said. "I should do that next time."

It hit me as I took in the hollows under Istrella's eyes and the unbrushed tangle of her hair that this was the first time I'd seen her since my encounter with Marcello in the foggy streets of Ardence. I tugged my lace cuffs down over my bandages, apprehension rising up in my chest.

I had to tell her. He was her *brother.*

Zaira caught my eye and shook her head, glaring murder at me. As Istrella plopped down in a chair, Zaira mouthed over her head, *Don't you dare.*

"I need to come up with some new designs for those cannons," Istrella said, her cheerfulness sounding a little more forced than usual. Her hands trembled slightly as she pulled a pouch of beads and a spool of wire out of her box. "Yesterday I was watching the battle, and I thought, all right, that was very effective, but what about ways to win battles *without* slaughtering thousands of people?"

Zaira winced and slumped back into her own chair. Istrella pressed on, oblivious. "It's a design challenge. Killing people is easy, but keeping them out of battle for prolonged periods *with-*

out killing them? Tricky! But I think it can be done." A certain strain showed through the cracks in her enthusiasm.

"That sounds excellent, Istrella," I said, through a tightening throat. "Listen, about Marcello—"

"Yes!" Istrella interrupted, before Zaira could lunge across the table at me. "I've been thinking about him. I have a solution."

I blinked in shock. "You do?"

She nodded vigorously. "You need a way to capture him without hurting him, right? So we can bring him back to the Mews and figure out how Ruven's controlling him, since it's clearly not the potion."

She hadn't heard that he was a chimera after all. My heart twisted. "Istrella..."

"I thought for sure he'd seal my power after he saw the cannons firing, but he didn't—which means whatever Ruven did to him, he's still fighting the control on some level. So that's encouraging." She rummaged in her box of parts. "If he's fighting, we can fix him. Right?"

I swallowed. "I hope so."

Istrella drew a tiny canvas bag out of her box. "Here it is. I made you another paralysis ring, like the one you used at the Mews. And then once you've got him paralyzed, slide the second ring on his finger—the one that's pure obsidian. It'll keep him unconscious for as long as he's wearing it. Don't put that one on yourself!" She frowned. "Though come to think of it, I have no idea whether being unconscious for a long time is bad for people, so maybe also don't leave it on him for days and days."

I accepted the bag. "Thank you, Istrella." I took a breath to say more, but Zaira kicked me under the table, hard enough to bruise my shin.

"I'm giving them to you because he's bound to come after you again," Istrella said, meeting my eyes with her imploring round ones. They were the same exact shade as Marcello's. My breath caught painfully in my lungs. "I've been tracking him, and he's still in the area, some distance north of here, probably with Ruven. I know you're the best person to catch him, Amalia. Because he'll try to talk to you, and he wouldn't hurt you."

I clasped my hands behind my back to hide my bandaged forearms, ignoring the twinge of pain as my healing wounds pressed against each other. "About that," I began, my voice thick with unshed tears.

Zaira sprang to her feet. "Hey, Istrella. There's something I wanted to ask you." She shoved her dangling jess under Istrella's nose. "My jess got a bit melted yesterday. Will it still work all right?"

Istrella took Zaira's thin wrist in her hand and peered at the jess, pushing her artifice glasses down over her eyes. "Looks like the magical flows are all intact," she said. "It should be fine. The wire is a bit weakened, though. I'd watch it for further damage whenever you unleash for more than a few minutes. The enchantments on a jess make them virtually indestructible—but, well, balefire is awfully good at destruction."

From the looks Zaira was giving me, if I made any further attempts to tell Istrella about Marcello, I should expect a knife in my throat. The guilty knot in my gut only tightened with an accumulating pressure of dread.

A knock came at the half-open door. "Lady Cornaro?" one of the Serene Envoy's servants called, before poking her head hesitantly around the door. She flinched when she saw Zaira; by the set of her jaw, Zaira noticed.

"Yes?" I asked.

The servant entered the room, glancing with open terror at Zaira before bowing deeply to me. "There are people here to see you and the Lady Zaira. A Falcon and Falconer." She hesitated. "I believe they said their names were Jerith and Balos."

Chapter Thirty-One

*C*ompletely clear of that wretched poison, as you can see."
Jerith swept into a florid bow, gracefully plucking a drink from
the tray a servant offered on his way back up. "Now only Balos
can tell me what to do."

"I wouldn't count on that," Balos murmured, declining
a drink himself as he eased into one of the more comfortable
chairs in the rose-draped drawing room.

"Is everyone in the Mews free, then?" I asked, as the rest of us
settled as well.

"Yes," Jerith said. "And we're all ready to do our part to make
sure Ruven gets fed to the sharks one small piece at a time."

"That's a plan I can agree with," Zaira approved.

Jerith's demeanor changed, then, the usual mocking gleam
leaving his eyes. "I've been wanting to thank you. I try not to
dwell on the various ways things could have gone worse that
night in the Mews, but some possibilities do tend to leap to
mind."

Balos nodded. "Thank you for not killing my husband," he
said. "All I could think while he was up there—besides trying to say *Revincio* and failing—was that it would be so easy to
shoot him."

"There was no way in the Nine Hells I was going to let that happen," Zaira said firmly.

I hid my face behind a wineglass, taking a long sip.

"Yes, well, I'm glad you didn't shoot me, but I'm also glad I didn't get to find out exactly how long it would take me to wipe the Serene City off the lagoon like a piece of flotsam." Jerith grimaced. "That would have been hard to live with."

Zaira grunted. "I wasn't going to let *that* happen, either."

"Which brings me to part of the reason we're here." Jerith leaned his elbows on his knees, staring intently at Zaira. "Tell me about it."

She snorted. "Please tell me they didn't send you all the way from Raverra to pat me on the head and tell me not to feel bad about burning all those people."

"No, they sent us to help protect Ardence and be in position to move against Ruven," Jerith said. "I frankly don't care how you feel. But as your teacher, it's my job to help you improve your control, and I want to know how long you kept it."

I rather doubted Jerith cared as little as he pretended to about Zaira's emotional well-being, but it was the right thing to say. Some of the tension in Zaira's shoulders eased. "A while," she said. "It got away from me when some chimeras jumped us."

"It was quite impressive," I put in. "She maintained a vast wall of balefire with precise control for some time. I've never heard of a fire warlock doing anything of the sort."

Jerith grinned. "Well done, then. Wish I could have seen that."

Zaira shrugged uncomfortably. "I was motivated."

"Now." Jerith lifted a finger. "Why did you lose control?"

"I told you, some chimeras—"

"Not when," he interrupted gently. "Why."

"How should I know?" Zaira frowned at him. "I guess I let it loose to burn the chimeras and it just kept going."

Jerith closed his eyes, as if he could watch what had happened on the inside of his lids. "Do you remember what I told you on the watchtower, when you asked me how I kept control while I was raising the storm?"

"That you'd tell me if we both made it through alive." Zaira took a long breath, as though bracing herself. "All right. What's the secret?"

"You have to stop fighting it." Jerith opened his eyes again, and the silver rings of his mage mark stood out bright and keen. "Stop being afraid of your fire, and stop trying to beat it down. You need to embrace it."

Zaira stared at him for a moment in flat disbelief. Then she lurched to her feet, throwing an arm vaguely northward. "Did you see what's out there, Jerith? Did you see what I did?"

"It was hard to miss," Jerith said calmly.

"*That's* what happens if I stop fighting it. Death feeding on death, until someone knocks me out and puts an end to it. And you're telling me to *hug* it?"

Jerith grimaced. "More accept than hug. But yes." He rose to his feet, too, and put his hands on his hips. "I've watched you in training session after training session, Zaira, and every time you unleash so much as a spark of balefire, you're fighting it every second."

"Yes, to hold it back from killing you!" Zaira threw her hands up. "Would you rather I let it burn you, and the whole Mews, and keep killing and spreading to the ends of the Grace-forsaken earth?"

Nothing could compel me to intervene in this argument, but I couldn't help but agree with Zaira. I'd felt the searing heat of her balefire's pure, wicked hunger. It was beautiful, but the idea of letting it go unchecked was terrifying.

Jerith jabbed a finger at Zaira. "It's a part of you. You can't treat it as an enemy, any more than you can treat your own arm as an enemy."

"Damned right, it's an enemy!" Zaira stepped toward Jerith, fists balled at her sides. "That's what I call something that kills my family and wants to murder my friends."

"Do you want to control it, or not?" Jerith snapped.

"Not if it means I have to get friendly with *that*." She waved toward the valley, invisible from here but looming large in my memory, a vast wasteland of bones and cinders. "I'd rather not unleash my fire at all. To the Nine Hells with it! I'll move to the country and take up beet farming."

Jerith and Zaira glared at each other, a few feet apart, chests heaving, the air between them crackling with suppressed power. I shifted uncomfortably in my chair. I wouldn't put it past either of them to start throwing punches; perhaps it was just as well they had jesses on.

Balos cleared his throat. "My family are farmers, and I have to admit, I can't see you raising good beets," he said mildly.

Jerith didn't break eye contact with Zaira. "Well, *my* family are Loreician nobles, and they hid me from the Falcons until I was eight, when I lost control and murdered my best friend and three other children." His gaze narrowed to intense silver slits. "And I *still* managed to stop fighting my power, for the sake of control. Because I didn't want anything like that to ever happen again."

Grace of Mercy. I'd known Jerith had some tragedy in his past, as most warlocks did, but I'd always hoped with the small corner of my mind willing to think about it that it had been some narrow escape, ending perhaps in injury rather than death.

But I should have known better. Lightning knew no kindness, and balefire no mercy.

"Good for you, rich brat," Zaira growled, but some of the fight had gone out of her stance.

The tension eased visibly from Jerith's spine, too. They were like two cats who'd decided not to fight after all, and now glanced around the room as if uncertain how they'd come to be facing off with each other, tails still lashing.

"Ignore my advice if you want," Jerith said at last. "But the fact that I followed it is the reason we still have a city to go home to."

"There you are. I was wondering where you kept disappearing to." I leaned over the railing of the sending spire platform, my coat drawn tight around me. The air had gone quite still with the coming twilight, and soft gray clouds muffled the sky, seeming low enough over our heads that I could almost reach up and touch them.

Kathe sat on the roof not far off, his arms resting on his knees and his feathered cloak spread out on the red tiles around him. Perhaps half a dozen crows had gathered to him, and he was stroking one's glossy neck.

"I've set up a meeting with the Lady of Spiders, as you asked," he said, without looking up.

"Thank you," I said, though leggy memories of our last encounter crept up my spine. She'd *said* I'd need something from her someday. "You mentioned she'd want a price, and I suspect you don't mean in ducats. Do you have any idea what she'll ask for?"

The feathers on Kathe's shoulders rustled. "All the secrets

you most wish to hide, scavenged from the shadows of your mind."

I swallowed. "Is that a metaphor, or..."

"Oh, I'm being quite literal." Kathe's piercing eyes flicked up to meet mine. "That's why she's one of the most influential Witch Lords. She accumulates knowledge and secrets—magical and personal, ancient lore and buried shame." His mouth twisted in a bitter smile. "Everyone comes to her eventually, when a question burns so brightly it outshines their better judgment. So no one dares go against her, because she knows the precise threads to pull on to unravel them."

The edge in his tone made me wonder if he was speaking from personal experience. "Can she be trusted?"

He tipped his head, appearing to think it over. "She herself is unlikely to use the knowledge she gleans against you so long as you leave her alone. But others could trade their secrets for one of yours, if they wanted it badly enough. And the process itself is...unpleasant. It's not a bargain to enter lightly."

I pulled my coat closer around me. "I'm not certain we have a choice."

"There's always another move you can make," Kathe said, tapping a crow gently on the beak. It nibbled his finger affectionately. "There may not be another one that will win you the game, though."

"So long as we can win and end it swiftly." I leaned my elbows on the stone railing, looking out at the blasted wasteland below. The line separating life from death was so stark and sudden. I shivered. "I spoke to my mother over the courier lamps, and I have the full backing of the Empire, though it took some persuasion. We can leave tomorrow morning, if that's all right with you."

"Of course." A crow hopped onto his hand and he lifted it to stare into its beady black eyes, avoiding mine. "Let is on the way, as it happens. Will you visit my home with me?"

"I would love to see it." A certain unexpected fluttering occurred in my chest at the thought. "Though I fear we'll be in something of a hurry."

"We can dally more on the way back." He grinned and rose to his feet, without any apparent care for the rounded sloping tiles beneath him. His crows scattered to give him space as he paced toward me. "Assuming we're not all dead, of course."

"It's so kind of you to include yourself in that 'we,'" I said dryly. "You're far too clever a bird to get caught."

"Oh, I make my share of rash mistakes." Kathe grimaced. "Just ask my Heartguard."

"Perhaps I will." I stared out over the blackened valley. No traffic traveled down the River Arden or the road beside it from the north. No one moved across the scorched fields, searching for remnants of their lives among the homes that had burned there. It was a place the Graces had forsaken utterly, and all the bustling people of Ardence and the lands beyond looked away from it, as if to gaze upon it might be to become cursed. "I hear Ruven's withdrawn northward," I said slowly. "There were farms and villages and towns there, in the land he marched through coming down from the hills. I don't have much intelligence yet on what state they're in."

Kathe leaned on the stone railing beside me, from the other side. The platform I stood on gave me extra height, putting me slightly above the soft, black-tipped locks of his hair. A sudden urge to run my fingers through it possessed me, and I forced my gaze back to the valley, where dusk had begun softening the hills to purple.

"I do have some news on that front, from my crows," Kathe said carefully.

Foreboding gripped my chest like an overtightened corset. "I miss the days when news was sometimes good."

"It's not very romantic, is it? I didn't want to tell you and spoil the mood." He gestured grandly out over the desolate ruin of the valley.

"You have a strange notion of what's romantic. But go on."

"Well, the good news is that he didn't kill everyone." Kathe paused. "If you can call that good."

Somehow, I doubted it. "What has he done to them?"

"Some he's given his potion. Some he's turned into chimeras." Kathe flicked a chip of loose mortar off the railing and watched it go skittering off down the roof tiles. "And some died fighting, of course. But most of them he's sending back to Kazerath, to make his own."

The winter air found a gap in my coat and slid its cold hands up my back. "We have to save them."

"I believe that is the plan, yes. By killing Ruven."

I stared north. The hills rose crowned with snow at the far end of the valley, lifting pure white heads above the black and gray waste of ash and cinders. Smoke and coming dusk hazed the air too much for the Witchwall Mountains to be visible beyond them, but I knew they were out there, looming against the sky.

"This isn't the world I wanted to build," I said quietly.

Kathe surveyed the scorched wasteland below us. "If it were, I admit I would have to question your objectives."

"I don't want to always have to protect my people through killing." I gripped the railing, the stone cold beneath my hands. "I want it to be more like when I passed the Falcon Reserve Act. Using my mind and my words to chart a course for the Empire by which justice and decency can prevail. But I have the tools for both war and peace in my hands now, and if I move with the wrong hand at the wrong time, everything will shatter, like glass in a crowded shop."

He laid his cool, elegant fingers over mine. The touch demanded nothing, but changed us instantly from separate lonely figures on a windswept roof to a pair standing together. "That doesn't change," he said softly. "It's terrifying."

"What do we do, then, Kathe?" I asked desperately, searching the sharp, ageless lines of his face for an answer.

"The best we can. And we hope it's enough."

"I should be going with you," Lucia fretted.

She sat restlessly on the most comfortable chair in my guest room, only barely keeping herself from leaping to her feet and helping the servants who packed my things because the physician had threatened to send her back to bed if she did. Two days and the attentions of an alchemist and the Serene Envoy's personal physician had done wonders; she didn't look well, certainly, but neither did she appear ready to expire at any moment. Her regimen of potions and strict limits on activity would continue for some time, however, so accompanying us to Vaskandar was out of the question.

Which was just as well, and not only because of my irrational fear that anyone besides Kathe and Zaira who crossed into Vaskandar with me would wind up dead.

"I need you here," I said sternly. "There's too much work to be done, and I won't be in the Empire to do it."

"You're just saying that to make me feel better." She tried out half a smile. "My lady."

"Not in the slightest." I dragged a chair directly opposite hers and sat down so that I could stare directly into her eyes. "The Falcon Reserve Act is just as important as stopping Ruven. More so, in the long run. I need you to defend it for me while I'm out of the country."

Lucia frowned. "Defend it, my lady?"

"Yes." I lowered my voice. "Its opponents may well attempt to sabotage it while I'm gone. Even if they don't, this is a delicate moment. We need to make certain the transition happens smoothly—that the Mews and the Empire comply with the law. That there's no retaliation against the mage-marked. That any Falcons who choose to leave active duty and join the reserve can live comfortable and safe civilian lives. That newly discovered mage-marked and their families understand their options. That no one attempts to capitalize on the system by gathering up mage-marked to create a power base."

Lucia's eyes grew wider and wider as I spoke. "I see what you mean, my lady."

"I wouldn't leave the Serene Empire now if there were anyone else who could do this," I told her, and I meant it. "There's too much at stake. I'm trusting you to handle this in my name until I return."

"My lady, I . . ." She hesitated. "I wish I could be certain I was worthy of your trust."

I squeezed her hand. "This is why Ciardha picked you." I had to believe it. "Because you're a scholar. Because you can be a leader. She could have picked anyone to be my aide if I only needed a bodyguard who could run errands for me. But Ciardha knew what I would need, because she's Ciardha, and she's basically perfect."

Lucia nodded vigorously, and I almost laughed.

"And she chose you, Lucia," I told her. "That's how I know you can do this. Ciardha chose you."

"Then I'll do it." Lucia drew herself up, then winced and pressed a hand to her ribs. "I'll have a full report for you when you return, my lady."

When I return. It was hard to think of coming back to Raverra. Even if we defeated Ruven, how could I come home, with a wake of death and ashes behind me? How could I come home without Marcello?

But I'd given Lucia the answer already. I had done at least one good thing, by the Graces. And for the sake of all the mage-marked in the Serene Empire, I would see it through, for all the days of my life.

I lifted my chin with resolve. "I look forward to it."

Chapter Thirty-Two

There was no avoiding the bones. They crunched beneath our horses' feet, falling to brittle blackened shards. Our mounts stepped nervously, tossing their heads, snorting at the trailing clouds of ash that rose with the wind and settled again over the charred remains of several thousand soldiers.

There wasn't much left of them. The balefire had taken clothes and flesh and armor, faces and hair and the last screams from their lungs. The fragments of bone that remained could have been sticks and coals left over from last night's fire.

But they weren't. And Zaira knew it.

She bowed over her horse's neck, looking pale and ill, her hands clenched on the saddle. She'd never learned to ride, but that wasn't an issue with Kathe along; her horse followed his, well-behaved despite the uneasy shivers that sometimes crossed its shoulders when the ash blew past. I was hardly any better a rider, but the road wasn't passable for a coach.

Because of all the people we had killed.

A certain queasy dizziness washed over me, and I wished I could close my eyes. But it wouldn't be right to look away. I had done this, as much as Zaira had. I could have spared these people with one word, and I hadn't.

"I could give them flowers," Kathe said softly.

Zaira lifted her head, blinking as if she were coming back from far away. "What?"

"I could give them flowers," Kathe said again, looking back. "The seeds are there in the earth. It's winter, so they would die before morning. But I could grow flowers along the road, at least, if you like."

Zaira seemed to think it over. "No," she said, her voice rough. "No, don't cover over the truth. The Grace of Bounty will give them flowers when those seeds are good and ready."

I tried to imagine green grass growing over the smoking mounds of ash, and flowers blooming all through the valley, coming out in a blaze as bright as balefire. It seemed impossible, now, but life was inexorable. It would always triumph over death in the end.

That, I supposed, was what made Witch Lords so dangerous.

We climbed up out of the valley into the hills, and soon our horses' hooves fell on snow. With the smoky haze left behind us, Mount Whitecrown emerged from hiding, its glacier-mantled shoulders rising with breathtaking glory above the surrounding peaks. I pulled on a fur hat and mittens I'd made certain to acquire after my last trip to Vaskandar in entirely insufficient winter clothing, and turned up the collar on my fur-lined coat, the gold embroidery tickling my chin. My breath still made clouds in the air, and I wished I had a scarf to wrap around my cold nose.

The three of us were completely alone on the broad trade road. We'd decided that with Kathe and Zaira along, an escort of soldiers would be superfluous and only slow us down—but the land itself was eerily empty. Farms and houses scattered across the hills, and the road threaded past villages and towns and wayside inns; all of them stood silent. This land had been evacuated as Ruven's troops approached, and if anyone had been so foolish as to stay behind, there was no sign of them now. No smoke rose from the chimneys, despite the cold, and windows showed dark and still.

"Quiet as the Hell of Despair," Zaira muttered as we rode past another shuttered village. "I thought you said we were avoiding Ruven's army."

"We are." Instinct kept my voice low, even with no one around for miles to hear us. "His forces followed the west fork of the River Arden down out of the mountains, and we're following the east fork, to cross into Vaskandar in my great-grandmother's domain of Atruin."

"So why are there no people, if he didn't come this way?"

"We should reach inhabited areas soon," I said, trying to sound more certain than I felt. "The courier lamp relay lines were sabotaged in this area, so I don't know exactly where, but soon."

A crow had dropped from the sky to land on Kathe's shoulder and mutter in his ear—a frequent occurrence thus far on this journey—and he tipped his head as if listening. "Ruven's pulled back toward Kazerath and is blooding his claim in the hills to the west," he reported. "No sign of people on the road ahead, for a few miles at least. But I've found something else interesting."

"It's not an enemy Witch Lord this time, is it?" Zaira asked warily.

Kathe only grinned in answer.

A moment later he trotted off the road at an abandoned inn; our horses followed his around the back of it, their ears pricked and alert. Zaira and I exchanged worried glances, but found nothing more alarming than Kathe gesturing proudly at a red-painted sleigh. Hoofprints churned up the thin crust of snow in the yard around it, and a bare rectangle of ground and the ruts of wheel marks suggested the inn's residents had taken the wagon rather than the sleigh for the journey to safety in the snowless valley.

"There," Kathe said, with satisfaction. "This will let us go *much* faster. You two are terrible riders."

"We use boats in Raverra, not horses," I apologized.

Kathe hitched two of our horses to the sleigh and let the third go, whispering to each the entire time. The one he freed trotted purposefully back toward Ardence, and I had no doubt it would find its stable. Zaira, meanwhile, raided the inn for blankets and food, while I left money to pay for everything, hoping that thieves wouldn't find it before the innkeeper did. Soon the three of us settled comfortably into the sleigh, with me in the middle and Zaira and Kathe to either side. I worried for a moment about who would drive before I remembered that Kathe needed no reins to guide the horses.

Kathe turned to me and grinned. "Brace yourself," he warned us. "When we were setting out, I picked horses who liked to run. And I can let them run as fast as they want for as long as they want, without getting injured or tired."

"What are you—" I began, but then the sleigh sprang forward.

Zaira whooped, and I couldn't blame her; it was exhilarating, the snow flying beneath us, the breeze in our hair, the sleigh hissing along the road. It was so much smoother than a coach, and with Kathe enhancing the horses, our speed was just short of terrifying. The wind stung my face with cold, but the rest of me was snug and warm under Zaira's blankets, with Kathe pressed against me on one side and Zaira putting out heat like an oven on the other.

Crows swooped alongside us as we raced through the hills, calling back and forth to Kathe and to each other. The clouds passed and the sky broke blue above us, and snow fell in clumps off the branches of evergreens, which sprang up to greet the sun with the weight gone from them. I let my mind blow clean with the white snow and the clear sunlight and the stark black writing of the trees against the sky, and my heart let some of the weight on it go as well, at least for a short while.

But the dark empty windows of every farmhouse we passed and the unnerving lack of other travelers on the road reminded me that this was no wintry pleasure jaunt. The bright veneer of snow and sun over everything couldn't hide that we had already slid off the perilous edge into war, at the cost of thousands of lives. If we didn't want the whole empire to wind up like this—a desolate ghost country, its people in hiding or dragged off to serve as consumable fuel for Ruven's magic—we had work to do.

A crow swooped down out of the sky and landed on the hand Kathe raised to meet it, looking ruffled and quite offended. Kathe listened to its raucous complaints, then peered up at the sky and muttered, "I should have expected this."

I followed his gaze and saw a large dark bird circling overhead, its broad wings rocking against the gray sky. "What is it?"

"A vulture chimera." The crow perched on Kathe's hand cawed harshly at the offending creature; I suspected its remark was rude. "Ruven's, no doubt. It's tracking us."

"I could try to set it on fire," Zaira offered, squinting dubiously up at it. "I've never tried to burn something in the air before, though."

"That reminds me," I murmured. "Since we're not surrounded by innocent bystanders anymore . . . *Exsolvo*."

Zaira winced as if I'd shouted a curse at her, but made no objection. Perhaps I should have asked before releasing her within a few hours of passing through the valley of death we had created.

Kathe was still staring upward, absently stroking his bird's glossy chest. "My crows would be delighted to mob it and chase it off, for that matter, but it wouldn't solve anything. We're close enough to Kazerath that another spy would take its place." He glanced at me. "Especially now that his domain has the taste of your blood."

The healing wounds in my arms itched at the thought, and I rubbed them uneasily; the bandages were off now, thanks to a good healing salve, and the scars passed rough and raw beneath my hands. "I hadn't thought of that. Does this mean everything in Kazerath is going to attack me on sight?"

"It means everything that's part of his domain will know you, and he can put out domain-wide standing commands about you." Kathe loosed his bird, which fluttered off to a roadside tree. "So if he wants you tracked, he has an entire nation full of animals to track you, all of which know you by scent and sight."

"At least the big stinking bird is easy to spot," Zaira grumbled.

"The question," Kathe said, leveling the vivid yellow rings of his mage mark at me, "is what he'll do, now that he knows you've left Ardence. What does he want from you, my lady?"

I shifted uncomfortably. "He wants me to accept his offer. He'll probably try to put pressure on me." And he'd made it quite clear how he intended to do that. I swallowed. "Which means Marcello."

"So we know his next move." Kathe rubbed his hands. "Excellent. Shall we try to take his piece?"

I rubbed my thumb across the ring Istrella had given me. "Yes," I said, lifting my chin with determination. "Yes, I think we will."

Kathe's crows picked out another deserted inn for us to sleep in—which was somewhat unsettling, especially since I would have expected to be past the evacuated area by now. With no need for stealth and our enhanced horses, we'd made it into the foothills of the Witchwall Mountains, approaching the Vaskandran border. Most likely the local people had withdrawn to Greymarch fortress to the north for safety, taking no chances with an invading army in the area, but with the courier lamp relay mirrors shattered, there was no way to be sure.

We gathered in the inn's empty dining room. No fire burned in the hearth, and the shadowy emptiness made the place feel haunted despite the lack of dust or disorder. Nothing was out of place; everything looked as if the innkeeper and all the guests had just stepped outside for a moment, and would be back shortly.

"Well, there's a kitchen, so we can make a hot dinner," Zaira reported.

We all stared at each other.

My mouth twitched. "Not one of us knows how to cook, do we?"

Zaira shook her head. "I never had a kitchen."

"I always had a chef," I admitted.

Kathe shrugged, looking strangely embarrassed. "I, ah, don't need to eat."

"That's just weird." Zaira poked him in the arm. Kathe gave her a startled look, then tipped his head, frowning, as if trying to figure out what this puzzling action could mean. But Zaira had already turned away from him. "Well, let's see what they've got that's good cold."

We had a meal of stale bread, oil-cured olives, a decent sharp country cheese, dried apricots, and honey. Zaira ate about five times what I did, still replenishing her energy after all the balefire she'd unleashed. When she was done she stretched, sighed, and patted her tummy.

"What do you think?" she asked, eyeing me with speculation. "Is it late enough for some fishing?"

My stomach clenched the food I'd eaten into a hard knot. "I suppose I should give it a try."

Kathe pushed his plate away. He'd taken at least a taste of everything and wound up eating half the olives, so apparently he didn't mind eating, even if it wasn't strictly necessary. "It may be ironic at best for me to say this, but I have misgivings about using you as bait." He paused. "Again."

"This time it was my idea." I rose, pressing my palms on the table to hide their trembling. "He probably won't show up anyway. And if he does, I'm certain I can get him to talk. Ruven doesn't want me dead."

Kathe nodded slowly, holding my gaze. "I'll have crows watching you. Good luck."

My breath made crisp white puffs in the cold night air. The clouds had begun to clear, and diamond-hard stars peeked through the shredding gaps. I hugged my coat around me as I ambled in front of the inn, taking the longest possible route through the grounds toward the stables. A crow eyed me beadily from the branches of a pear tree, puffed up to a black sphere against the cold.

"Here I am, all alone, going to get something I forgot from my baggage," I muttered, turning Istrella's ring on my finger to make certain it was loose. "Totally not a trap at all."

The snow blanketing the patch of rolling fields around the inn shone in the muffled starlight, a stark contrast to the ragged dark edge of the forest and the looming black shadow of the surrounding hills. I wished I could have brought a lantern, more for the comfort of a warm spark in the vast darkness than for the light it would have shed, but I needed my hands free.

Still, it was hard not to hurry as I crossed the snow, boots crunching, toward the hulking barn behind which we'd left the sleigh. Knowing that we were hoping something *would* leap at me out of the shadows made it even worse.

I caught a whiff of hay as I passed the barn; one of our horses let out a sharp, short whinny, no doubt questioning my sanity for being outside on a night like tonight. The moon came out from behind a cloud just as I rounded the corner, throwing a patch of bright silver light on the sleigh and the baggage we'd left in the back to give me an excuse to wander out here alone.

The scent of anise struck me, faint in the open night air and sickly sweet.

Marcello bent over our bags, one of my elixir bottles empty and upside-down in his hand, his orange eye blazing with reflected light like a cat's.

Chapter Thirty-Three

He straightened when he saw me, for all the world like a guilty child, even as my insides performed an extraordinary set of acrobatics.

"What are you *doing*?" I demanded. Another empty bottle caught my eye, gleaming in the moonlight at his feet; the sight cut me like broken glass. That was both of the large bottles I'd had in my bag—I had some small ones in my satchel up in my room, thank the Graces, but this was still a disaster.

Marcello lifted a hand. "I don't want to do this, Amalia. Graces know I don't. Please, hear me out; I have a message."

It was *his* voice, worried and a bit embarrassed, as if he were himself again. I could almost believe we were back at the Mews and he was apologizing for some annoying regulation or order he had to follow, if it weren't for the empty bottles shining in the snow.

He'd poured out my survival onto the frozen ground, and now he was sorry for the inconvenience. Ruven could twist him to murder, but couldn't make him rude. My eyes stung.

"Fine," I said, clinging to the pretense that this was normal, that he was all right, trying to ignore the horrifying scent of anise surrounding us. "What's your message?"

Marcello took a deep breath. "My lord Ruven wishes to extend—"

I hurled his sister's ring at him as hard as I could.

It hit him in the chest and stuck there, runes flaring to life. He went utterly still, the breath he'd gathered easing out in a vague huff rather than whatever word he'd intended. His eyes stayed fixed on me, the human one wide with shock and perhaps a touch of betrayal, the inhuman one glaring with its slit pupil wide to drink in the darkness.

I fumbled in my pocket and found the obsidian ring, careful not to accidentally slip it on my own finger. Trembling, I approached Marcello where he stood with his hand still raised, feeling his gaze on me.

"We'll save you," I whispered to him, staring into his green eye. "We'll bring you home. I promise."

And I slipped the obsidian ring over his finger.

His eyes went vague and glassy at once, and he collapsed to the snow.

Zaira and Kathe helped me settle Marcello on a bed in one of the inn guest rooms. I drew the blanket up over his chest, careful not to dislodge the obsidian ring. Zaira left at once, with a glance at me and an announcement that she was going to forage for some wine, but I lingered by Marcello's side.

I couldn't help staring at his face. With his eyes closed, I could almost pretend that the silver scales running down his temple, cheek, and neck were just an effect of the moonlight. He looked relaxed, peaceful, without any trace of the torment that had pulled at his face ever since that terrible night in the Imperial Palace. I wished he could sleep like this until we found a way to cure him, and then wake believing it had all been a terrible dream.

Feathers rustled at my side. "What will we do with him, now that we have him?" Kathe asked.

"We can take him with us to Greymarch fortress and ask them to hold him there for now." I itched to smooth Marcello's tangled hair back from his face, but it seemed inappropriate to do so with Kathe standing next to me. "I have to stop there to ask their alchemist to make me more elixir, anyway. I only have my backup bottles left, about four days' worth."

I turned from Marcello's bedside. I suddenly couldn't bear to watch him sleep anymore, knowing that the appearance of peace was an illusion. That I'd only postponed the reckoning I dreaded, not avoided it. Kathe followed me into the narrow hallway with its yellow-painted walls and creaky old board floors; I closed Marcello's door, gently as if I could actually wake him, and leaned my forehead against it.

Kathe hesitated, then laid a hand on my shoulder—an awkward gesture, as if he'd seen someone do it in a woodcut illustration and knew this was how one expressed sympathy, but had never tried it before. For all I knew, that might be exactly the case.

"I'm sorry this happened to your friend," he said quietly.

"Could you tell whether he..." I couldn't finish, or meet Kathe's eyes.

"The transformation is clearly more than skin deep, but I could also sense Ruven's presence wound through him." Revulsion laced Kathe's voice. "So I can't tell how much is Ruven's external influence versus permanent physical changes. In all honesty, chimeras are much more closely bound to their creator's will than creatures naturally born in a Witch Lord's domain; I'm surprised his own personality and principles are able to break through at all."

I closed my eyes. Marcello's principles were stronger than the pillars of the Empire. There was a strange comfort in knowing that his honor and loyalty were rocks that even the vast ocean of Ruven's magic couldn't wash away. "I see. Thank you."

"One way or another, we'll kill him," Kathe promised.

It took me a moment to realize he meant Ruven. I turned to him, a complex tangle of feelings winding tighter in my chest. "Is that what you think I want? Vengeance?"

He blinked. "Don't you?"

I shook my head. "I want Ruven dead to end the threat he poses. But I'd leave him alive if it would fix all the damage he's done." As soon as the words left my mouth, I thought of Ruven's offer; it might well be the only way to restore Marcello. The knowledge twisted at my gut. "My mother taught me that vengeance inevitably comes to rule the one seeking it. And nothing must rule a Cornaro."

Kathe grimaced and rubbed the back of his head, mussing up his pale, black-tipped hair. "I must confess I find it rather satisfying, myself."

"I suppose you would." I sank down against the wall, exhaustion dragging on me like a damp wool blanket. "I can't hoard grievances like jewels the way you do in Vaskandar. If my fists are closed around grudges, my hands aren't free to work. I have to let them go and focus on doing what needs to be done."

Kathe crouched next to me, frowning, reminding me for all the world of one of his own birds hunkering inside its feathers against the cold. "Maybe I'm going about this wrong, then."

"Going about what wrong?"

"If you were a Witch Lord, you would hold a serious grievance against me for what I did to you at the Conclave." Kathe glanced down, drawing patterns in the dust on the floor with his finger. "If I wanted to keep you as an ally, or a friend, I would need to offer you favors in return until you were satisfied."

"I see." I reached out and barely brushed the feathers of his cloak, their softness sliding beneath my fingertips. "You're still my friend, Kathe. And my ally, too, I hope."

He caught my hand gently in his, lifting it so the lace fell away from my wrists and the first few of the raw, half-healed claw wounds showed on my forearm. "You forgive too easily," he murmured, tracing a tingling path between the red marks. "You let people too close, for a leader of a great empire. It's dangerous."

"Yes, well, I do question my sanity sometimes, particularly where my courtship choices are concerned," I said, a bit breathlessly. "Don't think you can get away with anything you like just because I'm willing to give you another chance, though."

Kathe's lips quirked in a one-sided smile. "It wouldn't be much fun if you *let* me get away with anything. I prefer it to be more of a contest." He rose, offering his hand. "Speaking of which, Zaira found a deck of cards while you were outside, and promised to teach me some Raverran games. A wound won't heal if you poke at it. Would you like to come allow yourself to be distracted for a while?"

Part of me rebelled at the idea of playing cards when three thousand people were dead at our hands and Ruven had twisted and broken Marcello, perhaps beyond mending. It seemed almost indecent to grasp after joy when everything was so terrible.

But to completely surrender joy would be to allow Ruven a victory. I took Kathe's extended hand, slim and strong in mine.

"All right," I said softly. "For a while."

He drew me to my feet, and we went downstairs together.

Zaira and Kathe played cards far more competitively than I did. After a couple of hours, I was yawning, ready to collapse into the oblivion of sleep; Kathe, on the other hand, finally had a solid grasp of the rules and strategy and had a fire in his eyes.

"Ooh, you're not just a pretty face after all," Zaira said appreciatively, after he beat her for the first time in a close-fought game that I'd been knocked out of in the third round. "Keep getting better at this rate, and I'm going to have to start cheating."

"Is cheating acceptable, then?" Kathe asked eagerly, sweeping his cards up off the table. "Because if you're cheating, I'm cheating."

I rose, rubbing my eyes. "I, on the other hand, am going to bed," I announced. "Enjoy yourselves."

Zaira waved me off like a fly. "The grown-ups are busy, Cornaro. Go get your baby rest."

I paused at the top of the stairs, in the darkened hallway, as one board let out a slow creak beneath my feet. Marcello's door stood at the far end. I paced toward it as if some current drew me that way. One look, I told myself, to make sure he was all right. To see his face looking almost human as he slept.

I eased the door open and peeked in. And then I took three quick steps across the room in shock, reaching out with a shaking hand to verify what my eyes refused to believe.

His bed was empty. The obsidian ring lay neatly on the center of his pillow.

Claws folded gently around my neck from behind.

"Shh," Marcello whispered. "Let's talk."

Chapter Thirty-Four

My pulse hammered against the sharp points of his claws. I held utterly still. "It's difficult to talk when one can't move one's throat," I said carefully.

"Sorry about that. I'm going to let go in a moment." His words stirred my hair. "I have a message for you. I'm going to deliver it, then leave. That's all." He took a ragged breath. "But if you call for help or attack me again, I have to cripple you on my way out."

"That seems uncivil and unlike you," I said, struggling to sound calm.

Marcello's fingers trembled on my throat. "My lord Ruven is upset that you didn't listen to his message the first time, so he melted my flesh and bone to get the ring off and gave me new orders." His voice dropped to a whisper. "Please don't test those orders, Amalia. I don't have the power to resist them."

I didn't doubt it was true, any more than I doubted Marcello's ability to rip my hamstrings or put out my eyes in the time it took me to blink, with his chimera's speed. "All right," I agreed unsteadily.

His claws eased away from my throat. "Let's try this again, then."

Slowly, keeping my hands in plain sight, I turned around.

The moonlight caught in Marcello's scales and glowed in his inhuman eye. He wore the same frayed uniform, his unkempt black hair brushing its collar. Now that he was awake, pain once again haunted and hollowed his face.

He had my satchel slung over one shoulder.

I started to reach for it in instinctive panic. My notes were in there, and one of my favorite magical theory books, and my remaining elixir bottles—and worst of all, the jess I'd gotten from the garrison in Ardence, just in case we had a chance to use it on Ruven. I couldn't let that fall into his hands.

"Don't!" Marcello raised a hand in warning, claws unsheathed, eyes widening with real fear. "Don't come any closer, or reach for your flare locket, or call for the others. *Please.*" He took a shuddery breath, as if he were fighting something inside him. "I don't want to take your personal things, and I know how you feel about your books. If you talk to me, I'll simply complete my orders, then return your satchel. But if you give me a reason to run, I'll have to take the whole thing, and…" A muscle in his jaw jumped. "And hurt you very badly."

My pulse raced like quicksilver through my veins. "What are your orders? I thought you just had a message."

"This is part of the message." His human eye shone bright with unshed tears in the moonlight. "I'm sorry. I don't want to do this."

He reached into my satchel and pulled out one of my backup elixir bottles.

"What are you doing? Leave that alone!" I checked myself from lunging at him in panic, with some difficulty.

Marcello flicked the stopper out with one claw, turned the bottle upside down, and began pouring my elixir out on the floor.

"Marcello, no! I need that!" Fear spiked my voice louder than I'd meant. I had an emergency vial in the inner pocket of the coat I still wore, but that would only cover tonight's dose. Without the bottles in that bag, I'd resume dying in the morning.

"I'm sorry, Amalia," he said again, his voice rough with emotion. "Ruven made me tell him everything I knew about your weaknesses."

He shook out every last drop from the bottle; the smell of anise filled the room. Then he pulled the next bottle out of my satchel and ripped the cork out of that one, too.

"You're going to *kill* me!" I protested, desperate, as Zaira's laughter drifted up from below. "Why should I talk to you if you're destroying my elixir?"

"Oh, you'll listen," he said through his teeth. A vicious edge crept into his voice. "Not so easy to overlook now, am I?"

The sickly-sweet smell of anise strengthened as more potion spattered to the floor. "I'm listening, damn you! Look, you have my attention, you can stop!"

"Lord Ruven has asked me to tell you," Marcello said, biting off each word as if he hated the taste of his own tongue, "that he can cure you."

My breath froze in my throat. "What?"

"He's a Skinwitch and a scholar. He can purge the Demon's Tears from your veins. You won't need this elixir anymore." Marcello tossed the empty second bottle onto his bed and opened the third. "That's what you want, isn't it? Not to have to depend on anyone."

"I depend on you," I whispered, reaching toward him despite myself. "Fight him, Marcello. You don't have to do this. Don't let him make you kill me."

He bared his teeth as if he were in agony. "Accept his offer, and you won't have to die. He can get here in plenty of time to save you. Just swear you'll serve him, and you can live."

A clear stream flowed from the third bottle, splashing onto shining floorboards already dark with the rest of it.

"You know I can't do that," I said desperately, as the well-worn wood soaked up the elixir I needed to live like dry earth.

"You'd best consider it, or you're going to die in agony." Marcello's orange eye remained merciless, but his green one pleaded with me as the stream slowed to a trickle. "My lord asks for your help claiming more domains, your blood, and your lifelong service. In return, he can cure you permanently and save your life. He can restore me to the way I was. And he can withdraw all his forces from the Empire."

"He *can* do all of those things, yes," I snapped. "But I'm not such a fool as to believe he *will* do them, in good faith, with no strings attached. I'm on the Council now—I can't take a bad bargain like that, even to save my life. I'm calling Ruven's bluff. If he wants me alive, I need that elixir."

Marcello drew out my last elixir bottle. He pulled the cork and paused. "It's not a bluff," he rasped. "My Lord Ruven doesn't bluff. Take his bargain, Amalia. You can live, and I can be human again, and the Empire will be safe. All he wants in return is you."

My eyes stayed fixed on the small glass bottle, and the line of liquid tipping toward its round rim. "Stop. *Stop*, Marcello. I know you don't want to do this."

"I don't," he agreed softly. "But I have to, unless you agree to my lord's offer."

"Did he command you?" I took an urgent step toward him; he hissed like an angry cat, and I stopped, my stomach clenching. "Tell me what he said, and we can find a way around it!"

"It's not like that." Marcello shook his head fiercely. "His will is my will. It's not a verbal command I can try to outwit. Now give me your answer."

"I need time to think."

"Time to stall, you mean. I know you, Amalia. Give me your answer now, before Zaira or Kathe can wander up here and find us."

The bottle tipped in his hand. A single drop quivered from the rim, sparkling in the moonlight.

I could lie. I could get as much as Ruven would give me, then back out before giving him anything too risky in return. If all I gained was just this one elixir bottle, well, at least I'd still be alive to keep fighting him.

"Fine," I said. "I'll do it. I'll work with him, if he cures you first. Just put that down, and we can negotiate the details."

Marcello winced as if I'd struck him. "You always were a terrible liar, Amalia."

He flipped the bottle, and the last of my elixir gushed out, wasted and gone.

My legs wavered under me. I sank on the edge of the bed, stunned. I was all too aware of the tiny precious vial inside my coat that would buy me twelve more hours of life in which to find an alchemist. Marcello knew about it, too, and by the way he was eyeing me, he hadn't forgotten.

Marcello rummaged in my satchel. "Is that the last one in here? If so, next I'm afraid I'll need—" He froze, frowning. "What's this?"

Oh, Hells. He'd found the jess. My hand stole slowly toward my flare locket.

But what he lifted from the satchel was much smaller than a jess. It was a round golden button, embossed with a falcon—the one he had given me months ago when we parted for a time, so that something of his would go with me.

He stared at it, the color draining from his face. "You still have this," he whispered.

"Of course I do." My throat ached so much I could hardly speak. "I carry it to remind me of your good advice when I want to do dangerous things, like you asked." My voice cracked. "I ignore it, of course, but it makes me feel better to hear your voice in my mind."

He closed his fist tight around the button, and squeezed his eyes shut. I didn't dare move. Tears leaked from his human eye, streaming down his cheek.

Then he dropped the button back in my satchel and set it carefully down on the floor, in the damp patch of anise-scented potion seeping into the floorboards.

"I'll be going now," he said, his voice low and husky. "Say hello to Zaira for me."

"Wait!" I lunged for him at last, but he leaped up into the window as if it were something he practiced all the time.

"Take care of yourself, Amalia," he said, and the shadow of his old wistful smile flitted across his face.

And then he leaped down, a jump that would likely have broken his legs when he was human. By the time I made it to the window, he was halfway across the field to the waiting black forest, leaving a sparse line of footprints behind him in the snow.

Our sleigh hissed along through the night, beneath the cold stars, taking corners fast enough that one runner came up off the snow. Every muscle in my body locked with fear that we'd plummet off a cliff or slam into a tree, but Kathe had enhanced the horses' eyes to see in the dark, even if we couldn't. I huddled between Kathe and Zaira, alternately praying for the dawn to come faster, so we could see, and slower, so I could live.

Zaira gripped the bench with white knuckles. "Slow down, you crazy bastard! Do you get more points in some demon-cursed Witch Lord contest if we *all* die?"

Kathe's teeth flashed white in the moonlight. "No, but that's an intriguing idea. Would I get a better score if we all die at once, or sequentially?"

"Don't make it a game," I groaned.

After a tense discussion at the inn, we'd decided to continue north to Greymarch rather than turning back to Ardence; it was closer, and as a major fortress, it had at least one Falcon alchemist and a few minor ones without the mage mark, any of whom could make more of my elixir. Kathe thought we could get there not long after dawn; with any luck, I'd have a new batch ready before I even started to have symptoms. The single dose Marcello had left me inside my jacket had bought me enough time to save my life.

We flew along through the dark, ragged hours of the night, Zaira and I hanging on tight and muttering curses, until the sky went gray and then gold above the silhouetted peaks to the east. As the rosy light of dawn drew receding fingers of shadow across the snow, the great fortress of Greymarch came into view at last. The Grace of Luck had been with me, for once; we'd made it.

Greymarch perched upon a hill above the River Arden in the looming shadow of Mount Whitecrown. Its stout outer walls sprawled across most of the hilltop, and a massive stone keep reared up within them, with smaller buildings clustering around it. Proud round towers jutted from the castle and at intervals along the curtain wall, set to glowing by the sunrise. Ranks of cannons pointed down at the road as it ran alongside the river toward the Vaskandran border. Great artifice circles marked the road itself here; unlike the simpler trap circles we'd used outside Ardence, these could be triggered from a control circle in the fortress if anyone was foolish enough to try to march an enemy army this way, but otherwise lay safe and dormant for normal traffic on the road. More artifice circles decorated the bare rocky bluffs beneath the castle, ready to start landslides to block the pass.

The fortress teemed with activity, which was a relief after how empty the countryside had been all along our journey. Even from a distance it was easy to spot movement on the battlements, and smoke rose from the chimneys. If I recalled my reports correctly, there were some two thousand imperial troops stationed here to guard the pass, including half a dozen Falcons; if they'd been taking in farmers and villagers from the hill country to ensure their safety, well, there was certainly room for another thousand within those walls. I'd seen smaller towns.

The great fortress gates stood open, showing glimpses of swarming activity as troops mustered in the yard beyond. A handful of officers rode out to meet us, and the sight of their smart blue and gold imperial uniforms eased a knot of fear that had clenched my chest all night. I wondered wistfully if perhaps we could prevail upon them for soft beds and a few hours' sleep while their alchemists prepared my elixir; it had been a long night's travel.

Our sleigh slowed as the welcoming contingent approached. The woman riding in front was a colonel, by the insignia and trim on her coat, and likely the fortress commander.

"Good morning, Colonel," I greeted her, as she eyed my finely embroidered coat and Kathe's feathered cloak with a frown. "I'm afraid something of an emergency brings us here. I am—"

"Lady Amalia Cornaro." The colonel bowed deeply; the other officers followed suit. "I'd heard you might be stopping here on your way north. I'm sorry we're not more ready to receive you, but we're preparing to march."

"Did our messengers get through, then?" I asked. "We've been concerned, with the courier lamp relays broken and no word from your fortress."

The colonel grimaced. "Yes, we've received our orders at last. My apologies that we were unable to march sooner and come to Ardence's aid. Please, accept what hospitality we can offer, and be welcome at Greymarch."

"I'd be delighted, though we can only stop briefly. I need

to borrow the services of your alchemists; it's something of an emergency."

"Of course, my lady. Come inside, and we'll get you everything you need."

She reined her horse aside to fall in beside our sleigh, and the other officers followed suit. Kathe lifted his eyebrows in inquiry, and I nodded wearily, leaning back in the sleigh. The horses blew white puffs of steam and started forward again, toward the welcoming arch of the castle gate.

But something caught my eye: a V-shaped black fleck on the rose-tinged sky, high above the fortress. The vulture chimera.

Ruven knew we were here, and he'd made no move to stop us through all the long night.

I grabbed Kathe's hand. He shot me a puzzled glance, and I gave my head a sharp shake; the horses, who'd begun drawing our sleigh forward again, clattered to a confused stop. They flicked annoyed ears back at Kathe, as if wishing he'd make up his mind.

"Excuse me, Colonel," I asked politely, "but how did you know I was coming, with the courier lamp relays broken? There's no way a rider beat us here from Ardence with the news."

The colonel didn't quite meet my eyes. "A runner came from Stonewatch, five miles east. The courier lamps are working there."

One of the other officers stared at me intently, almost rudely. Zaira straightened in her seat, eyes narrowing. "Wait. You're marching to Ardence, you say?"

"Of course," the colonel said immediately. "We received orders for our entire garrison to march south and reinforce the city."

"No, you didn't." The cold certainty woke my sleepy brain like a bucket of water to the face. "We requested one thousand troops from Greymarch, with the rest to stay and guard the pass."

"I assure you, my lady, we did in fact receive orders for every soldier in the castle to march to Ardence," the colonel said, her words hard and precise. "Now if you'll come with me, I also have orders to make you quite comfortable if you happened to stop here."

Her eyes urged me to understand. And I did, all too well.

She must have seen it in my face. She mouthed a curse and gave a curt wave of her hand; the officers began fanning out into an arc. One of them laid a hand on her pistol.

Hells have mercy. They were under Ruven's control. All of them.

Chapter Thirty-Five

"I see where this is going," Kathe murmured.

He rose to his feet, and suddenly the air choked with the weight of his presence, as if he had swept aside the curtain with which he concealed the full force of his power.

"Enough," he said, and his voice echoed with the growling force of thunder.

The soldiers swore, drawing weapons; but their horses bucked and reared, eyes rolling, blowing great clouds of steam as their hooves kicked up snow. Pistols and swords clattered to the ground; the colonel and her officers had to hang on for dear life.

Kathe sat again, cloak spreading around him. The sleigh was already moving, our horses calmly turning around to head back down the spur road we'd taken to reach the fortress.

"That's unfortunate," he sighed, his tone normal again.

"Wait, stop!" the colonel called, clinging to her horse's heaving back. Behind her, a commotion broke out on the battlements of the fortress. Our horses started pulling away, their ears turned back in annoyance.

I gripped the bench, the full horrifying weight of what had just happened crushing me like a falling mountain. "They're controlled," I breathed. "Do you think Ruven just got the commanding officers, or—"

"Oh, I'll bet your fortune it's the whole damned castle," Zaira said. We picked up speed, hurtling down the mountain, snow flying beneath our horses' hooves as their manes blew behind them. "You said they had alchemists, right? Once he got them, he wouldn't have to worry about running out. He could just serve up his potion three meals a day to the whole cursed fortress, and with the courier lamps broken no one would even notice they were acting strangely."

A gunshot broke the stillness of the air, then another; wood chips flew off a tree as we passed it. I braced for a third shot, but it didn't come. Soldiers poured out of the fortress gate behind us, some of them with muskets ready, but they milled in confusion as we sped too far ahead of them to catch. It felt deeply wrong to be fleeing from soldiers in the familiar blue and gold uniforms of the Serene Empire, which should have meant protection and safety.

"And now there's a small army of imperial soldiers about to march on Ardence." I could hear my own voice rising and taking on an edge, but I couldn't rein it in any more than I could have slowed down the breakneck pace of our sleigh. "And when they get there, Jerith and the others are going to have to kill our own people, while Ruven watches and laughs."

Kathe made a disgusted sound. "He's got the common folk, too, from the farms and villages around here. My crows can see them mustering with the soldiers inside the castle. Old folk and children—anyone who can walk. He's going to march them all at your city and force your friends to kill them, or be conquered."

"Like Hells he is." Zaira looked half-ready to throw herself out of the sleigh and go storming after Ruven right now. "I don't care if he's immortal. I'll cut him into pieces, roast the pieces separately, and then feed the roasted bits to my dog just so he can shit him out later."

"You see, Amalia?" Kathe flashed a sharp grin my way. "Lady Zaira understands the appeal of vengeance."

"You're damned right I do."

We reached the bottom of the spur road with no sign of further pursuit; Ruven's orders must not have extended to the eventuality of our escape. The sleigh swung out behind the horses as they swerved onto the main road that followed the River Arden through a valley pass, the great white-capped peaks of the Witchwall Mountains rising in glory against the sky on either side. I was all too aware of the artifice trap circles lying beneath the snow; if Ruven decided he wanted us dead, all he had to do was give the order, and the officers up at the fortress could activate them and kill us with a word.

But then, if he wanted *me* dead, all he had to do was wait. And it would take a lot more than an artifice trap to kill Kathe.

Zaira nudged me with a sharp elbow. "All right, we need to find you another alchemist. How much time do we have?"

I tried to swallow, but my throat was too dry. "I normally would take my next elixir dose around midmorning. A couple of hours after that, my previous dose will wear off, and the Demon's Tears will start working again."

Kathe gave me a strange look, his face still and wary instead of animated with its usual mischief. "And what does that mean? How does it work? I've tailored herbs to cure poisons and illnesses before."

"Unfortunately, it's not that simple." I tried to pretend it was a theoretical question a younger student had asked me at the University of Ardence, and not a matter of my own survival. "Demon's Tears doesn't work like other alchemical poisons. It binds itself permanently to your heart and lungs, then cycles its magical influence through your blood until it completely infiltrates your body. Only then does it begin its attack, so that by the time you have symptoms it's too late for a true cure."

"And your uncle did that to you?" Zaira snorted. "Charming. Can't say I'm sorry he's dead."

Right now, I wasn't about to disagree. "My elixir doesn't fight the Demon's Tears directly. It suppresses the poison's ability to attack me. So unless you can make an herb that counteracts malign magical energy, I doubt you can help."

Kathe shook his head. "I've never wished I were an alchemist before." His gaze fell to his hands, which curled into fists in his lap. I suspected he liked feeling helpless even less than I did. "How long before it's too late?"

"The good news is that it's a lengthy and unpleasant death." That startled a nervous laugh out of him; despite the seriousness of my situation, I mentally chalked up a point for myself and smiled back. I ran the math in my head, a grim calculation of how many hours I had remaining. "If I can't get more elixir, I don't think I'm likely to survive more than a couple of hours past sunset."

Unless I agreed to Ruven's deal. Then he could cure me, restore Marcello, and save the thousands of lives even now preparing to march to their own deaths.

"We can't have that. It'd be no fun if you died now," Kathe said, squeezing my hand tightly enough to belie his light tone. "Write a couple of notes with the recipe. I'll send one crow back to Ardence, and one ahead to an alchemist of mine in Let. A crow can't carry more than a small vial, but we can at least hope to buy time."

I nodded, giddy with relief, and pulled out paper, pen, and ink from my satchel. "That way I can tell Lucia to warn my mother about Greymarch, as well. Thank you."

"Don't thank me yet," he said grimly. "Crows aren't courier lamps. It'll be many hours yet before we have any chance of a response."

"How many is many?" Zaira demanded.

Kathe shook his head. "We'll find out."

It was a bleak ride to the border. We passed through a small town below Greymarch, and its empty streets seemed especially ominous knowing that everyone who lived there was mustering even now to march to their deaths: the woodcarver whose porch so proudly displayed dozens of whimsical sculpted animals, the family who had painted bright flowers above their windows, the children who had left tracks running dizzily through the snow.

Unless we could kill Ruven in time to free them, no one would come home to the little cottage with a dried wedding posy hanging over the door, too bright to be more than a month old. No one would finish clearing the snow from the little shrine to the Grace of Love tucked up against an ancient tree in the town green. This place would stand empty forever, a monument to an abandoned moment, without even the peace of a grave.

"That pus-rotted eel." Zaira glared at a small wooden sled leaning against the wall of a cottage. "Why does he take the little brats and the old relics who can't even fight?"

The yellow rings in Kathe's eyes burned with a fury I was glad wasn't turned on me. "They're just fuel to him," he said. "And shields, to make your Empire's warlocks hesitate while he claims more land."

"Well, *this* warlock sure as Hells won't hesitate to set his smug, pasty face on fire," Zaira growled.

The sun climbed up past the shadow-shrouded mountains looming in icy, forested splendor to the east. I watched it with dread, knowing too well what would begin when it reached its zenith. Zaira thumped my shoulder once or twice in sympathy, but didn't say much, staring back broodingly toward Greymarch and the town beneath it even when it had disappeared from sight. Kathe frequently glanced my way, seemed on the verge of speaking, and then visibly stopped himself.

The vulture chimera still soared above us, a hateful black smudge on the cold blue sky. Occasionally, it dipped down low enough to catch my eyes with its beady black ones, waiting, as if to say *And will you take my master's offer now?*

The sun was still on the rise when we got our first glimpse of Vaskandar. As our sleigh rounded a shoulder of Mount White-crown, the sprawling ancient forest spread out beneath us, pines dusted gray with snow. Open patches of crisp snowbound fields punctuated the rolling forest, with white puffs of smoke rising up from neat clustered villages. It was a far cry from the tangled, bloodthirsty forests of Sevaeth, or the rough brooding pines of Kazerath; but only a fool would think this orderly, rolling land-scape any less dangerous. This was Atruin, the domain of the Lady of Eagles, one of the eldest and most powerful of the Witch Lords.

I knew the moment we crossed the border, even though I didn't spot the boundary stones. A prickling sense of magic coursed through my veins, and a surge of familiarity, like a homecoming. My blood *knew* this place. I was linked to this land, like it or not, as sure as the jess linked me to Zaira.

I wasn't the only one who noticed the change at the border. A vast-winged shadow swooped out of the sun at the vulture chi-mera, talons extended; the chimera veered off and turned back toward Greymarch, crying in alarm. The eagle circled over the road, silent and proud, daring the interloper to return.

There went my last chance of accepting Ruven's bargain. Now I had to get more elixir by tonight or die.

Great rough-trunked pines rose around us, blocking out the light and swallowing sound with their long, brooding silence. I could feel the Lady of Eagles' magic and her presence every-where, like the premonition of thunder in the air before a storm, refraining from killing us only so long as we stuck to the road and followed her rules.

It was, perhaps, enough to make my heart race and my breath quicken. But I knew that wasn't what was happening. The weakness stealing into my limbs wasn't solely from exhaustion, nor was the wavering of my vision around the edges merely from staring at the snow too long.

Kathe gave me an alarmed glance and tentatively settled an arm over my shoulders. When I didn't object, he asked in a low voice, "You're not well, are you."

"No," I admitted.

He stared off through the vast, gloomy hall created by the moss-decked columns of the towering pines. "When I was a child," he said softly, "my mother laid a command on her domain to protect me. It was absolutely stifling." He shook his head in frustration. "If I swam in the river, an overzealous bear might pull me out, thinking I was drowning. If I dared myself to climb a challenging tree, the tree would rearrange its branches to make it safe and easy for me. If I played stick swords with another child, they'd get bitten by angry squirrels or swarmed by bees—honestly, I'm lucky no one died."

"Your childhood was weird," Zaira said fervently.

"No," I said, thinking of my own mother, "I understand."

"I imagine you might." Kathe chuckled. "Anyway, before long I started sneaking across the border into other domains to play. And I did all manner of shockingly foolish things, because I had no sense of personal danger."

"This explains a lot. About you, and every Witch Lord I've met," Zaira muttered.

I considered my own current circumstances and laughed; my shortened breath left me dizzy.

"When I was about ten years old, I finally managed to hurt myself badly enough to be laid up in bed for a week," Kathe sighed.

"How did you manage that, with all the life magic in you?"

Zaira asked, sounding impressed. "I've seen how quickly the vivomancers at the Mews mend, even if you can't outright heal yourselves. A brat broke her leg falling out of a tree in the garden once and was limping on it the next day."

"Oh, I started a fight with a pack of whiphounds." Kathe grimaced. "Suffice to say I didn't win, and it was messy. But my point is that while I was recovering, my mother would come and sit with me, to help keep me distracted." He gave me a sidelong look, then, humor gleaming in his eyes.

"Let me guess," I said dryly. "You played a game."

"I'm not good at soothing noises, and trust me, you don't want to hear my singing voice," he apologized. "So I'm afraid it's games or silence, whichever you find more comforting. You choose."

I reached up and squeezed his hand on my shoulder, a warm rush of gratitude softening the edge of the terrible knowledge that my life depended on a pair of crows, and might last no longer than the descending sun. "All right," I said. "I'll play."

The next few hours were among the strangest of my life. Apparently the game Kathe's mother had played with him was a circle storytelling game; at first I could pretend I was merely weak and ill with laughter, as I struggled to keep the story plodding ahead in some sensible fashion on my turns while Kathe kept adding improbable twists and Zaira raunchy ones. It felt daring and nearly blasphemous to laugh with death creeping through my veins and the oppressive, watchful power of the Lady of Eagles lying deeper than the blanketing snow across the open fields, and gathering thicker than shadows beneath the ancient trees.

But as my vision swam and narrowed, and the fog in my mind thickened, I ran out of the breath and wit to finish my sentences.

I leaned my head on Kathe's shoulder because I couldn't hold it up anymore, struggling to listen as they continued the story without me because that was better than the sound of my own labored breath.

Even with my eyes closed, I could feel the pulse of the land around me, in my own veins. Deer listened to my faltering heartbeat from the forest, their delicate ears tilting to follow me while the rest of them stood still as statues. Pines swayed in the wind, needles rubbing, whispering in time to the surge of blood in my ears. Birds watched the speck of me huddled under blankets in the back of the sleigh from far above, knowing I was dwindling like a candle flame drowning in its own pooled wax. But death was a part of the tapestry of life, woven through it in thick red ribbons; and while the land knew I was dying, it didn't care.

Something sharp jabbed my shoulder. "Hey. Hey, Cornaro."

My eyes flew open to find Zaira frowning at me. "Sorry. I was listening."

"No sneaking out early like this was a bad play, you hear me? I don't want to have to get a new Falconer."

That was right. If I died, Zaira's jess could kill her if she didn't get a new one within a few days. "If you need one..." I sucked in a shallow breath. "I have a jess...in my satchel."

She shook my shoulder, her fingers digging in. "Idiot. That's not what I meant."

"It's true, not just anyone...could put up with you." I managed a smile.

Hells take it, I couldn't die now. It wasn't just her jess. Someone had to champion the mage-marked and see the Falcon Reserve Act through. I had confidence that Lucia would try, but without me, she wouldn't have the necessary power.

I pulled myself straighter in my seat, with a groan. "If I don't survive...tell my mother that my last request was for her to see my Falcon law through."

"That's low," Zaira approved. "I like it. But here's a better idea: don't die."

"Yes, I'd rather spare you the need for deathbed emotional manipulation," Kathe agreed. "You're the only person in my life who I can talk to as an equal without needing to constantly be on my guard, and I'd miss you."

That woke me up more than Zaira's poking. He was staring out at the passing landscape as if he found it riveting, the warm light of the lowering sun gilding the planes of his face.

Before I could find an answer to such an extraordinary statement, the cramps struck, twisting chimera claws into my middle. I doubled over, gasping.

Graces have mercy. This was the final stage.

"Amalia?" Kathe asked, alarm sharpening his voice.

"I'm sorry," I managed, forcing the words between my teeth.

His arms went around me with a rustle of feathers. But another spasm ripped through me, and I could barely feel the warmth of them. He was saying something, his tone raw and urgent, but I was beyond understanding.

For a time, I lost myself to pain.

It couldn't have been more than an hour, but it felt like days of suffering, trapped in the prison of my failing body as hoofbeats thudded in the snow and voices murmured tensely over my head. But I couldn't let go, couldn't surrender—I had too much to do. *Defeat Ruven. Save Marcello. Protect the Falcons. Preserve the Empire.* I had to live one moment longer, and another, and another, no matter how much it hurt.

At last, Zaira burst out, "Took your time, you poxy sky-rat!" and jarred me back to awareness of the world around me.

The sleigh had stopped in the middle of a snowbound field; the homey scent of woodsmoke from a nearby village tinged the air. The black silhouettes of bare branches speared the sun like a slice of blood orange to the west, and rosy gold light spilled across the sky from it. Kathe held a ruffled-looking crow, untying a gleaming vial from its leg with an inexplicably unsteady hand.

I gulped the elixir down, the taste of anise as sweet on my tongue as the relief that coursed down my throat. I leaned against Kathe, utterly spent. The knot of pain in my gut began to untie itself, and all the world came pouring back in around me from where I'd shuttered it away to focus on the simple act of surviving.

"Going to stay with us after all?" Zaira asked.

"Mmmh," I agreed. I felt as if I'd been pounded flat and left to dry.

Kathe closed his eyes and covered his face with one elegant hand. "Please don't do that again," he said, his voice more subdued and serious than I'd ever heard it.

I stared at him. It must be the aftereffects of the poison playing tricks on my eyes; that couldn't possibly be moisture shining on his cheek through the gaps in his fingers.

"I'll try not to," I promised.

Chapter Thirty-Six

The first bones lay scattered in pieces at the foot of a tree.

Zaira didn't seem to have noticed, her eyelids drooping after trying to sleep in the sleigh as we traveled all night and well into the morning, with less success than I'd had. My body had been exhausted enough from the ravages of the poison to sleep through much worse than a sleigh ride. I'd only awakened when Zaira poked me to take my morning dose of elixir, delivered in the night by the second crow. I'd woken to the expected splitting headache and the far more surprising warmth of a Witch Lord all along my side; I'd apparently spent the night slumped against Kathe, his cloak draped around us both.

Now he half stood up as the sleigh began to slow, his eyes alight, leaning eagerly over the edge and taking great deep breaths as if he wanted to drink in everything around him. I could almost convince myself that I'd imagined the bones in my poison-weakened state, or at least that the skull couldn't have been quite so round, so obviously human.

Then we passed a tree with what was undeniably a human skeleton impaled on it, a sharp branch protruding like a spear through its ribs. A violet uniform hung from it in tatters, and the bones bore scrapes and scratches from the animals that had picked them so very clean.

Zaira sucked in a sharp breath. Kathe, seeming oblivious, leaped out of the sleigh with a gleeful whoop as if we had arrived at some beautiful sparkling lake or perhaps a particularly fine bakery, while the horses shuffled to a confused halt.

Deeper in the woods off the road, more skeletons sprawled, some with scraps of flesh still on them. Muskets and pikes lay abandoned in the underbrush beside some of them. One tree farther along the road had skulls festooning its branches like fruit, with no sign of the rest of the bones that must once have accompanied them.

I met Zaira's eyes; hers stretched wide as my own, fully ringed with white. "What in the Hell of Death," she whispered.

Kathe didn't so much as glance at the bones. He laid a hand on a tree trunk, sighing fondly. Birds twittered in the branches above him, fluttering close, some of them coming to land on him. Something I took at first to be a dog gamboled up to him, tongue lolling gleefully, tail wagging; then I glimpsed its mad yellow eyes and knew it must be a coyote. Kathe threw a snowball for it to chase.

When it seized a human femur up out of the snow a moment later, shaking it vigorously, I couldn't take any more.

"Kathe," I called sharply, pressing my fingers to my temple to constrain the flare of my headache.

He turned to face us, grinning. He flung his arms wide, his cloak flapping out around him like dark wings.

"Welcome to Let," he declared.

I stared at him, completely at a loss for words.

"Of course," Zaira muttered, her voice heavy with irony. "Silly me. Must have missed the boundary markers because I was too busy staring at all the dead people."

"Is this, ah," I managed, then licked my dry lips and tried again. "Is your entire domain decorated in this, ah, motif?"

Kathe looked around, then, as if he were only now noticing

all the bones, and gave a sort of shy grimace as if we'd caught him practicing some silly but harmless hobby, like designing fashions for cats. "Ruven launched an attack on my border here. It's customary in Vaskandar to leave the remains of those who attempt to violate one's borders as a warning. I forgot you don't do that in the Empire."

"You made a *tree of skulls*," Zaira pointed out. "That's not just leaving the bodies where they fell."

Kathe regarded the tree in question, and his eyes narrowed in something like satisfaction. "Well, I was angry."

Zaira gave me a meaningful look that I interpreted as, *You're courting him. This is your fault.* I shook my head to disavow all responsibility for Kathe's grisly welcome signs.

"And no, it's not all like this. Just the border with Kazerath," Kathe said. "Come on, I'll show you."

Songbirds had continued to gather around him on every available branch, even perching on the skulls, singing out their welcome. The coyote pranced off as if it intended to tell the rest of its family; with it gone, a trio of squirrels chased themselves up and down and around a nearby tree, their bushy tails twitching excitedly as they chattered to Kathe. The animals didn't seem to be controlled in any way; they were all just happy to see him.

Kathe gave us a beckoning wave and began striding off down the road, his feathered cloak flowing behind him. Our horses seemed to exchange a glance between them, then followed at a modest trot. The sleigh slid along the road, passing between hanging skulls and scattered human bones as if they were nothing more than the trees and bushes we'd seen on the Atruin side of the border.

"And I was just thinking he might be all right after all." Zaira shook her head. "No such thing as a tame Witch Lord, I guess."

I could only nod in stunned agreement. It was too easy to forget, when Kathe was being clever and charming, that I'd seen him stab a woman in the back and bury her alive. One who was trying to kill me, granted, but the bone knife he'd used still rode at his hip, pale and wicked.

The love the creatures of his domain clearly had for him had blindsided me, though, and it shouldn't have. "He's got more layers than a Loreician torte," I murmured.

Zaira cast a glance at a partial skeleton that hung upside-down from a writhing tangle of mossy vines in the boughs of an ancient tree. "Uh-huh. Some of them are a bit dark and bitter for my taste."

Kathe dropped back to walk beside our sleigh, his unnaturally quick stride keeping up with the trotting horses. His breath misted in the air as he pointed things out to me, with great enthusiasm.

"That tree is six hundred years old. It makes your Empire look like a baby. And there, see that snowy gap in the trees? It doesn't look like much now, but in the summer it's a circle of the most velvety green moss, and it blooms with tiny flowers like a field of stars."

Zaira pointed at the inverted skeleton. "And what's that?" she asked ironically.

Kathe flashed his teeth. "That was an enemy vivomancer who thought he could sabotage one of my boundary stones. He's lucky it was me who caught him; there are plenty of Witch Lords who would have made his death last for days." Kathe caught the looks we were giving him, then, and sighed, a weight seeming to fall on his shoulders. "You think me barbaric, don't you."

"No," I protested hastily, even as Zaira said "A bit, yes."

"War is war. I'd prefer not to kill anyone, but if they bring violence to my borders, I will protect my own." He lifted an eyebrow at Zaira. "Much like you, warlock."

Zaira winced. I instinctively sucked in a breath to say something in her defense, but there was nothing to say; we'd left far more extensive and just as grisly evidence outside Ardence of what happened to those who threatened our people.

"Come on," Kathe said then, his voice gone serious, "and I'll show you what I'm protecting."

Kathe continued to accumulate a following of animals as we walked. Birds glided along from tree to tree beside us, and a pair of deer paced us in the woodline. A wolf came and sniffed his hand, and he scratched behind its ears absently, as if it were a dog; after it left, a red fox followed him for a few minutes, tongue lolling in a grin. He looked for all the world like one of the paintings of the Graces walking the countryside, with birds and animals gazing adoringly at them and flowers blooming in their footsteps; it formed a bizarre counterpoint to the grisly relics of battle around us. With my head pounding and my body still exhausted from the aftermath of the poison, I could only stare.

Soon the road swung away from the Kazerath border, however, and we gained a reprieve from such macabre warnings. We broke out of the forest into a farm village, the open fields wide and white with snow around us. Most of the houses stood in a rough square around the village green; their weathered gray boards and peaked slate roofs were more practical than pretty, but they seemed in good repair, and cheery smoke rose from their chimneys. The green itself stood clear of snow, and a handful of goats nibbled surprisingly lush grass at one end, while at the other a fence kept the goats mostly out of a garden plot growing decidedly out-of-season vegetables, no doubt thanks to their local vivomancer.

We had barely reached the edge of the village square when a pair of dogs came charging out to meet us, barking with great excitement, tails wagging madly. The wild animals who'd followed Kathe dispersed in a huff, and he crouched down, laughing, to greet the dogs, who wriggled with ecstasy at his attention. Not far behind them came a small pack of children, shouting with nearly as much excitement, and doors opened all over the village as the adults came out to see what was happening.

"Lord Kathe! Lord Kathe! My cat had kittens!" one little girl squealed, with evident conviction that he would find this news of utmost importance.

"Lord Kathe! Will you grow cherries for us?" a boy pleaded.

"Will you do your trick with the crows?"

"Did more soldiers from Kazerath come, Lord Kathe? Did you kill them *all*?"

"Are you staying overnight? You can sleep in my bed! I'll sleep on the floor, I don't mind!"

Kathe laughed and answered each of them as he could, still crouched down from greeting the dogs, reaching out to ruffle hair and pat shoulders. "I know! Six healthy kittens! Their mama should be proud. No soldiers this time, Rika, I'm happy to say. Cherries...let's see..." Kathe snapped his fingers, and in the yard of a house across the square behind him, one bough of a tree burst suddenly into bloom. Flowers blossomed and dropped in an instant, fluttering down like pink snow, and the branch bent under the rapidly growing weight of plump red cherries.

The children shrieked with glee and raced off toward it; Kathe straightened, calling after them, "Now, don't eat so much you get sick, or your parents will be angry with me!"

I exchanged glances with Zaira as we climbed down out of the sleigh. First the bones, now this...But it all made a strange sort of sense. He would do anything for his domain. It was all a part of him, pumping through his heart with his blood: the children, the dogs, the ancient tree he'd pointed out to me. Ruven thought of the lives in his domain as power that was his to spend;

to Kathe, these were his children, for whom he would equally perform the sweet miracle of cherries in winter or rip those who would threaten them to pieces and decorate the forest with their skulls.

The village adults approached next, more deferential than their offspring, greeting Kathe with deep bows.

"Lord Kathe," an old woman with a blacksmith's brawny arms and burned leather apron greeted him. "I hope they weren't bothering you."

"Not at all," Kathe said. "We're only passing through today, but I'm always glad to stop and say hello."

While Zaira and I hung awkwardly behind him, nearly the same scene unfolded as had with the children, except the adults' questions and requests were somewhat more serious. Should they expect any more attacks near the village? They'd heard rumors he'd be levying an army, was it true? The red cow had taken sick again and the local Greenwitch couldn't figure out what was wrong with her, could he take a look?

Kathe assured them that Ruven's attention was turned south and he could keep the border safe without needing an army. He closed his eyes for a moment before announcing that the red cow had been eating baneleaf, and he'd cured her of the poison and given her some resistance to it, but they'd want to pull it up where it grew in the west pasture so that no other livestock fell afoul of it.

"We're going to be here all day," Zaira muttered to me. "Look at him. He can't say no."

I opened my mouth to protest that Kathe had said himself we were just passing through, and surely in a moment we would move on, but then I saw his face. He was deep in a serious discussion of baneleaf with one of the farmers gathered around him, now, their breaths making a cloud of mingled steam in the winter air around them.

This could not be more unlike Ruven's domain of Kazerath, where the people had made warding signs against evil whenever they spoke of him and had hand-shaped burn marks on their faces. And it wasn't much like Atruin, either, where the people were happy and safe but treated their Witch Lord with distant and reverent awe, as if she were the Grace of Majesty or the great and terrible sun itself.

It occurred to me with a sudden, deep pang that he reminded me most of Marcello, and the careful attention he gave to the concerns of every Falcon in the Mews.

I hugged my coat closer around me against the cold. "Perhaps I should give him a gentle reminder of the urgency of our errand," I murmured.

At that moment, the sounds of hooves thudding in snow and jingling harness broke through the conversation. From across the square, a great voice bellowed, "Thought you could just slip past the border without us noticing, eh?"

Everyone looked up in surprise except Kathe, who instead turned slowly around, grinning widely. "I shouldn't have to tell you where I am," he called. "A good Heartguard simply *knows*."

Three newcomers rode into the square, and it took only a casual glance to see they were no farmers. They carried themselves with the dangerous assurance of warriors, and grinned at Kathe like old friends.

"May I introduce three of my Heartguard?" Kathe gestured grandly as they approached. "Verin, whose family has served in the Heartguard for three generations." The woman who bowed from her saddle in acknowledgment was lean and long as a hunting knife, with deep golden-brown skin and short dark hair ruffed up like a hawk's feathers. "Hal, who used to get me into trouble when I was small, and keeps me out of trouble now." The man who'd yelled to Kathe laughed heartily; he sported a great red beard, streaked with gray, and a chest like a wine barrel. He must be in his forties; it was unsettling to think that Kathe was closer to Hal's age than mine. The years that showed in light creases and general weathering on Hal's mortal face had passed by Kathe without marking him. "And Glass, whose aim is the only thing sharper than their tongue." The third, an androgynous youth with pale shoulder-length hair, grinned in greeting as they slouched in a splendidly embroidered emerald-green riding coat, a long musket across their back.

"And my friends," Kathe concluded, "meet Lady Amalia Cornaro and Lady Zaira the fire warlock."

The three offered us deep bows, as best they could from horseback. "Lady Amalia! I've been dying to meet you ever since our Lord Kathe told us he was courting a Raverran," Hal boomed, his red brows rising.

"Yes, we were all wondering who he'd found that might be willing to put up with him," Glass added, their pale eyes scrunching with humor.

"We should get moving," Verin said, glancing at the afternoon sun. Her hand dropped casually to check the lie of some of the several daggers strapped to her person, as if this were a routine she no longer noticed herself performing. "Your crow said you were in a hurry, my lord."

"Finally," Zaira muttered.

"I am," Kathe said seriously. "It wouldn't do to keep the Lady of Spiders waiting."

Chapter Thirty-Seven

So, what do you think of our lord?" Hal asked, his gruff voice carrying easily over the thud of hooves and jingle of harness as our sleigh once more hissed along the snowy road. Kathe rode up in front with Verin, who was having some kind of serious conversation with him about Ruven's troop movements; I wished I could participate, but Hal and Glass had brought their horses up alongside the sleigh, an eager gleam of curiosity in their eyes.

"He's a good man," I said, and when Hal's eyebrows flew up and Glass snorted, I added, "mostly."

Hal guffawed. "That's one way to put it."

"He's good to us, anyway," Glass amended. "So you understand, my lady, if we want to verify that he's not making terrible mistakes with his romantic decisions."

"It's our job," Hal agreed, with an expression of mock piety. "We guard his heart, after all."

Zaira laughed. "That one? His heart is made of razors. It can damn well guard itself."

"Now, now, you'll put us out of a line of work," Glass said. "So Lady Amalia, we must assure ourselves of your worthiness. Do you have a sense of humor?"

"She must, to tolerate Lord Kathe." Hal chuckled. "What about *your* heart? Do you have a good heart, my lady?"

"Well," I began, realizing with some distress that I was uncertain of the answer.

"But not *too* good," Glass cut in. "If you're a simpering do-gooder, you won't last long around here."

"No fear of that," Zaira said. Despite the lightness of her tone, I couldn't help a pang at the words.

"Clearly you've got courage," Hal said, "because we don't see a lot of Raverrans this deep in Vaskandar. I hear you tell each other scary stories about us."

"Maybe it's all the bones," Zaira suggested, with a great pretense of seriousness.

Glass cocked their head in a way that reminded me of Kathe. "I'd never thought of that. Do you think they discourage visitors?"

I couldn't tell if they were throwing Zaira's irony right back at her. Before I could try to formulate some kind of response, Kathe dropped back to join us, shaking a finger at his Heartguard.

"Are you two interrogating the Lady Amalia? She's not a prisoner, you know."

"Of course not, my lord." Hal bowed from his saddle. "Only making conversation."

"Well, why don't you go up ahead and make conversation with Verin, or perhaps the Lady Zaira," Kathe suggested firmly.

Hal slapped Glass on the back. "We're being dismissed, my friend."

"But we were only getting started," Glass sighed. They obediently moved around to the other side of the carriage, however, and Hal rode forward to catch up with Verin.

"Forgive them," Kathe said. "It's been years since I've courted anyone, and they're excited."

"You seem very close to your Heartguard." I couldn't quite keep a trace of envy from my voice. I'd had precious little easy camaraderie in my life, and now that I was on the Council, it would become even rarer. Though I hoped that perhaps Lucia could become something very like a Heartguard, with time.

"Of course we're close." Kathe turned his wrist up, showing blue veins through his pale golden skin. "This domain is my blood and bone. Like everyone else in Let, they're a part of me."

Zaira gave him a deeply dubious look. "You Witch Lords are creepy," she declared, and turned away from us to start chatting with Glass. In a moment they were laughing together, as if they'd always been friends.

Kathe watched them with an odd, bittersweet expression. "See, the problem I run into is that I already feel a closeness with everyone in my domain, but it's a rather lopsided closeness."

"They look up to you," I said.

"They don't just look up to me. I am their lord." He dropped his voice so Glass wouldn't hear the weariness in it. "I sustain them, I protect them, and I could kill them with a thought. No matter how I treat them, or they treat me, it can never be an equal relationship." He grimaced. "And I'm terrible at making friends in the normal way, as you may have noticed, so it's rather difficult to get close to anyone outside my domain."

"I don't know," I said. "I like you all right."

He lifted an amused eyebrow. "I'm not certain you know how to make friends in the normal way, either."

"Fair point."

"Maybe that's why I get along better with you than I do with anyone else outside Let." He tapped his chin, thinking. "Except possibly the Fox Lord. He's a friend, too, I think."

An unexpected stab of sympathy slipped between my ribs. I knew what it was like to never be entirely certain whether your friends were really your friends, or just people who were being nice because they wanted something from you. "I can see why you've found it difficult to find people to court."

He laughed. "Am I that bad, then?"

I thought about protesting that that wasn't what I meant, but I smiled instead. "No worse than I am."

"We haven't played a game with just the two of us in a while," he said, reaching out across the moving air between us, then letting his hand fall again as a swaying of the sleigh opened more distance. "Not since I visited you in Raverra."

My cheeks warmed as I remembered our kisses in the mask shop. "That was a nice visit."

"When we're not on a desperate mission, we'll have to pick up where we left off." He grinned. "But in the meantime, perhaps we can play a game we've been postponing."

"We've been postponing a game?"

"Yes. A dreadfully serious one called Does It Make Any Sense at All That We're Courting?' We can take turns bringing up the obvious problems with a potential marriage alliance, and you get a point for each one you solve."

Something lurched in my chest, an anxious bird half-afraid of flight. But I kept my expression smooth and lifted an eyebrow. "Is the prize a marriage proposal?"

"Oh, no." Kathe put his hand to his chest. "I'd come up with a much better game for that."

"In Raverra, such details are usually negotiated in writing, with wine and advisers present, but all right." My insides buzzed like a nest of bees. I'd always half assumed that our courtship was a joke—one Kathe was playing on me, or on his fellow Witch Lords, or perhaps on the Serene Empire. It was easy enough to play along when every kiss was part of the game. He would tire of it at some point, and move on when the gambit had outlasted its usefulness. I could surprise my grandchildren someday by telling them, *Did you know I once courted a Witch Lord?*

He'd told me he was courting me in earnest. Perhaps I should have believed him. He was just so present in the now, seizing it with both hands and squeezing everything he could get from it, that it was hard to imagine a future with him—unlike Marcello, whose every look seemed to carry promises of family and home.

But Kathe was right. Our courtship might be a game, but it was one with rules and stakes and, one way or another, an ending.

"I'll go first," I said, striving to keep my tone light to match his. "We govern two different countries hundreds of miles apart, and neither of us can be away from our duties at home for long."

Kathe nodded, as if he'd been expecting this. "Since Let is certainly not going to become part of the Empire, we'd have to content ourselves with frequent visits, I suppose," he said. "I can enhance horses to make the trip go quite quickly. If we spent a week per month in each other's domains, we'd only be apart half the year."

"That could get lonely," I said softly.

Kathe shrugged. "No lonelier than we are now."

I thought of all the nights my father struggled to stay awake until my mother came home from the Imperial Palace, then finally gave up and put us both to bed, murmuring, *We'll see your mother in the morning.* "I suppose we wouldn't spend much time together regardless."

"Just as well. I'm told I'm best in small doses." Kathe's eyes crinkled at the corners. "Do I get a point?"

"It's a workable solution, I think, if not a perfect one. Your turn."

"Heirs." He raised his pale brows. "I believe we both need them, and have rather different requirements in terms of magical ability."

My face heated. It was an entirely logical question, but I couldn't help thinking about how those heirs would be conceived. "We'd have to hope for one with the mage mark and one without, to make our lives easier," I said. "If we weren't so lucky, well, I suppose we'd have to, ah, keep trying."

The Graces weren't hearing my silent prayers, because Zaira whipped around from her conversation with Glass. "That'd be such a trial," she leered. "All that trying and trying."

Kathe flashed her a grin. "I find that solution entirely acceptable. A point for you. Your turn, Lady Amalia."

I wished I could grab up a handful of the nice cold snow around us and rub it on my face. I cleared my throat, waited for Zaira to go back to chatting with Glass, and then pointed out in a low voice, "You're immortal, and I'm not. I'll grow old and die at the usual rate."

The glee slid off Kathe's face, leaving it somber. He glanced at his Heartguard, one by one, and then turned his gaze back to me. "That's something I'll have to come to terms with, one way or another. There are those among the Witch Lords who train themselves to think of all the rest of humanity as passing shadows, not worth getting to know because they're doomed to an early death." He shrugged. "I think that's dreadfully arrogant. We do get killed off, after all. Not letting yourself care for someone who won't live past a hundred is ridiculous when odds are decent you won't live to see three hundred yourself."

"How practical of you! Well, if it doesn't bother you, it doesn't bother me." The idea of him remaining untouched by time as it passed was oddly comforting, in fact. Kathe was a force of nature, like my mother or Ciardha; it seemed more wrong that they *would* age than that Kathe wouldn't. "Your turn."

"Saying it wouldn't bother me might be an exaggeration, but it certainly shouldn't affect our decisions. Let's see." Kathe studied his hands, folded in front of him on the saddle. "You cut to the quick with that one, so perhaps I shouldn't hold back, either."

My belly tightened. "I know what you're going to say."

"I imagine you do." He met my eyes, the yellow rings of his mage mark piercing and relentless. "Captain Verdi."

Hells. This was supposed to be a game, and not one called Wring the Blood from Amalia's Heart. "You know I put my duty to the Empire first," I said stiffly. "I wouldn't allow other romantic entanglements to disrupt a marriage alliance."

Kathe sighed. "To be clear, for all I've enjoyed poking at the good captain, it doesn't bother me that you care about him. And I would consider a marriage that allowed other lovers. But—"

"But it's not what I want," I interrupted, the words bursting out of me from the sheer force of anguish I'd invested in the question over the past months. "I remember what it was like for my parents. When you're married to an empire, there are only so many other relationships you can maintain. I'm barely going to have time for one husband; I'd never want either of you to become an afterthought. And—" I took a breath and mustered half a smile. "I'm an only child. I never did learn to share. I admire those who can, but I don't want to."

Kathe's expression changed several times, settling on something unreadable, his yellow-ringed eyes gleaming. "That's just as well," he said. "I don't like sharing, either. But that wasn't what I meant."

"Oh?" I might as well simply keep on blushing, if I was going to spend half this conversation embarrassed.

"I fear," Kathe said, with the care of a man stepping out onto a bridge one strong wind gust short of collapsing, "you may, ah, overestimate my confidence that we can restore Captain Verdi to himself."

My hands clenched inside my fur mittens, cold fingertips curling against my palms.

"I have to find a way. If I can't, it doesn't matter. He's gone." The words cut me on the way out, like coughing up swords.

"I profoundly hope, for your sake, that is not the case." Kathe edged closer to the sleigh and reached out again, his hand lighting on my hair like a bird for one brief moment. "But if it is, well, suffice to say I've learned there are problems that come with carrying around someone's ghost." His voice roughened, and I knew he must be thinking of Jathan.

"In Raverra, we look toward the future," I said. "We strive not to let the ghosts of the past haunt us." It was easy to say, a sentiment my mother would approve. It was more difficult to banish my last memory of Marcello's two green eyes, pleading with me not to leave him alone in a room decorated with scenes of torture while he fought to keep some shred of himself alive. "But sometimes..." I swallowed. "Sometimes it's hard."

"I may know someone who failed to do that, once," Kathe said. "Who carried his grief and guilt around with him and honed it into a weapon."

I couldn't look away from his eyes. "And does he regret it?" I asked.

Kathe tipped his head, seeming to ponder this. "He doesn't regret getting vengeance. That part was extremely satisfying."

"I see."

"But he regrets losing track of other things that mattered along the way." He reached out across the air scented with snow and horses for my hand. I took off my mitten and laced my fingers through his, feeling the familiar hum of magic beneath his skin.

"I'll remember that," I said.

"This is probably it, isn't it?" The firelight traced patterns of orange light and shadow on the side of Zaira's face. "One way or another."

She regarded me with an odd, pensive frown from her seat on a sawn-off log in the huntsman's shelter where we huddled before a fieldstone fireplace. Kathe had offered to let us rest here while he made a side trip up a hill too steep and rocky for the sleigh to collect my elixir from the alchemist who had brewed it. I had been more than happy to stay behind; my head was still pounding, and I was glad to be out of the sleigh for a while. I certainly hadn't recovered enough to climb up what looked like a small mountain in the dark. Glass and Verin had gone with him, and they'd left a grumbling Hal to look after the horses outside.

"Us or Ruven, you mean?" I asked. It had, in fact, occurred to me that if our trap for him failed, matters would likely go poorly for us.

"No. I mean the last time we do this sort of thing." Zaira waved at the cold night beyond the three-sided stone shelter, where snow stretched white and dreaming beneath the black spears of tree trunks. I shivered at the sight, drawing my own stump seat closer to the fire. "You and me, off doing mad things by ourselves that nobody else has the guts to do."

I felt an inexplicable piercing loss at the idea. "Maybe not. This sort of thing will still need to get done."

Zaira snorted. "Not by one of the Council, it won't. You'll be locked up in the Imperial Palace all day, frowning over maps and papers and ordering people killed."

"That's not..." I let my protest die, sighed, and finished, "inaccurate."

"And I'll be, well, not here. And not in your palace, either."

I raised an eyebrow. "Where *will* you be?"

Zaira let out a gusty breath. "Terika wants to get married. She won't say it in as many words, because she doesn't want to scare me off, but it's pretty damned obvious."

"Would that be so bad?" I asked, trying very hard to sound neutral, and not at all as if I were wondering whether they'd let me buy them a nice little town house in the city as a wedding gift.

"I dunno." Zaira picked up a stick from a basket beside the fireplace and began poking the fire; the flames flared up, reflected in her eyes. "I don't understand how she can still like me. I'm like a dog that keeps biting her hand and chewing up her boots and pissing on her floor, but she keeps feeding me anyway. And I've been a stray for so long."

"Well, my understanding is that usually you get married if you find someone you want to spend the rest of your life with." Or to seal a political alliance, but never mind that. "Do you want to spend the rest of your life with Terika?"

"I used to think the rest of my life would be about five years."

"And now?"

She laughed. "At the rate we're going? Two days. So I suppose it's not much of a commitment." She tossed her burning stick entirely into the fire. "I should probably ask her, I guess."

A noise escaped me that I could only have described as a squeal, though I attempted to smother it with a cough. Zaira scowled at me.

Then her eyes slid past me to the dark woods beyond the shelter, and she frowned. "Is that what I think it is?"

She didn't seem alarmed, and we should theoretically be quite safe in Kathe's domain. But it was still one of those questions that set the pulse to pounding in anticipation of the worst possible answer, much like *What's that in your hair?*

When I followed her gaze, however, the shape teased by the farthest edge of the ruddy firelight was neither a massive slavering chimera nor some fresh dangling human corpse—both entirely real possibilities, this close to the Kazerath border—but a tall rough stone carved with timeworn swirls and slashes.

"A boundary stone." I rose and approached it, trying to make out the lines of its ancient patterns. It stood on the far side of the road from the huntsman's shelter, some fifty feet from our fire. "I knew we were close to the border, but I didn't realize we were *this* close."

"Maybe you should stand back farther, then," Zaira suggested. But she followed at my shoulder, fingers flexing.

"So long as we stay on this side of the stone, we should be safe. Remember how it acted like a wall when those chimeras were after us?" We were close enough now that I could pick out the symbols clearly in the flickering firelight. "This is definitely a Kazerath stone. I recognize the patterns."

I traced a jagged line, feeling the rough rock slide beneath my fingertip. And something more, too—magic tingled beneath my touch. The stone didn't warm in recognition like the ones marking Atruin had, but I still felt a certain resonance vibrating in my fingers. It knew me, and recognized my great-grandmother's blood.

Halfway down the monolith, which stood taller than my head, several patterns converged in a divot carved into the stone. The niche was no bigger than a child's fist, and the bottom of it bore stains that looked black in the reddish light.

"That must be where he bloods it, to mark the boundary of his claim." I reached for my dagger.

Zaira seized my wrist. "What in the Hells are you doing? Did that poison rot your brain?"

"We need to lure Ruven north if we want to trap him," I said. "It'll take him time to get here. He's still down at the border, and the last thing we want is him personally supporting his controlled army as it invades the Empire. If we can get him moving toward us now, we can spring our trap much sooner, and have a chance of killing him before those poor controlled people from Greymarch reach Ardence."

"Don't get me wrong, I like the idea of spitting in his wine.

But last time you got that strange look on your face and started poking one of these rocks, we wound up getting arrested by a bunch of angry deer."

I sighed. "Maybe I should wait for Kathe to get back."

I let Zaira tug me back to the fireside, and we settled on the stumps again. Hal stuck his broad bearded face into the shelter to check on us, then stepped in to warm his hands at the fire.

"Don't worry, I'll be leaving you alone again soon," he said cheerfully. "Those poor horses have been in harness for too long, even with Lord Kathe taking good care of them; I've got them out of it, but I want to give them a thorough brushing." He hesitated a moment, then turned to face me, mischief in his eyes. "I only have one question for you first, my lady, while my lord is away."

"Oh?" I asked warily. Zaira looked back and forth between us, grinning, clearly expecting something good.

"Do you love him?"

"*Well.*" I seized up a stick and became very busy poking the fire. "That's a complicated question."

Hal snorted. "Nothing complicated about it. I've got a dog back home, and he loves everyone. Me, I love my friends, and my brother and his little girls, and my lord. As for Lord Kathe, he'd never admit it, but he loves all of Let, every little piece of it." He chuckled. "My heart's not that big. I can't love more people at once than I can count on my fingers. So I won't judge you if you say no."

I poked the fire so vigorously my stick snapped. "I . . . you see, that's . . ."

"Define *love*," Zaira said dramatically, and then howled with laughter when I glared at her.

"Let me make this easier for you," Hal rumbled. "Do you like him?"

"Yes, definitely," I replied immediately.

He nodded, seeming pleased. "Would you take a musket ball for him?"

"Well, that would be a foolish thing to do, because a musket ball could kill me and would barely bother him," I reasoned.

"Ugh. That's not an answer." Hal shook his head. "You're like he is; I'd get a straight answer out of a cat sooner. Fine. Would you wrestle a bear chimera for him?"

"I don't..." I paused. "I think you and I define love differently."

Hal sighed. "I give up. By your definition, then. Do you love him?"

"You're not going to get her to tell you," Zaira said. "She's so stiff she can't even admit she loves her mother."

"I'll ask you, then," Hal said, his bushy brows set in a determined line. "You seem to know her pretty well. Does she love Lord Kathe?"

My entire face burned. Zaira grinned from ear to ear. "Weeeeeeeeeeeelll," she began, drawing the word out to some seven or eight syllables.

I sprang to my feet. "Kathe will be back soon, won't he? Didn't you want to brush those horses?"

Hal guffawed, holding his belly. Then he slapped my back hard enough to rock me onto my toes, exchanged a knowing look with Zaira, and laughed some more. "You're redder than a ripe apple! Hah! All right, I have my answer." He collected himself as best he could and bowed. "I'll go take care of those horses, then, my lady."

He left the shelter, whistling.

I could have lit another fire with the heat from my face. "What was that all about?" I demanded of Zaira, whose grin hadn't faded.

She shook her head. "If you don't know, I'm sure as Hells not going to explain it to you."

Before I could frame a response, a gleam of light from the dark woods caught my attention, near the boundary stone. A round, glassy flash, like the eye of a predator. But instead of a pair of eyes, there was only one.

My lungs filled with sudden frost. *Marcello.*

Chapter Thirty-Eight

I stared into the darkness, struggling to pull a familiar human outline from the black shadows beyond the firelight. The glowing eye blinked once, but didn't move.

Slowly, with exquisite care, as if I were trying not to startle a wild animal, I took three steps to the edge of the shelter and down onto the trampled snow.

Zaira's hand fell on my shoulder. "I see him," she whispered. "Do we try to take him?"

I paused, fear and longing and anguish driving urgently through my veins. It was all Nine Hells in one question. "I don't know," I whispered. "I don't know if we can. Or what we'd do if we captured him."

"Nothing I could do to catch him would be pretty," Zaira said. "You could stall him until Mr. Decorates With Bones gets back."

"Ruven has near absolute power on that side of the border, and Kathe has it here. Unless one of us steps across, there's not much we can do to each other." I took a shaky breath. "So I'm going to talk to him."

Zaira sighed a "this is a terrible idea" sort of sigh. "Fine. I'll hang back a few steps and chaperone. Don't do anything to make me have to light him on fire."

My steps crunched in the snow, each one taking me farther from the warm firelight and closer to the blazing eye waiting in the forest. With each step, the glare of the fire faded, and I could make out more of him. His familiar silhouette, shoulders canted as he rested one hand on the boundary stone. His uniform buttons, gleaming with reflected firelight. The dark waves of his hair. The swath of silver scales trailing down his cheek.

Exhaustion or sorrow hollowed his face, and stubble softened the clean lines of his chin. He watched me approach, unmoving, both eyes bright in the firelight.

I stopped too close to him, well within lunging range, my breath misting between us. My heart pounded hard enough to set the bedraggled lace at my collar to trembling.

"Amalia." He swallowed, as if my name hurt his throat. "I'm glad you're alive."

All the things I might say crowded in my mind. I could try to reach the real Marcello, to help bolster him against Ruven's influence. I could get him talking, to stall until Kathe returned, in the hopes of capturing him. I could attempt to get information about Ruven from him. Or I could tell him all the things I should have said long ago, when I thought I would have forever to get around to saying them.

"What am I going to do with you, Marcello?" I whispered.

"My lord Ruven's offer still stands." His voice remained soft and weary, as if I'd caught him just before going to bed. "He felt your touch on his boundary stone, and assumes you were signaling that you wanted to talk. I'm here to ask if you've made your choice."

"You hate him," I said, staring into the hard-edged shadows of his one green eye.

"Yes," he said quietly. "More than you could ever know."

"That's not like you. You never hated anyone."

"I do now."

I closed my eyes so that I could see the face I knew, warm and honest and stubborn. But that Marcello was never coming back, not even if we cured him somehow. There had been an innocence in him that was shattered now, as surely as mine had been when I had killed Roland.

"People change," I murmured. "People have to change. They're only different, not gone."

"I need your answer, Amalia."

I opened my eyes again. Marcello was waiting, resigned, for the *no* he was certain he was getting. But my mother had trained me never to reject an offer on instinct alone. *Think through all the implications and all the possibilities*, she'd told me. *Your instincts may be correct, but they are far from your only adviser.*

We had other, better ways of driving Ruven out of the Empire. I could live with poison in my veins, as I had for half my life. But Ruven was the only one who could make Marcello human again.

I had already sacrificed someone I loved for the Empire once. But that didn't mean that I always had to make that same choice, over and over. I didn't have to become that person, cold and ruthless, drowning the ashes of my heart for the sake of Raverra.

"What do *you* want, Marcello?" It was the question I hadn't been able to ask Roland.

Marcello let out a puff of breath, a white cloud drifting across his face and dissipating into the winter air. "Are you asking the man I was, or this thing I've become?"

"You aren't a thing," I said sharply. "And I'm asking *you*. Take that as you will."

"I don't know." He pushed a hand through his hair in frustration. "I want what Ruven wants—but I also want to kill him. I'm horrified at what I've done and proud of it. I want you to be happy, and I want you to suffer." An unstable edge came into his voice. He raised his hand before him, unsheathing the curving claws whose marks I still bore on my arms; I flinched. "I want to stay like this forever," he whispered, staring at them with apparent fascination. "To be strong and fast and better than human. But I also want to rip these claws out of my fingers, and rip this eye out of my head."

I reached out without thinking, heedless of his claws, grabbing his hand before it could move toward his face. "Please don't hurt yourself."

"The old me would rather cut off my own hands than hurt you again." He slid his fingers through mine, his touch heartbreakingly gentle, linking us across the border. "But it doesn't matter what I would choose. I'm only going to do what Ruven wants, anyway." He met my eyes; both of his, green and orange, held the same hopeless intensity. "I always trusted you to make the decisions, Amalia. I can tell you that Ruven wants you to say yes, because he's afraid. But I can't tell you what I want, because I don't know what's me, and what's him, and what's some animal instinct he gave me to make me better at killing." Marcello shook his head, as if throwing off invisible insects that plagued him. "My task is to ask for your decision. Whatever it is, I trust you to make the right one."

I should have known. There was no way out of this; just like with Roland, I would have to make the choice myself. But this time, instead of a simple trade of one life for thousands, it was giving power to my enemy in return for... what? I would have to be a much greater fool than I already was to believe for a minute that Ruven would give up his hold over Marcello. Even if he turned him human again, it would be a change he could reverse at any time. He would keep Marcello close and torment him whenever Ruven felt he needed to keep me in line.

I unlaced my fingers from Marcello's, tenderly, carefully. The warmth of his touch lingered on my winter-chilled skin.

"I have a return message for you to take to Ruven," I said.

Something flickered across Marcello's face—disappointment? Recognition? It was gone too quickly for me to guess. But he nodded. "That's why I'm here."

"Tell him I said thank you."

Marcello's brows lowered. "Thank you? For what?"

I drew my dagger. "For teaching me how to conquer him."

"Amalia, what in the Hells are you doing?" Zaira called from behind me.

I pricked a finger, cutting deeper than was probably necessary in my wild surge of determination, and shoved it into the niche in the boundary stone.

"Have you lost your *mind*?" Zaira's footsteps crunched rapidly in the snow.

"Stop!" Marcello cried, panic in his voice.

I squeezed my finger, and three drops of blood pattered rapidly to the rough stone.

Every tree on the Kazerath side of the border began thrashing, as if a fierce wind swept through them. Birds cried angrily, their calls rising in the night air.

"You *dare*!" Marcello hissed, lunging half across the border to grab my wrist. His face twisted in furious contempt; there was nothing of himself in his expression.

A branch stabbed down from beside and above me, sharpened to a spear, and pierced through his shoulder.

"Marcello!" I cried.

He staggered backward, releasing me, blood spreading a darker crimson across his ragged Falconer uniform. His hand went to his shoulder; his eyes met mine, full of betrayed shock.

I whirled around, but there was no sign of Kathe returning;

only Hal, running around the shelter with a sword in one hand and a currycomb in the other to see what was the matter. The tree had detected an invading chimera and acted on its own.

I spun back to face Marcello, but he had already fled. His footsteps receded with unnatural speed into the darkness, and only a trail of blood drops remained on the cold white snow.

"Is there some reason you didn't ask the Lady of Horrible Crawly Things to meet you someplace closer?" Zaira asked Kathe as our sleigh whizzed along the forest road through Let the next morning, his Heartguard riding around us.

"No, I just like making things as complicated as possible," Kathe said, so easily that for a moment I wasn't sure whether he was kidding.

Zaira laughed, however. "All right, what's the reason?"

A smile teased Kathe's lips. It was good, by the Graces, to see someone I cared about smiling. It eased the knots that had settled into my shoulders since last night.

"I know a secret," he said.

"And naturally, you're going to tell us, because nothing brightens a gloomy winter day quite like ruining a nice fresh secret," Zaira said.

"Naturally. Especially because this is Ruven's secret." Kathe's grin spread wider. "I know the location of one of his blooding stones."

I made an appreciative noise, but Zaira's eyes stayed half-lidded. "I'm sure that's a big coup you can brag about when you're sitting around the Witch Lord coffee house, but how is that different than the rock Amalia bled on last night?"

"Boundary stones mark the limits of your claim." Kathe cupped his hands. "Like the walls of a bowl that keep the water from spilling uselessly across the table. You can't use them to make a new claim, only to define one."

Zaira frowned. "So if bleeding on the rock didn't do anything, why were the trees so angry?"

"It was a declaration of intent," I said.

"A declaration of war, more like it." Kathe shook his head. "We don't touch each other's boundary stones. To tamper with one is to brazenly announce your plans to seize territory from your neighbor's domain. It's a challenge Ruven can't ignore." He gave me an approving look. "Which was the entire point, of course."

"So it was a slap in the face," Zaira said.

"Yes," I agreed. "To get his attention."

"But the blooding stone is a different matter." Kathe rubbed his hands. "The blooding stones disperse your blood into the rivers and spread your claim through the land. A threat to one of *those* Ruven will have to deal with personally. Since we need to lure him into the center of the ring of Truce Stones to activate them against him, we need something with the urgency of a rival claim threatening one of his blooding stones to draw him into our trap."

"And then he comes rushing in to defend his blooding stone and attacks Amalia?" Zaira's voice dripped skepticism. "That doesn't leave her in a good place, does it? Again."

"Actually, we have the opposite problem." I forced the words out. "I'm not sure we can count on him attacking me. Not in a way that would trigger the Truce Stones. He's as likely to try to paralyze me, or knock me unconscious. He wants me alive."

"I'll do it," Zaira offered. "He doesn't want *me* alive."

I shook my head. "You can't. Remember, if you put your blood on the Truce Stones, you can't attack him, either. We need your balefire to overcome his healing."

"I fear Witch Lords tend to be reluctant to attack one

another," Kathe said, frowning. "Plus, if he sees me at all, he'll assume it's a trap."

"I hate to say it, but we need to recruit a volunteer." A queasiness in my belly knew that if Marcello were here and himself, he would have spoken up by now, and I would try halfheartedly to dissuade him but would know that he was perfect. Graces curse me, I was too willing to make these sacrifices. "The problem is that Ruven is as likely as not to do something horrible to them, like bend their bones in knots or simply stop their heart. The harm he does may well be permanent."

"I'll do it," Hal said, kneeing his horse closer to the sleigh.

Glass shot him an annoyed look and sighed. "Beat me to it, but I suppose that's just as well. I'm not really the self-sacrificing type."

"You know I don't want you to," Kathe said to Hal, his frown deepening.

Verin lifted an eyebrow. "My lord. With due respect, you dare say that in front of the Lady Amalia? After you set her up to take exactly the same risk without her knowledge or permission?"

I stopped myself before I could utter a demurral. On reflection, he deserved that.

Kathe grimaced. "I'm sorry, Amalia. I didn't want you to get hurt, either. I just..." He trailed off.

"You decided it was worth an injury to destroy your enemy," Verin supplied. "And in this case I agree, and am adding my voice to Hal's and volunteering. Which, my duty as your Heartguard obliges me to point out, you did not give the Lady Amalia a chance to do."

"Sometimes I suspect you enjoy your duty as my Heartguard a bit much, Verin," Kathe said.

I smiled at her. "Someone has to keep him in line."

She nodded gravely. "Even so."

"Now, that's not fair, coming after a piece of my glory, Verin."

Hal wagged a finger at her. "I called it first. Besides, you have a wife and son waiting for you at home."

"All right, Hal," Kathe agreed reluctantly. "You can be our bait. Try to get him to hurt you but not kill you."

"Ha! You hear that, Verin?" Hal smacked his own chest smugly. "I'm more disposable than you!"

"A true honor," Glass said dryly. "Don't let it go to your head."

"You're not disposable, Hal," Kathe protested. "None of you are. Don't make me change my mind about this."

"So," I asked, "this place where we're meeting the Lady of Spiders is near Ruven's blooding stone?"

Kathe nodded. "The blooding stone is just across the border, by a pool at the headwaters of one of Kazerath's streams. If we can get the Truce Stones, we'll want to set up the trap immediately, before Ruven hears of the meeting and suspects what we're up to."

An alarming thought occurred to me. "If we're in his domain, can we truly hide the Truce Stones from him? Won't he sense them?"

Kathe shook his head. "They're not alive, and they're not part of his domain. He'd have to see them with his own eyes, the same as you or I."

"Do you truly think we can convince the Lady of Spiders to let us use them?" I asked.

"If not, we'll find out soon," Kathe said.

A silence fell, then, as our thoughts turned to the challenges ahead of us. Kathe kept watching Hal, a frown marring his brow.

When we stopped to water the horses in a crystal clear stream, Kathe abruptly jumped down from the sleigh and strode off into the trees, his boots crunching through the snow. Verin and Glass exchanged meaningful looks; Hal was whistling cheerfully as he tended to the horses, and seemed not to notice.

Glass and Verin put their heads together beside the sleigh, barely within my hearing. "Is this yours or mine?" Glass muttered.

Verin folded her arms, staring off after her lord. "Normally, I'd say yours, since he needs cheering. But I think if you talk to him right now, he'll leave you stuck in a tree."

Glass laughed. "Come now, I'm the soul of tact."

"Mmm," Verin said noncommittally.

"But you're no good, either." Glass scratched their head. "You're too much of a scold."

"Only because you all need scolding so often." Verin shook her head in disgust. "It should be Hal, but he's the one person who *can't* handle this."

"Excuse me," I put in tentatively. "If you're discussing who should go talk to Kathe, I can do it."

The two Heartguards turned assessing looks on me. I felt rather like my mother was deciding whether my outfit would pass muster for meeting with the doge. Finally, Verin gave a sharp nod.

"If you think you can keep this from becoming a mood, you have my blessing," she said.

"Better you than me," Glass agreed.

I had none of Kathe's grace as I struggled through the knee-deep snow. Chunks of it fell into my boot-tops at once and melted to frigid ice water, seeping through my stockings. I tried to remember the high-stepping gait my Callamornish cousins had used on the few occasions that I'd visited them in winter and we'd gone out into the hills; we never had snow like this in the Serene City.

I couldn't believe how exhausting it was to move through the stuff, especially when still weak from the ravages of poison.

Soon I was huffing like a bellows, my legs burning. I had to put a hand on a tree and stop to catch my breath after an embarrassingly short distance. I closed my eyes, trying to block out the knowledge that Verin and Glass were probably watching me.

A warm touch stirred my hair, brushing it back from my face.

"You're so excessively Raverran," Kathe said, a laugh in his voice.

I opened my eyes to find him beside me, his feathered black cloak stark against the snow. He wore a quizzical smile, but the pain shone sharp as ice in his eyes.

He was in his element here, a creature of winter, all gray and black and white. If he wanted to stalk off and brood gorgeously in his own forest, it felt more than a little ridiculous for me to stumble after him in my brocade and velvet and gold-stitched embroidery, my nose pink from the cold. Yet here I was.

"You're worried about Hal," I said quietly.

Kathe shrugged, feathers rustling. "Do I look like the type to worry?"

He started to pull back his hand from my hair, but I caught it in my thick, clumsy mittens instead. "Frankly, no," I said. "And yet, you do."

He didn't retrieve his hand, but he stood silent, shadows passing through the gray of his eyes behind the mage mark. Finally, he whispered, "Ruven will kill him. You know he will."

I swallowed. "He's not known for his mercy. But he's just as likely to incapacitate him, so he can use him against you."

Kathe let out a humorless bark of a laugh. "That's some consolation. You're as bad at this as I am."

"Sorry." I pressed his hand between mine. His strong, bare fingers curled around my mitten, squeezing back. "My mother taught me many things, but gentleness was not one of them."

"That's all right. Vaskandar isn't a gentle country." He let out a steaming cloud of breath. "I hate this."

"What? Having to send someone into danger?"

"No." His mouth crooked. "Being powerless."

"I can imagine it's something a Witch Lord doesn't have much opportunity to get used to," I said.

He released my hand, turning to stare off through the trees. "You know how my mother died," he said, so softly I almost didn't hear it.

Hell of Nightmares. I did. I nodded, words fading from my tongue like a letter dropped in the rain.

"Trapped and endlessly drowning far beneath the sea, with all the weight of the ocean pressing her down into darkness." Kathe closed his eyes. His lashes were nearly as pale as the snow around us. "We were very close, and I was her heir, and she reached for my help in her panic. For days and days I felt a shadow of what she felt—the terror, the utter darkness, the water filling her lungs like blood. And there was nothing I could do for her. Nothing." He met my gaze then, a bitter fury in his eyes that I knew must be for himself. "I can't bear to sit back and watch while Ruven kills or maims my friend, and do nothing again."

I pulled my mitten off and reached out to lay my palm tentatively against his chest. The tingling energy of his power coursed up my arm. Beneath my hand I could feel his heart, fluttering like a crow's wings. "You did do something for your mother," I said softly. "You did what she wanted most. The same thing Hal wants from you, and that Jathan wanted."

Kathe flinched at Jathan's name, and I wondered if I'd gone too far. "Is this a riddle, then?" he asked, his voice harsh as one of his crows'.

"If you want it to be."

He watched me warily for a moment, still as a wild animal on the brink of spooking. Then, slowly, he raised a hand to lay it over mine on his chest, covering his heart. The beats reverberating beneath my fingertips slowed, their pace less agitated.

"To live and be happy," he said.

"It's what we all want, for those we love." I tried a smile, uncertain and tender.

"That's odd." Kathe reached out and cupped my cheek, his hand almost painfully warm against the numbing winter chill.

"Oh? Why is that?"

He tipped his head like a curious bird, a smile ghosting across his lips. For a moment, a word hovered there, unspoken, so real I could almost hear it reverberating in the air. But then he shook his head.

"I'm glad you didn't die before you got your elixir," he said. "Let's leave it at that, for now."

But the words he didn't speak caught in the branches of the trees, and seeped down into the earth. And my blood was in the earth, too, mingled with his, so I heard them.

That's what I want for you.

The forest cottage might have been quaint and cozy with a different occupant. Its log walls were neatly cut and sanded smooth, its shutters lovingly painted red. The fieldstone chimney was in good repair, with inviting woodsmoke wafting from it. Bumps in the snow and the occasional spray of winter-bare sticks suggested a garden.

But what crawled up the walls and in and out the tidy windows was not ivy. Spiders of varied sizes scuttled across the logs, from tiny dots the size of a pinhead to leggy black monstrosities larger than my hand. One the size of a dowager's lapdog and nearly as hairy waited faithfully on the front steps, quite still until it made a tiny motion that turned my stomach with the realization it was real.

Zaira froze. "Hell of Nightmares. I'll just stay outside."

"I'm afraid she asked for you specifically," Kathe said.

"She, ah, didn't ask for *me*, did she?" Glass asked.

"No," Kathe confirmed. "My Heartguard can wait outside."

"Pity," Verin sighed, staring in fascination at the house. "I actually like spiders. They're so elegant."

"Elegant," Zaira said flatly. "One of us is wrong about what that word means."

I drew in a steadying breath. "All right. Let's get this over with."

We let Kathe go first. Zaira put me firmly between her and the puppy-sized spider on the doorstep, and I, in turn, stood as far from it as I could. Kathe strode up to the red door without any apparent unease whatsoever, gently brushed a few spiders off it, and knocked.

"You're late," a smooth, resonant voice responded. But the door opened, and there stood the Lady of Spiders.

Her long silver-gray hair trailed to the ground, but she was no withered crone. She might almost have been beautiful if it were not for the dead look in her round dark eyes and the mirthless predatory line of her smile. She wore a Raverran-style corset, faded with age and at least fifty years out of fashion, over trailing skirts slimmer than anything I was used to. I had braced myself, this time, for the beadwork: beautiful, intricate designs in subtle, shining colors that constantly shifted in mesmerizing patterns—because every bead was actually a live spider.

Zaira swayed at my side. Despite all my mental preparation, I still had to swallow an undignified noise.

"My apologies, my lady," Kathe was saying, with a gracious bow. "An incident on the road to Let delayed us."

The Lady of Spiders stepped aside, inviting us in. "You must learn not to apologize in your own domain, young crow. Enter, if you do not fear the truth you carry like poison inside you."

I couldn't help it; my hand stirred toward the satchel slung over my shoulder, where my new elixir bottles nestled.

Zara swallowed. "Out of curiosity, what if we *do* fear the truth?"

The Lady of Spiders' grin broadened. "Then enter anyway, but be afraid."

Chapter Thirty-Nine

I stepped into the cottage too close behind Kathe, clinging to the shadow of his feathered cloak like a child. I expected the floor to be crawling, and was relieved to find scrupulously clean-swept boards and cheery, spider-free rag rugs. But Zaira sucked in a breath behind me, and she gripped my wrist.

"Don't look up," she whispered hoarsely.

It took all my willpower not to. I fixed my gaze on the Lady of Spiders' face, struggling to ignore the flickers of movement on the ceiling, forcing my attention away from the shifting patterns on her gown.

"Thank you for speaking with us," I said, inordinately proud of my ability to make words.

"You say that now." She chuckled, a dark rich sound. "Sit, Amalia Cornaro and Zaira of Raverra, and tell me what cruel need has driven you here at last."

She settled herself in a rocking chair, her silvery hair and antique silk gown spreading out to transform it to a queen's throne. A steaming cup of tea waited on a tiny table by her elbow. Zaira and I eased delicately into rustic wooden chairs by the fire; I wasn't the only one who checked for spiders first. Kathe remained standing, leaning against the mantel behind us. He had arranged this meeting, but it was the Empire's negotiation, which meant I was the one who had to attempt rational conversation in a room where I didn't dare raise my eyes too far.

"We're hoping that the current extraordinary circumstances might permit us to make use of the Truce Stones," I said.

"An artifact created for peace, and you would use it in war." She ran a strand of silver hair through her fingers, as if testing the pull of her web. Jewel-backed spiders glittered on her hands like rings. "You're not the first to come to me seeking this, but I've never granted such a request. Do you know the history of the Truce Stones?"

"No," I admitted.

The Lady of Spiders regarded me from her dark, dark eyes in silence. It was Kathe who finally spoke. "The Yew Lord and his mother created them together, in the early days of Vaskandar. Before then, Witch Lords wouldn't meet and speak with each other peacefully, since to enter another's domain is to place yourself in their power. It was the Truce Stones that made Conclaves possible."

"Power is a strange thing," the Lady of Spiders said. "Ones like Ruven crave its strength, believing it will make them unassailable. Yet the more of it they gather, the more enemies and dangers they see." She emitted a hissing noise that might have been a laugh. "The Truce Stones exist so that we ancient and terrible Witch Lords, the most powerful beings Eruvia has ever known, can feel safe. When you use them as a trap, that purpose is damaged, perhaps even destroyed."

Kathe smiled a charming smile. "Sorry."

"You are a nuisance, Crow Lord, like the screaming pests from which you take your name." There was neither rancor nor affection in the Lady of Spiders' voice; she was stating a fact. "I've barely managed to keep silent how you killed the Lady of Thorns. If you misuse the Truce Stones again so soon, hiding the truth and keeping the trust placed in the stones intact will be much harder. You would threaten the order that keeps all our domains from descending into blood and chaos."

"Doesn't Ruven threaten it more?" I asked, leaning to the edge of my chair. "He's a Skinwitch. He's making human chimeras. He's using up lives as if they meant nothing."

"Ah, Ruven." The Lady of Spiders shook her head. A delicate golden spider caught the light, gleaming like a jeweled pin in her hair. "That poor boy."

"*Poor* Ruven?" Zaira exploded, throwing up her hands. "Do you seriously expect anyone to piss out one drop of sympathy for that pox-licker?"

"Sympathy is for the warm-blooded," the Lady of Spiders said dismissively. "He chose his road and walked it of his own free will. But there was a little boy, once, who could have become something else. Perhaps a healer, if someone had taught him to bind himself by rules and codes when he felt no spark of kinship with his own kind." She curled a hand pensively over the great black spider perched over her heart like a brooch. "Instead, he faced a world that wanted him dead because of what he could do. Everyone that child met besides his own mother thought he should be exterminated like vermin. Of *course* he grew up twisted by fear."

Zaira snorted. "The world wants *me* dead because of what I can do, too. I'm no bastion of virtue, but I'm not a vile sting-roach like him."

"Give it time," the Lady of Spiders murmured. "Give it time."

"Do you really want to see what Ruven will do to Vaskandar, if he's left unchecked?" I demanded, frustrated. "If he expands his domain enough, even the combined power of the other sixteen Witch Lords might not be enough to stop him. He's breaking all your rules, and he'll keep pushing his power in new and terrible directions. Is that what you want?"

The Lady of Spiders sighed. "Amusing as it might be to watch, no. Which is why I'm willing to allow you to use the Truce Stones."

I blinked. "You are?"

"Why would I have come all the way to Let if I were not?" She exchanged a knowing look with the ceiling, as if sharing a joke at our expense. I barely checked myself from following her gaze, and caught a glimpse of a shifting mass of movement before yanking my eyes back down to her face. "I will, of course, require a surety."

"A surety?" I glanced at Kathe, uncertain. He grimaced and nodded, as if he'd expected this but was less than happy about it.

"My price. There is always a price." Her dead black eyes glittered. "The secrets you guard in the dark corners of your heart. The rot you've hidden and let fester. The empty places where life has cut pieces from your soul with its jagged knife. Your demons and your curses, your foolish hopes and bitter dreams."

"Why do you even *want* that?" Zaira asked, leaning as far away from the Lady of Spiders as her chair would allow.

"Because aside from being lovely things, secrets hold power, my dear." The Lady of Spiders lifted her teacup and took a tiny sip. "When I've drunk down the bitter dregs of your soul, I will know how to break you. To control you. To destroy you. And if you do not wish me to give this knowledge freely to your enemies, well, I can rest assured that you will never betray our agreement or turn your powers against me or my domain." She set her teacup down with a satisfied *clink*.

"And how would you, ah, obtain this information?" I asked, my throat dry.

She reached up to her hair and took down the golden spider from it, holding it cupped in her palm with all the care of a collector handling a rare and precious treasure. "Aelie's venom will crack open your mind. Then I can suck out the marrow."

Zaira and I stared at her in silence, and then at each other. Zaira shook her head, eyes wide.

I turned back to the Lady of Spiders, fixing as polite an expression as I could manage to my face. "I must confess, I'm not certain I understand."

"You don't need to. You will see." The Lady of Spiders stroked Aelie's golden abdomen as the creature's reaching legs explored her wrist. "Either of you will suffice. One of you is on Raverra's Council of Nine, and the other is a fire warlock who has proven herself one of the few living beings who can kill a Witch Lord; you are both intriguing, both useful. I am content to wait for the other to come to me again in due time. These are extraordinary circumstances, after all."

Kathe cleared his throat. "Would you consider—"

"No," the Lady of Spiders said. "You've had your turn, Crow Lord. I want someone new."

Sweet Hell of Nightmares. *The secrets you guard in the dark corners of your heart. The rot you've hidden and let fester.* A swarm of possibilities coursed through my mind: the elixir that kept me alive. My father's murder. The sweet smell of anise, and the sinking realization that my own kin had betrayed me. Drawing a rune in my own blood that condemned my cousin to death. The stink of thousands of burning corpses. The pleading look in Marcello's eyes as he begged me not to leave him alone.

But there was more to consider. The intricacies of the Empire's magical wards and weapons, and how to subvert them. Passwords that could activate Raverran spies in deep cover. The thousand small crimes an empire hides from its allies. Troop numbers smaller or larger than we wanted Vaskandar to think. The soft spots in the steely armor around my mother's heart.

I could brace myself well enough to face my own inner horrors; after all, I lived with them every day. But I was on the Council of Nine now. All my secrets were state secrets. The murky shadowed places in my mind belonged to the Empire, and were not mine to give.

The Lady of Spiders watched me, expectantly, waiting for a hesitating insect to step into her web. If we didn't stop Ruven, there might not be an Empire left for me to protect.

I took in a shaky breath. "All right. I—"

"I'll do it," Zaira interrupted.

I stared at her. "Are you sure?"

Zaira rolled her eyes. "Oh, yes, I'm eager as a puppy to let some fanged horror bite me and poison me so that this Demon of Nightmares can poke around in my brain. I'm looking forward to it like the Festival of Bounty, let me tell you. But you can't do it, and you know it."

"You know dangerous information, too," I pointed out. Like the Mews and its defenses, and the Falcons and their weaknesses, not to mention a fair salting of military secrets. "And as the sole fire warlock in Eruvia, you're honestly more important than I am."

"Better looking, too. But I try to ignore the rest of you when you ramble about strategy, and I don't sit in meetings with you nine pox-withered demons who run the Empire. I've got a thimbleful of secrets, and you have buckets." She shook her head. "Don't be a fool. One of us has to do this, and it can't be you."

The rigid line of her shoulders and the wide white margins of her eyes betrayed the fear her casual tone denied. I touched her arm, gently. "I would never ask you to do this."

"If you'd asked, I'd tell you to go bugger yourself." Zaira turned to the Lady of Spiders. "What do I need to do? Let's get this over with."

The hollow eyes and savoring smile of the Lady of Spiders grew so unsettling I almost would rather look at the ceiling. "Choose who will stay, to be near you in your suffering and hear your buried truth," she said. "Or would you prefer to endure this alone?"

"You make it sound so cursed enticing," Zaira muttered. Then she lifted her head. "Crow Lord, out."

Kathe bowed. "I would say good luck, but luck isn't what you need. Be strong."

As he opened the door, I started to rise. But Zaira caught my sleeve.

"Amalia," she said sharply. "You stay."

"Really?" I couldn't keep the surprise from my voice.

"I need someone to make sure that crone doesn't put spiders in my mouth as a funny joke or something." Her grip on my sleeve was like iron. I sank back down beside her.

"You may wish to seal your friend's magic," the Lady of Spiders said to me. "Lest you perish."

I gave Zaira a questioning glance, and she nodded. "*Revincio*," I said.

"Give me your hand," the Lady of Spiders told Zaira, her voice deep and solemn.

Zaira bared her teeth and gripped my hand so hard I felt something pop.

"Or I could put her on your face," the Lady of Spiders suggested, smiling.

"No! No. Here's my hand, Graces help me." Zaira stuck out her thin, trembling fingers.

"Oh, they won't," the Lady of Spiders assured her sweetly.

She seized Zaira's wrist. As Zaira instinctively tried to yank it away, the Lady of Spiders tipped Aelie onto the back of her hand.

"Gently, gently," she crooned. I squeezed Zaira's other hand, my breath frozen with horror.

The spider's sharp fangs twitched, then sank into Zaira's olive-bronze skin.

"Holy Hells! Get it off get it off get it off!" Zaira cried, her voice rising to a higher pitch than I'd ever heard it.

The Lady of Spiders scooped Aelie from Zaira's hand and placed her in the window beside her chair with something like reverence. As soon as her wrist was free, Zaira shoved her chair back along the floor until it jerked to a stop against the hearthstone.

She clutched her hand, eyes wide. "That *hurts*!"

"I'm told it's quite agonizing," the Lady of Spiders said, calmly setting her chair to rocking. "Now, shhh. She begins."

A shadow fell over the room, as if clouds had covered the sun. I caught movement from the corners of my eyes.

Like a wave creeping up the beach, an irregular tide of spiders scuttled down the walls. I bit my own knuckle to stifle a shriek as they descended with sinister, leggy grace like some horrid lacy curtain.

They left an open circle at the bottom of Aelie's window, all facing inward as if to watch her work with their excess of shining black eyes as the spider spun her web, working furiously. A dreamy smile spread over the Lady of Spiders' pale round face. She rocked and hummed, like a knitting grandmother. My stomach clawed its way up into my rib cage.

Zaira looked ready to faint; she doubled over, sweat glistening on her temples, and hissed out a string of curses. I offered her my hand, tentatively, and she crushed it in hers.

The creaking of the rocking chair stopped. The Lady of Spiders leaned forward to peer at the web in the window, the silk of her gown rustling and swarming with glittering motion.

"Ahhh," she breathed. "And there you are."

The web formed three distinct concentric rings, each in a different pattern; the outermost was a rough and tangled weave of coarse, prickly threads. The Lady of Spiders reached out one hooked, slender finger and touched it.

Zaira flinched as if she'd been struck. "What in the Nine Hells? I felt that!" Her eyes went wide and black like a frightened cat's.

"Now let's unravel you," the Lady of Spiders purred, "and see what you're hiding."

Dread knotted my chest like Aelie's web. We'd made a mistake, a terrible mistake; I'd sacrificed a friend again, and now something awful was going to happen. I started to surge from my chair, but Zaira yanked me back down.

"I can do this," she hissed.

The Lady of Spiders cast an unreadable glance at Zaira. Then, with long sharp fingernails, she began to carefully separate the rough-spun outermost ring from the web.

Zaira cried out in pain, as if those clawlike nails ripped her own insides.

"No," I blurted. "This is wrong. We shouldn't do this, we can't—"

Aelie ran up her mistress's arm to a dangling thread of her hair and settled back in her place of pride. The Lady of Spiders smiled sweetly and dropped the severed shred of web into her teacup.

Zaira choked down a scream and swayed where she sat, her eyes squeezed shut. I held her up, glaring at the Lady of Spiders. "Stop this! We've changed our minds."

"I fear it's far too late for that," she said, her eyes dead shining black as she stirred her tea. With every circle of her spoon, shudders ran through Zaira's thin frame.

Shards of color flickered in the steam rising from the teacup, like broken glass. I caught the scent of smoke, and the crackling hiss of flames, as if her tea were somehow on fire. The Lady of Spiders lifted the cup to her lips, eyes half-closed, and savored the aroma.

She took a sip, and Zaira stiffened in my arms.

"Get out of my head, you pus-rotted sack of maggots," she spat.

"I'm just skimming the surface, child." The Lady of Spiders licked flecks of tea from her lips. "So astringent."

"Zaira," I began, my voice shaking, "if you don't want—"

Zaira whipped around to glare in my direction. Her mage mark stood out black as night against eyes hazed and unseeing.

"When did you ever give a dead rat's moldy bollocks about what I want?" she snarled. "You grew up pissing in a golden privy while I was eating garbage."

I froze, shocked as if she'd thrown ice water in my face. "I do care. You know I do."

"That's just her mask." The Lady of Spiders laughed, deep in her throat. "Let's see what's beneath it."

She set her cup down and reached for the web again. The second ring was entirely different, a confection of shining silken threads, the patterns intricate as artifice wirework. The Lady of Spiders tore it free with delicate pinches; Zaira twisted in agony at every snapped strand. The spiders on the walls converged on the window glass, crawling in closer around the web and plunging the room deeper into shadow. All I wanted was to drag Zaira out of there, unleash her power, and beg her to burn the whole house down until nothing was left but ashes.

The Lady of Spiders held up the section of lacelike webbing, admiring it in the light. "Much more complex on the inside, aren't we." She laughed and dropped it in her tea. Zaira made no sound this time, but bit her lip until it bled.

Now the hues that flickered in the steam were richer, warmer, like shades of summer sunlight and green fields. I thought I heard the faint sound of laughter; it sounded like Terika. The tea smelled of chocolate, cinnamon, and...dog? I wrinkled my nose.

The Lady of Spiders took a sip. Zaira swayed, her eyes still remote as if she couldn't see the room around us, and buried her face in her hands.

"I can't do it, Amalia," she whispered.

"You don't have to. Let's leave," I said fervently, ready to spring to my feet.

"She doesn't know me," Zaira groaned. "*You* saw what I did. I'm worse than a demon. I can't ask Terika to marry that."

I hesitated. The Lady of Spiders was watching, her obsidian eyes amused. Her horrific pets swarmed the walls, trapping us in a dark cave of too many legs and eyes and a thousand kinds of secret poison. But the pain in Zaira's voice was too real to ignore.

I bent close to her ear. "Don't underestimate Terika," I whispered. "I thought you were smarter than that. Of course she knows you."

"Shouldn't have let her get close." Zaira's voice dropped so low I almost couldn't hear her. "You, too. Curse you both. Too much to lose."

I squeezed her hand. "Like it or not, you're not alone anymore. And you can't get rid of us, so you may as well like it."

"So sweet," the Lady of Spiders sighed. "Plenty to work with here if anyone ever wanted to destroy you, child."

I whirled on her, pointing a finger that trembled with wrath. "If you dare come after our friends, Witch Lord, you'll learn that we can protect them. Look to what lies outside Ardence if you harbor any doubt."

The Lady of Spiders clicked her tongue reprovingly. "Threatening a person's loved ones is crass. I don't do it. But I've dealt with those who do."

Her gleaming black eyes flicked to me, piercing me with cold. *Ruven.* I wasn't sure how I was so certain, but she meant Ruven. She'd sold him something that could hurt us, and she was warning me.

I didn't have time to try to parse out what she might have told him. The steam rising from the tea had changed; it flickered with the unearthly blue light of balefire, and smelled of burning meat.

The Lady of Spiders let out a pleased sigh. "And now we see what else you've been hiding, here in your darkest corners."

She sipped a mouthful despite the terrible stench, savoring it as if nothing tasted quite so fine as scorched human flesh. My stomach turned over.

Zaira went rigid; a hiss like a cornered cat's slid between her teeth.

A sound filled the cottage, like faint and distant screaming. A chill penetrated deep into my bones. I knew those screams. They kept me awake at night.

"My, my," the Lady of Spiders said, her eyes closed as she breathed in the steam. "You've killed a lot of people. Let's see, so many! An old woman...Was she dear to you?"

Zaira groaned, her eyes squeezed shut, her lids flickering as if they strained to open but couldn't.

"She was like a second mother to her, so leave it alone," I snapped.

"She should have been more careful with the first one. Now, who's this? A boy who tried to kiss you—well, he should have asked, no loss there. An old drunk who startled you when you were sleeping, and my, quite an assortment of petty street ruffians! The Wolf Lord, of course. Spectacular. And...Most impressive! An entire army." She eased her eyes open to black, gleaming slits. "But there's more," she breathed.

The faint screams had faded. A new sound rose with the steam: a sweet voice, singing softly. A lullaby.

Zaira went still as death. "No," she whispered.

The Lady of Spiders took a sip, almost reverently. "And down, and down, into the darkness." Her voice had grown lulling, mesmerizing, flowing like an ancient black river that disappeared into a cavern. A rustling filled the room, as the spiders on the walls and ornamenting her gown seethed with restless agitation. "What have you buried in such a deep grave, Lady Zaira, beneath a headstone marked with Love? What terror is this, that sings so sweetly?"

"No," Zaira said again, the word sliding out between clenched teeth.

"A mother's lullaby," the Lady of Spiders hissed, her eyes narrowed to gleaming slits. "How much she must have loved you, little one, to hold you close while you screamed and spat at her. All that fuss because you didn't want to take the potion she got from the Temple of Mercy to cure your pox."

I could only stare at Zaira's sweat-drenched, pain-creased face in horror. I knew what came next. "Don't say it," I demanded, my fist clenching on my knee. "She knows what happened. Don't rub salt in it."

"Is *that* why you killed them?" The Lady of Spiders sounded genuinely surprised. "Just because you didn't want to take your medicine?"

Zaira dug her fingers into her own face. Alarmed, I pulled them back, but she was strong. The tendons stood out in her thin wrists like iron cables.

"But they burned so beautifully," the Lady of Spiders sighed. "That was well done, at least."

"Leave her alone," I growled. My own cheeks were wet, and helpless fury clogged my chest. "She didn't do that. Her fire got out of control. It wasn't her fault."

"Mmm." The Lady of Spiders pressed her lips together, like a merchant unconvinced of the quality of goods I was selling. "Now, why were all these memories buried so deep, child? Why did you lock each and every killing away like that, so you couldn't call them up even if you tried?"

Zaira stayed curled in a tight ball, face in her knees, and didn't respond. Anger at this woman who had delighted in tormenting her flooded me in a hot rising tide, and I heaved myself to my feet.

"She doesn't remember because *she* didn't kill them!" I balled my hands into fists at my sides. "It was her balefire, not her! When she loses control, the fire takes over. Don't try to make her out to be some murderer when she wasn't even effectively *conscious* when any of this happened!"

"Is that what you think?" The Lady of Spiders' lips curved in a humorless smile. "Has she let you believe that? You are a scholar, Lady Amalia Cornaro. You know perfectly well that balefire has no mind of its own."

"I've seen it," I insisted. "When it takes control, Zaira is gone. It's hungry and wicked and—"

"You shouldn't talk about your friend that way," the Lady of Spiders chided, shaking her head. "She can hear you, you know."

I whirled and knelt by Zaira again. "Then listen to me, Zaira, not to her. It wasn't you who killed them. It was the fire. It wasn't you."

Zaira hauled in a ragged breath. She pulled her head back and opened red eyes swamped with unshed tears. They were no longer distant, but hard, present, and haunted.

"It was me," she rasped.

"No," I insisted. "I've seen the change that comes over you in the moment you lose control. You're not yourself anymore. The flame takes over."

"I *am* the flame, curse you." She tipped her head back, uncurling, and ground the heels of her hands into her eyes. "Everything she said is true. I lose control of my fire in the way a brat with a temper gets lost in her own tantrum, or a wastrel gets lost in drink. It's still me."

"But you change completely," I protested. "You would never—"

"Shut up," Zaira growled. "You're making it worse, idiot." She glared at me. "Of course I change. It comes over me like a madness. Like a hot blue wave. But it's still me."

The Lady of Spiders smiled serenely and pointed one tapered fingernail at the final, central circle of Aelie's web. "Indeed."

My breath caught in my throat. It was beautiful. The silk shimmered pure and bright, catching all the colors of the light, and it formed a heartbreakingly perfect geometric design that unfolded from the center like a flower. There was something almost holy about it; it reminded me of the spectacular stained glass rose window in the Temple of Beauty in Raverra.

The Lady of Spiders lifted it reverently in her hands. "I hate to destroy this," she murmured. "But it was never meant to catch flies. You are a rare creature, Lady Zaira."

This time, when she dropped it into the tea, Zaira's eyes narrowed, but not with pain. A great hissing cloud of steam rose up all at once. The spiders on the window scuttled away from the few wispy remains of the web in a panic, and light flooded back into the room; the patterns on the Lady of Spiders' dress writhed faster than ever.

"Ah, well. I suspected as much," she sighed, tipping her cup over.

It was empty. The tea had boiled away to nothing, leaving not even dregs.

I stared at Zaira, struggling to think what I could say that might help ease the devastation graven into her face. And then something slid into place, like a loose cuff fastened at last.

"That's why you didn't burn down the city," I breathed.

Zaira blinked red-rimmed eyes at me in confusion. "What madness are you spouting now?"

I gripped her shoulder. "Don't you see?" Excitement bubbled up in my chest, and I had to swallow it down so I wouldn't smile at her, not now, not when she was hurting so much. "Jerith was right. If it's a part of you, you can control it. You *have* controlled it. That's why your fire didn't spread throughout Raverra when you lost command of it as a child, even though no one was there to put a jess on you. *You* stopped it." I shook her shoulder gently, while she stared at me with deep suspicion. "Yes, you lost control and lashed out, as a child does. And it had terrible consequences, because you could do much more than hit or bite. But you came back, Zaira. Whatever place of divine violence your mind goes to when you unleash your fire, whatever state of transcendent madness and fury, you came back on your own."

Zaira's brows drew together, throwing eddies into the shadows that haunted her face. But before she could reply, a soft, urgent rap sounded at the door.

"If you're done, I have news." Kathe's voice was subdued, as if he knew what he might be interrupting.

Zaira rose, perhaps too hastily, as she had to reach for the mantel to steady herself. "Go piss yourself. I need a moment here."

"When you're done, then," he said through the muffling wood, "we'd best hurry. I have a report from a crow. Your challenge last night was quite effective, Amalia. Ruven is already closer than we thought, and heading this way."

Chapter Forty

Even the grass around Ruven's blooding stone was sick.

The waist-high pillar of ancient stone perched at the peak of a rocky spit that jutted out into a still, deep lake. No snow had settled on or around the rune-carved stone, despite the pristine white that blanketed the woods and the scab of gray ice across the water. But any warmth the presence of magic lent to the scrabble of earth clinging to the near-island on which the stone stood did the plants huddled on it little good. The grass was withered and yellow, the trees stunted and twisted.

A shallow basin carved into the top of the blooding stone bore old black stains that trailed down a granite channel to vanish beneath the ice-skimmed water. Ruven's blood, and his father's before him. The river that fed this lake came from Let, bearing the leftover dregs of Kathe's claim across the nearby border; but the streams that flowed from it carried Ruven's blood, to spread his claim throughout Kazerath.

Magic lay thick and heavy in the air, pressing down on me like the low steely clouds in the sky above. Zaira and I stood shoulder to shoulder, not quite leaning on each other. I could tell that with everything that had happened, her legs were as unsteady as mine.

I gripped the hilt of my dagger, still sheathed at my hip. "Should I do this now?"

Kathe scanned the trees, poised with the still readiness of an animal preparing to bolt or to pounce. "We need to place the Truce Stones in a circle in the woods first. This outcrop is too small; if we set up the trap here, he could kill you without ever stepping onto it. Glass and Verin, come with me, and we'll hide them in a ring around the lake. Lady Amalia, I'll send you a crow when we're ready, and you can proceed."

Hal had already dripped a few drops of blood into the receptacle of each of the borrowed Truce Stones, and I had poured in a bit of Ruven's potion. Zaira had chipped off flakes of dried stuff from the blooding stone with her knife to add to the mix, just to make sure it was enough. In theory, anyone whose blood mixed in the Truce Stones was bound against harming each other within their ring; if someone broke the truce, their blood would turn against them. From what I'd seen when Kathe killed the Lady of Thorns, this was agonizing and debilitating—but most important of all, it temporarily cut off a Witch Lord from their blood link to their own domain.

"I hope this works," I fretted, as Kathe, Verin, and Glass gathered up the stones that would mark the perimeter of the enchantment. Zaira had already hidden the center stone among some rocks a few paces away. "I can't think of any reason the blood should have to be fresh, but this isn't my area of particular expertise."

"If it doesn't, I'll buy time for everyone to escape," Kathe said grimly. "I don't stand a chance of defeating Ruven here, in his own domain, but I can probably delay him enough for you to reach the border."

"I don't like where that leaves you, my lord," Verin said, frowning.

Kathe shrugged. "If Witch Lords were easy to kill, we wouldn't be having this conversation."

"I'll guard his back," Glass told Verin, patting their musket.

"That's not your job," Kathe said sternly. "You guard my heart. And for that, I need to know that at least some of us will leave here alive. Once we place the Truce Stones, you two go back across the border into Let and wait for us there."

Glass straightened from their habitual slouch. "Bury that. My lord, I'm not going slinking back to Let like some whipped dog. Let us stay and fight."

"Our place is with you, my lord," Verin agreed.

"Bah," Hal scoffed. "If you stay, you'll just get killed." I winced. He could have been less callous about it, though I suspected he wasn't wrong. Ruven would see them as Kathe's point of weakness, and target them.

"What about you, then?" Glass lifted their eyebrows. "I suppose you'll be sipping beer the whole time, delivering witty commentary about the battle?"

"Hal will be injured and possibly dying," Kathe said sharply. "Which is why I need you waiting across the border with a physician, Glass. This is an order."

Glass bowed their head, lips pressed tight. After a moment, they managed, "Yes, my lord."

"You, too, Verin. You've got a son. I'm not telling him I took his mother into Kazerath and got her killed."

Verin sighed. "Yes, my lord. But if you need help, I'm coming back for you."

"If *I* need help, you're better off evacuating the border towns." Kathe took my hand, then, and lifted it to his lips. Electricity shivered through my fingers. "Good luck, Lady Amalia. I'll be waiting in hiding, ready to help when you need it."

He, Verin, and Glass headed back along the natural causeway to shore, then broke up and disappeared into the forest. I couldn't help but feel a pang of worry for them. These were Ruven's woods; his presence breathed from every tree, stirring the branches of the restless pines. The few birds that watched from their stark branches were his, and the limp grass beneath our feet. At any moment, if Ruven figured out what we were up to, the land itself could try to murder us.

"Are you ready?" I asked Hal.

He patted his sword hilt and shrugged. "When he approaches us, I'll step in to guard you. He'll have to get past me to blood the stone again and wipe out your claim. If for any reason he doesn't attack, I'll bellow a lot and swing this around and generally menace him until he comes at me."

"He won't hold back." I held his bright blue eyes. "There's a good chance he'll kill you."

"I know that," he grunted. "I always figured I'd die in battle. I can't think of a better way than protecting my home from a monster like the Skin Lord."

I had to get used to this, somehow. Sending people to their possible deaths was now part of my job. But still, my throat tightened, and I could only nod and whisper, "Thank you."

I turned to Zaira, who still seemed somewhat paler than usual; the sweat hadn't had time to dry from her temples. Aelie's bite showed red and swollen on the back of her hand.

"How about you? Are you ready?"

Zaira let out a harsh bark of a laugh. "My part is to set Ruven's face on fire. I've been ready for this for months."

I tried an experimental and rather tentative punch of her shoulder. She punched mine back, hard enough to leave a bruise.

"All right, then," I said, wincing. "*Exsolvo.*"

Zaira took in a shuddery breath. "I'm trusting you to bring me back again, Cornaro."

"Of course."

"And you?" Zaira asked. "Are you ready to pee on Ruven's tree?"

"My part is the easiest of all." I tried out a smile, though I wasn't entirely sure it fit. "All I have to do is bleed, and then possibly bluff like mad if things don't go as expected. Both of which are areas in which I've amassed a certain amount of practice."

It wasn't long before a crow fluttered down to land on the twisted, dying branch of a nearby stunted tree. It cawed at me urgently, then took off again.

"That's the signal." I drew my dagger and stepped forward to the blooding stone.

I didn't have nearly as strong a connection to the land here as I'd had in Atruin. There, the Lady of Eagles was the only and true master of the domain, having claimed it with her own blood for hundreds of years. Here her claim was secondary to Ruven's, her magic flowing up the rivers and streams of Vaskandar to insinuate its way into land claimed by another. But still, when I touched the rim of rough ancient rock, I could feel a pulse in the earth beneath my feet. *Ruven's heartbeat.* This was his blood. This was his bone.

I drew my dagger across the back of my arm, wincing at the pain. It was hard to make the cut, with every instinct rebelling against it, and I only managed a shallow slice. But red beads welled up along it, and I held my stinging arm over the basin and squeezed.

The first drop fell, shining crimson. The moment it hit the stone, everything changed.

The whispering trees stilled. I had their absolute attention. Birds rose up from the forest around us, crying in consternation. I became precisely, acutely aware of each blade of grass around me, sickened and dying as Ruven pulled more from his domain than he gave back; the lives closest to the source of his power were most harshly affected by his reckless greed. I could feel the tormented straining of the branches within reach, and how they held their breath, waiting to see if someone would truly challenge their master. I had a vague sense of the lake, deeper than it looked, its bottom lost in inky darkness. Cold fish moved sluggishly there beneath the ice. I could feel the snow-locked ground, and the waiting spring sleeping within it, biding its time.

I couldn't touch any of it, as I might have if I were a vivomancer. And my awareness didn't stretch even to the far shore. But the land thrummed in my mind, tense as a plucked harp string.

Another drop of blood fell, and another. Barely enough to trickle toward the mouth of the channel that led down to the lake. But it was enough. I was forming a connection; one I couldn't use, but the Lady of Eagles might, if she chose.

Ruven's attention fell on me like a burning building. He *knew*.

And he was coming.

"Get ready," I gasped. "He's close."

Hal drew his sword and stepped forward. "How long?"

"Not long. He's almost—"

A gunshot shattered the wintry stillness of the air, cracking across the sky like thunder.

Hal staggered and fell, blood blooming on his barrel chest.

"Hal!" I cried, abandoning the blooding stone to rush toward him. But though he still moved feebly against the rocks and the dying grass, I knew in the sick twisting of my gut that it was too late.

At the far end of the rocky spit, where it met the shore, Marcello and Ruven stood side by side, the snow-dusted forest rearing up behind them. Smoke still rose from Marcello's pistol. A light breeze stirred the collar of Ruven's long dark coat, lifting strands of his ponytail to mingle with the winter air.

"That was a very good try, Lady Amalia Cornaro," Ruven called. "It might have worked, if I hadn't happened to notice this Truce Stone."

He took one from behind his back, where his hands had been folded, showing me its bloodstained crown with a sharp grin. Then he threw it in the lake. It crunched through the thin ice, leaving a black, rippling hole as the water swallowed it.

At my feet, Hal gave a short, wet gasp and went still.

Chapter Forty-One

Ripples of horror spread through my chest, cold and dark as the lake that trapped us here. I couldn't comprehend how so much had been destroyed in a few fleeting seconds: Hal dead, the circle of Truce Stones broken, and us left at Ruven's mercy in his own domain. Surely, I could turn back time, somehow, and try again. This couldn't have gone so terribly, irrevocably wrong.

"Hells take it," Zaira breathed, flexing her fingers at her sides.

From a patch of trees along the shoreline, a flock of crows burst skyward, cawing.

Kathe stepped out of the woods, his black feathered cloak mantling behind him like the bristling hackles of some furious beast. He paced toward Ruven, head down, deadly intent in the line of his shoulders. The bone knife he'd used to kill the Lady of Thorns gleamed in his hand, unsheathed and ready at his side.

Ruven turned with slow menace to face him.

"Are you truly so mad as to challenge me here, in my own domain, Crow Lord?" he asked incredulously.

"At this moment, I am precisely that mad." The lethal intensity of Kathe's voice struck a chill through me. "You killed my friend."

Zaira's hand fell on my shoulder. "Do we run, or do I try to burn him?" she whispered.

I shook my head. Marcello was reloading his pistol, still staring straight at us. The impossibility of our situation sat in my stomach like a gulp of icy lake water. "We already know your balefire alone isn't enough. And they're blocking the only way out. We have to hope Kathe can give us a chance somehow." I gripped my flare locket in one hand and my bloody dagger in the other.

Ruven smiled at Kathe, baring shining teeth. "Let's see if I can kill you, too."

A roaring groan shook the trees along the bank. Branches stabbed at Kathe like spears, lethally fast and sharp, one after another. Within two heartbeats, dozens of them clawed at him from every angle.

But Kathe ducked and dodged with careless grace as he continued his relentless advance on Ruven. He flicked his head barely out of the way of one deadly lance, then lifted his knife to shear through another as if it were clay before it could touch him.

One tore the sleeve of his gray tunic as he twisted aside. Another struck the feathered mantle of his cloak and rebounded as if it were impenetrable armor. He blocked yet another with his bone knife, and the branch shattered like glass. He couldn't turn Ruven's domain against him, but he could still use the pieces of his own domain he'd brought with him. I hardly dared breathe—he was unstoppable. He was going to make it.

Ruven frowned and backed a step, then another, but not enough. Kathe lunged between two grasping tree-talons, cloak flying, and was upon him.

He stabbed at Ruven's face, once, twice. Ruven screamed, staggering back, his hands flying up to cover the bloody ruin of his eyes.

"Serves the bastard right," Zaira said, awe in her voice.

Kathe struck a third time, burying his bone knife in Ruven's chest, punching through his sternum as if it were a loaf of soft bread. But I could see even from here the desperation straining his eyes.

Not enough. Graces help us, he didn't think this was nearly enough.

Ruven's pain-clawed hands relaxed. He wiped the blood away from his face, revealing fresh new eyes, the violet mage mark in them blazing with anger.

"You'll pay for that," he said, ignoring the knife hilt sticking from his chest. He grabbed at Kathe, who leaped back out of his range. Kathe flashed Ruven a sharp taunting smile, but fear for him tightened a band around my lungs.

"You are nothing but a nuisance," Ruven spat. "But you are a nuisance for which I have prepared. You should have stayed in Let."

From the woods, three chimeras paced, like horses crossed with serpents. Their snakelike heads bore flaring hoods, and they hissed with fangs bared; reptilian tails lashed the air, and scales covered their long lean bodies and powerful legs. Kathe faced them warily, his hands bare and empty.

Zaira tugged at my sleeve. "We need to do something about *him*."

I tore my eyes reluctantly from the battle of the Witch Lords to find Marcello advancing up the causeway, pistol in one hand, rapier in the other. The determined furrows in his brow were achingly familiar, but his orange eye stared with inhuman ferocity. The breeze stirred the black waves of his hair, lifting it from the collar of his tattered, bloodstained uniform.

He moved smoothly, and the hole in his scarlet doublet was the only sign of the wound to his shoulder from last night. Ruven must have healed him. Relief and consternation mixed queasily in my stomach.

"I don't have any way to take him down without hurting him." The flare locket I gripped for reassurance would do little in the bright daylight, a distraction at best. I'd used up Istrella's last ring, and my satchel was empty of magical surprises.

"Then we'll have to hurt him," Zaira said grimly.

On the shore, all three chimeras leaped at Kathe at once. I couldn't look away, couldn't breathe.

Kathe tossed his cloak over the head of the first one; it screamed as if the feathers had become knives, and blood ran down its sides as it collapsed. He ducked quickly past another, using its body to shield him from the third. He laid one hand on its neck as he went by, as if to push it away from him; it let out a screech and collapsed. He must have stopped its heart, just as Ruven could do to humans.

One left. He could handle this. The pressure in my chest eased slightly.

The third chimera circled and lunged at Kathe again. But as he braced himself to meet it, a root thick as my arm and sharpened to a stiletto point lanced up from the ground behind him. It struck him in the back, spearing through him.

"Kathe!" I screamed. But it was too late.

The blood-streaked tip of the spike protruded from his lower chest. Kathe staggered, staring down at it, caught.

Something yanked my arm, and I realized I had started down the causeway toward him. Zaira's fingers dug into my skin.

"What do you think you're going to do?" she hissed, pulling me back. I shook my head, throat aching too much to speak.

Kathe touched the impaling root with a trembling hand, and it crumbled instantly to dry powder. He wove on his feet, blood still spreading alarmingly across his tunic, as the remaining chimera lunged at him.

He flung up an arm to ward it off, and the chimera sank its serpentine fangs into it. For a moment it froze like that, teeth buried in Kathe's arm, eyes gone suddenly glassy; then it slid to the ground, dead as its compatriot.

Kathe fell to his knees, clutching his arm.

"What is this?" he demanded, his voice hoarse. The fear in it sent a sliver of frost through the core of me.

"A venom my father developed in his spare time, in case he had to defend his domain against his fellow Witch Lords." Ruven plucked Kathe's dagger from his chest, casual as pulling a splinter, and began to clean his nails with it. "It would kill a mortal a thousand times over. It won't kill you, alas, but it should stop your heart and your breath for a time, and make it quite impossible for you to move."

"Leave him alone," I shouted, shaking my arm free of Zaira and starting forward. But Marcello stood between me and the causeway, his human eye brimming with anguish, his pistol leveled at my chest.

"I can't let you interfere, Amalia," he said.

Kathe slumped over, clutching his arm to his bloody chest. "You..." he began, but he couldn't seem to finish.

A tangle of roots reached up from the ground, slithering over him. "You see," Ruven said, clearly relishing each word, "you are not the only one who has made bargains with the Lady of Spiders, Crow Lord. I know your greatest fear."

"No," I whispered, clutching at the claws around my neck.

The roots dragged Kathe's unresisting body toward the lake. I knew in my bones how deep it was, and how dark, and how smothering the weight of water at the lightless bottom.

"Zaira, can you burn those off him?" I asked desperately.

"Not without getting your crow friend, too."

"If you unleash your balefire," Marcello said to Zaira, his voice low and uneven, "I'll shoot Amalia in the gut. My lord can heal her later if he wants her alive."

He wouldn't meet my eyes. My veins filled with ice to match the gray surface of the lake—fear of dying in slow agony, fear for Kathe, and fear that shooting me would utterly destroy whatever remained of the true Marcello.

"Marcello, we're your friends," I urged, searching desperately for some sign of the good man I knew in the taut lines of his shoulders, the tension in his jaw. "Let us pass. Let us help him."

"Friends?" He glanced deliberately at Hal's still, bloody form. "I've seen how you use your friends and cast them aside. I have my orders. Don't test me."

The claws of Kathe's necklace dug into my palm, and my chest hurt as if I were the one with a hole speared through me. Zaira cursed, squeezing her hands into fists until her knuckles showed white.

The roots broke through the ice and hauled Kathe's still, bloody form down into the watery darkness.

"We'll see if you last as long as your mother did, before you choose to die," Ruven called gleefully after him.

The black water scattered silent ripples beneath the shattered ice.

Chapter Forty-Two

That's enough." A blue spark kindled in Zaira's eyes. She raised her hands, facing Ruven across the water. "I don't care if it won't kill you, you festering blister, I'm setting you on fire."

Marcello cocked back the hammer of his pistol. "Please don't."

Deep lines furrowed his face, but his hand remained steady. The round eye of the pistol's muzzle stared at me, his slit orange eye glaring above it.

"Fine," Zaira growled. "I'll burn you, too. Sorry, Amalia, but it's that or let him kill us."

Despite her callous words, sweat beaded on her brow, and her cheeks tightened up under her eyes. Balefire kindled at her fingertips; the spider bite on her hand was livid in the harsh blue light.

The moment slowed until the heartbeat throbbing through me became a gradual roar. The crows screaming angrily in the sky barely moved, their wings frozen as they thrashed the air. This was it: the last precious second before Zaira killed Marcello, or Marcello killed me. Either way, a friendship on which my life had pivoted was over.

No. If there had ever been an Amalia who would have stood by and let it happen, she was gone long ago.

"*No!*" I threw myself between the two of them, facing Zaira, my arms spread wide to shield Marcello from her fire. "I won't let you do it!"

"Don't be a sentimental idiot," Zaira snapped. But moisture shimmered at the corners of her eyes, and her voice trembled at the edge of breaking. "He's gone, Amalia. It doesn't make sense to get us both killed trying to save someone who's already dead."

"He's *not* dead!" The words scraped my throat raw. "I can't let you kill him. He's not gone, Zaira."

I could feel Marcello's presence behind me. He was part of Ruven's domain, too, and close enough that I could sense the beat of his heart, the quickening of his breath, through my blood still on the stone. I didn't have to look to know the moment the pistol began to waver in his hand.

I took a deep, ragged breath. "That's why I have to do this myself."

Before I could think, before I could stop myself, I spun and lunged at Marcello. The dagger I'd used to cut my arm was still in my hand, and all his chimera's speed was useless with the pure shock widening his eyes. I drove the dagger into his side, throwing the full force of my weight behind it.

Warm blood spread against my hand. Marcello staggered, choking, staring at me in horror. His pistol discharged with a bone-jarring crack and a puff of smoke, the ball ricocheting harmlessly off rock.

He collapsed to the ground, his breath wet and labored, clutching at the spreading bloodstain on his side. I fell to my knees beside him, half-blind with tears.

"Holy Hells, Amalia!" Zaira cried out.

"I'm sorry," I whispered. "Marcello, I'm sorry, I'm so sorry."

"You did it," he wheezed, shock slurring his words. "You actually stabbed me."

"Oh, my. Oh, very nicely done, Lady Amalia." On the shore, Ruven tucked Kathe's dagger through his belt and clapped.

Zaira whirled toward him, teeth bared in a snarl. Ruven laughed and stepped back toward the forest.

"Much as it pleases me to demonstrate my immortality, Lady Zaira, I must confess that your balefire causes me some discomfort. So I will risk being labeled an ungracious host and leave the entertainment of my guests to others for the moment."

The three dead chimeras sprawled on the ground suddenly jerked and twitched, like puppets with jostled strings, and then lurched unsteadily to their feet. Their eyes remained blank and empty, glazed with death, and no breath expanded their sunken ribs. They shambled toward us with the dull gracelessness of broken clockwork.

It was *wrong*. The delicate tracery of life to which I was still barely connected shuddered with it, and nausea wrenched my belly strongly enough to distract me even from Marcello dying on the ground in front of me. I braced myself on the earth and felt it cringing under my fingers.

"There are so many foolish rules and taboos in Vaskandar," Ruven sighed. "Laid down by the oldest Witch Lords in the name of preserving the cycle of life—but frankly, I think they only want to keep themselves in power. If we can shape wood and bone, why not use the dead as our puppets, after all? It's the same thing."

All around the lake, a tumult shook the snow, and black mounds of earth heaved up from beneath the blanketing white. Bones reached up into the daylight, bones picked bare by time and ones with ragged flesh still hanging off them; bones still cloaked in moldering fur, skulls with decaying eyes still pooled in them. Rotting carcasses trailing startled beetles, and ancient skeletons clean and pure as the snow itself.

"Hell of Corruption," Zaira breathed, the flush of rage draining from her face.

Some of them had been human, with scraps of armor hanging off them, and rusted weapons caught in their rib cages from an ancient battle. But beside them stumbled deer with grinning skulls and spreading sharp antlers, great shaggy bears with stinking holes rotted in their fur, and wolves with wisps of gray pelt clinging to their yellowed skeletons. They followed the three venomous chimeras as they advanced up the causeway toward us, the vanguard of a terrible army.

"Please enjoy this modest entertainment," Ruven called, with a mocking bow, and retreated into the woods.

"Get out of my way, Cornaro," Zaira said, and she unleashed her fire.

I slipped my arm beneath Marcello's shoulders and dragged him back from the blast of heat and light, away from the smoke and stench, almost to the tip of the rocky spit. Ice stretched around us, thin and brittle as the barrier that kept me from screaming, with black water stretching deep and dark below it. Crows circled above, cawing frantically. Marcello's blood soaked through my shirt.

I pulled him half into my lap and fumbled with shaking hands in my satchel in a desperate search for something that could help him, some forgotten alchemical salve to stop the bleeding, but all I had was Terika's vial of reinvigoration potion.

"Oh Graces, please tell me he's going to heal you." I couldn't stop crying. My dagger had fallen from his side and was gone, and now there was only the terrible spreading bloodstain on his ruined uniform, and Marcello's struggling breath, and the blood he coughed up onto my already scarlet hands as I pressed them over the wound. "You're too valuable to let die. Right? Please let him heal you."

Marcello tried to push my hands away. "It's all right, Amalia," he said weakly. "Let me go. I'm done being Ruven's toy."

"I can still cure you," I insisted, furiously blinking away tears. "Somehow. We'll make you human again, you'll see."

"He took away so much." Pain twisted Marcello's face; his scales wrinkled like a lizard's skin. "And he filled me up with bloodlust and cruelty. But he couldn't make me stop loving you."

I seized his hand, then, claws and all. "I love you, too," I said desperately, at last. Grace of Mercy, what kind of fool was I, that I always waited until one of us was dying? "Do you hear me? I love you."

He nodded, and managed the barest, thinnest echo of his wistful smile. And then his eyes closed.

"Don't you dare die," I whispered, crushing his hand in mine. "Don't you dare, Marcello."

But his heart was still beating. I could feel it, pulsing in time with Ruven's. A thin trickle of vivomancy threaded through him: not enough to close his wound, but enough to pause the bleeding and keep him alive.

Ruven wasn't done with either of us yet.

Rage swelled in me, so strong I could feel the heat of it scorching my skin. But no. That wasn't mere anger; anger wouldn't focus exclusively on my landward side. Nor would it come with a harsh blue glare and a thick pall of black smoke.

I lifted my head to find a wall of balefire creeping toward me. Zaira stood within the heart of the blaze, arms stretched wide to embrace it. The entire spit was burning, pale flames leaping skyward with hungry exaltation, except for the tip where I knelt with Marcello. Blue fire clawed its way closer over the rocks, a finger's width at a time, melting the stone beneath it.

"Zaira," I called. "You can stop now. They're gone. You burned them all."

She gave no sign that she heard me. The madness of the flames had taken her, and she was lost to it.

I squeezed my eyes shut against the heat, against the sight of Marcello's pale face and bloodstained body, against the knowledge that Kathe was fighting to live and trapped in his own worst nightmare hundreds of feet beneath the ice. How in the Nine Hells had this gone so wrong? We were supposed to save the Empire.

I *still* had to save the Empire. Somehow. No matter what happened to me, no matter what happened to my friends, that was my duty. It might be tempting to let Zaira's flames rage unabated, to let them wash over me and absolve me of everything I had done, but that was not an option I possessed.

I opened my eyes and dragged in a breath. "*Revincio*," I said.

Nothing happened.

Balefire still raged all along the spit, spreading out onto the surface of the lake, licking hungrily toward the clouds above. The ice retreated before it, a clear space spreading rapidly, freeing a scattered reflection of glowing blue ripples in the black water.

I cleared my throat of smoke and tears and fear. "*Revincio*," I said again, as clearly as possible.

The balefire edged closer, withering grass and charring sticks to ash, scorching the rock beneath. I dragged Marcello back a few feet, down the slope toward the water's edge, but we were almost out of land. I might be a decent swimmer, but not good enough to keep an unconscious man afloat with me in icy cold water—and the blazing lake was proof enough, if I'd needed it, that water was no protection.

"*Revincio*," I cried, in a panic now. "*Revincio, revincio, revincio!*"

Zaira stood wreathed in a glorious mantle of fire, her head tilted back to the sky. On one upraised wrist, the jess gleamed— but the shape was wrong, blurred and uneven.

It was melting. Istrella had warned that it might become further damaged after the apocalyptic fire she'd unleashed outside Ardence, and now it was melting altogether. *Sweet Grace of Mercy.*

As I watched, it sloughed off her wrist in a dribble of molten gold.

Lightning-blue flames danced and writhed all around her, consuming everything but Zaira herself, reveling in absolute destruction. All that remained of Ruven's dead army was ashes. *There is nothing we cannot make beautiful*, the flames said. *There is nothing so dark we cannot turn it into light.*

Graces preserve us all. Without the jess, her flames could rage to the far border of Kazerath, consuming everything in their path. That might even be her intent; it was the one thing that could destroy Ruven.

But I'd promised to always bring her back.

I reached into my satchel. My trembling fingers brushed across Marcello's button before finding the cool, complex weave of wire they sought. *The jess.*

I rose, the jess clenched in my hand, and faced the flames.

Zaira twirled slowly within them, her bare wrists gracefully extended, her hair an aura of fire. Flames fluttered from her arms like wings. She was dancing, exultant, drinking in the destruction with the pure hunger of the flames themselves.

She was free.

The jess dangling from my hand suddenly felt as heavy as an iron chain.

I'd put this on her once, to save Raverra from burning. I couldn't force it on her again. Not even to save my life.

I gritted my teeth and slipped the jess over my own wrist, pushing it up my arm to get it out of the way. I didn't need it. I had taken one bright thing out of the Lady of Spiders' cottage, and I clasped it to my heart: No matter how far gone she might seem, Zaira could quench her flames on her own.

I tried not to think about how that had come *after* she'd killed the people she loved most.

"Zaira!" I called. "Zaira, listen to me! Your balefire is spreading too far!"

She turned, slowly, to face me. Her eyes were full of blue fire. It burst from every inch of her skin: the wild, fierce magic of her own soul escaping, leaping with joy and yearning into the light.

"I know you don't want to kill me," I pleaded. "Zaira, you're my friend. You're the best friend I have, in fact. We've been through so much together."

The balefire kept creeping toward me. Even with the additional distance I'd opened, it was less than ten feet away. The cold waters of the lake lapped over Marcello's limp hand; I had nowhere else to run. If I couldn't get through to Zaira, Marcello and I were both going to die, and no amount of healing from Ruven could restore our scattered ashes.

I steeled myself and stepped forward. The heat rolling off the flames sucked all the moisture from my skin, leaving my eyes dry and raw. The fire burned shifting patterns into my vision, and every time I blinked, orange flames danced behind my eyelids, the inverse of what raged before me.

"I trust you, Zaira," I said quietly. "And if your fire is part of you, I trust that, too." I struggled not to cough from the smoke; the fire was close enough now that the bare skin on my face was tightening. Zaira stepped closer with it, trailing a wake of eddying flames, her expression a distant mask within the twisting curtains of fire.

"I put my life in your hands," I breathed. "My friend."

I reached out a hand toward her, empty, offering. Pain seared my fingertips.

I closed my eyes and waited to see if I would die.

Chapter Forty-Three

A warm hand slid into mine. Slim, confident fingers clasped my palm close against hers.

There was no pain.

I opened my eyes and met Zaira's. They gleamed black and clear, with the fire still rising all around her.

Around *us*. The balefire raged all about me, deadly streams of blue-white light shifting and snapping, a myriad of shapes in light created and destroyed every instant. I still felt its heat, but I wasn't burned.

"Amalia," she said, her voice clear and calm. "Stab him in the face for me."

All at once, the fire winked out.

Zaira's eyes closed, and her hand slipped from mine as she collapsed to the ground.

I stood alone on the rocks, over the unconscious bodies of my friends, with a stretch of smoking ruin making a path to shore. I sucked in a deep breath, coughed on the lingering smoke, then pulled in another. My whole body trembled with the unspent energy of fear and love and grief.

I didn't have time for shock. I groped in my satchel and drew out Terika's reinvigoration potion. My hands trembled so violently I almost couldn't break the wax seal and work out the cork, but I managed to splash some over Zaira's parted lips.

"Come on," I whispered. "I need you. This has to work."

The wind blew a fine grit of ash across her face and teased her dark curls, but she didn't stir. Crows called overhead with desperate urgency.

From the shadow of the woods, out onto the cindered shore, stepped Ruven.

"Lady Amalia Cornaro." His smile spread wide. No stray trace of blood on his face remained to suggest he'd had both eyes stabbed out not half an hour ago. His black leather coat flowed behind him as he advanced across the stony causeway toward me, his boots crunching on the remains of his creatures. "Just the two of us again, I see. Exactly as I planned."

Hells. I had nothing left in me to deal with Ruven right now. Even my dagger was gone, for what little good it would have done, melted to a slick pool of steel by Zaira's fire. I had driven him off with words alone before, but they had always been words backed by some kind of power: that of the Serene Empire, or of his fellow Witch Lords at the Conclave. Now we were in his domain, and I was out of allies and resources. I had no way to protect myself, let alone my friends.

When you're taken off guard, get your opponent talking, my mother's remembered voice whispered in my mind. *It will buy you time to make a plan.*

"What do you want, Ruven?" I asked, my voice rough and broken as the heat-shattered stones beneath my boots.

He spread his hands wide, pacing nearer. "A fine question, Lady Amalia! It seems to me that I can ask you for anything I desire."

"You can ask," I agreed coldly.

Ruven chuckled. "Spoken like a queen sitting on her throne. But my lady, forgive me, you are no queen here. You cannot dictate terms to me. You have only one choice left to make." He came closer, every step shattering charred bone. "You can leave here as my vassal, bound to my service by the potion you so detest. Or you can leave here as my willing partner, to stretch the bounds of what magic can accomplish together, forging new realms of scholarship and dominion."

"And why should I make such a choice?" I had to stall him to give the reinvigoration potion time to work, or in case some other desperate chance presented itself. "For that matter, what makes you think I'd stay loyal to you if I said I'd join you?" *Keep talking.*

"You know why." Ruven snapped his fingers; behind me, Marcello groaned weakly with pain. "Accept my offer, and Captain Verdi becomes human again—and remains so only for so long as you serve me well. Reject it, and he stays a chimera for the rest of his life, which is likely to be a rather short one. I have no reason to keep him alive if he gives me no sway over you."

"What about Zaira?" I asked. "And Kathe?"

Ruven sighed. "Alas, they are both too dangerous to live. Much as I like the idea of a fire warlock under my command, I have no illusions that she would prove anything but trouble. As for the Crow Lord, he will lie under this lake until he dies. Given what I learned of his greatest fear from the Lady of Spiders, it won't be long." He stopped at last, only a few paces from me. His violet-ringed eyes narrowed with satisfaction. "No, Lady Amalia, your position is too weak to negotiate. You may purchase one mercy from me, and only one."

I knew how I must look to him: tears streaking my face, barely standing. My coat stained with blood, my tangled hair blowing loose in the wind.

But if he thought that tears and pain made a person weak, he understood nothing of what it was to be human.

"Duly noted," I said, like a tomb door grinding shut, stone on stone.

"You have already lost." Ruven didn't bother to hide how he savored the words. "You only have to decide whether to save your friend, or to damn him."

I closed my eyes to shut out Ruven's face. I had promised myself not to abandon Marcello again, not after I'd walked out of the room while he begged me to stay, leaving him to his fate. And yet I might well have killed him. My mother had advised me to draw hard lines I would not cross. Where could I draw such a line, if not at the abandonment of a friend to death, or to life as a monster?

I'd told Kathe I'd die before bending the knee to Ruven. But there were so many fates worse than death.

"You are out of time, Lady Amalia," Ruven said. I opened my eyes to find him holding out a hand to me, an eager glint in his violet-ringed gaze. "You have spurned my hand before, no matter how many times I have offered it in good faith. Take it now, and accept my dominion at last."

I stared at his offered hand, lean and elegant and well-manicured. He extended it farther, insistent.

"Take it," he repeated, his voice gaining an edge of urgency.

This mattered to him. For all he pretended indifference to what I chose, he desperately wanted me to say yes.

Of course he grew up twisted by fear, the Lady of Spiders had said. He was afraid, surrounded by enemies; he craved the power in my blood, and the power of the Empire that I could wield, to make him safe.

After all he'd done to me and those I loved, the arrogant bastard was begging me to save him.

I crossed the few steps between us, forcing myself to come within his reach. Ash stirred up at my every step. Ruven held his hand ready, smile spreading, already triumphant.

"I'm going to regret this," I murmured.

"You may," he said. "But I doubt that I will."

"We'll see."

I swallowed to stop the bile that tried to rise at the back of my throat and forced myself to reach out and clasp his offered hand.

Ruven's fingers tightened over mine, as if he were afraid I might change my mind and try to pull them back. Immediately, his magic began crawling up my arm, a pins-and-needles numbing pain that made my stomach turn.

I met his gloating eyes and smiled. "In Callamorne, they shake hands to seal a deal."

I jerked my hand sharply down, then up. The jess I'd pushed up my arm slid down to my wrist, and then over his.

"*Revincio*," I whispered.

The ache of magic in my arm cut off immediately. Ruven's eyes widened, and he sucked in a sharp breath through his teeth.

I didn't dare give him a chance to recover from his shock. I snatched Kathe's dagger from Ruven's belt and started stabbing everything I could reach, blind panic erasing all of Ciardha's training.

Kathe's knife was sharp as starlight, and blood slicked my hands as it found Ruven's stomach, then his chest, then opened a deep slash in his cheek. *There you go, Zaira. I stabbed him in the face for you.*

Ruven staggered back, lifting his arms to ward me off, the jess gleaming bright on his wrist. But when I lunged at his neck with the wild hope of severing it, his hands shot out and clamped on my throat.

"You vile common filth," he snarled. "You *dare!*"

I struggled to breathe, my pulse pounding against his grip, and kept stabbing at him. Ruven bared his teeth and squeezed harder. "I would have spared you!" he hissed. "I could have used you! But now you give me no choice but to kill you."

It was no good. Sparks swarmed at the edges of my vision, and Kathe's knife grated on a rib and twisted from my loosened grasp. Even without Ruven's magic, it simply took too much to kill him. My lungs heaved, but Ruven's fingers dug into my throat like steel.

"Hey, leave some for me," Zaira rasped from the ground behind me.

Twin lines of blue fire arced around me, scribing a circle on the ground, and crossed through Ruven like scissor blades closing.

He burst into flame. A scream rose from his throat, of pure agonized terror, as balefire roared up from his coat, his boots, his flesh. He released my throat and I fell to my knees, gasping, surrounded by a circle of fire.

Ruven tugged frantically at the jess on his wrist with fingers withering to bone in furious, moon-pale flames. He pulled his belt knife from a sheath of flames and sawed desperately at his own arm with it, but the blade's edges had already blurred and melted. Fire devoured his shining golden hair, caressed the flesh from his fine-boned face, clothed him in a robe of glory such as the Demon of Death would tremble to wear.

He was a charred ruin of a man, still standing in the heart of a pillar of flame that shouted his destruction to the heavens. The trees on the shore thrashed in his agony, raining down pine needles upon the snow as he sucked the life from them to stay alive. But he couldn't heal himself, and piece by piece the balefire was gnawing him to ashes.

He staggered at me. He reached out, whether to plead for his life or to attack; the jess dangled golden from his wrist. Blistering heat rolled off him, and the violet rings of his mage mark still blazed somehow in eyes that were nearly gone.

Zaira stepped up beside me, into my circle of fire. Her eyes held a cold, pure clarity, breathtaking as the geometric perfection of the rose-window center of Aelie's web. But there was nothing distant or divine about the raw, human pain and triumph on her face.

She lifted one hand palm-out toward Ruven, and the flames devouring him roared up higher still. And she reached out the other hand, without looking, to me.

I took it and heaved myself to my feet. We stood there, side by side, holding hands, as Ruven at last crumpled to ash and scattered across the rocks on the wind.

Chapter Forty-Four

Zaira lowered her hand, and the flames flickered out. A winter chill descended immediately, stinging my parched skin. She swayed on her feet, and I caught her under the elbow.

"Is it wrong of me to want to piss on his ashes?" she murmured, her eyes sagging shut despite all her attempts to keep them open.

"Maybe later," I said. "Rest now."

She nodded, and slid down my side to lean against a rock, its sides blackened and slicked by fire.

I sucked in a shuddering breath. This wasn't over. "I have to see if I can help Marcello and—"

A series of sharp cracks escalated to a shattering noise as if all the wineglasses in the Imperial Palace had been dropped at once. The ice coating the lake exploded in a shower of shards like falling snow, and a great tangle of roots rose up out of the churning water.

Kathe rode them, braced on the twisting branches, hunched over as he coughed up bloody lake water. The crows that had been circling and crying in the air above swooped down at once to greet him, settling around him protectively.

I ran to the water's edge. He was alive, at least, thank the

Graces. "Kathe! Are you all right?" I called, but as I did, I dropped to my knees beside Marcello.

His face was pale, his eyes closed, and he was barely breathing. Hells have mercy, if I'd killed him despite everything, I would never forgive myself.

Kathe straightened, dripping, his ripped tunic plastered to his chest. The roots braided a bridge in front of his feet; as he walked toward the shore, a murder of crows carried his cloak to him, draping its feathered warmth over his shoulders. He hardly looked in better shape than Marcello, with blue lips and washed-out bloodstains, but his mage mark shone fierce as ever from his shadowed eyes.

"How is Captain Verdi?" he asked, in a voice ragged around the edges.

"I don't know." I bit my lip so fiercely I tasted blood. I'd never learned anything about treating wounds; I didn't have the faintest idea what to do to help him. It was always easier to break things than to fix them.

Kathe splashed through the last few feet to shore. He stumbled as he set foot on land, but caught himself, and crouched down beside me in a rustle of feathers. Icy cold poured off him, and his skin looked waxy and pale.

"Are you *sure* you're all right?" I asked him in alarm, and then realized he'd never answered my question in the first place.

Kathe closed his eyes and laid two fingers to the pulse in Marcello's neck. "I'll be fine," he said. "I just...It wasn't good."

I slipped an arm around his cold, wet back, under his cloak, and steadied him. He shivered, so minutely I wouldn't have noticed if I hadn't been touching him.

After a moment, he rocked back on his heels and let out a breath. "The good news is that Ruven appears to have permanently altered Captain Verdi's ability to withstand grievous injuries and heal quickly, so he may survive." He met my eyes. "The bad news is that he does appear to have made far more extensive alterations than you can see on the surface, and they're permanent, too. I'm sorry, Amalia."

And we had killed the only man who could restore him to what and whom he had been. I covered my eyes with a hand for a moment, trying not to think, trying to stop terrible possibilities from unfolding in my mind.

"Let's make sure he lives, first," I said. "We'll figure out the rest later."

When we arrived at the closest village across the Let border, they had mulled wine, fresh clothes, soft beds, and a physician waiting, courtesy of Glass and Verin. They must have told the residents to leave us alone; the struggle not to ask questions or express concern was plain on the villagers' faces as they welcomed us into the largest house in town, which they'd quickly emptied for their lord and his guests, and made themselves scarce.

The physician took immediate charge of Marcello, shaking her head at the state of him. Zaira and Kathe were in hardly better shape. Zaira didn't even make it inside before collapsing as the temporary energy from Terika's reinvigoration potion abandoned her. As for Kathe, Witch Lords might be hard to kill, but being impaled, poisoned, *and* drowned was still quite a lot to recover from. His lips still had a blue tinge, and his face was pale and exhausted. I hesitated, torn between making certain Kathe and Zaira were well and following after the physician to anxiously await news of Marcello's prospects.

"Will you be all right?" I asked Kathe, as Verin and Glass saw Zaira safely bundled into a warm bed to sleep and regain her strength.

"I must admit I've been better." He winced and put a hand to his chest. From what I could see through the tear in his tunic, while his wound had stopped bleeding, it was far from healed. "I think I need to fall into bed like Zaira." His voice dropped to a subdued murmur. "But first I have to tell Verin and Glass about Hal."

I laid a hand on his still-damp arm; his whole body was tense as a drawn bow. "They know," I said.

"I know they do. But I still have to tell them." He squeezed my shoulder with an icy hand, his gaze solemn. "Go watch over your captain. Verin and Glass will take good care of me."

A burst of anguish for all of them surged raggedly through me, and I planted a hurried near-miss kiss on his sharp cheekbone before whirling and running after Marcello.

The physician had taken him to an upstairs bedroom to treat him. I paced and waited outside its plain wooden door, worrying my ragged lace cuffs to shreds. Kathe's voice rose and fell below, incomprehensibly quiet, punctuated occasionally by Verin's and Glass's higher tones. At last, the physician opened the door, a somber frown further creasing her age-lined face.

"How is he?" I asked, tucking my hands behind my back so I wouldn't seize her to shake news out of her.

"He'll live," she said, sounding dubious.

I let out a long breath and leaned against the yellow-painted wall of the upstairs hallway where I'd been pacing.

"Only because he isn't human, though," the physician said. "The bleeding stopped on its own, and the wound was already starting to heal. I've never seen anything like it. He's already awake."

Instead of lifting at the news, my heart seemed to slip from my chest and slither to the floor. "He is? Did he say anything?"

"He asked for you." The physician gave me an odd, wary look. "You can talk to him if you want."

"I do," I said, despite her look of skepticism. I could only pray to the Graces that it was because he looked like a monster, and not because he spoke like one.

The physician moved aside and waved me in.

I stepped into what must have been a child's room, painted by hand with a lovely field of bright flowers on the walls, and puffy clouds drifting across a deep blue ceiling. Carved wooden animals had been hurriedly pushed into a corner to make room for a guest, and some child had piled blocks on top of a chest rather than putting them properly away. The sun had set while I waited, and beeswax candles graced the bedside table and almost every other available surface, bathing the room in golden light and the scent of honey.

Marcello lay propped in bed, his face so pale his scales stood out darkly. He stared at me from beneath lids drooping with exhaustion, but both his green eye and the orange one focused on me with sharp intensity.

I approached him like I would a wild animal, hardly daring to breathe. Whatever he saw in my face, it made his tighten with pain.

"I'm sorry," I whispered. There was no chair, so I sat down on the edge of the narrow bed, atop a bright patchwork quilt.

"For which? Stabbing me, or saving my life?" He grimaced, and his voice softened. "I'm sorry, too."

"How do you feel?" I asked, watching every tiny shift in his face, every flicker in his eyes, searching to sift out what was the man I knew and what might be something else Ruven had put there.

He pushed his hair back from his face, weariness dragging at his arm. "You mean who am I? I would very much like to know."

I reached out to where his hand lay on the quilt and took it gently in mine, avoiding his claws as best I could. Their hard, curving tips still lightly pricked my skin. "You're Marcello Verdi. A captain of the Falconers and my dear friend." I tried to say it with inarguable confidence, as if I had no doubt whatsoever it was true.

His lids squeezed shut, and relief washed through me at the reprieve from his unsettling inhuman eye, followed by a stab of guilt. This was his face, now, and it still belonged to a person I loved. That wasn't Ruven glaring at me from the slit pupil, or some wild animal; it was Marcello.

"That's who I want to be," he said, his voice subdued. "But I keep having these flashes of anger, Amalia, sometimes for no reason at all. I wanted to hurt the physician, when she was in here, and I barely stopped myself."

I squeezed his hand, my chest aching. "But you did stop yourself."

His eyes opened again, his brows lifting. "I did," he said, sounding surprised. "I wouldn't have, before Ruven died."

"Maybe the alchemists can try to come up with a potion to help you, when you get back to the Mews."

Marcello shifted uncomfortably on his pillows. "If the Mews will take me back."

"Why wouldn't they?" I asked.

He stared at me incredulously. "Amalia, I'm a chimera. How can I ask people to trust me to command them? How can I teach children? How can I..." He broke off, and covered his face with both hands. "Grace of Mercy. How can I face Istrella?"

"She's your sister. She loves you."

"My father always did say I'd come to a bad end." The muffled laughter escaping through his fingers had an unhealthy edge to it. "Even he will have to be impressed by how far I exceeded his expectations."

"It's not the end." I touched the backs of his hands, gently, and he slid them down off his face. "So you've changed. I've changed, too."

His lips tightened. "Not like I have."

"No," I agreed. "But Hells, I've killed my cousin and stabbed my friend, not to mention helping slaughter several thousand people. If you're a monster, I'm a worse one." It was a bitter admission, but I forced a smile. "This world will keep trying to make us harder, and more broken. But if we know who we want to be, we can keep striving to become that person." Like Kathe, with his Heartguard. "I was worried, before you woke up, whether you would be yourself, or whether Ruven had truly killed the man you were and twisted you into something terrible."

Marcello winced. "And? Did he?"

"I'm not worried anymore." I couldn't quite keep my voice steady. "You care again. You *want* to be good. That's what matters. If we keep working at it, you and I, that will be enough."

"Why didn't you let me burn him?"

Zaira asked the question in hushed tones, so as not to wake Marcello. She'd come to see how he was doing and found him sleeping; I'd nearly nodded off, myself, in the chair I'd dragged in from the kitchen.

I blinked at her, coming more fully awake. "What?"

She shrugged uncomfortably, as if the question were an itchy coat she couldn't take off. "When we had to take down Captain Creepyface, here. Why did you stop me from burning him? You shouldn't have had to stab him. You care too damned much."

I tried not to remember the feeling of the knife punching through skin and muscle, sinking into his side. "Well, for one thing, he was more likely to survive a knife wound than balefire."

"Bollocks," Zaira said flatly. "You struck to kill. You were hoping he'd survive, but you weren't planning on it. That wasn't why—or at least, it wasn't the only reason."

"No, it wasn't," I said quietly. "I thought you should never have to kill a friend again. I've always had the luxury of being the one who gives the word and keeps her hand clean. I thought if I was going to make the decision that Marcello had to..." Words caught in my throat, but I forced them out. "If we had to kill him, it was only right that I do it myself."

Zaira shook her head. "You're a strange one, Cornaro."

"Perhaps." Silence fell, then, broken only by the stutter of the candles and Marcello's faintly labored breath. His brow creased even in sleep. He looked more like himself, worried and earnest. I could almost imagine that the scales were merely some strange mud streaked across his skin, or the scar of a nasty burn.

Now was the time to do my staring, while he wasn't awake to see it, relearning the new map of his face.

Out of the corner of my eye, I caught Zaira rubbing her bare wrist. I nodded at it, smiling faintly. "So, what now? Your jess is off, and you can control your fire without it. Ruven is dead. The world is yours. What will you do?"

Zaira's eyes narrowed. "You take this ghoulish delight in asking me about my plans."

I grimaced. "Sorry. It's my job to think of the future, so that's where my mind goes. I don't mean to put you on the spot."

She stared down at her wrist, then out the window at the darkness. The wind shushed through the trees and drew a faint moaning from the chimney. "I miss Terika," she said at last. "Every time I think of going anywhere but back to her, it hurts."

"Mmm," I said, hoping she'd go on if I could keep my mouth shut.

My restraint was rewarded. Zaira sighed. "I guess if I've found the one woman on earth mad enough to put up with me, I should propose before she wakes up and changes her mind."

I impulsively moved to hug her, but corrected the motion to clasp her shoulder instead. "That's the spirit."

"Hmph. It's something, anyway. Maybe the Demon of Madness cursed me, too."

"So you'll go back to the Empire, then?" I asked.

"Seems like it. And anyway, it's home." Zaira waved a dismissive hand around the room. "Vaskandar has far too much nature and not enough decent pastry. Now that you've gotten that law passed and I can do whatever I damn well please with my life instead of being shut up in the Mews, there's no reason to stay away."

I hesitated, trying to think of a delicate way to broach the matter, then recalled I was speaking to Zaira and delicacy was pointless. "You'd have to get another jess."

She rubbed her wrist again. "I've been thinking about that," she admitted, her voice low. "When you can open a pit to the Nine Hells anytime, there are too many ways to miss a step and fall in. Look what Ruven did to Jerith. If that had been me, Raverra would be cinders now. And even if I can get my fire back under control now, that doesn't mean I won't ever lose it again—when I'm startled, when I'm mad, when I'm drunk, when I'm waking up from a nightmare." She shook her head. "I don't mind having a jess, so long as my Falconer isn't an idiot."

"I'm inclined to take that as a compliment. But, Zaira..." I swallowed an unaccountable lump in my throat. "You do realize that they'll never let me be your Falconer, now that your jess is off."

Zaira frowned. "Bugger that. I don't want some random fuzz-mouthed green brat. It took me months to train you up to be tolerable."

My mouth twitched. "And I, too, would regret the end of our fond partnership. But it's very much against the law, and even more so now that I'm on the Council of Nine."

"Curse it, there's got to be something we can do." Zaira crossed her arms. "Get your mamma to make an exception."

"She can't." Unbelievably, Zaira's eyes moistened, and I felt mine stinging, too. "Not even the doge is above the law."

Marcello stirred, blinking open sleepy eyes. "I have a jess in my pouch," he mumbled.

"What?" I leaned over him, anxious. "How are you feeling? Do you need the physician?"

"I have a jess in my pouch," he repeated, more clearly, and waved at the top of a brightly painted clothes chest, where someone had neatly stacked his personal effects. "Officers in the Falconers carry a jess when they leave the Mews, in case of a magical emergency. Like an out-of-control fire warlock, as you may recall."

I stared at him. "I was so worried about Ruven getting his hand on one, and you had one all this time?"

"He never thought to ask, so I didn't have to tell him. All his questions were about the Falcons, not the Falconers, because he thought that only mages truly mattered."

Hope quickened my heartbeat. "But you're only allowed to use that jess in emergencies," I pointed out.

Zaira laughed. "I'm a walking emergency. I can make one if you really want."

Marcello shrugged, then winced in pain. "I suspect the old me would have cared more about following regulations. But I can tell you that no one will notice it's a different jess if we don't tell them. You could only see that the knot was melted if you looked quite closely, and no one goes around staring at other peoples' jesses like that."

Hearing Marcello advise us to circumvent the rules was like

trying to put a glove on the wrong hand. But Zaira broke out into a broad smile. "All right, then! I like the new you."

She lifted a hand as if to slap him on the shoulder, but then reconsidered; whether out of respect for his near-fatal wound, or because his shoulder was bare and sweaty, I couldn't guess. Instead, she scooped up his pouch from the pile on the chest and began rummaging through it.

"What's this?" she asked, pulling out a clumsily wire-wrapped chunk of quartz.

Marcello flushed. "Istrella gave me that when she was small. It was her first pocket luminary. I used it up long ago, but I carry it as a good-luck charm."

"Ugh, you're revolting." Zaira made a gagging face and tucked it carefully back into his pouch. "Here it is."

She pulled out the jess. Its complex weave gleamed in the candle-light, clean and bright and unmarred by fire. The red gems winked as it dangled from her hand. Zaira stared at it, her mouth set in a skeptical line.

"We don't have to do this," I said softly. "Not if you don't want to."

"You're a terrible listener. I said I wanted it." She stuffed the jess into my hand. "I guess I trust you, more or less. And you're better than a toothache."

"Promise me one thing," I murmured.

"What?" Zaira asked warily.

"That you won't say anything like that when you propose to Terika."

"Do I look like I want to be poisoned?" Zaira laughed. "I'm an idiot sometimes, but I'm not stupid."

She stuck out her hand, waiting. I slid the jess over it, settling it carefully on her wrist; a shiver of magic hummed under my fingertips.

I met her eyes. "*Exsolvo*," I said.

Zaira turned her wrist this way and that, peering at the jess. "Huh. It's more comfortable when the knot isn't all melted."

My shoulders relaxed, tension fleeing them that I hadn't known was there. "Thank you," I said softly. "For entrusting me with this. I'm honored."

"Don't let it go to your head."

Then, to my extreme shock, Zaira reached over and gave me a quick, bony-armed hug.

Chapter Forty-Five

The next morning, I came downstairs from my cozy borrowed bedroom to find Kathe, Marcello, and Zaira already having breakfast at the simple oak dining room table. Kathe had collapsed into bed after his talk with his Heartguard, slept the whole night through, and looked entirely refreshed and reinvigorated this morning. No sign remained that he'd been grievously wounded and trapped under a lake in a state bordering on death; even his leather tunic was mended. Marcello, on the other hand, looked as if he shouldn't be up at all. He held himself with the careful fragility of someone wary of setting off pain with the tiniest move.

"Sit down, Cornaro," Zaira said through a mouthful of sausage. "Look, Vaskandran breakfast is a pile of meat!"

I sighed and slid onto the bench next to Kathe and opposite Marcello. "It's like that in Callamorne, too." And tea instead of chocolate, but that at least was better than coffee. I spread butter on a slice of bread, soaking up the welcome sight of their faces. They might be worn and scarred, each in their way, but they had all come through this alive; and that was a miracle of the Graces for which I was profoundly thankful. "What world have we awakened to this morning? Is there any news?"

"Buckets of it," Zaira said. "Your crow beau here has been getting feathery messengers all morning."

Kathe nodded. "All of the controlled imperial soldiers were, of course, freed when Ruven died, and promptly turned to drive the remaining Kazerath forces out of the Empire. Ruven's troops on the border are in disarray, as well, with mass desertions and infighting, and some of his mage officers trying to retain control. They'll be lucky if they can manage an orderly withdrawal. His former allies among the Witch Lords have already withdrawn from the border. The Vaskandran threat to the Empire is over."

Marcello let out a relieved breath. "Thank the Graces."

"What about Kazerath?" I asked. "Ruven didn't have an heir, did he?"

Zaira snorted. "Such a shame. He'd have made a great dad."

Kathe pushed his plate away; he hadn't eaten much. "No, he had no heir. Kazerath is like a slab of fresh meat thrown to a pack of dogs. I need to quickly decide how much of it I want to carve off for myself, and blood my claim before anyone else moves in."

"So you're going to dive in first and start the fight?" Zaira asked. "You don't seem like the type."

Kathe managed a shadow of his usual sharp grin. "My close associates and I have been involved in the deaths of three Witch Lords in the past few months. That's almost unheard of in our history. So long as I mind my own business, my dear peers should be willing enough to leave me alone for a while. And since I was the only Witch Lord involved in killing Ruven, by rights I could claim all of Kazerath if I wished."

"Will you?" I asked.

His smile faded. "No. You've seen the way I rule. I like having a small domain. I want to know the faces of my people. And taking in too much of Kazerath might be like eating spoiled fruit. I'll content myself with a small bite, and offer the rest to certain of my fellows as favors."

"That seems shrewd," I approved. "How soon will you be doing that?"

"First I have to go back to collect the Truce Stones and return them to the Lady of Spiders." Kathe's voice went soft and solemn. "And collect Hal's remains, such as they are, to return to his family."

Hells. My friends might have survived, but not all of his had. "I'm so sorry," I murmured, and laid a hand on his shoulder. "Do you need any help?"

He shook his head, avoiding my eyes. "I've called the rest of the Heartguard. I'm going to wait for them to arrive, and we'll go together."

Marcello rose then, his lips pale. "Excuse me," he said hoarsely, "I think I need to lie down." And he left the dining room with the unsteady tread of a man on the brink of fainting.

I lifted a hand to my mouth. "I forgot that he was the one who shot Hal."

"I didn't." Kathe's voice took on an edge. "He apologized the moment he saw me this morning, and offered his life in return. I didn't take him up on it. But neither will I spare his feelings by dancing around the subject of my good friend's death."

"I wouldn't ask you to. Hal deserves to be spoken of with honor and pride." I stood, my heart aching for both of them. "If you'll excuse me a moment, I should make sure he's all right."

I found Marcello sitting on the worn floorboards in the upstairs hallway, leaning against the pale plastered wall, his eyes closed. I sat down beside him in silence, feeling his warmth along my hip and shoulder even if we didn't quite touch.

"You didn't have to come after me," he said quietly.

"I left you alone when you were hurting once, and I don't think I'll ever forgive myself for it," I said. "I'm not going to do it again."

He turned his mismatched eyes on me. It was easier to meet them both this time; I could start to see the human pain in both of them, green and orange alike.

"The hardest part," he said, "is that I'm not as upset as I should be."

"About Hal?" I asked.

"About all of it." He gestured around as if the ghosts of the people he'd killed stood silently in the hall. "I murdered the doge, for Graces' sakes. I'm not happy about it—I don't have Ruven's sick joy poisoning me anymore—but the place where that horror should live is locked away. Or empty." His fists curled tight on the floor beside him.

I laid my hand over his; the ridges of his knuckles stood out like a handful of dice. "It could just be shock."

"Or Ruven scooped out my ability to feel guilt. I don't know, Amalia. I hate that for every thought and feeling, I have to second-guess whether it's the real me feeling that way, or whether it's the monster he tried to make me." He turned his palm up, lying flat so that my hand lay in his. His claws curled past the tips of his fingers, unsheathed and hooking a good half inch into the air. "Look at me. I'm not the man you knew anymore."

I slid my fingers carefully through his, claws and all, and met his gaze squarely. "But you're still the man I love."

That was his own dear worried expression, the familiar divot between his brows. I brushed the hair back from his orange eye, then ran my fingertips down the scales on the side of his face. They were softer and smoother than I expected, and no stubble grew on them like it did on the rest of his jaw.

"You need a shave," I said.

He let out a surprised, helpless laugh that was half a sob. "Yes. Yes, I do."

"I'm not certain how I feel about stubble," I sighed. "But I suppose I'll kiss you anyway."

His eyes widened. Before he could say something foolish about being a chimera, I touched my lips to his, which were warm and soft as I remembered. I kissed him tenderly, lingeringly, trying to pour how much I cared about him into that one small melting moment.

At first he pulled away, his breath catching in shame. "You don't have to—"

"I know I don't have to," I said. "I want to. Because I love you."

A shiver ran through him, and he closed his eyes. Our lips met again, slow and gentle. I didn't want it to end, by the Grace of Love—he was still Marcello, still sunlight on warm green grass and the scent of leather and the comfort of a home that had never been mine, except in dreams. I wanted to lean against his shoulder and hold him in my arms forever, especially after how close I'd come to ending everything that was good about him with my own hands.

But eventually he drew back, still clasping my shoulders. His sheathed claw tips caught the fabric of my jacket.

"Wait. You said you love me." His brows lifted in surprise, as if the words had only now reached his ears.

"I should have said it a long time ago." I laid my hand along his stubble-roughened cheek, my eyes stinging. "You were right. I took you for granted, and I'm sorry. But I was afraid."

"You mean those awful things I said when I was under Ruven's influence?" He waved an anxious hand. "I said all that to be cruel, Amalia, it wasn't—"

"It was true," I interrupted. "Sometimes the truth is cruel."

He swallowed. The old Marcello would have denied it, even to himself. But for all I missed his innocence, he had traded it for a deeper, less comfortable knowledge, graven into the harder lines of his handsome face.

"What were you afraid of?" he whispered instead.

"A choice." I let my fingers slide down his jaw to his collarbone, the one Ruven had broken; it was wholly mended now, with no sign it had ever been injured. "If I admitted I loved you, it wasn't just a fancy or flirtation that could go on forever. If I loved you, I had to decide what I was going to do about it, once and for all. No more ifs and maybes and somedays." I met his eyes squarely; I owed him too much to avoid facing the truth any longer. "If I acknowledged how much I was giving up, it would be harder to...to..." My throat betrayed me, seizing up in a hard knot.

His hands closed over mine. "You don't have to say it. I know you can't court the chimera who murdered the doge." Bitterness edged his voice, though I could tell he tried to keep it out.

"No! That's not why." I couldn't let him think that. A pressure built in my chest until I felt certain something would tear. "If that were all, I would fight them for you—my mother and the Council and all of Raverran society, anyone who tried to tell us no—and I would win." I took a deep, shuddery breath. "If we weren't who we were, I would ask you to marry me. I have this little dream, Marcello, this selfish dream, of coming home to your smile every day." The image lodged in my heart like a thorn: those wonderful dimples I hadn't seen in too long, warmed by the clear light of the sun slanting through my palace windows. "Of having children together, and watching you play with them. You would be such a good father." The tears brimmed over at last, running hot down my cheeks, but I let them fall.

Marcello closed his own eyes as if my words hurt him. "I

never had a dream like that," he said hoarsely. "I couldn't afford one. I couldn't think of marrying you because I knew it would never happen. I only wanted—" He broke off and shook his head.

"What?" I asked, my voice husky with tears. "What would you want, if our ranks didn't matter?"

He gazed down at our clasped hands. "I want you to be happy."

It's what we all want for those we love. The words lodged in my chest like a broken arrowhead. But that wasn't what I needed to know. "Not what you want for me," I said gently. "What you want for yourself."

He was quiet a moment. A faint frown creased his forehead. When he lifted his eyes to meet mine, they shone damp but unclouded. "To be with you. To change the world with you. We're better together than apart, Amalia. You've got vision and insight I'll never have. And I..."

"You have a truly good heart and an unwavering sense of honor." I touched his chest; his heartbeat pulsed strong beneath my fingers. "I need you, Marcello. To be my rudder, so I won't crash on the rocks or lose my way." *My Heartguard.*

"And I need you as my pilot, to show me where to go." His mouth twisted into something that wasn't quite a smile. "I've been thinking about how to atone for everything I've done. To put more good in the world, to balance the harm Ruven made me do. There's still a lot I want to accomplish to help the Falcons—getting the jesses changed so they won't kill the mage if their Falconer dies, making sure Colonel Vasante's successor is a Falcon, reorganizing the Falconers to support and protect the mage-marked living outside the Mews as well as those on active duty. There's so much left to be done. I want to do it together with you, Amalia."

"Yes. I want that, too." The ache inside me deepened until I felt sure I would crack into pieces. My fingers slipped from Marcello's chest, and the world seemed cold and empty without his heartbeat. "And that's why we can never court, no matter how much we want to."

His lips pressed together, and his throat jumped.

"Never," he whispered.

Graces help me, this hurt like ripping out my own insides. "If you married me, you couldn't be a Falconer, Marcello. You'd be a noble. It's against the law."

His eyes went wide. "I can't quit the Falconers. It's everything I've worked for. It's my entire life."

"You'd have to resign." It had been hard enough to force the Council and the military to accept me as Zaira's Falconer when her jess was accidentally fused shut with balefire and none of us had any choice. They'd never make an exception for Marcello if he gained noble status voluntarily by marrying me. "Istrella would need a new Falconer, and you'd have to leave the service. I wish it weren't true, but the law is crystal clear."

"I can't leave *Istrella*," Marcello protested, his face pale with anguish. "I can't abandon her and all the rest of the Falcons to a command chain that sometimes doesn't even think of them as people."

"I know." I rubbed my damp cheeks, but the tears kept coming, wearing channels into my face. "And I can't ask you to, Marcello. No more than I can throw away all the advantages of a political marriage, especially when I can use that power to protect the mage-marked. Everything you just said you wanted— we can do it together. We *will*. But we can't do it as a couple."

"I see." He let out a soft sigh, as if he'd cradled that one breath for a very long time. "As friends, then?"

"Of course," I said. "Always."

"I'll never stop loving you, Amalia," he murmured.

At first, I could only manage a nod. But I forced the words

out through my burning throat. "And I'll never stop loving you, Marcello. I swear it."

We folded each other in our arms, then. I held him gently, careful of the wound I'd made in his side, and rested my head on his shoulder to hear the beating of his heart. His arms came around me, warm and supporting, and he leaned his scaly cheek on my head.

"Just like this," I whispered, and closed my eyes to stop the tears.

We held each other that way for a long time, safe from everything the world might send against us. And for the first time in a long while, like the earliest green shoot unfolding from the damp black soil in spring, I felt that everything would be all right.

I found Kathe out in the back garden with Glass, talking solemnly, their breath making puffs of mist in the winter air. A soft, feather-gray blanket of cloud smothered the sky, and the first light flakes of snow drifted down over the two of them. Pure white fields stretched beyond them, broken only by the meandering line of a low stone wall, and then the gray-green watching presence of the forest.

Glass spotted me over Kathe's shoulder and waved, their face breaking into a knowing sort of grin. They bowed to Kathe and took their leave as I approached, slipping me a wink on their way out.

Kathe turned, his smile of greeting chasing the lingering shadows of his conversation with Glass from his face. "Hello, Lady Amalia. I hope all is well?"

"Yes." I pulled my coat tighter around me as I approached,

my boots crunching shallow footprints into the snow. "How are you? We haven't really spoken since...since yesterday."

His smile faded. He stood still as a deer pausing at the edge of a wood for a moment, snowflakes gathering one by one on the puff of black feathers around his shoulders. The muted light softened his fine features, lending depth to the gleaming gold and gray of his eyes.

"Do you want a true answer," he asked at last, "or a flippant one? I'm better at flippant, but for you, my lady, I could consider honesty."

"A true one," I said.

"Then I'm well enough." He sighed, releasing a great cloud of steam. "I've got enough experience with grief to know that the beast loosens its teeth over time. I have plenty to keep me busy. You know as well as I do, I expect, how it goes."

"I do," I said softly.

"I imagine you'll be heading back to Raverra soon?" he asked, a wistful note in his voice. "To receive your due glory as the savior of the Empire, and plot its course through the changing waters ahead?"

"I don't know about glory," I laughed. "I've got so much to do, I'm going to be working before I step out of my boat. I'll be lucky to see sunlight before spring."

"And..." He paused, seeming uncertain. Then he sighed, kicked at a chunk of snow, and stared off over the fields. "You've seen Let now, and I suppose you've seen me for what I am. I'm neither gentle nor good, Amalia."

"Neither am I." Snow caught in my eyelashes, and I blinked it off. "But we're both trying, in our own way. That's got to count for something."

"Intent wins you no points in any game," Kathe said dryly. "It's your actions that count."

I touched his elbow, and my fingertips hummed with the power around him. "I've seen your actions, and I'm still standing here beside you."

"About that." He met my gaze then. "You formed a partnership with me to defeat Ruven. Now that he's dead, well, if you don't have any further interest in courting, I'll understand." His mouth twisted into a wry smile. "I don't want you to feel trapped because you don't dare offend the mad Witch Lord who decorates his borders with his enemies' bones."

My stomach dropped as if I'd missed a step. Was this it, then? His polite way of letting me know that with our objective achieved, our courtship was over?

It was still a highly valuable alliance for the Serene Empire. I was all too aware that marrying Kathe would be a coup for Raverra and for the Cornaro family, and that I was unlikely to find another suitor who could offer so much advantage. But that wasn't why the idea of breaking off our courtship felt like losing a finger. He was strange and difficult and as hard to hold on to as quicksilver, but if he departed from my life now, he'd leave an odd-shaped hole in it no one else could fill.

"My lord Kathe," I said, drawing myself up with great dignity, "you have known me long enough by now that you should realize there is very little I won't dare, with sufficient motivation."

He lifted an eyebrow. "And how motivated are you to keep courting? Because I like you a great deal, Amalia Cornaro. I like talking to you. I like conspiring with you. And I rather enjoy kissing you. But for all the wonders we could accomplish together, if you're only courting me out of some sense of duty, well, I wouldn't want to waste another minute of your time."

Kathe awaited my answer with an air of polite interest, as if he were not particularly invested in the outcome, but I knew him well enough now to spy the tension in the line of his shoulders beneath those feathers, and a trace of anxiousness lurking behind the yellow rings in his eyes.

He cared. This mattered to him as much as it did to me.

A surge of affection welled up in me for this complex, contradictory creature, watching me with his head tilted like one of his own crows hoping for a snack. How could I best show him that he was more to me now than a mere political opportunity?

I felt a smile breaking across my face. "Let's play a game," I said.

His face lit up. "What kind of game?"

"For every reason you give me why our next visit should be in Let, I'll give you one why it should be in Raverra. When one of us concedes, the winner gets a prize."

"What's the prize?" Kathe asked, his eyes crinkling.

"It's a surprise." I gestured grandly to him. "Would you like to go first?"

"All right." He rubbed his hands together. "You should visit me in Let next, because you haven't met all my Heartguard. They'll be most cross with me if I don't introduce you."

"They're welcome to come to our palace anytime," I countered. "And you should visit me in Raverra because you have all manner of exciting intelligence collaboration opportunities to discuss with my mother."

"True," Kathe conceded, his eyes sparkling. "But you've only seen Let in the winter, when everything is dull and gray. Soon it will be spring, and the starlaces will be blooming in the dappled forest shadows, and the moss will glow with a thousand shades of green." He leaned in conspiratorially close. "And there will be *baby foxes*. Have you ever held a baby fox?"

I laughed. "You're going to lose your terrifying reputation, Kathe. How can I maintain a proper Raverran dread of Witch Lords if you go about cuddling baby animals?"

"Foxes are very fierce," he protested.

"Hmm. You make a strong argument." I shivered in the frosty air. "Spring would certainly be better than winter, at least."

He offered an arm, and I leaned against his side under the feathered cloak, slipping my own arm around his waist. I didn't think I'd ever get used to the tingling shock that coursed through me when I touched him. "Do you concede, then?" he asked.

"Not yet! You need to visit Raverra in the spring for the Festival of Victory. There are all manner of athletic competitions and games and sailing races. It's quite the spectacle."

"Games?" Kathe put a hand to his chest. "You know my weak spots, my lady. But I must hold out for Let, I'm afraid. You haven't even seen my home, after all. I want to show you the castle I grew up in."

"I do want to see that, very much." I tightened my arm around Kathe's waist, enjoying the feel of the hard muscles in his back. "But you're forgetting something very important about Raverra."

"Oh?" He angled to face me more directly; we stood nearly eye to eye, with his cloak folded about me like a great black wing.

"We have better food," I said, very seriously.

Kathe's chuckle rustled the feathers on his shoulders. "That you do."

"Have you a rebuttal for my devastating argument?" I asked archly.

"No." Kathe's tone shifted, becoming serious. "Only that either way, I hope we can see each other again soon, because I'll miss you, Amalia Cornaro."

A warmth stirred within me, and the winter air lost its bite. "I suppose I must concede, then," I sighed.

"Really?" Kathe's pale brows lifted. "Why?"

"I want to show you the sights of Raverra," I said simply, "but you want me to meet your friends and see your home."

He shook his head. "There I go, ruining my reputation again. You'll think I'm sentimental."

"That's a very real danger," I agreed.

"Now, what's my prize?" he asked, grinning.

"This." I pulled him closer, closing my eyes.

Our kiss was lightning and sweet thunder, and warm rain melting away the snow. We held each other with the desperation of two people unexpectedly alive in a stark winter world of sorrow and death, on the cusp of turning the page into spring.

Chapter Forty-Six

They must have had advance news of our return at the Mews, because a crowd waited in the entrance hall. We had scarcely stepped through the gates when Terika squealed and ran to meet Zaira. She caught her around the waist and spun her in the air; Zaira's hair whipped behind her like a banner as she laughed.

"Put me down, you madwoman! What do you think I am, a puppy?"

Some of the people gathered around Zaira, laughing and talking and welcoming her back. But much of the crowd still stood frozen, staring at Marcello, who hung half a step behind me, head ducked.

Right at the front of the waiting Falcons and Falconers was Istrella.

Marcello sucked in an audible breath, lifted his head, and stepped up beside me. The light fell full on his silver scales and his inhuman eye.

A murmur ran through the crowd. More than a few of them blanched, or stepped back. Istrella winced as if she'd been struck.

"I'm back," Marcello announced, his voice faltering. I squeezed his shoulder.

Istrella stared at him, eyes wide. "Marcello?"

He nodded. "It's me, 'Strella."

She came forward from the whispering crowd, one step, then another. The clear winter light streaming through the open doors fell on her face; she squinted at Marcello, as if to determine whether he were actually her brother, but she kept approaching.

Finally, she stood directly before him, her expression torn between doubt and wonder. The hall fell silent, everyone watching, waiting to see what would happen. I frantically searched for something I could say, something that would help; but in the end, this was between the two of them.

Istrella frowned. Slowly, tentatively, she reached out toward her brother's face. He swallowed visibly.

She poked him right in his orange eye.

"Ow!" Marcello's hand flew up to cover his eye, and he reeled back a step. "What did you do that for?"

"I wanted to see if it had feeling," Istrella said curiously.

"Yes! Of course it has feeling! It's my eye!"

I wasn't the only one in the hall who smothered a nervous laugh. Istrella tipped her head, considering. "Is your vision different on that side?"

"I, ah..." Marcello lowered his hand, blinking a watery eye now even redder than usual. "It sees better in the dark. But it can't see colors very well."

"So interesting." Istrella reached out again, this time toward Marcello's scales. "What are those for? Are they hard, like armor?"

"No! Don't poke me again!" But Marcello was smiling now, and he ruffled her hair.

"Perhaps they're for radiating heat when you use unnatural bursts of speed or strength," Istrella suggested.

A girl of perhaps ten or eleven with a jess on her wrist sighed and said loudly, "I wish they'd let *me* make a chimera. Not a human one, of course, but I want a flying bunny."

Everyone laughed, and the tension was broken. People came

and clustered around Marcello, welcoming him, asking him questions. I heard Namira, Terika's mentor, inquire whether she might possibly have a blood sample, "for research purposes only, of course."

I stood back and watched, relief washing through me. "He'll be all right," I murmured.

"We'll take care of him," Jerith agreed, appearing at my elbow with Balos at his side. "The colonel won't accept if he tries to resign, or any such foolishness."

Balos glanced around, then added, "And we're going to quietly keep an eye on him, too, to make sure his behavior isn't too badly affected. If it looks like he's not fit for certain duties, well, we'll deal with it then."

"Thank you," I said, with feeling.

"He may have to give up his ambitions to take over when Colonel Vasante retires, though," Jerith said, frowning. "Even if he were acting perfectly normal, which I gather from your message he isn't, it would frankly be hard to get everyone to accept someone with a creepy lizard eye and claws in charge of the most critically important military unit in the Empire."

"That's all right." I clapped Jerith on the shoulder. "Marcello doesn't want to command the Falcons anymore. He wants you to do it."

Jerith started to laugh, but it died on his lips as he realized I was serious. "He's gone mad," he said. "Maybe he shouldn't be allowed to remain an officer after all, if he thinks I should be in charge."

"We talked about it a lot on the journey back," I told Jerith. "We both believe the next commander of the Falcons should *be* a Falcon. You've got the brains and the seniority, and you're highly respected."

Jerith shook his head, diamond earring flashing. "If you think they'd have trouble accepting a chimera, wait until you try to stuff a warlock down their throats."

"It'll be a long-term project," I admitted, "but I don't think the colonel has any intention of retiring soon, so we have time."

"Besides," Jerith demanded, "what do you mean, respected? I'm the archenemy of respect. There's a reason they demoted me, remember?"

"I'm sure Balos can keep you in line," I said serenely.

Balos chuckled. "You may overestimate me, Lady Amalia."

I watched the milling crowd. A knot had formed around Istrella and Marcello, excitedly talking magical theory, and another around Zaira, who kept one arm about Terika as she told some dramatic and doubtless exaggerated story of our adventures that seemed to involve a great deal of swearing. It was back to the same Mews I remembered, before the attack—but at the same time, it wasn't.

There was a difference in how some of the Falcons stood, a boldness and confidence replacing ironic resignation. The snippets of conversation that reached my ears had changed, too; there was the usual Mews gossip and chatter about lessons and research and assignments, but now I heard people talking about plans and futures as well.

"Oh, Lamonte is getting married in the spring! They're going to live in Loreice, to be near family."

"Thinking of starting a little farm in the country, using my vivomancy to grow crops finally..."

"Yes, an artifice carousel! It's always been my dream project, but the colonel said it was too frivolous—now I can build it at last."

"I can't wait to move back in with my sister and my fathers. Captain Verdi gave me plenty of leave to go see them, but it's not the same, and I've missed them *so much*."

A warm feeling stole over me. I wiped my eyes under the pretense of brushing hair from them.

"This will all change, you know," Balos said softly. "The war is over. Many of the Falcons will leave, to start new lives. The Mews will become a different place."

"Yes," I said, with bittersweet satisfaction. "A better one."

"I can't believe I'm about to do this. Ugh, I'm sweating like an old cheese." Zaira wiped her palms on her skirts. "Hells take it, I'm going to run."

I gently seized her arm. "You are not going to run," I said. "It was very nice of my mother to allow you to use this spot, and very nice of Marcello to come up with a pretext for why they need an alchemist at the Imperial Palace. It's far too late for you to back out of this."

We stood on the sending spire platform atop the courier lamp tower in the Imperial Palace, wind tugging at our hair. The railing was an elegant confection of white marble, and embellished runes chased round with delicate spiraling wire decorated the spire thrusting toward the sky above us. It was the highest point in Raverra, and the view of the Serene City was stunning. The labyrinth of green canals and red roofs spread out below us on one side, and the palace courtyard with its white marble statues on the other. I'd had a sweet little table and two pretty chairs brought up here, along with the finest picnic the palace kitchens could prepare and an excellent bottle of Loreician sparkling white wine. Four discreet artifice heat lamps beat back the winter chill in the air.

"If she says no, I'm jumping off the edge in humiliation," Zaira warned darkly.

I patted her shoulder. "Forgive me if I don't start writing your eulogy. Now, if you think you can refrain from scaling the walls to escape your fate, I should get to the Council meeting."

Zaira gave a nervous jerk of a nod. But as I headed for the stairs, she blurted out, "Amalia."

I turned back to face her. "Yes?"

"I don't have any family." Zaira gave a kind of embarrassed shrug. "If she's actually dumb enough to marry me, at the wedding... Will you stand for me?"

My eyes misted at once, and a ridiculous grin spread across my face. "I would be more honored than words can express."

"Don't let it go to your head." Zaira straightened her spine, shook out her hands, and then made a shooing motion at me. "All right, get out of here. I've got to talk Terika into making the worst mistake of her life, and I don't need you around spoiling everything."

"Grace of Luck go with you," I wished her.

Zaira grunted. "So long as She doesn't piss in my eye, I should be fine."

Lucia met me at the bottom of the stairs, poised and alert. It was good to see her whole and healthy, with no sign of the chest wound she'd suffered. "Do you wish to take the long way around to the Map Room, my lady?"

I blinked. "Why would I do that?"

She couldn't quite suppress a smile. "Because if you go directly there, you risk running into Terika on her way to the courier lamp tower, and I assure you that the grin on your face will entirely give the game away."

I laughed. "Very well, then. The long way it is."

Passing through the less private areas of the palace meant I ran into advisers and courtiers seeking a moment of my time, and I didn't yet have my mother's skill at brushing them off; before I knew it, I was in danger of being late to the meeting. Still, as I passed through an empty audience chamber, I paused by a window that looked out over the grand square before the Imperial Palace.

People thronged the plaza below, completely at ease, with the casual complacency of peacetime. Patricians with a seat on the Assembly hurried into the same coffeehouses as laborers from the Tallows, seeking a cup of the foul black liquid to warm themselves against the winter chill. Families from the country pointed up at the palace, gathering their children close. Best of all, I spotted a pair of young men whom I knew to be Falcons wandering across the plaza, hot pastries in hand, their breath misting in the air as they talked. They wore fashionable coats instead of scarlet uniforms, their jesses invisible beneath their lace cuffs, and no Falconers trailed behind them; no one in the busy crowd gave them a second glance.

A crow fluttered down behind them and snapped up a crumb of fallen pastry, its glossy black feathers ruffled in the winter breeze, and I smiled.

"My lady," Lucia called from behind me, "I think Terika's arrived."

I hurried across the room to where Lucia stood at a window on the opposite side, looking out over the palace courtyard. I followed her gaze to the sending spire, hoping for a glimpse of Zaira's picnic. Sure enough, there they were, leaning close together across the table, the wind playing with their hair and the sending spire gleaming gold above them.

And then suddenly Terika leaped to her feet and sprang at Zaira, nearly knocking her out of her chair. Alarm flared in my chest for one brief moment—was she somehow controlled again?—but no. She'd just tackled her with an overly enthusiastic hug. And now they were kissing, standing atop the height of power in the strongest empire in the world, holding a bright future in each other's arms.

It looked as if Terika had said yes. I exchanged a gleeful glance with Lucia and turned away from the window, struggling to wipe the smile off my face before I reached the Map Room. It wouldn't do to walk into the Council meeting giggling like a loon.

It was easy enough to sober up when Lucia opened the door and I found the rest of the Council waiting for me. My mother sat at the head of the table, only a faint lingering stiffness from her wound marring her posture of commanding grace. All nine of them fell silent as I entered, staring at me.

There was something different in the set of their canny faces. A wariness I'd never seen there before, or at least not when they looked at me. A grudging respect even in the eyes of my some-time adversaries, like Lord Caulin and Scipio da Morante. They were analyzing me, considering, weighing the shift of power in the room as it tilted inexorably toward the Cornaro palace.

That's right. I had passed a major law, saved the Empire, and both courted and slain Witch Lords. I wasn't just the newest and youngest member of the Council, an apprentice learning her place in the innermost secret halls of power. I had already taken the world in my hands and shaken it.

I held my chin up and kept my face impassive as I strode to the one empty chair, my boots ringing loud across the Eruvia inlaid on the floor. As I settled in my seat, I met my mother's eyes.

"I'm ready," I said.

A faint, proud smile stirred her lips, warming her dark eyes.

"I know you are," she said. "Let's begin."

Acknowledgments

Wow. We made it. Swords and Fire is done—a whole trilogy!

It's hard to believe that this journey—which started way back in October 2012 when I had a conversation in the car with my husband about how societies might shape themselves around magical power—is over, at least for now. Thank you for walking this road with me, from Raverra to Vaskandar and back again, and for sticking with Amalia and Zaira all the way to the end.

It's a piece of magic, that you have this book in your hand and can use it to turn a bunch of words I wrote into pictures and people and places in your head. A lot of wonderful people helped create this particular enchantment, and I'm incredibly grateful to all of them:

My mom and dad, who nurtured my creativity and taught me the skills I needed to complete big projects and always helped me believe in myself. My big brother Dave, who taught me more about writing than I think he realizes. My husband, Jesse, who has been an unflagging bastion of patience and support, and my amazing daughters, Maya and Kyra, who've cheered me on and been incredibly understanding when I'm on deadline.

My friends, who've done everything from consult on names to help me brainstorm ways to kill immortals and who've occasionally coaxed me out into the sunlight or fed me. My forever beta readers, Deva Fagan and Natsuko Toyofuku, for being with me throughout all this epic quest. I'm glad you're with me, here at the end of all things.

My amazing agent, Naomi Davis, literary fairy godmother and all-around co-conspirator, without whose brainstorming help this book would be a lot less wrenching. My wonderful editor, Sarah Guan, whose unfailing insight and urging to be more evil has improved this book immensely. My fantastic UK editor, Emily Byron, whose excellent feedback has shaped this entire trilogy all the way through from the first book to the last.

My cover designer, Lisa Marie Pompilio, and cover artists Crystal Ben and Arcangel, who created a breathtaking cover which somehow is *even better than the other two*, which I would never have dreamed was possible. My US publicist, Ellen Wright, and my UK publicist, Nazia Khatun, who brought these books to far more people than they would ever have reached otherwise, and who answered all my clueless questions along the way. And the entire Orbit team, who are all completely amazing people possessed of more awesomeness than seems remotely fair or even plausible, to be honest. I am so incredibly honored and proud to work with all of you.

And finally, you, my readers. This story is alive because you read it. Thank you, from the bottom of my heart, for that gift.

extras

extras

about the author

Melissa Caruso graduated with honors in creative writing from Brown University and holds an MFA in fiction from University of Massachusetts Amherst.

Find out more about Melissa Caruso and other Orbit authors by registering online for the free monthly newsletter at www.orbitbooks.net.

about the author

Michael Carter graduated ...

if you enjoyed
THE UNBOUND EMPIRE

look out for

THE SISTERS OF THE WINTER WOOD

by

Rena Rossner

Every family has a secret . . . and every secret tells a story.

In a remote village surrounded by forests on the border of Moldova and Ukraine, sisters Liba and Laya have been raised on the honeyed scent of their Mami's babka and the low rumble of their Tati's prayers. But when a troupe of mysterious men arrives, Laya falls under their spell — despite their mother's warning to be wary of strangers. And this is not the only danger lurking in the woods.

As dark forces close in on their small village, Liba and Laya discover a family secret passed down through generations. Faced with a magical heritage they never knew existed, the sisters realise the old fairy tales are true . . . and could save them all.

1

Liba

If you want to know the history of a town, read the gravestones in its cemetery. That's what my Tati always says. Instead of praying in the synagogue like all the other men of our town, my father goes to the cemetery to pray. I like to go there with him every morning.

The oldest gravestone in our cemetery dates back to 1666. It's the grave I like to visit most. The names on the stone have long since been eroded by time. It is said in our *shtetl* that it marks the final resting place of a bride and a groom who died together on their wedding day. We don't know anything else about them, but we know that they were buried, arms embracing, in one grave. I like to put a stone on their grave when I go there, to make sure their souls stay down where they belong, and when I do, I say a prayer that I too will someday find a love like that.

That grave is the reason we know that there were Jews in Dubossary as far back as 1666. Mami always said that this town was founded in love and that's why my parents chose to live here. I think it means something else—that our town was founded in tragedy. The death of those young lovers has been a pall hanging over Dubossary since its inception. Death lives here. Death will always live here.

2

Laya

I see Liba going
to the cemetery with Tati.
I don't know
what she sees
in all those cold stones.
But I watch,
and wonder,
why he never takes me.

When we were little,
Liba and I went to
the Talmud Torah.
For Liba, the black letters
were like something
only she could decipher.
I never understood
what she searched for,
in those black
scratches of ink.
I would watch

the window,
study the forest
and the sky.

When we walked home,
Liba would watch the boys
come out of the *cheder*
down the road.
I know that when she looked
at Dovid, Lazer and Nachman,
she wondered
what was taught
behind the walls
the girls were not
allowed to enter.

After her Bat Mitzvah,
Tati taught her Torah.
He tried to teach me too,
when my turn came,
but all I felt was
distraction,
disinterest.
Chanoch l'naar al pi darko,
Tati would say,
*teach every child
in his own way*,
and sigh,
and get up
and open the door.
Gey, gezinte heit—
I accept that you're different, go.

And while I was grateful,
I always wondered
why he gave up
without a fight.

3

Liba

As I follow the large steps my father's boots make in the snow, I revel in the solitude. This is why I cherish our morning walks. They give me time to talk to Tati, but also time to think. "In silence you can hear God," Tati says to me as we walk. But I don't hear God in the silence—I hear myself. I come here to get away from the noises of the town and the chatter of the townsfolk. It's where I can be fully me.

"What does God sound like?" I ask him. When I walk with Tati, I feel like I'm supposed to think about important things, like prayer and faith.

"Sometimes the voice of God is referred to as a *bat kol*," he says.

I translate the Hebrew out loud: "The daughter of a voice? That doesn't make any sense."

He chuckles. "Some say that *bat kol* means an echo, but others say it means a hum or a reverberation, something you sense in the air that's caused by the motion of the universe—part of the human voice, but also part of every other sound in the world, even the sounds that our ears can't hear. It means that sometimes even the smallest voice can have a big opinion." He grins, and I know that he means me, his daughter; that my opinion matters. I wish it were true. Not everybody in our town sees things the way my father does. Most women and girls do not study Torah; they don't learn or ask questions like I do. For the most part, our voices don't matter. I know I'm lucky that Tati is my father.

Although I love Tati's stories and his answers, I wonder why a small voice is a daughter's voice. Sometimes I wish my voice could be loud—like a roar. But that is not a modest way to think. The older I get, the more immodest my thoughts become.

I feel my cheeks flush as my mind wanders to all the things I shouldn't be thinking about—what it would feel like to hold the hand of a man, what it might feel like to kiss someone, what it's like when you finally find the man you're meant to marry and you get to be alone together, in bed . . . I swallow and shake my head to clear my thoughts.

If I shared the fact that this is all I think about lately, Mami and Tati would say it means it's time for me to get married. But I'm not sure I want to get married yet. I want to marry for love, not convenience. These thoughts feel like sacrilege. I know that I will marry a man my father chooses. That's the way it's done in our town and among Tati's people. Mami and Tati married for love, and it has not been an easy path for them.

I take a deep breath and shake my head from all my thoughts. This morning, everything looks clean from the snow that fell last night and I imagine the icy frost coating the insides of my lungs and mind, making my thoughts white and pure. I love being outside in our forest more than anything at times like these, because the white feels like it hides all our flaws.

Perhaps that's why I often see Tati in the dark forest that surrounds our home praying to God or—as he would say—the *Ribbono Shel Oylam*, the Master of the Universe, by himself, eyes shut, arms outstretched to the sky. Maybe he comes out here to feel new again too.

Tati comes from the town of Kupel, a few days' walk from here. He came here and joined a small group of Chassidim in the town—the followers of the late Reb Mendele, who was a disciple of the great and holy Ba'al Shem Tov. There is a small *shtiebl* where the men pray, in what used to be the home of Urka the Coachman. It is said that the Ba'al Shem Tov himself used to sit under the tree in Urka's courtyard. The Chassidim here accepted my father with open arms, but nobody accepted my mother.

Sometimes I wonder if Reb Mendele and the Ba'al Shem Tov (*zichrono livracha*) were still with us, would the community treat Mami differently? Would they see how hard she tries to be a good Jew, and how wrong the other Jews in town are for not treating her with love and respect. It makes me angry how quickly rumors spread, that Mami's kitchen isn't kosher (it is!) just because she doesn't cover her hair like the other married Jewish women in our town.

That's why Tati built our home, sturdy and warm like he is, outside our town in the forest. It's what Mami wanted: not to be under constant scrutiny, and to have plenty of room to plant fruit trees and make honey and keep chickens and goats. We have a small barn with a cow and a goat, and a bee glade out back and an orchard that leads all the way down to the river. Tati works in town as a builder and a laborer in the fields. But he is also a scholar, worthy of the title Rebbe, though none of the men in town call him that.

Sometimes I think my father knows more than the other Chassidim in our town, even more than Rabbi Borowitz who leads our tiny *kehilla*, and the bare bones prayer *minyan* of ten men that Tati sometimes helps complete. There are many things my father likes to keep secret, like his morning dips in the Dniester River that I never see, but know about, his prayer at the graveside of Reb Mendele, and our library. Our walls are covered in holy books—his *sforim*, and I often fall asleep to the sound of him reading from the Talmud, the Midrash, and the many mystical books of the Chassidim. The stories he reads sound like fairy tales to me, about magical places like Babel and Jerusalem.

In these places, there are scholarly men. Father would be respected there, a king among men. And there are learned boys of marriageable age—the kind of boys Tati would like me to marry someday. In my daydreams, they line up at the door, waiting to get a glimpse of me—the learned, pious daughter of the Rebbe. And my Tati would only pick the wisest and kindest for me.

I shake my head. In my heart of hearts, that's not really what I want. When Laya and I sleep in our loft, I look out the skylight above our heads and pretend that someone will someday find his way to our cabin, climb up onto the roof, and look in from above. He will see me and fall instantly in love.

Because lately I feel like time is running out. The older I get, the harder it will be to find someone. And when I think about that, I wonder why Tati insists that Laya and I wait until we are at least eighteen.

I would ask Mami, but she isn't a scholar like Tati, and she doesn't like to talk about these things. She worries about what people say and how they see us. It makes her angry, but she wrings dough instead of her hands. Tati says her hands are baker's hands, that she makes magic with dough. Mami can make something out of nothing. She makes cheese and gathers honey; she mixes bits of bark and roots and leaves for tea. She bakes the tastiest *challahs* and cakes, *rugelach* and *mandelbrot*, but it's her *babka* she's famous for. She sells her baked goods in town.

When she's not in the kitchen, Mami likes to go out through the skylight above our bed and onto the little deck on our roof to soak up the sun. Laya likes to sit up there with her. From the roof, you can see down to the village and the forest all around. I wonder if it's not just the sun that Mami seeks up there. While Tati's head is always in a book, Mami's eyes are always looking at the sky. Laya says she dreams of somewhere other than here. Somewhere far away, like America.

4

Laya

I always thought
that if I worshipped God,
dressed modestly,
and walked in His path,
that nothing bad
would happen
to my family.
We would find
our path to Zion,
our own piece of heaven
on the banks
of the Dniester River.

But now that I'm fifteen
I see what a life
of pious devotion
has brought Mami,
who converted
to our faith—
disapproval.
The life we lead
out here is a life apart.

I wish I could go to Onyshkivtsi.
Mami always tells me stories
about her town
and Saint Anna of the Swans
who lived there.

Saint Anna
didn't walk with God—
she knew she wasn't made
for perfection;
she never tried
to fit a pattern
that didn't fit her.
She didn't waste her time
trying to smooth herself
into something
she wasn't.
She was powerful
because she forged
her own path.

The Christians
in Onyshkivtsi
built a shrine
to honor her.
The shrine marks a spring
whose temperature
is forty-three degrees
all year,
rain or shine.
Even in the snow.

It is said
that it was once home
to hundreds of swans.
Righteous Anna used to
feed and care for them.
But Mami says the swans
don't go there anymore.

There is rot
in the old growth—
the Kodari forest
senses these things.
I sense things too.
The rot in our community.
Sometimes it's not enough
to be good,
if you treat others
with disdain.
Sometimes there's nothing
you can do
but fly away,
like Anna did.

5

Liba

When we get back from our morning walk, Mami is in the kitchen making breakfast and starting the doughs for the day. Tati shakes the snow off his boots as he walks in. "*Gut morgen*," he says gruffly as he pecks a kiss on Mami's cheek. She pins her white-gold hair up and says, "*Dubroho ranku*. Liba, close the door quickly—you're letting all the cold in."

I let the hood of my coat drop down. "Where's Laya?"

"Getting some eggs from the coop," Mami sings. She and Laya love mornings, not like me, but I'd wake up early every morning if it meant I got time alone with Tati.

I shrug my coat off and hang it on a hook by the door as Mami pours tea at the table. "*Nu?* Come in, warm up," she says to me.

I shake the chill off and start braiding my hair, which is the color of river rocks. Long and thick. I can't pin it up at all. "Your hair is beautiful like moonstone, *dochka*," Mami says. "Leave it down."

"More like oil on fur," I say, because it's sleek and shiny and I never feel like I can tame it. It will never be white and light like hers and Laya's.

"Do you want me to braid it for you?" Mami asks.

I shake my head.

"Come here, my *zaftig* one," Tati says. "Your hair is fine; leave it be."

I cringe: I don't like it when he calls me plump, even though it's a term of endearment, and anyway, I know what comes next. Laya walks in and he says, "Oh, the *shayna meidel* has decided to join us." The pretty one. I concentrate on braiding my hair.

Laya grins. "*Gut morgen.* How was your walk?" She looks at me.

I shrug my shoulders and finish braiding my hair, then sit at the table and lift a cup of tea to my mouth. "*Baruch atah Adonai eloheinu melech haolam, shehakol nih'ye bidvaro—Blessed are you, Lord our God, king of the universe, by whose word all things came to be.*" I make sure to say every word of the blessing with meaning.

"*Oymen!*" Tati says with a smile.

Instead of trying to be something I will never be, I do everything I can to be a good Jew.

6

Laya

When I was outside
gathering eggs,
I searched the sky,
hoping to see something—
anything.
One night I heard
feathers rustling
and turned around
and looked up—
a swan had landed
on our rooftop.
It was watching me.
I didn't breathe
the whole time
it was there.
Until it spread
its wings
and took off
into the sky.

Every night I pray
that it will happen again
because if I ever see
another swan,
I won't hold my breath—
I will open the window
and go outside.

That's why I rake my gaze
over every flake of bark
and every teardrop leaf,
hoping. I see that
every finger-branch
is reaching for something.
I am reaching too.
Up up up.

At night I feel
the weight
of the house
upon my chest.
It's warm
and safe inside,
but the wooden planks
above my head
are nothing like
the dark boughs
of the forest.
Sometimes I wish
I could sleep outside.
The Kodari is
the only place
I feel truly at home.

But this morning
I'm restless
and that usually means
something is about to change.
That's what the forest
teaches you—
change can come
in the blink of an eye—
the fall of one spark
can mean total destruction.

There is a fever
that burns in me.
It prickles every pore.
I'm not happy with
the simple life we lead.
A life ruled
by prayer and holy days,
times for dusk and dawn,
the sacred and the profane.
A life of devotion,
Tati would say.
The glory
of a king's daughter
is within.

But I long for what is
just outside my window.
Far beyond
the reaches of the Dniester,
and the boundaries
of our small *shtetl*.

It hurts,
this thing I feel,
how unsettled
I've become.
I want to fit
in this home,
in this town.
To be the daughter
that Tati wants me to be.
To be more
like Liba.
Prayer comes
so easily to her.

Mami understands
what I feel
but I also think
it scares her.
She is always sending me
outside, and I'm grateful
but I also wonder
why she doesn't
teach me how to bake,
or how to pray.
It's almost like she knows
that one day
I will leave her.

Sometimes I wish
she'd teach me
how to stay.

I close my eyes
and take deep breaths.
It helps me
resist the urge
to scratch my back.
I want to crawl out
of this skin I wear
when these thoughts come
and threaten to overwhelm
the little peace I have,
staring at the sky,
praying in my own way
for something else.

Something is definitely
inside me.
It is not glory,
or devotion.
It is something
that wants to burst free.

Enter the monthly
Orbit sweepstakes at

www.orbitloot.com

With a different prize every month,
from advance copies of books by
your favourite authors to exclusive
merchandise packs,
**we think you'll find something
you love.**